DOVER · THRIFT · EDITIONS

Great Horror Stories

Tales by
Stoker, Poe, Lovecraft and Others

Edited by
John Grafton

Introduction by
Mike Ashley

DOVER PUBLICATIONS, INC.
Mineola, New York

Acknowledgments

"The White People" by Arthur Machen. Copyright © The Estate of Arthur Machen; reproduced by permission of A. M. Heath & Co. Ltd., on behalf of Janet Pollock as the Literary Executor of the Estate.

"The Lottery" from *The Lottery* by Shirley Jackson. Copyright © 1948, 1949 by Shirley Jackson. Copyright © renewed 1976, 1977 by Laurence Hyman, Mrs. Sarah Webster and Mrs. Joanne Schnurer. Reprinted by permission of Farrar, Straus and Giroux, LLC.

"The Colour Out of Space" by H. P. Lovecraft is reprinted by permission of Arkham House Publishers, Inc., and Arkham's agents, JABberwocky Literary Agency, P.O. Box 4558, Sunnyside, N.Y. 11104-0558.

Bibliographical Note

This Dover edition, first published in 2008, is a new anthology of fourteen stories reprinted from standard texts. A new Introduction, written by Mike Ashley, has been specially prepared for the present edition.

Library of Congress Cataloging-in-Publication Data

Great horror stories : tales by Stoker, Poe, Lovecraft, and others / edited by John Grafton ; [introduction written by Mike Ashley].
p. cm. — (Dover thrift editions)
ISBN-13: 978-0-486-46143-4
ISBN-10: 0-486-46143-2
1. Horror tales, English. 2. Horror tales, American. I. Grafton, John.

PR1309.H6G69 2008
823'.0873808—dc22

2007029255

Manufactured in the United States of America
Dover Publications, Inc., 31 East 2nd Street, Mineola, N.Y. 11501

Contents

INTRODUCTION

WHY DO WE read horror fiction? It's an interesting question and one that is often asked. There are people who will argue: isn't there enough horror in the world without wanting more? Yet books labeled "horror" continue to sell, often in vast numbers. Of course there's good horror and bad. On the surface that may sound like an absurd statement, but it's true. The stories in this book are "good" horror. That is, they are not stories that turn to acts of physical depravity or violence in order to sicken or repulse. So what is "good" horror and what caused these stories to be written?

Deep down, we all know why we read stories that frighten us. Stories are safe. In them we can confront those things that otherwise scare or unnerve us, but at a safe distance. If we want to, we can close the book. If we continue to read we know that we may not want to turn out the light, we may not want to open that dark door——. But we always do, and life goes on; and we're all just that little bit braver, that little bit bolder and better able to cope with the world. The stories perhaps, in some small way, have helped us discover something new about ourselves. And that discovery gives us a thrill. That's what the best writers can do, and that's what they do here. These horror stories are among the very best ever written. Some are over a hundred years old and yet they have not become dated—their impact remains undiminished. They have stood the test of time because they are good stories, well crafted, by great writers.

But that's only part of what "good" horror means. The writers chose to write these stories for a reason and that certainly wasn't to revolt or repulse. It was to release or express something from within themselves. Most of these stories were written either out of the author's direct experience or their outlook on the world. The very best horror stories give us an insight into that author and help us understand how they coped with life and the world about them.

Let's have a look now at these writers and their stories.

"The Mark of the Beast" is based on a clash of cultures and beliefs, as relevant today as it was in 1887 when the story was written. Joseph

Rudyard Kipling (1865–1936) was born in India, and spent many of his young adult years there, though he was educated in England. He thus had firsthand experience of the cultures of East and West. He lived in Lahore, where his father was the curator of the museum. Just outside the city, an army battalion was stationed that Kipling came to know well. He worked for seven years as an assistant editor on the *Civil and Military Gazette,* where many of his early stories were published. Kipling is best remembered today for *The Jungle Book* (1894), but some of his finest work explores the relationship between the cultures in India, as in "The Mark of the Beast" (*The Pioneer,* 12 and 14 July 1890), a story that begins and ends by also challenging our beliefs in the supernatural.

Montague Rhodes James (1862–1936) was an exact contemporary of Kipling, but his chosen career was behind the walls of academe. He was Dean and (from 1905) Provost of King's College, Cambridge, and later Provost of Eton College. While at King's College, James began the practice of reading ghost stories to his colleagues and pupils. The earliest of these was "Canon Alberic's Scrap-book," which he read on 28 October 1893. James was only thirty-one then, not a fusty old graybeard as some might imagine. Moreover, he was a noted mimic, and he told his stories with humor and an especial delight at lampooning various personages at the university. Although his ghost stories (as they're called, though they aren't anything like traditional ghost stories) are regarded as among the best in the English language, his narration of them was at once humorous and shocking. He begins a story in a commonplace setting with the characters going about their business, and then gradually—almost imperceptibly—he allows some strange elements to intrude, just a hint at first, but then gathering momentum until a sudden climactic eruption occurs. James was also a distinguished medieval scholar and antiquary—almost all of his nonfiction books deal with the subject of ancient manuscripts and buildings—so it is no surprise his protagonist undertakes similar pursuits. But delving into the unknown has its perils. The story presented here, "Oh, Whistle, and I'll Come to You, My Lad," was first recounted by James at a Christmas gathering of pupils at King's College in 1903, and was later published in his first story collection, *Ghost Stories of an Antiquary* (1904). It has all the key ingredients of a Jamesian story; and although its primary purpose was to entertain, there is that subtle undertone of warning: that life has a habit of surprising you when you expect it least, so always be on your guard. James's ghost stories were, in many ways, designed to help prepare his pupils for the wider world.

The life of William Hope Hodgson (1877–1918) was very different from the lives of Kipling and James. Hodgson was full of life and energy—at one time he ran a body-building gymnasium; and it was a significant loss to the genre of the supernatural when he was killed in action in the First World War—at Ypres in April 1918—at the age of forty. Hodgson had run away from his boarding school to join the merchant navy in 1891, when he was thirteen. He served a four-year apprenticeship and spent another four years before the mast until he settled on land and subsequently turned to writing. What he had witnessed and experienced during those years at sea—his accumulated fears and terrors—later inspired stories that were published in popular magazines of the day, as well as several novels. His most oft-reprinted story is "The Voice in the Night" (1907), wherein Hodgson considered how fungus, which attaches itself to all rotting matter, might also absorb human beings. But he wouldn't let the idea rest there and developed it into what Hodgson's biographer, Sam Moskowitz, called a "sea horror tale of near-genius inspiration," "The Derelict" (*Red Magazine*, 1 December 1912). Hodgson was expressing all those fears and terrors that build up in the months of isolation at sea.

Hector Hugh Munro (pen name, Saki; 1870–1916) was also a victim of the First World War when he was killed by a sniper on the Somme battlefield in November 1916. He also has at least two things in common with Kipling. Munro was born in the outposts of the Empire, in Burma (now Myanmar), where his father was an Inspector-General for the Burmese police. Munro's mother died when he was only two, and he was raised in England by two maiden aunts who were strict and severe. Kipling likewise had lived with a foster couple who ill-treated him. Munro, who went on to become a journalist and foreign correspondent, took his revenge upon his caregivers in his fiction. He was noted for his sardonic and often cruel short stories, which are finely honed as if he relished every word, each one tightening the screw. "Sredni Vashtar" (*The Westminster Gazette*, 28 May 1910) is perhaps his most savage story, serving as an outlet for his oppressed childhood.

The stories so far have all been to some extent by-products of the author's experiences, but not so with "The Monkey's Paw." The author, William Wymark Jacobs (1863–1943) enjoyed a reasonably comfortable life. His father worked in the London Docklands and was sufficiently prosperous to provide young William with a private education. He took employment in the post office as a clerk and accountant, and remained there twenty years—until he had sufficient income from his writing to retire. Most of Jacobs's stories are set around the Docklands area and are rather humorous tales of daily life mixed with homespun philosophy. Now and then Jacobs turned a hand to more macabre tales, such as "The Brown Man's Servant" (1896) and "Jerry Bundler" (1897), but these were few and far between and none prepared his readers for "The Monkey's Paw." In fact, the story so horrified the editor of *The Windsor Magazine* that he rejected the story as too powerful for his readers. It was, instead, published by *Harper's Magazine* in September 1902. It has since become the most popular of all classic horror stories—and you will see why when you read it. Jacobs knew that everything comes at a price.

The world of Algernon Blackwood (1869–1951) is about as far removed from that of W. W. Jacobs's as it can be. Blackwood enjoyed the wide open spaces of the world—the further from civilization he was, the happier: the northern wastes of Canada, the desolate Egyptian desert, the mountains of the Caucasus, anywhere he could be alone and commune with nature. Blackwood held the view that civilization had dulled mankind's innate senses, and that living close to nature would grant a person access to a higher level of awareness of the real world. Many of his stories draw upon that idea, and "The Willows" (from *The Listener and Other Stories*, 1907) is one of the best. Inspired by his several trips down the Danube in the early years of Britain's Edwardian era, the closing scene of the story is one that he actually witnessed. Blackwood believed that there are points on the earth where our own world comes close to that of other spiritual beings whose consciousness of us is normally limited; and if we trespass upon them—deliberately or not—we pay the penalty.

Izumi Kyōka (1873–1939) was born in Kanazawa, Japan, to an artistic family. His mother encouraged his literary interests but she died when Kyōka was only ten. He would frequently return to her memory by way of his fiction, which was also inspired by the myths and folktales of ancient Japan, as well as by the Noh musical theater. The dream-like quality of "A Tale of Three Who Were Blind" (1912) may owe something to Kyōka's poor health, since he sometimes fell into a state of delirium as a result of medication he took for the many ailments he suffered throughout his adult life. Yet the substance of the story comes as much from a yearning for things lost as it does for an escape from reality.

Ambrose Bierce (1842–1914?) also chose to escape from reality. At the end of his increasingly embittered life, Bierce took himself off to war-torn Mexico and was never seen or heard from again. Many believe that he was killed by one of the soldiers led by the revolutionary Pancho Villa; but others wonder whether that was exactly the impression Bierce hoped to create, and that in fact he committed suicide somewhere in California—or perhaps went into hiding. Whatever his fate, it was a remarkable end to the life of someone whose outlook was cynical and unyielding, and who managed to express his pessimism through a considerable output of strange and unusual stories. Bierce was twice wounded in the American Civil War, and looked back disdainfully on his battlefield experiences. From them came several stories including his most famous, "An Occurrence at Owl Creek Bridge" (1890), which contemplates the utter futility of life. Most of Bierce's stories are macabre reflections on the tragedy of existence, but occasionally he injected them with a dose of the inexplicable, and "The Damned Thing" (*Town Topics*, 7 December 1893) is one of the best.

Like Algernon Blackwood, the Welsh writer Arthur Machen (1863–1947) was fascinated by the occult; and both were members of the Hermetic Order of the Golden Dawn in the first decade of the twentieth century. Although Machen did not share Blackwood's personal beliefs about the world of nature, he still pondered that world and conjured up his own notions of what constitutes the substance of beauty and evil. "The White People" (*Horlick's Magazine*, January 1904) is one result of Machen's speculations, and according to the distinguished science fiction and fantasy scholar Everett F. Bleiler, the story is "probably the finest single supernatural story of the century, perhaps in the literature." The tale is all the more potent because it is written, for the most part, from a child's perspective.

On the face of it the Irish writer, Abraham "Bram" Stoker (1847–1912), seems an unlikely candidate for literary immortality. Although he trained as a barrister he became a journalist instead, until a fascination for the theater led him to become first a drama critic and then manager of one of the greatest actors of the day, Henry Irving. Stoker had been writing and selling stories since 1872, but none of them had much of an impact until he wrote *Dracula* (1897). While the book—or at least the character of Count Dracula—is among the most famous creations in all of English literature, few people remember the name of its creator; and Stoker never again achieved the same success, despite producing another half-dozen or so novels. Just before his death, he was working on a series of story collections, but he died before they were completed. His widow Florence compiled one volume, *Dracula's Guest* (1914), and included the hitherto unpublished title story believing it to be a chapter that had been dropped from the novel because of its length. Some Stoker scholars, however, believe it is in fact a separate story written before he began work on *Dracula*, and was to some extent a trial run. Stoker had become fascinated with the idea of vampires, but the true horror of the novel does not reside in the bloodsucking creature of the night, but in the mesmerizing power of one individual over another. Stoker was only too familiar with such a situation, since his employer Henry Irving had an overwhelming personality and dominating presence. In writing *Dracula*, perhaps Stoker could, through the character of Jonathan Harker, regain some control over his life.

Edgar Allan Poe (1809–1849) is undoubtedly the most tragic figure represented here. A literary genius with a powerfully perceptive mind, Poe's life was always beset by misfortune, poor health, alcoholism, and destitution. Poe knew neither of his parents since his father abandoned the family when Poe was hardly a year old, and his mother died soon after. He was raised by John Allan, from whom he took his middle name; but Poe was such an unstable young man that Allan eventually disowned him. Poe was also plagued by the constant ill-health of his wife, Virginia, whom he had married when she was only thirteen; she was ill with consumption for many years and died in 1847 at the age of twenty-four. Poe was frequently his own worst enemy, and time and again his stories reflect the paranoia of success followed by failure. Despite his remarkable intellect, he could do nothing to stop his world crumbling. Much of Poe's despair is evident in "The Facts in the Case of M. Valdemar" (*American Whig Review*, December 1845), one of his last and most powerful stories. The story is a genuine cry from the heart.

"The Lottery" by Shirley Jackson (1916–1965) is the most recent story in this collection, and somehow that makes it all the more unsettling. It was published in *The New Yorker* for 28 June 1948, and the reader reaction to the story was unprecedented—with the magazine and the author receiving hundreds of letters of complaint. It has long since been recognized as a classic, and yet the book in which the story was subsequently collected, *The Lottery* (1949), remains among the top twenty most banned books in American schools and libraries. Jackson, who was a private person and seldom wrote about herself or her work, was nevertheless provoked into stating that she hoped the story would jolt readers into recognizing the pointless violence and inhumanity in their lives.

William Fryer Harvey (1885–1937) is virtually forgotten today, yet in 1955, Sir Archibald Wilson, writing in the *Times Literary Supplement*, called him "the greatest of modern horror writers." Harvey trained as a doctor, but ironically his calling dealt him a cruel blow that prevented him from ever practicing his chosen profession. During the First World War, in which he served as a Surgeon-Lieutenant, he rescued a petty officer working as a stoker, who was trapped in the boiler room of a damaged destroyer. He saved the man's life but was overcome by the fumes from the escaping oil and collapsed. He was awarded the Albert Medal for Gallantry in October 1918, but the experience damaged his lungs and he was incapacitated for the rest of his life. Before this calamity befell him, Harvey had already turned to writing strange stories, inspired by an early reading of the tales of Edgar Allan Poe. He produced several classic stories, including the one reprinted here, "The Beast With Five Fingers" (*The New Decameron*, 1919), written soon after the war. It was filmed in 1946, starring Peter Lorre. Perhaps there is in this fiction some of Harvey's frustration with his own enfeebled body and a desire to take revenge upon a world that had dealt him a cruel blow.

Like Harvey, Howard Phillips Lovecraft (1890–1937) also died young, though there were no acts of gallantry connected with his fate. Lovecraft was an eccentric who felt disconnected from his time, yearning for the Regency period and longing for the colonial days. Although born in Providence, Rhode Island, he was a devoted Anglophile—hence the English spelling of the word color in his story, "The Colour Out of Space" (*Amazing Stories*, September 1927). Lovecraft was fascinated with the idea that the seeds of life might have the ability to travel through space and regenerate on other worlds. He considered his horrors on a cosmic scale, and was influenced to some degree by the work of Algernon Blackwood—including "The Willows," a story that also appears in this anthology. While Lovecraft earned an unfair reputation as a recluse who rarely emerged from his home, he did live much of his life in his imagination. He had an intense desire to know what might exist or have existed in the vast depths of space and time. "I have often wished that I had the literary power to call up visions of some vast & remote realm of entity beyond the universes of matter & energy," he wrote to his friend Donald Wandrei shortly after completing "The Colour Out of Space." And indeed he did, as his reputation as a writer of cosmic horror came from this very imagining.

⋆ ⋆ ⋆

These, then, are the authors and stories collected here and, if I may return to my original point about "good" horror, we can see how horror fiction has been used by these writers to help them come to terms with aspects of their life or the world about them. That these stories are still being read and enjoyed a hundred years or more after they were written is testament to how powerful a tool horror fiction can be and how successful the writers were in their efforts. Once you have read this book, these stories will forever remain a part of you.

MIKE ASHLEY
July 2007

The Mark of the Beast

Rudyard Kipling

Your gods and my gods—do you
or I know which are the stronger?
Native proverb

EAST OF SUEZ, some hold, the direct control of providence ceases, man being there handed over to the power of the gods and devils of Asia, and the Church of England providence only exercising an occasional and modified supervision in the case of Englishmen.

This theory accounts for some of the more unnecessary horrors of life in India: it may be stretched to explain my story.

My friend Strickland of the police, who knows as much of natives of India as is good for any man, can bear witness to the facts of the case. Dumoise, our doctor, also saw what Strickland and I saw. The inference which he drew from the evidence was entirely incorrect. He is dead now; he died in a rather curious manner, which has been elsewhere described.

When Fleete came to India he owned a little money and some land in the Himalayas, near a place called Dharmsala. Both properties had been left him by an uncle, and he came out to finance them. He was a big, heavy, genial and inoffensive man. His knowledge of natives was, of course, limited, and he complained of the difficulties of the language.

He rode in from his place in the hills to spend New Year in the station, and he stayed with Strickland. On New Year's Eve there was a big dinner at the club, and the night was excusably wet. When men foregather from the uttermost ends of the Empire, they have a right to be riotous. The Frontier had sent down a contingent o' Catch-'em-Alive-Os who had not seen twenty white faces for a year, and were used to ride fifteen miles to dinner at the next fort at the risk of a Khyberee bullet where their drinks should lie. They profited by their new security, for they tried to play pool with a curled-up hedgehog found in the garden, and one of them carried the marker round the room in his teeth. Half a dozen planters had come in from the south and were talking "horse" to the Biggest Liar in Asia, who was trying to cap all their stories at once. Everybody was there, and there was a general closing up of ranks and taking stock of our losses in dead or disabled that had fallen during the past year. It was a very wet night, and I remember that we sang "Auld Lang Syne" with our feet in the Polo Championship Cup and our heads among the stars, and swore that we were all dear friends. Then some of us went away and annexed Burma, and some tried to open up the Sudan and were opened up by fuzzies in that cruel scrub outside Suakim, and some found stars and medals, and some were married, which was bad, and some did other things which were worse, and the others of us stayed in our chains and strove to make money on insufficient experiences.

Fleete began the night with sherry and bitters, drank champagne steadily up to dessert, then raw, rasping Capri with all the strength of whisky, took Benedictine with his coffee, four or five whiskies and sodas to improve his pool strokes, beer and bones at half-past two, winding up with old brandy. Consequently, when he came out, at half-past three in the morning, into fourteen degrees of frost, he was very angry with his horse for coughing, and tried to leapfrog into the saddle. The horse broke away and went to his stables; so Strickland and I formed a guard of dishonour to take Fleete home.

Our road lay through the bazaar, close to a little temple of Hanuman, the monkey-god, who is a leading divinity worthy of respect. All gods have good points, just as have all priests. Personally, I attach much importance to Hanuman, and am kind to his people—the great grey apes of the hills. One never knows when one may want a friend.

There was a light in the temple, and as we passed we could hear voices of men chanting hymns. In a native temple the priests rise at all hours of the night to do honour to their god. Before we could stop him, Fleete dashed up the steps, patted two priests on the back, and was gravely grinding the ashes of his cigar-butt into the forehead of the red stone image of Hanuman.

Strickland tried to drag him out, but he sat down and said solemnly: "Shee that? 'Mark of the B-beasht! *I* made it. Ishn't it fine?"

In half a minute the temple was alive and noisy, and Strickland, who knew what came of polluting gods, said that things might occur. He, by virtue of his official position, long residence in the country and weakness for going among the natives, was known to the priests and he felt unhappy. Fleete sat on the ground and refused to move. He said that "good old Hanuman" made a very soft pillow.

Then, without any warning, a Silver Man came out of a recess behind the image of the god. He was perfectly naked in that bitter, bitter cold, and his body shone like frosted silver, for he was what the Bible calls "a leper as white as snow." Also he had no face, because he was a leper of some years' standing, and his disease was heavy upon him. We two stooped to haul Fleete up, and the temple was filling and filling with folk who seemed to spring from the earth, when the Silver Man ran in under our arms, making a noise exactly like the mewing of an otter, caught Fleete round the body and dropped his head on Fleete's breast before we could wrench him away. Then he retired to a corner and sat mewing while the crowd blocked all the doors.

The priests were very angry until the Silver Man touched Fleete. That nuzzling seemed to sober them.

At the end of a few minutes' silence one of the priests came to Strickland and said, in perfect English, "Take your friend away. He has done with Hanuman but Hanuman has not done with him." The crowd gave room and we carried Fleete into the road.

Strickland was very angry. He said that we might all three have been knifed, and that Fleete should thank his stars that he had escaped without injury.

Fleete thanked no one. He said that he wanted to go to bed. He was gorgeously drunk.

We moved on, Strickland silent and wrathful, until Fleete was taken with violent shivering fits and sweating. He said that the smells of the bazaar were overpowering, and he wondered why slaughterhouses were permitted so near English residences. "Can't you smell the blood?" said Fleete.

We put him to bed at last, just as the dawn was breaking, and Strickland invited me to have another whisky and soda. While we were drinking he talked of the trouble in the temple, and admitted that it baffled him completely. Strickland hates being mystified by natives, because his business in life is to overmatch them with their own weapons. He has not yet succeeded in doing this, but in fifteen or twenty years he will have made some small progress.

"They should have mauled us," he said, "instead of mewing at us. I wonder what they meant. I don't like it one little bit."

I said that the managing committee of the temple would in all probability bring a criminal action against us for insulting their religion. There was a section of the Indian Penal Code which exactly met Fleete's offence. Strickland said he only hoped and prayed that they would do this. Before I left I looked into Fleete's room, and saw him lying on his right side, scratching his left breast. Then I went to bed, cold, depressed and unhappy, at seven o'clock in the morning.

At one o'clock I rode over to Strickland's house to inquire after Fleete's head. I imagined that it would be a sore one. Fleete was breakfasting and seemed unwell. His temper was gone, for he was abusing the cook for not supplying him with an underdone chop. A man who can eat raw meat after a wet night is a curiosity. I told Fleete this and he laughed.

"You breed queer mosquitoes in these parts," he said. "I've been bitten to pieces, but only in one place."

"Let's have a look at the bite," said Strickland. "It may have gone down since this morning."

While the chops were being cooked, Fleete opened his shirt and showed us, just over his left breast, a mark, the perfect double of the black rosettes—the five or six irregular blotches arranged in a circle—on a leopard's hide. Strickland looked and said, "It was only pink this morning. It's grown black now."

Fleete ran to a glass.

"By Jove!" he said, "this is nasty. What is it?"

We could not answer. Here the chops came in, all red and juicy, and Fleete bolted three in a most offensive manner. He ate on his right grinders only, and threw his head over his right shoulder as he snapped the meat. When he had finished, it struck him that he had been behaving strangely, for he said apologetically, "I don't think I ever felt so hungry in my life. I've bolted like an ostrich."

After breakfast Strickland said to me, "Don't go. Stay here, and stay for the night."

Seeing that my house was not three miles from Strickland's, this request was absurd. But Strickland insisted, and was going to say something, when Fleete interrupted by declaring in a shamefaced way that he felt hungry again. Strickland sent a man to my house to fetch over my bedding and a horse, and we three went down to Strickland's stables to pass the hours until it was time to go out for a ride. The man who has a weakness for horses never wearies of inspecting them; and when two men are killing time in this way they gather knowledge and lies the one from the other.

There were five horses in the stables, and I shall never forget the scene as we tried to look them over. They seemed to have gone mad. They reared and screamed and nearly tore up their pickets; they sweated and shivered and lathered and were distraught with fear. Strickland's horses used to know him as well as his dogs; which made the matter more curious. We left the stable for fear of the brutes throwing themselves in their panic. Then Strickland turned back and called me. The horses were still frightened, but they let us "gentle" and make much of them, and put their heads in our bosoms.

"They aren't afraid of *us,*" said Strickland. "D'you know, I'd give three months' pay if Outrage here could talk."

But Outrage was dumb, and could only cuddle up to his master and blow out his nostrils, as is the custom of horses when they wish to explain things but can't. Fleete came up when we were in the stalls, and as soon as the horses saw him, their fright broke out afresh. It was all that we could do to escape from the place unkicked. Strickland said, "They don't seem to love you, Fleete."

"Nonsense," said Fleete; "my mare will follow me like a dog." He went to her; she was in a loose-box; but as he slipped the bars she plunged, knocked him down, and broke away into the garden. I laughed, but Strickland was not amused. He took his moustache in both fists and pulled at it till it nearly came out. Fleete, instead of going off to chase his property, yawned, saying that he felt sleepy. He went to the house to lie down, which was a foolish way of spending New Year's Day.

Strickland sat with me in the stables and asked if I had noticed anything peculiar in Fleete's manner. I said that he ate his food like a beast; but that this might have been the result of living alone in the hills, out of the reach of society as refined and elevating as ours for instance. Strickland was not amused. I do not think that he listened to me, for his next sentence referred to the mark on Fleete's breast, and I said that it might have been caused by blister-flies, or that it was possibly a birthmark newly born and now visible for the first time. We both agreed that it was unpleasant to look at, and Strickland found occasion to say that I was a fool.

"I can't tell you what I think now," said he, "because you would call me a madman; but you must stay with me for the next few days, if you can. I want you to watch Fleete, but don't tell me what you think till I have made up my mind."

"But I am dining out tonight," I said.

"So am I," said Strickland, "and so is Fleete. At least if he doesn't change his mind."

We walked about the garden smoking, but saying nothing—because we were friends, and talking spoils good tobacco—till our pipes were out. Then we went to wake up Fleete. He was wide awake and fidgeting about his room.

"I say, I want some more chops," he said. "Can I get them?"

We laughed and said, "Go and change. The ponies will be round in a minute."

"All right," said Fleete. "I'll go when I get the chops—underdone ones, mind."

He seemed to be quite in earnest. It was four o'clock, and we had had breakfast at one; still, for a long time, he demanded those underdone chops. Then he changed into riding clothes and went out into the veranda. His pony—the mare had not been caught—would not let him come near. All three horses were unmanageable—mad with fear—and finally Fleete said that he would stay at home and get something to eat. Strickland and I rode out wondering. As we passed the temple of Hanuman, the Silver Man came out and mewed at us.

"He is not one of the regular priests of the temple," said Strickland. "I think I should peculiarly like to lay my hands on him."

There was no spring in our gallop on the racecourse that evening. The horses were stale, and moved as though they had been ridden out.

"The fright after breakfast has been too much for them," said Strickland.

That was the only remark he made through the remainder of the ride. Once or twice, I think, he swore to himself; but that did not count.

We came back in the dark at seven o'clock, and saw that there were no lights in the bungalow. "Careless ruffians my servants are!" said Strickland.

My horse reared at something on the carriage drive, and Fleete stood up under its nose.

"What are you doing, grovelling about the garden?" said Strickland.

But both horses bolted and nearly threw us. We dismounted by the stables and returned to Fleete, who was on his hands and knees under the orange-bushes.

"What the devil's wrong with you?" said Strickland.

"Nothing, nothing in the world," said Fleete, speaking very quickly and thickly. "I've been gardening—botanising, you know. The smell of the earth is delightful. I think I'm going for a walk—a long walk—all night."

Then I saw that there was something excessively out of order somewhere, and I said to Strickland, "I am not dining out."

"Bless you!" said Strickland. "Here, Fleete, get up. You'll catch fever there. Come in to dinner and let's have the lamps lit. We'll all dine at home."

Fleete stood up unwillingly, and said, "No lamps—no lamps. It's much nicer here. Let's dine outside and have some more chops—lots of 'em and underdone—bloody ones with gristle."

Now a December evening in Northern India is bitterly cold, and Fleete's suggestion was that of a maniac.

"Come in," said Strickland sternly. "Come in at once."

Fleete came, and when the lamps were brought, we saw that he was literally plastered with dirt from head to foot. He must have been rolling in the garden. He shrank from the light and went to his room. His eyes were horrible to look at. There was a green light behind them, not in them, if you understand, and the man's lower lip hung down.

Strickland said, "There is going to be trouble—big trouble—to-night. Don't you change your riding-things."

We waited and waited for Fleete's reappearance, and ordered dinner in the meantime. We could hear him moving about his own room, but there was no light there. Presently from the room came the long-drawn howl of a wolf.

People write and talk lightly of blood running cold and hair standing up and things of that kind. Both sensations are too horrible to be trifled with. My heart stopped as though a knife had been driven through it, and Strickland turned as white as the tablecloth.

The howl was repeated, and was answered by another howl far across the fields.

That set the gilded roof on the horror. Strickland dashed into Fleete's room. I followed, and we saw Fleete getting out of the window. He made beast-noises in the back of his throat. He could not answer us when we shouted at him. He spat.

I don't quite remember what followed, but I think that Strickland must have stunned him with the long bootjack, or else I should never have been able to sit on his chest. Fleete could not speak, he could only snarl, and his snarls were those of a wolf, not of a man. The human spirit must have been giving way all day and have died out with the twilight. We were dealing with a beast that had once been Fleete.

The affair was beyond any human and rational experience. I tried to say "hydrophobia," but the word wouldn't come, because I knew that I was lying.

We bound this beast with leather thongs of the punkah-rope, and tied its thumbs and big toes together, and gagged it with a shoe-horn, which makes a very efficient gag if you know how to arrange it. Then we carried it into the dining room, and sent a man to Dumoise, the doctor, telling him to come over at once. After we had dispatched the messenger and were drawing breath, Strickland said, "It's no good. This isn't any doctor's work." I, also, knew that he spoke the truth.

The beast's head was free, and it threw it about from side to side. Anyone entering the room would have believed that we were curing a wolf's pelt. That was the most loathsome accessory of all.

Strickland sat with his chin in the heel of his fist, watching the beast as it wriggled on the ground, but saying nothing. The shirt had been torn open in the scuffle and showed the black rosette mark on the left breast. It stood out like a blister.

In the silence of the watching we heard something without, mewing like a she-otter. We both rose to our feet, and, I answer for myself, not Strickland, felt sick actually and physically sick. We told each other, as did the men in *Pinafore,* that it was the cat.

Dumoise arrived, and I never saw a little man so unprofessionally shocked. He said that it was a heart-rending case of hydrophobia, and that nothing could be done. At least any palliative measures would only prolong the agony. The beast was foaming at the mouth. Fleete, as we told Dumoise, had been bitten by dogs once or twice. Any man who keeps half a dozen terriers must expect a nip now and again. Dumoise could offer no help. He could only certify that Fleete was dying of hydrophobia. The beast was then howling, for it had managed to spit out the shoehorn. Dumoise said that he would be ready to certify to the cause of death, and that the end was certain. He was a good little man, and he offered to remain with us; but Strickland refused the kindness. He did not wish to poison Dumoise's New Year. He would only ask him not to give the real cause of Fleete's death to the public.

So Dumoise left, deeply agitated; and as soon as the noise of the cartwheels had died away Strickland told me, in a whisper, his suspicions. They were so wildly improbable that he dared not say them out aloud; and I, who entertained all Strickland's beliefs, was so ashamed of owning to them that I pretended to disbelieve.

"Even if the Silver Man had bewitched Fleete for polluting the image of Hanuman, the punishment could not have fallen so quickly."

As I was whispering this the cry outside the house rose again, and the beast fell into a fresh paroxysm of struggling till we were afraid that the thongs that held it would give way.

"Watch!" said Strickland. "If this happens six times I shall take the law into my own hands. I order you to help me."

He went into his room and came out in a few minutes with the barrels of an old shotgun, a piece of fishing-line, some thick cord, and his heavy wooden bedstead. I reported that the convulsions had followed the cry by two seconds in each case, and the beast seemed perceptibly weaker.

Strickland muttered, "But he can't take away the life! He can't take away the life!"

I said, though I knew that I was arguing against myself, "It may be a cat. It must be a cat. If the Silver Man is responsible, why does he dare to come here?"

Strickland arranged the wood on the hearth, put the gun-barrels into the glow of the fire, spread the twine on the table and broke a walking stick in two. There was one yard of fishing line, gut lapped with wire, such as is used for *mahseer*-fishing, and he tied the two ends together in a loop.

Then he said, "How can we catch him? He must be taken alive and unhurt."

I said that we must trust in providence, and go out softly with polo-sticks into the shrubbery at the front of the house. The man or animal that made the cry was evidently moving round the house as regularly as a night-watchman. We could wait in the bushes till he came by and knock him over.

Strickland accepted this suggestion, and we slipped out from a bathroom window into the front veranda and then across the carriage drive into the bushes.

In the moonlight we could see the leper coming round the corner of the house. He was perfectly naked, and from time to time he mewed and stopped to dance with his shadow. It was an unattractive sight, and thinking of poor Fleete, brought to such degradation by so foul a creature, I put away all my doubts and resolved to help Strickland from the heated gun-barrels to the loop of twine—from the loins to the head and back again—with all tortures that might be needful.

The leper halted in the front porch for a moment and we jumped out on him with the sticks. He was wonderfully strong, and we were afraid that he might escape or be fatally injured before we caught him. We had an idea that lepers were frail creatures, but this proved to be incorrect. Strickland knocked his legs from under him and I put my foot on his neck. He mewed hideously, and even through my riding-boots I could feel that his flesh was not the flesh of a clean man.

He struck at us with his hand- and feet-stumps. We looped the lash of a dog-whip round him, under the armpits, and dragged him backwards into the hall and so into the dining-room where the beast lay. There we tied him with trunkstraps. He made no attempt to escape, but mewed.

When we confronted him with the beast the scene was beyond description. The beast doubled backwards into a bow as though he had been poisoned with strychnine, and moaned in the most pitiable fashion. Several other things happened also, but they cannot be put down here.

"I think I was right," said Strickland. "Now we will ask him to cure this case."

But the leper only mewed. Strickland wrapped a towel round his hand and took the gun-barrels out of the fire. I put the half of the broken walking stick through the loop of fishing-line and buckled the leper comfortably to Strickland's bedstead. I understood then how men and women and little children can endure to see a witch burnt alive; for the beast was moaning on the floor, and though the Silver Man had no face, you could see horrible feelings passing through the slab that took its place, exactly as waves of heat play across red-hot iron—gun-barrels for instance.

Strickland shaded his eyes with his hands for a moment and we got to work. This part is not to be printed.

The dawn was beginning to break when the leper spoke. His mewings had not been satisfactory up to that point. The beast had fainted from exhaustion and the house was very still. We unstrapped the leper and told him to take away the evil spirit. He crawled to the beast and laid his hand upon the left breast. That was all. Then he fell face down and whined, drawing in his breath as he did so.

We watched the face of the beast, and saw the soul of Fleete coming back into the eyes. Then a sweat broke out on the forehead and the eyes—they were human eyes—closed. We waited for an hour but Fleete still slept. We carried him to his room and bade the leper go, giving him the bedstead, and the sheet on the bedstead to cover his nakedness, the gloves and the towels with which we had touched him, and the whip that had been hooked round his body. He put the sheet about him and went out into the early morning without speaking or mewing.

Strickland wiped his face and sat down. A night-gong, far away in the city, made seven o'clock.

"Exactly four-and-twenty hours!" said Strickland. "And I've done enough to ensure my dismissal from the service, besides permanent quarters in a lunatic asylum. Do you believe that we are awake?"

The red-hot gun-barrel had fallen on the floor and was singeing the carpet. The smell was entirely real.

That morning at eleven we two together went to wake up Fleete. We looked and saw that the black leopard-rosette on his chest had disappeared. He was very drowsy and tired, but as soon as he saw us, he said, "Oh! Confound you fellows. Happy New Year to you. Never mix your liquors. I'm nearly dead."

"Thanks for your kindness, but you're over time," said Strickland. "Today is the morning of the second. You've slept the clock round with a vengeance."

The door opened, and little Dumoise put his head in. He had come on foot, and fancied that we were laying out Fleete.

"I've brought a nurse," said Dumoise. "I suppose that she can come in for . . . what is necessary."

"By all means," said Fleete cheerily, sitting up in bed. "Bring on your nurses."

Dumoise was dumb. Strickland led him out and explained that there must have been a mistake in the diagnosis. Dumoise remained dumb and left the house hastily. He considered that his professional reputation had been injured, and was inclined to make a personal matter of the recovery. Strickland went out too. When he came back, he said that he had been to call on the Temple of Hanuman to offer redress for the pollution of the god, and had been solemnly assured that no white man had ever touched the idol, and that he was an incarnation of all the virtues labouring under a delusion. "What do you think?" said Strickland.

I said, "'There are more things . . .'"

But Strickland hates that quotation. He says that I have worn it threadbare.

One other curious thing happened which frightened me as much as anything in all the night's work. When Fleete was dressed he came into the dining-room and sniffed. He had a quaint trick of moving his nose when he sniffed. "Horrid doggy smell, here," said he. "You should really keep those terriers of yours in better order. Try sulphur, Strick."

But Strickland did not answer. He caught hold of the back of a chair, and, without warning, went into an amazing fit of hysterics. It is terrible to see a strong man overtaken with hysteria. Then it struck me that we had fought for Fleete's soul with the Silver Man in that room, and had disgraced ourselves as Englishmen for ever, and I laughed and gasped and gurgled just as shamefully as Strickland, while Fleete thought that we had both gone mad. We never told him what we had done.

Some years later, when Strickland had married and was a church-going member of society for his wife's sake, we reviewed the incident dispassionately, and Strickland suggested that I should put it before the public.

I cannot myself see that this step is likely to clear up the mystery; because, in the first place, no one will believe a rather unpleasant story, and, in the second, it is well known to every right-minded man that the gods of the heathen are stone and brass, and any attempt to deal with them otherwise is justly condemned.

"Oh, Whistle, and I'll Come to You, My Lad"

M. R. James

"I SUPPOSE you will be getting away pretty soon, now. Full term is over, professor," said a person not in the story to the professor of ontology, soon after they had sat down next to each other at a feast in the hospitable hall of St. James's College.

The professor was young, neat, and precise in speech.

"Yes," he said; "my friends have been making me take up golf this term, and I mean to go to the East Coast—in point of fact to Burnstow (I dare say you know it)—for a week or ten days, to improve my game. I hope to get off tomorrow."

"Oh, Parkins," said his neighbour on the other side, "if you are going to Burnstow, I wish you would look at the site of the Templars' preceptory, and let me know if you think it would be any good to have a dig there in the summer."

It was, as you might suppose, a person of antiquarian pursuits who said this, but, since he merely appears in this prologue, there is no need to give his entitlements.

"Certainly," said Parkins, the professor: "if you will describe to me whereabouts the site is, I will do my best to give you an idea of the lie of the land when I get back; or I could write to you about it, if you would tell me where you are likely to be."

"Don't trouble to do that, thanks. It's only that I'm thinking of taking my family in that direction in the Long, and it occurred to me that, as very few of the English preceptories have ever been properly planned, I might have an opportunity of doing something useful on off-days."

The professor rather sniffed at the idea that planning out a preceptory could be described as useful.

His neighbour continued: "The site—I doubt if there is anything showing above ground—must be down quite close to the beach now. The sea has encroached tremendously, as you know, all along that bit of coast. I should think, from the map, that it must be about three-quarters of a mile from the Globe Inn, at the north end of the town. Where are you going to stay?"

"Well, *at* the Globe Inn, as a matter of fact," said Parkins; "I have engaged a room there. I couldn't get in anywhere else; most of the lodging-houses are shut up in winter, it seems; and, as it is, they tell me that the only room of any size I can have is really a double-bedded one, and that they haven't a corner in which to store the other bed, and so on. But I must have a fairly large room, for I am taking some books down, and mean to do a bit of work; and though I don't quite fancy having an empty bed—not to speak of two—in what I may call for the time being my study, I suppose I can manage to rough it for the short time I shall be there."

"Do you call having an extra bed in your room roughing it, Parkins?" said a bluff person opposite. "Look here, I shall come down and occupy it for a bit; it'll be company for you."

The professor quivered, but managed to laugh in a courteous manner.

"By all means, Rogers; there's nothing I should like better. But I'm afraid you would find it rather dull; you don't play golf, do you?"

"No, thank Heaven!" said rude Mr. Rogers.

"Well, you see, when I'm not writing I shall most likely be out on the links, and that, as I say, would be rather dull for you, I'm afraid."

"Oh, I don't know! There's certain to be somebody I know in the place; but, of course, if you don't want me, speak the word, Parkins; I shan't be offended. Truth, as you always tell us, is never offensive."

Parkins was, indeed, scrupulously polite and strictly truthful. It is to be feared that Mr. Rogers sometimes practised upon his knowledge of these characteristics. In Parkins's breast there was a conflict now raging, which for a moment or two did not allow him to answer. That interval being over, he said: "Well, if you want the exact truth, Rogers, I was considering whether the room I speak of would really be large enough to accommodate us both comfortably; and also whether (mind, I shouldn't have said this if you hadn't pressed me) you would not constitute something in the nature of a hindrance to my work."

Rogers laughed loudly.

"Well done, Parkins!" he said. "It's all right. I promise not to interrupt your work; don't you disturb yourself about that. No, I won't come if you don't want me; but I thought I should do so nicely to keep the ghosts off." Here he might have been seen to wink and to nudge his next neighbour. Parkins might also have been seen to become pink. "I beg pardon, Parkins," Rogers continued; "I oughtn't to have said that. I forgot you didn't like levity on these topics."

"Well," Parkins said, "as you have mentioned the matter, I freely own that I do *not* like careless talk about what you call ghosts. A man in my position," he went on, raising his voice a little, "cannot, I find, be too careful about appearing to sanction the current beliefs on such subjects. As you know, Rogers, or as you ought to know; for I think I have never concealed my views—"

"No, you certainly have not, old man," put in Rogers *sotto voce.*

"—I hold that any semblance, any appearance of concession to the view that such things might exist is equivalent to a renunciation of all that I hold most sacred. But I'm afraid I have not succeeded in securing your attention."

"Your *undivided* attention, was what Dr. Blimber actually *said,*" Rogers interrupted, with every appearance of an earnest desire for accuracy. "But I beg your pardon, Parkins: I'm stopping you."

"No, not at all," said Parkins. "I don't remember Blimber; perhaps he was before my time. But I needn't go on. I'm sure you know what I mean."

"Yes, yes," said Rogers, rather hastily—"just so. We'll go into it fully at Burnstow, or somewhere."

In repeating the above dialogue I have tried to give the impression which it made on me, that Parkins was something of an old woman—rather henlike, perhaps, in his little ways; totally destitute, alas! of the sense of humour, but at the same time dauntless and sincere in his convictions, and a man deserving of the greatest respect. Whether or not the reader has gathered so much, that was the character which Parkins had.

On the following day Parkins did, as he had hoped, succeed in getting away from his college, and in arriving at Burnstow. He was made welcome at the Globe Inn, was safely installed in the large double-bedded room of which we have heard, and was able before retiring to rest to arrange his materials for work in apple-pie order upon a commodious table which occupied the outer end of the room, and was surrounded on three sides by windows looking out seaward; that is to say, the central window looked straight out to sea, and those on the left and right commanded prospects along the shore to the north and south respectively. On the south you saw the village of Burnstow. On the north no houses were to be seen, but only the beach and the low cliff backing it. Immediately in front was a strip—not considerable—of rough grass, dotted with old anchors, capstans, and so forth; then a broad path; then the beach. Whatever may have been the original distance between the Globe Inn and the sea, not more than sixty yards now separated them.

The rest of the population of the inn was, of course, a golfing one, and included few elements that call for a special description. The most conspicuous figure was, perhaps, that of an *ancien militaire,* secretary of a London club and possessed of a voice of incredible strength and of views of a pronouncedly Protestant type. These were apt to find utterance after his attendance upon the ministrations of the vicar, an estimable man with inclinations towards a picturesque ritual, which he gallantly kept down as far as he could out of deference to East Anglian tradition.

professor Parkins, one of whose principal characteristics was pluck, spent the greater part of the day following his arrival at Burnstow in what he had called improving his game, in company with this colonel Wilson; and during the afternoon—whether the process of improvement were to blame or not, I am not sure—the colonel's demeanour assumed a colouring so lurid that even Parkins jibbed at the thought of walking home with him from the links. He determined, after a short and furtive look at that bristling moustache and those incarnadined features, that it would be wiser to allow the influences of tea and tobacco to do what they could with the colonel before the dinner-hour should render a meeting inevitable.

"I might walk home tonight along the beach," he reflected—"yes, and take a look—there will be light enough for that—at the ruins of which Disney was talking. I don't exactly know where they are, by the way; but I expect I can hardly help stumbling on them."

This he accomplished, I may say, in the most literal sense, for in picking his way from the links to the shingle beach his foot caught, partly in a gorse-root and partly in a biggish stone, and over he went. When he got up and surveyed his surroundings, he found himself in a patch of somewhat broken ground covered with small depressions and mounds. These latter, when he came to examine them, proved to be simply masses of flints embedded in mortar and grown over with turf. He must, he quite rightly concluded, be on the site of the preceptory he had promised to look at. It seemed not unlikely to reward the spade of the explorer; enough of the foundations was probably left at no great depth to throw a good deal of light on the general plan. He remembered vaguely that the Templars, to whom this site had belonged, were in the habit of building round churches, and he thought a particular series of the humps or mounds near him did appear to be arranged in something of a circular form. Few people can resist the temptation to try a little amateur research in a department quite outside their own, if only for the satisfaction of showing how successful they would have been had they only taken it up seriously. Our professor, however, if he felt something of this mean desire, was also truly anxious to oblige Mr. Disney. So he paced with care the circular area he had noticed, and wrote down its rough dimensions in his pocket-book. Then he proceeded to examine an oblong eminence which lay east of the centre of the circle, and seemed to his thinking likely to be the base of a platform or alter. At one end of it, the northern, a patch of the turf was gone—removed by some boy or other creature *ferae naturae*. It might, he, thought, be as well to probe the soil here for evidences of masonry, and he took out his knife and began scraping away the earth. And now followed another little discovery: a portion of soil fell inward as he scraped, and disclosed a small cavity. He lighted one match after another to help him to see of what nature the hole was, but the wind was too strong for them all. By tapping and scratching the sides with his knife, however, he was able to make out that it must be an artificial hole in masonry. It was rectangular, and the sides, top, and bottom, if not actually plastered, were smooth and regular. Of course it was empty. No! As he withdrew the knife he heard a metallic clink, and when he introduced his hand it met with a cylindrical object lying on the floor of the hole. Naturally enough, he picked it up, and when he brought it into the light, now fast fading, he could see that it, too, was of man's making—a metal tube about four inches long, and evidently of some considerable age.

By the time Parkins had made sure that there was nothing else in this odd receptacle, it was too late and too dark for him to think of undertaking any further search. What he had done had proved so unexpectedly interesting that he determined to sacrifice a little more of the daylight on the morrow to archeology. The object which he now had safe in his pocket was bound to be of some slight value at least, he felt sure.

Bleak and solemn was the view on which he took a last look before starting homeward. A faint yellow light in the west showed the links, on which a few figures moving towards the club-house were still visible, the squat martello tower, the lights of Aldsey village, the pale ribbon of sands intersected at intervals by black wooden groynes, the dim and murmuring sea. The wind was bitter from the north, but was at his back when he set out for the Globe. He quickly rattled and clashed through the shingle and gained the sand, upon which, but for the groynes which had to be got over every few yards, the going was both good and quiet. One last look behind, to measure the distance he had made since leaving the ruined Templars' church, showed him a prospect of company on his walk, in the shape of a rather indistinct personage, who seemed to be making great efforts to catch up with him, but made little, if any, progress. I mean that there was an appearance of running about his movements, but that the distance between him and Parkins did not seem materially to lessen. So, at least, Parkins thought, and decided that he almost certainly did not know him, and that it would be absurd to wait until he came up. For all that, company, he began to think, would really be very welcome on that lonely shore, if only you could choose your companion. In his unenlightened days he had read of meetings in such places which even now would hardly bear thinking of. He went on thinking of them, however, until he reached home, and particularly of one which catches most people's fancy at some time of their childhood. "Now I saw in my dream that Christian had gone but a very little way when he saw a foul fiend coming over the field to meet him." "What should I do now," he thought, "if I looked back and caught sight of a black figure sharply defined against the yellow sky, and saw that it had horns and wings? I wonder whether I should stand or run for it. Luckily, the gentleman behind is not of that kind, and he seems to be about as far off now as when I saw him first. Well, at this rate he won't get his dinner as soon as I shall; and, dear me! it's within a quarter of an hour of the time now. I must run!"

Parkins had, in fact, very little time for dressing. When he met the colonel at dinner, Peace—or as much of her as that gentleman could manage—reigned once more in the military bosom; nor was she put to flight in the hours of bridge that followed dinner, for Parkins was a more than respectable player. When, therefore, he retired towards twelve o'clock, he felt that he had spent his evening in quite a satisfactory way, and that, even for so long as a fortnight or three weeks, life at the Globe would be supportable under similar conditions—"especially," thought he, "if I go on improving my game."

As he went along the passages he met the boots of the Globe, who stopped and said, "Beg your pardon, sir, but as I was a-brushing your coat just now there was something fell out of the pocket. I put it on your chest of drawers, sir, in your room, sir—a piece of a pipe or something of that sort, sir. Thank you, sir. You'll find it on your chest of drawers, sir—yes, sir. Good-night, sir."

The speech served to remind Parkins of his little discovery of that afternoon. It was with some considerable curiosity that he turned it over by the light of his candles. It was of bronze, he now saw, and was shaped very much after the manner of the modern dog-whistle; in fact it was—yes, certainly it was—actually no more nor less than a whistle. He put it to his lips, but it was quite full of a fine, caked-up sand or earth, which would not yield to knocking, but must be loosened with a knife. Tidy as ever in his habits, Parkins cleared out the earth on to a piece of paper and took the latter to the window to empty it out. The night was clear and bright, as he saw when he had opened the casement, and he stopped for an instant to look at the sea and note a belated wanderer stationed on the shore in front of the inn. Then he shut the window, a little surprised at the late hours people kept at Burnstow, and took his whistle to the light again. Why, surely there were marks on it, not merely marks, but letters! A very little rubbing rendered the deeply-cut inscription quite legible, but the professor had to confess, after some earnest thought, that the meaning of it was as obscure to him as the writing on the wall to Belshazzar. There were legends both on the front and on the back of the whistle. The one read thus:

FLA.
FUR BIS
FLE

The other:

卐 QUIS EST ISTE QUI VENIT 卐

"I ought to be able to make it out," he thought; "but I suppose I am a little rusty in my Latin. When I come to think of it, I don't believe I even know the word for a whistle. The long one does seem simple enough. It ought to mean, 'Who is this who is coming?' Well, the best way to find out is evidently to whistle for him."

He blew tentatively and stopped suddenly, startled and yet pleased at the note he had elicited. It had a quality of infinite distance in it, and, soft as it was, he somehow felt it must be audible for miles round. It was a sound, too, that seemed to have the power (which many scents possess) of forming pictures in the brain. He saw quite clearly for a moment a vision of a wide, dark expanse at night, with a fresh wind blowing, and in the midst a lonely figure—how employed, he could not tell. Perhaps he would have seen more had not the picture been broken by the sudden surge of a gust of wind against his casement, so sudden that it made him look up, just in time to see the white glint of a sea-bird's wing somewhere outside the dark panes.

The sound of the whistle had so fascinated him that he could not help trying it once more, this time more boldly. The note was little, if at all, louder than before, and repetition broke the illusion—no picture followed, as he had half hoped it might. "But what is this? Goodness! what force the wind can get up in a few minutes! What a tremendous gust! There! I knew that window-fastening was no use! Ah! I thought so—both candles out. It's enough to tear the room to pieces."

The first thing was to get the window shut. While you might count twenty Parkins was struggling with the small casement, and felt almost as if he were pushing back a sturdy burglar, so strong was the pressure.

It slackened all at once, and the window banged to and latched itself. Now to relight the candles and see what damage, if any, had been done. No, nothing seemed amiss; no glass even was broken in the casement. But the noise had evidently roused at least one member of the household: the colonel was to be heard stumping in his stockinged feet on the floor above, and growling.

Quickly as it had risen, the wind did not fall at once. On it went, moaning and rushing past the house, at times rising to a cry so desolate that, as Parkins disinterestedly said, it might have made fanciful people feel quite uncomfortable; even the unimaginative, he thought after a quarter of an hour, might be happier without it.

Whether it was the wind, or the excitement of golf or of the researches in the preceptory, that kept Parkins awake, he was not sure. Awake he remained, in any case, long enough to fancy (as I am afraid I often do myself under such conditions) that he was the victim of all manner of fatal disorders: he would lie counting the beats of his heart, convinced that it was going to stop work every moment, and would entertain grave suspicions of his lungs, brain, liver, etc.—suspicions which he was sure would be dispelled by the return of daylight, but which until then refused to be put aside. He found a little vicarious comfort in the idea that someone else was in the same boat. A near neighbour (in the darkness it was not easy to tell his direction) was tossing and rustling in his bed, too.

The next stage was that Parkins shut his eyes and determined to give sleep every chance. Here again over-excitement asserted itself in another form—that of making pictures. *Experto crede*, pictures do come to the closed eyes of one trying to sleep, and are often so little to his taste that he must open his eyes and disperse them.

Parkins's experience on this occasion was a very distressing one. He found that the picture which presented itself to him was continuous. When he opened his eyes, of course, it went; but when he shut them once more it framed itself afresh, and acted itself out again, neither quicker nor slower than before.

What he saw was this. A long stretch of shore—shingle edged by sand and intersected at short intervals with black groynes running down to the water—a scene, in fact, so like that of his afternoon's walk that, in the absence of any landmark, it could not be distinguished therefrom. The light was obscure, conveying an impression of gathering storm, late winter evening, and slight cold rain. On this bleak stage at first no actor was visible. Then, in the distance, a bobbing black object appeared; a moment more, and it was a man running, jumping, clambering over the groynes, and every few seconds looking eagerly back. The nearer he came the more obvious it was that he was not only anxious, but even terribly frightened, though his face was not to be distinguished. He was, moreover, almost at the end of his strength. On he came; each successive obstacle seemed to cause him more difficulty than the last. "Will he get over this next one?" thought Parkins; "it seems a little higher than the others." Yes; half climbing, half throwing himself, he did get over, and fell all in a heap on the other side (the side nearest to the spectator). There, as if really unable to get up again, he remained crouching under the groyne, looking up in an attitude of painful anxiety.

So far no cause whatever for the fear of the runner had been shown; but now there began to be seen, far up the shore, a little flicker of something light-coloured moving to and fro with great swiftness and irregularity. Rapidly growing larger, it, too, declared itself as a figure in pale, fluttering draperies, ill-defined. There was something about its motion which made Parkins very unwilling to see it at close quarters. It would stop, raise its arms, bow itself towards the sand, then run stooping across the beach to the water's-edge and back again; and then, rising upright, once more continue its course forward at a speed that was startling and terrifying. The moment came when the pursuer was hovering about from left to right only a few yards beyond the groyne where the runner lay in hiding. After two or three ineffectual castings hither and thither it came to a stop, stood upright, with arms raised high, and then darted straight forward towards the groyne.

It was at this point that Parkins always failed in his resolution to keep his eyes shut. With many misgivings as to incipient failure of eyesight, overworked brain, excessive smoking, and so on, he finally resigned himself to light his candle, get out a book, and pass the night waking, rather than be tormented by this persistent panorama, which he saw clearly enough could only be a morbid reflection of his walk and his thoughts on that very day.

The scraping of match on box and the glare of light must have startled some creatures of the night—rats or what not—which he heard scurry across the floor from the side of his bed with much rustling. Dear, dear! the match is out! Fool that it is! But the second one burnt better, and a candle and book were duly procured, over which Parkins pored till sleep of a wholesome kind came upon him, and that in no long space. For about the first time in his orderly and prudent life he forgot to blow out the candle, and when he was called next morning at eight there was still a flicker in the socket and a sad mess of guttered grease on the top of the little table.

After breakfast he was in his room, putting the finishing touches to his golfing costume—fortune had again allotted the colonel to him for a partner—when one of the maids came in.

"Oh, if you please," she said, "would you like any extra blankets on your bed, sir?"

"Ah! thank you," said Parkins. "Yes, I think I should like one. It seems likely to turn rather colder."

In a very short time the maid was back with the blanket.

"Which bed should I put it on, sir?" she asked.

"What? Why, that one—the one I slept in last night," he said, pointing to it.

"Oh yes! I beg your pardon, sir, but you seemed to have tried both of 'em; leastways, we had to make 'em both up this morning."

"Really? How very absurd!" said Parkins. "I certainly never touched the other, except to lay some things on it. Did it actually seem to have been slept in?"

"Oh yes, sir!" said the maid. "Why, all the things was crumpled and throwed about all ways, if you'll excuse me, sir—quite as if anyone 'adn't passed but a very poor night, sir."

"Dear me," said Parkins. "Well, I may have disordered it more than I thought when I unpacked my things. I'm very sorry to have given you the extra trouble, I'm sure. I expect a friend of mine soon, by the way—gentleman from Cambridge—to come and occupy it for a night or two. That will be all right, I suppose, won't it?"

"Oh yes, to be sure, sir. Thank you, sir. It's no trouble, I'm sure," said the maid, and departed to giggle with her colleagues.

Parkins set forth, with a stern determination to improve his game.

I am glad to be able to report that he succeeded so far in this enterprise that the colonel, who had been rather repining at the prospect of a second day's play in his company, became quite chatty as the morning advanced; and his voice boomed out over the flats, as certain also of our own minor poets have said, "like some great bourdon in a minster tower."

"Extraordinary wind, that, we had last night," he said. "In my old home we should have said someone had been whistling for it."

"Should you, indeed!" said Parkins. "Is there a superstition of that kind still current in your part of the country?"

"I don't know about superstition," said the colonel. "They believe in it all over Denmark and Norway, as well as on the Yorkshire coast; and my experience is, mind you, that there's generally something at the bottom of what these countryfolk hold to, and have held to for generations. But it's your drive" (or whatever it might have been: the golfing reader will have to imagine appropriate digressions at the proper intervals).

When conversation was resumed, Parkins said, with a slight hesitancy, "Apropos of what you were saying just now, colonel, I think I ought to tell you that my own views on such subjects are very strong. I am, in fact, a convinced disbeliever in what is called the 'supernatural.'"

"What!" said the colonel, "do you mean to tell me you don't believe in second-sight, or ghosts, or anything of that kind?"

"In nothing whatever of that kind," returned Parkins firmly.

"Well," said the colonel, "but it appears to me at that rate, sir, that you must be little better than a Sadducee."

Parkins was on the point of answering that, in his opinion, the Sadducees were the most sensible persons he had ever read of in the Old Testament; but, feeling some doubt as to whether much mention of them was to be found in that work, he preferred to laugh the accusation off.

"Perhaps I am," he said; "but—Here, give me my cleek, boy!—Excuse me one moment, colonel." A short interval. "Now, as to whistling for the wind, let me give you my theory about it. The laws which govern winds are really not at all perfectly known—to fisher-folk and such, of course, not known at all. A man or woman of eccentric habits, perhaps, or a stranger, is seen repeatedly on the beach at some unusual hour, and is heard whistling. Soon afterwards a violent wind arises; a man who could read the sky perfectly or who possessed a barometer could have foretold that it would. The simple people of a fishing-village have no barometers, and only a few rough rules for prophesying weather. What more natural than that the eccentric personage I postulated should be regarded as having raised the wind, or that he or she should clutch eagerly at the reputation of being able to do so? Now, take last night's wind: as it happens, I myself was whistling. I blew a whistle twice, and the wind seemed to come absolutely in answer to my call. If anyone had seen me—"

The audience had been a little restive under this harangue, and Parkins had, I fear, fallen somewhat into the tone of a lecturer; but at the last sentence the colonel stopped him.

"Whistling, were you?" he said. "And what sort of whistle did you use? Play this stroke first." Interval.

"About that whistle you were asking, colonel. It's rather a curious one. I have it in my—No; I see I've left it in my room. As a matter of fact, I found it yesterday."

And then Parkins narrated the manner of his discovery of the whistle, upon hearing which the colonel grunted, and opined that, in Parkins's place, he should himself be careful about using a thing that had belonged to a set of papists, of whom, speaking generally, it might be affirmed that you never knew what they might not have been up to. From this topic he diverged to the enormities of the vicar, who had given notice on the previous Sunday that Friday would be the Feast of St. Thomas the Apostle, and that there would be a service at eleven o'clock in the church. This and other similar proceedings constituted in the colonel's view a strong presumption that the vicar was a concealed papist, if not a Jesuit; and Parkins, who could not very readily follow the colonel in this region, did not disagree with him. In fact, they got on so well together in the morning that there was no talk on either side of their separating after lunch.

Both continued to play well during the afternoon, or, at least, well enough to make them forget everything else until the light began to fail them. Not until then did Parkins remember that he had meant to do some more investigating at the preceptory; but it was of no great importance, he reflected. One day was as good as another; he might as well go home with the colonel.

As they turned the corner of the house, the colonel was almost knocked down by a boy who rushed into him at the very top of his speed, and then, instead of running away, remained hanging on to him and panting. The first words of the warrior were naturally those of reproof and objurgation, but he very quickly discerned that the boy was almost speechless with fright. Enquiries were useless at first. When the boy got his breath he began to howl, and still clung to the colonel's legs. He was at last detached, but continued to howl.

"What in the world *is* the matter with you? What have you been up to? What have you seen?" said the two men.

"Ow, I seen it wive at me out of the winder," wailed the boy, "and I don't like it."

"What window?" said the irritated colonel. "Come, pull yourself together, my boy."

"The front winder it was, at the 'otel," said the boy.

At this point Parkins was in favour of sending the boy home, but the colonel refused; he wanted to get to the bottom of it, he said; it was most dangerous to give a boy such a fright as this one had had, and if it turned out that people had been playing jokes, they should suffer for it in some way. And by a series of questions he made out this story: The boy had been playing about on the grass in front of the Globe with some others; then they had gone home to their teas, and he was just going, when he happened to look up "at the front winder and see it a-wiving at him." *It* seemed to be a figure of some sort, in white as far as he knew—couldn't see its face; but it waved at him, and "it warn't a right thing—not to say not a right person." Was there a light in the room? No, he didn't think to look if there was a light. Which was the window? Was it the top one or the second one? The "seckind one it was—the big winder what's got two little uns at the sides."

"Very well, my boy," said the colonel, after a few more questions. "You run away home now. I expect it was some person trying to give you a start. Another time, like a brave English boy, you just throw a stone—well, no, not that exactly, but you go and speak to the waiter, or to Mr. Simpson, the landlord, and—yes—and say that I advised you to do so."

The boy's face expressed some of the doubt he felt as to the likelihood of Mr. Simpson's lending a favourable ear to his complaint, but the colonel did not appear to perceive this, and went on, "And here's a sixpence—no, I see it's a shilling—and you be off home, and don't think any more about it."

The youth hurried off with agitated thanks, and the colonel and Parkins went round to the front of the Globe and reconnoitred. There was only one window answering to the description they had been hearing.

"Well, that's curious," said Parkins; "it's evidently my window the lad was talking about. Will you come up for a moment, colonel Wilson? We ought to be able to see if anyone has been taking liberties in my room."

They were soon in the passage, and Parkins made as if to open the door. Then he stopped and felt in his pockets.

"This is more serious than I thought," was his next remark. "I remember now that before I started this morning I locked the door. It is locked now, and, what is more, here is the key." And he held it up. "Now," he went on, "if the servants are in the habit of going into one's room during the day when one is away, I can only say that—well, that I don't approve of it at all." Conscious of a somewhat weak climax, he busied himself in opening the door (which was indeed locked) and in lighting candles. "No," he said, "nothing seems disturbed."

"Except your bed," put in the colonel.

"Excuse me, that isn't my bed," said Parkins. "I don't use that one. But it does look as if someone had been playing tricks with it."

It certainly did: the clothes were bundled up and twisted together in a most tortuous confusion. Parkins pondered.

"That must be it," he said at last: "I disordered the clothes last night in unpacking, and they haven't made it since. Perhaps they came in to make it, and that boy saw them through the window; and then they were called away and locked the door after them. Yes, I think that must be it."

"Well, ring and ask," said the colonel, and this appealed to Parkins as practical.

The maid appeared, and, to make a long story short, deposed that she had made the bed in the morning when the gentleman was in the room, and hadn't been there since. No, she "hadn't no other key." Mr. Simpson he "kep' the keys"; he'd be able to tell the gentleman if anyone had been up.

This was a puzzle. Investigation showed that nothing of value had been taken, and Parkins remembered the disposition of the small objects on tables and so forth well enough to be pretty sure that no pranks had been played with them. Mr. and Mrs. Simpson furthermore agreed that neither of them had given the duplicate key of the room to any person whatever during the day. Nor could Parkins, fair-minded man as he was, detect anything in the demeanour of master, mistress, or maid that indicated guilt. He was much more inclined to think that the boy had been imposing on the colonel.

The latter was unwontedly silent and pensive at dinner and throughout the evening. When he bade good-night to Parkins, he murmured in a gruff undertone, "You know where I am if you want me during the night."

"Why, yes, thank you, colonel Wilson, I think I do; but there isn't much prospect of my disturbing you, I hope. By the way," he added, "did I show you that old whistle I spoke of? I think not. Well, here it is."

The colonel turned it over gingerly in the light of the candle.

"Can you make anything of the inscription?" asked Parkins, as he took it back.

"No, not in this light. What do you mean to do with it?"

"Oh, well, when I get back to Cambridge I shall submit it to some of the archaeologists there, and see what they think of it; and very likely, if they consider it worth having, I may present it to one of the museums."

"'Mm!" said the colonel. "Well, you may be right. All I know is that, if it were mine, I should chuck it straight into the sea. It's no use talking, I'm well aware, but I expect that with you it's a case of live and learn. I hope so, I'm sure, and I wish you a good-night."

He turned away, leaving Parkins at the bottom of the stairs, about to make some reply; soon each was in his own bedroom.

By some unfortunate accident, there were neither blinds nor curtains to the windows of the professor's room. The previous night he had thought little of this, but tonight there seemed every prospect of a bright moon rising to shine directly on his bed, and probably wake him later on. When he noticed this he was a good deal annoyed, but, with an ingenuity which I can only envy, he succeeded in rigging up, with the help of a railway-rug, some safety-pins, a stick and an umbrella, a screen which, if it only held together, would completely keep the moonlight off his bed. And shortly afterwards he was comfortably in that bed. When he had read a somewhat solid work long enough to produce a decided wish for sleep, he cast a drowsy glance round the room, blew out the candle, and fell back upon the pillow.

He must have slept soundly for an hour or more, when a sudden clatter shook him up in a most unwelcome manner. In a moment he realised what had happened: his carefully constructed screen had given way, and a very bright frosty moon was shining directly on his face. This was highly annoying. Could he possibly get up and reconstruct the screen? or could he manage to sleep if he did not?

For some minutes he lay and pondered over the possibilities; then he turned over sharply, and with all his eyes open lay breathlessly listening. There had been a movement, he was sure, in the empty bed on the opposite side of the room. Tomorrow he would have it moved, for there must be rats or something playing about in it. It was quiet now. No! the commotion began again. There was a rustling and shaking: surely more than any rat could cause.

I can figure to myself something of the professor's bewilderment and horror, for I have in a dream thirty years back seen the same thing happen; but the reader will hardly, perhaps, imagine how dreadful it was to him to see a figure suddenly sit up in what he had known was an empty bed. He was out of his own bed in one bound, and made a dash towards the window, where lay his only weapon, the stick with which he had propped his screen. This was, as it turned out, the worst thing he could have done, because the personage in the empty bed, with a sudden smooth motion, slipped from the bed and took up a position, with outspread arms, between the two beds, and in front of the door. Parkins watched it in a horrid perplexity. Somehow, the idea of getting past it and escaping through the door was intolerable to him; he could not have borne—he didn't know why—to touch it; and as for its touching him, he would sooner dash himself through the window than have that happen. It stood for the moment in a band of dark shadow and he could not see what its face was like. Now it began to move, in a stooping posture, and all at once the spectator realized, with some horror and some relief, that it must be blind, for it seemed to feel about it with its muffled arms in a groping and random fashion. Turning half away from him, it became suddenly conscious of the bed he had just left, and darted towards it, and bent over and felt the pillows in a way which made Parkins shudder as he had never in his life thought it possible. In a very few moments it seemed to know that the bed was empty, and then, moving forward into the area of light and facing the window, it showed for the first time what manner of thing it was.

Parkins, who very much dislikes being questioned about it, did once describe something of it in my hearing, and I gathered that what he chiefly remembers about it is a horrible, an intensely horrible, face *of crumpled linen.* What expression he read upon it he could not or would not tell, but that the fear of it went nigh to maddening him is certain.

But he was not at leisure to watch it for long. With formidable quickness it moved into the middle of the room, and, as it groped and waved, one corner of its draperies swept across Parkins's face. He could not—though he knew how perilous a sound was—he could not keep back a cry of disgust, and this gave the searcher an instant clue. It leapt towards him upon the instant, and the next moment he was halfway through the window backwards, uttering cry upon cry at the utmost pitch of his voice, and the linen face was thrust close into his own. At this, almost the last possible second, deliverance came, as you will have guessed: the colonel burst the door open, and was just in time to see the dreadful group at the window. When he reached the figures only one was left. Parkins sank forward into the room in a faint, and before him on the floor lay a tumbled heap of bedclothes.

Colonel Wilson asked no questions, but busied himself in keeping everyone else out of the room and in getting Parkins back to his bed; he himself, wrapped in a rug, occupied the other bed for the rest of the night. Early on the next day Rogers arrived, more welcome than he would have been a day before, and the three of them held a very long consultation in the professor's room. At the end of it the colonel left the hotel door carrying a small object between his finger and thumb, which he cast as far into the sea as a very brawny arm could send it. Later on the smoke of a bonfire ascended from the back premises of the Globe.

Exactly what explanation was patched up for the staff and visitors at the hotel I must confess I do not recollect. The professor was somehow cleared of the ready suspicion of delirium tremens, and the hotel of the reputation of a troubled house.

There is not much question as to what would have happened to Parkins if the colonel had not intervened when he did. He would either have fallen out of the window or else lost his wits. But it is not so evident what more the creature that came in answer to the whistle could have done than frighten. There seemed to be absolutely nothing material about it save the bedclothes of which it had made itself a body. The colonel, who remembered a not very dissimilar occurrence in India, was of the opinion that if Parkins had closed with it it could really have done very little, and that its one power was that of frightening. The whole thing, he said, served to confirm his opinion of the Church of Rome.

There is really nothing more to tell, but, as you may imagine, the professor's views on certain points are less clear-cut than they used to be. His nerves, too, have suffered: he cannot even now see a surplice hanging on a door quite unmoved, and the spectacle of a scarecrow in a field late on a winter afternoon has cost him more than one sleepless night.

The Derelict

William Hope Hodgson

"IT'S THE *Material,*" said the old ship's doctor . . . "The *Material,* plus the conditions; and, maybe," he added slowly, "a third factor—yes, a third factor; but there, there . . ." He broke off his half-meditative sentence, and began to charge his pipe.

"Go on, Doctor," we said encouragingly, and with more than a little expectancy. We were in the smoke-room of the *Sand-a-lea,* running across the North Atlantic; and the doctor was a character. He concluded the charging of his pipe, and lit it; then settled himself, and began to express himself more fully:

"The *Material,*" he said, with conviction, "is inevitably the medium of expression of the Life-Force—the fulcrum, as it were; lacking which, it is unable to exert itself, or, indeed, to express itself in any form or fashion that would be intelligible or evident to us.

"So potent is the share of the *Material* in the production of that thing which we name Life, and so eager the Life-Force to express itself, that I am convinced it would, if given the right conditions, make itself manifest even through so hopeless-seeming a medium as a simple block of sawn wood; for I tell you, gentlemen, the Life-Force is both as fiercely urgent and as indiscriminate as Fire—the Destructor; yet which some are now growing to consider the very essence of Life rampant . . . There is a quaint seeming paradox there," he concluded, nodding his old grey head.

"Yes, Doctor," I said. "In brief, your argument is that Life is a thing, state, fact, or element, call-it-what-you-like, which requires the *Material* through which to manifest itself, and that given the *Material,* plus the conditions, the result is Life. In other words, that Life is an evolved product, manifested through Matter and bred of conditions—eh?"

"As we understand the word," said the old doctor. "Though, mind you, there *may* be a third factor. But, in my heart, I believe that it is a matter of chemistry; conditions and a suitable medium; but given the conditions, the Brute is so almighty that it will seize upon anything through which to manifest itself. It is a force generated by conditions; but nevertheless this does not bring us one iota nearer to its *explanation,* any more than to the explanation of electricity or fire. They are, all three, of the Outer Forces—Monsters of the Void. Nothing we can do will *create* any one of them; our power is merely to be able, by providing the conditions, to make each one of them manifest to our physical senses. Am I clear?"

"Yes, Doctor, in a way you are," I said. "But I don't agree with you; though I think I understand you. Electricity and fire are both what I might call natural things; but life is an abstract something—a kind of all-permeating wakefulness. Oh, I can't explain it; who could? But it's spiritual; not just a thing bred out of a condition, like fire, as you say, or electricity. It's a horrible thought of yours. Life's a kind of spiritual mystery . . ."

"Easy, my boy!" said the old doctor, laughing gently to himself; "or else I may be asking you to demonstrate the spiritual mystery of life of the limpet, or the crab, shall we say?"

He grinned at me, with ineffable perverseness. "Anyway," he continued, "as I suppose you've all guessed, I've a yarn to tell you in support of my impression that life is no more a mystery or a miracle than fire or electricity. But, please to remember, gentlemen, that because we've succeeded in naming and making good use of these two forces, they're just as much mysteries, fundamentally, as ever. And, anyway, the thing I'm going to tell you, won't explain the mystery of life; but only give you one of my pegs on which I hang my feeling that life is, as I have said, a force made manifest through conditions (that is to say, natural chemistry), and that it can take for its purpose and need, the most incredible and unlikely matter; for without matter, it cannot come into existence—it cannot become manifest . . ."

"I don't agree with you, Doctor," I interrupted. "Your theory would destroy all belief in life after death. It would . . ."

"Hush, sonny," said the old man, with a quiet little smile of comprehension. "Hark to what I've to say first; and, anyway, what objection have you to material life, after death; and if you object to a material framework, I would still have you remember that I am speaking of life, as we understand the word in this our life. Now do be a quiet lad, or I'll never be done:

"It was when I was a young man, and that is a good many years ago, gentlemen. I had passed my examination; but was so run down with overwork, that it was decided that I had better take a trip to sea. I was by no means well off, and very glad, in the end, to secure a nominal post as doctor in a sailing passenger-clipper, running out to China.

"The name of the ship was the *Bheotpte,* and soon after I had got all my gear aboard, she cast off, and we dropped down the Thames, and next day were well away out in the Channel.

"The captain's name was Gannington, a very decent man; though quite illiterate. The first mate, Mr. Berlies, was a quiet, sternish, reserved man, very well read. The second mate, Mr. Selvern, was, perhaps, by birth and upbringing, the most socially cultured of the three; but he lacked the stamina and indomitable pluck of the two others. He was more of a sensitive; and emotionally and even mentally, the most alert man of the three.

"On our way out, we called at Madagascar, where we landed some of our passengers; then we ran eastward, meaning to call at North-West Cape; but about a hundred degrees east, we encountered very dreadful weather, which carried away all our sails and sprung the jib-boom and fore t'gallant mast.

"The storm carried us northward for several hundred miles, and when it dropped us finally, we found ourselves in a very bad state. The ship had been strained, and had taken some three feet of water through her seams; the main topmast had been sprung, in addition to the jib-boom and fore t'gallant mast; two of our boats had gone, as also one of the pigsties (with three fine pigs), this latter having been washed overboard but some half-hour before the wind began to ease, which it did quickly; though a very ugly sea ran for some hours after.

"The wind left us just before dark, and when morning came, it brought splendid weather; a calm, mildly undulating sea, and a brilliant sun, with no wind. It showed us also that we were not alone; for about two miles away to the westward was another vessel, which Mr. Selvern, the second mate, pointed out to me.

"'That's a pretty rum-looking packet, Doctor,' he said, and handed me his glass. I looked through it, at the other vessel, and saw what he meant; at least, I thought I did.

"'Yes, Mr. Selvern,' I said, 'she's got a pretty old-fashioned look about her.'

"He laughed at me, in his pleasant way.

"'It's easy to see you're not a sailor, Doctor,' he remarked. 'There's a dozen rum things about her. She's a derelict, and has been floating round, by the look of her, for many a score of years. Look at the shape of her counter, and the bows and cut-water. She's as old as the hills, as you might say, and ought to have gone down to Davy Jones a long time ago. Look at the growths on her, and the thickness of her standing rigging; that's all salt encrustations, I fancy, if you notice the white colour. She's been a small barque; but don't you see she's not a yard left aloft. They've all dropped out of the slings; everything rotted away; wonder the standing rigging hasn't gone too. I wish the Old Man would let us take the boat, and have a look at her; she'd be well worth it.'

"There seemed little chance, however, of this; for all hands were turned-to and kept hard at it all day long, repairing the damage to the masts and gear, and this took a long while, as you may think. Part of the time I gave a hand, heaving on one of the deck-capstans; for the exercise was good for my liver. Old Captain Gannington approved, and I persuaded him to come along and try some of the same medicine, which he did; and we grew very chummy over the job.

"We got talking about the derelict, and he remarked how lucky we were not to have run full tilt on to her, in the darkness; for she lay right away to leeward of us, according to the way that we had been drifting in the storm. He also was of the opinion that she had a strange look about her, and that she was pretty old but on this latter point, he plainly had far less knowledge than the second mate; for he was, as I have said, an illiterate man, and he knew nothing of sea-craft beyond what experience had taught him. He lacked the book knowledge, which the second mate had, of vessels previous to his day, which it appeared the derelict was.

"'She's an old 'un, Doctor,' was the extent of his observations in this direction.

"Yet, when I mentioned to him that it would be interesting to go aboard, and give her a bit of an overhaul, he nodded his head, as if the idea had been already in his mind, and accorded with his own inclinations.

"'When the work's over, Doctor,' he said. 'Can't spare the men now, ye know. Got to get all shipshape an' ready as smart as we can. But we'll take my gig, an' go off in the Second Dog Watch. The glass is steady, an' it'll be a bit of jam for us.'

"That evening, after tea, the captain gave orders to clear the gig and get overboard. The second mate was to come with me, and the skipper gave him word to see that two or three lamps were put into the boat, as it would soon fall dark. A little later, we were pulling across the calmness of the sea with a crew of six at the oars, and making very good speed of it.

"Now, gentlemen, I have detailed to you with great exactness, all the facts, both big and little, so that you can follow step by step each incident in this extraordinary affair; and I want you now to pay the closest attention.

"I was sitting in the stern-sheets, with the second mate and the captain, who was steering; and as we drew nearer and nearer to the stranger, I studied her with an ever-growing attention, as, indeed, did

Captain Gannington, and the second mate. She was, as you know, to the westward of us, and the sunset was making a great flame of red light to the back of her, so that she showed a little blurred and indistinct, by reason of the halation of the light, which almost defeated the eye in any attempt to see her rotting spars and standing rigging, submerged as they were in the fiery glory of the sunset.

"It was because of this effect of the sunset, that we had come quite close, comparatively, to the derelict before we saw that she was surrounded by a sort of curious scum, the colour of which was difficult to decide upon, by reason of the red light that was in the atmosphere; but which afterwards we discovered to be brown. This scum spread all about the old vessel for many hundreds of yards, in a huge, irregular patch, a great stretch of which reached out to the eastward, upon our starboard side, some score, or so, fathoms away.

"'Queer stuff,' said Captain Gannington, leaning to the side, and looking over. 'Something in the cargo as 'as gone rotten an' worked out through 'er seams.'

"'Look at her bows and stern,' said the second mate; 'just look at the growth on her.'

"There were, as he said, great clumpings of strange-looking sea-fungi under the bows and the short counter astern. From the stump of her jib-boom and her cutwater, great beards of rime and marine growths hung downward into the scum that held her in. Her blank starboard side was presented to us, all a dead, dirtyish white, streaked and mottled vaguely with dull masses of heavier colour.

"'There's a steam or haze rising off her,' said the second mate, speaking again; 'you can see it against the light. It keeps coming and going. Look!'

"I saw then what he meant—a faint haze or steam, either suspended above the old vessel, or rising from her; and Captain Gannington saw it also:

"'Spontaneous combustion!' he exclaimed. 'We'll 'ave to watch w'en we lift the 'atches; 'nless it's some poor devil that's got aboard of her; but that ain't likely.'

"We were now within a couple of hundred yards of the old derelict, and had entered into the brown scum. As it poured off the lifted oars, I heard one of the men mutter to himself—'dam treacle!' and indeed, it was something like it. As the boat continued to forge nearer and nearer to the old ship, the scum grew thicker and thicker; so that, at last, it perceptibly slowed us.

"'Give way, lads! Put some beef to it!' sung out Captain Gannington; and thereafter there was no sound, except the panting of the men, and the faint, reiterated suck, suck, of the sullen brown scum upon the oars, as the boat was forced ahead. As we went, I was conscious of a peculiar smell in the evening air, and whilst I had no doubt that the puddling of the scum, by the oars, made it rise, I felt that in some way, it was vaguely familiar; yet I could give it no name.

"We were now very close to the old vessel, and presently she was high above us, against the dying light. The captain called out then to—'in with the bow oars, and stand-by with the boat-hook,' which was done.

"'Aboard there! Ahoy! Aboard there! Ahoy!' shouted Captain Gannington, but there came no answer, only the flat sound of his voice going lost into the open sea, each time he sang out.

"'Ahoy! Aboard there! Ahoy!' he shouted, time after time; but there was only the weary silence of the old hulk that answered us; and, somehow as he shouted, the while that I stared up half expectantly at her, a queer little sense of oppression, that amounted almost to nervousness, came upon me. It passed, but I remember how I was suddenly aware that it was growing dark. Darkness comes fairly rapidly in the tropics, though not so quickly as many fiction-writers seem to think; but it was not that the coming dusk had perceptibly deepened in that brief time, of only a few moments, but rather that my nerves had made me suddenly a little hypersensitive. I mention my state particularly; for I am not a nervy man, normally; and my abrupt touch of nerves is significant, in the light of what happened.

"'There's no one on board there!' said Captain Gannington. 'Give way, men!' For the boat's crew had instinctively rested on their oars, as the captain hailed the old craft. The men gave way again; and then the second mate called out excitedly—'Why, look there, there's our pigsty! See, it's got *Bheotpte* painted on the end. It's drifted down here, and the scum's caught it. What a blessed wonder!'

"It was, as he had said, our pigsty that had been washed overboard in the storm, and most extraordinary to come across it there.

"'We'll tow it off with us, when we go,' remarked the captain, and shouted to the crew to get down to their oars; for they were hardly moving the boat, because the scum was so thick, close in around the old ship, that it literally clogged the boat from going ahead. I remember that it struck me in a half-conscious sort of way, as curious that the pigsty, containing our three dead pigs, had managed to drift in so far, unaided, whilst we could scarcely manage to *force* the boat in now that we had come right into the scum. But the thought passed from my mind; for so many things happened within the next few minutes.

"The men managed to bring the boat in alongside, within a couple of feet of the derelict, and the man with the boat-hook hooked on.

"''Ave you got 'old there, forrard?' asked Captain Gannington.

"'Yessir!' said the bow man; and as he spoke there came a queer noise of tearing.

"'What's that?' asked the Captain.

"'It's tore, Sir. Tore clean away!' said the man; and his tone showed that he had received something of a shock.

"'Get a hold again then!' said Captain Gannington, irritably. 'You don't s'pose this packet was built yesterday! Shove the hook into the main chains.' The man did so gingerly, as you might say; for it seemed to me, in the growing dusk, that he put no strain on to the hook, though, of course there was no need; you see, the boat could not go very far, of herself, in the stuff in which she was embedded. I remember thinking this, also, as I looked up at the bulging side of the old vessel. Then I heard Captain Gannington's voice:

"'Lord! but she's old! An' what a colour, Doctor! She don't half want paint, do she! . . . Now then, somebody—one of them oars.'

"An oar was passed to him, and he leant it up against the ancient, bulging side, then he paused, and called to the second mate to light a couple of the lamps, and stand by to pass them up; for darkness had settled down now upon the sea.

"The second mate lit two of the lamps, and told one of the men to light a third, and keep it handy in the boat; when he stepped across, with a lamp in each hand, to where Captain Gannington stood by the oar against the side of the ship.

"'Now, my lad,' said the captain, to the man who had pulled stroke, 'up with you, an' we'll pass ye up the lamps.'

"The man jumped to obey; caught the oar, and put his weight upon it, and as he did so, something seemed to give a little.

"'Look!' cried out the second mate, and pointed, lamp in hand . . . 'It's sunk in!'

"This was true. The oar had made quite an indentation into the bulging, somewhat slimy side of the old vessel.

"'Mould, I reckon,' said Captain Gannington, bending towards the derelict, to look. Then to the man:

"'Up you go, my lad, and be smart . . . Don't stand there waitin'!'

"At that, the man, who had paused a moment as he felt the oar give beneath his weight, began to shin up, and in a few seconds he was aboard, and leant out over the rail for the lamps. These were passed up to him, and the captain called to him to steady the oar. Then Captain Gannington went, calling to me to follow, and after me the second mate.

"As the captain put his face over the rail, he gave a cry of astonishment:

"'Mould, by gum! Mould . . . Tons of it! . . . Good Lord!'

"As I heard him shout that, I scrambled the more eagerly after him, and in a moment or two, I was able to see what he meant—everywhere that the light from the two lamps struck, there was nothing but smooth great masses and surfaces of a dirty-white mould.

"I climbed over the rail, with the second mate close behind, and stood upon the mould-covered decks. There might have been no planking beneath the mould, for all that our feet could feel. It gave under our tread with a spongy, puddingy feel. It covered the deck-furniture of the old ship, so that the shape of each article and fitment was often no more than suggested through it.

"Captain Gannington snatched a lamp from the other man, and the second mate reached for the other. They held the lamps high, and we all stared. It was most extraordinary, and somehow, most abominable. I can think of no other word, gentlemen, that so much describes the predominant feeling that affected me at the moment.

"'Good Lord!' said Captain Gannington, several times. 'Good Lord!' But neither the second mate nor the man said anything, and for my part I just stared, and at the same time began to smell a little at the air, for there was a vague odour of something half familiar, that somehow brought to me a sense of half-known fright.

"I turned this way and that, staring, as I have said. Here and there, the mould was so heavy as to entirely disguise what lay beneath, converting the deck-fittings into indistinguishable mounds of mould, all dirty-white, and blotched and veined with irregular, dull purplish markings.

"There was a strange thing about the mould, which Captain Gannington drew attention to—it was that our feet did not crush into it and break the surface, as might have been expected, but merely indented it.

"'Never seen nothin' like it before! . . . Never!' said the captain, after having stooped with his lamp to examine the mould under our feet. He stamped with his heel, and the mould gave out a dull, puddingy sound. He stooped again, with a quick movement, and stared, holding the lamp close to the deck. 'Blest if it ain't a reg'lar skin to it!' he said.

"The second mate and the man and I all stooped, and looked at it. The second mate progged it with his forefinger, and I remember I rapped it several times with my knuckles, listening to the dead sound it gave out, and noticing the close, firm texture of the mould.

"'Dough!' said the second mate. 'It's just like blessed dough! . . . Pouf!' He stood up with a quick movement. 'I could fancy it stinks a bit,' he said.

"As he said this, I knew suddenly what the familiar thing was, in the vague odour that hung about us—it was that the smell had something animal-like in it; something of the same smell only *heavier*, that you will smell in any place that is infested with mice. I began to look about with a sudden very real uneasiness . . . There might be vast numbers of hungry rats on board . . . They might prove exceedingly dangerous, if in a starving condition, yet, as you will understand, somehow I hesitated to put forward my idea as a reason for caution, it was too fanciful.

"Captain Gannington had begun to go aft, along the mould-covered main-deck, with the second mate; each of them holding his lamp high up, so as to cast a good light about the vessel. I turned quickly and followed them, the man with me keeping close to my heels, and plainly uneasy. As we went, I became aware that there was a feeling of moisture in the air, and I remembered the slight mist, or smoke, above the hulk, which had made Captain Gannington suggest spontaneous combustion in explanation.

"And always, as we went, there was that vague animal smell; and suddenly I found myself wishing we were well away from the old vessel.

"Abruptly, after a few paces, the captain stopped and pointed at a row of mould-hidden shapes on each side of the main-deck . . . 'Guns,' he said. 'Been a privateer in the old days, I guess; maybe worse! We'll 'ave a look below, Doctor; there may be something worth touchin'. She's older than I thought. Mr. Selvern thinks she's about three hundred years old; but I scarce think it.'

"We continued our way aft, and I remember that I found myself walking as lightly and gingerly as possible; as if I were subconsciously afraid of treading through the rotten, mould-hid decks. I think the others had a touch of the same feeling, from the way that they walked. Occasionally the soft mould would grip our heels, releasing them with a little, sullen suck.

"The captain forged somewhat ahead of the second mate, and I know that the suggestion he had made himself, that perhaps there might be something below, worth carrying away, had stimulated his imagination. The second mate was, however, beginning to feel somewhat the same way that I did; at least, I have that impression. I think if it had not been for what I might truly describe as Captain Gannington's sturdy courage, we should all of us have just gone back over the side very soon; for there was most certainly an unwholesome feeling abroad, that made one feel queerly lacking in pluck, and you will soon perceive that this feeling was justified.

"Just as the captain reached the few, mould-covered steps, leading up on to the short half-poop, I was suddenly aware that the feeling of moisture in the air had grown very much more definite. It was perceptible now, intermittently, as a sort of thin, moist, fog-like vapour, that came and went oddly, and seemed to make the decks a little indistinct to the view, this time and that. Once, an odd puff of it beat up suddenly from somewhere, and caught me in the face, carrying a queer, sickly, heavy odour with it, that somehow frightened me strangely, with a suggestion of a waiting and half-comprehended danger.

"We had followed Captain Gannington up the three mould-covered steps, and now went slowly aft along the raised after-deck.

"By the mizzen-mast, Captain Gannington paused, and held his lantern near to it . . .

"'My word, Mister,' he said to the second mate, 'it's fair thickened up with the mould; why, I'll g'antee it's close on four foot thick.' He shone the light down to where it met the deck. 'Good Lord!' he said, 'look at the sea-lice on it!' I stepped up, and it was as he had said; the sea-lice were thick upon it, some of them huge, not less than the size of large beetles, and all a clear, colourless shade, like water, except where there were little spots of grey in them, evidently their internal organisms.

"'I've never seen the like of them, 'cept on a live cod!' said Captain Gannington, in an extremely puzzled voice. 'My word! but they're whoppers!' Then he passed on, but a few paces farther aft, he stopped again, and held his lamp near to the mould-hidden deck.

"'Lord bless me, Doctor!' he called out, in a low voice, 'did ye ever see the like of that? Why, it's a foot long, if it's a hinch!'

"I stooped over his shoulder, and saw what he meant; it was a clear, colourless creature, about a foot long, and about eight inches high, with a curved back that was extraordinarily narrow. As we stared, all in a group, it gave a queer little flick, and was gone.

"'Jumped!' said the captain. 'Well, if that ain't a giant of all the sea-lice that ever I've seen! I guess it's jumped twenty-foot clear.' He straightened his back, and scratched his head a moment, swinging the lantern this way and that with the other hand, and staring about us. 'Wot are *they* doin' aboard 'ere?' he said. 'You'll see 'em (little things) on fat cod, an' such like . . . I'm blowed, Doctor, if I understand.'

"He held his lamp towards a big mound of the mould, that occupied part of the after portion of the low poop-deck, a little foreside of where there came a two-foot high 'break' to a kind of second and loftier poop, that ran away aft to the taffrail. The mound was pretty big, several feet across, and more than a yard high. Captain Gannington walked up to it:

"'I reckon this 's the scuttle,' he remarked, and gave it a heavy kick.

The only result was a deep indentation into the huge, whitish hump of mould, as if he had driven his foot into a mass of some doughy substance. Yet, I am not altogether correct in saying that this was the only result; for a certain other thing happened—from a place made by the captain's foot, there came a little gush of a purplish fluid, accompanied by a peculiar smell, that was, and was not, half familiar. Some of the mould-like substance had stuck to the toe of the captain's boot, and from this, likewise, there issued a sweat, as it were, of the same colour.

"'Well!' said Captain Gannington, in surprise, and drew back his foot to make another kick at the hump of mould; but he paused, at an exclamation from the second mate:

"'Don't, Sir!' said the second mate.

"I glanced at him, and the light from Captain Gannington's lamp showed me that his face had a bewildered, half-frightened look, as if it were suddenly and unexpectedly half afraid of something, and as if his tongue had given way to his sudden fright, without any intention on his part to speak.

"The captain also turned and stared at him.

"'Why, Mister?' he asked, in a somewhat puzzled voice, through which there sounded just the vaguest hint of annoyance. 'We've got to shift this muck, if we're to get below.'

"I looked at the second mate, and it seemed to me that, curiously enough, he was listening less to the captain, than to some other sound.

"Suddenly, he said, in a queer voice—'Listen, everybody!'

"Yet we heard nothing, beyond the faint murmur of the men talking together in the boat alongside.

"'I don't hear nothing,' said Captain Gannington, after a short pause. 'Do you, Doctor?'

"'No,' I said.

"'Wot was it you thought you heard?' asked the captain, turning again to the second mate. But the second mate shook his head, in a curious, almost irritable way; as if the captain's question interrupted his listening. Captain Gannington stared a moment at him, then held his lantern up, and glanced about him, almost uneasily. I know I felt a queer sense of strain. But the light showed nothing, beyond the greyish-dirty-white of the mould in all directions.

"'Mister Selvern,' said the captain at last, looking at him, 'don't get fancying things. Get hold of your bloomin' self. Ye know ye heard nothin'?'

"'I'm quite sure I heard something, Sir!' said the second mate. 'I seemed to hear —' He broke off sharply, and appeared to listen, with an almost painful intensity.

"'What did it sound like?' I asked.

"'It's all right, Doctor,' said Captain Gannington, laughing gently. 'Ye can give him a tonic when we get back. I'm goin' to shift this stuff.'

"He drew back and kicked for the second time at the ugly mass, which he took to hide the companion-way. The result of his kick was startling; for the whole thing wobbled sloppily, like a mound of unhealthy-looking jelly.

"He drew his foot out of it, quickly, and took a step backwards, staring, and holding his lamp towards it:

"'By gum!' he said, and it was plain that he was generally startled, 'the blessed thing's gone soft!'

"The man had run back several steps from the suddenly flaccid mound, and looking horribly frightened. Though, of what, I am sure he had not the least idea. The second mate stood where he was, and stared. For my part, I know I had a most hideous uneasiness upon me. The captain continued to hold his light towards the wobbling mound, and stare.

"'It's gone squashy all through!' he said. 'There's no scuttle there. There's no bally woodwork inside that lot! Phoo! what a rum smell!'

"He walked round to the after-side of the strange mound, to see whether there might be some signs of an opening into the hull at the back of the great heap of mould-stuff. And then:

"'*Listen!*' said the second mate, again, in the strangest sort of voice.

"Captain Gannington straightened himself upright, and there succeeded a pause of the most intense quietness, in which there was not even the hum of talk from the men alongside in the boat. We all heard it—a kind of dull, soft Thud! Thud! Thud! Thud! somewhere in the hull under us, yet so vague that I might have been half doubtful I heard it, only that the others did so, too.

"Captain Gannington turned suddenly to where the man stood:

"'Tell them —' he began. But the fellow cried out something, and pointed. There had come a strange intensity into his somewhat unemotional face; so that the captain's glance followed his action instantly. I stared, also, as you may think. It was the great mound, at which the man was pointing. I saw what he meant.

From the two gaps made in the mould-like stuff by Captain Gannington's boot, the purple fluid was jetting out in a queerly regular fashion, almost as if it were being forced out by a pump. My word! but I stared. And even as I stared, a larger jet squirted out, and splashed as far as the man, spattering his boots and trouser-legs.

"The fellow had been pretty nervous before, in a stolid, ignorant sort of way, and his funk had been growing steadily; but, at this, he simply let out a yell, and turned about to run. He paused an instant, as if a sudden fear of the darkness that held the decks between him and the boat had taken him. He snatched at the second mate's lantern, tore it out of his hand, and plunged heavily away over the vile stretch of mould.

"Mr. Selvern, the second mate, said not a word; he was just staring, staring at the strange-smelling twin streams of dull purple, that were jetting out from the wobbling mound. Captain Gannington, however, roared an order to the man to come back; but the man plunged on and on across the mould, his feet seeming to be clogged by the stuff, as if it had grown suddenly soft. He zigzagged as he ran, the lantern swaying in wild circles as he wrenched his feet free, with a constant plop, plop; and I could hear his frightened gasps, even from where I stood.

"'Come back with that lamp!' roared the captain again; but still the man took no notice, and Captain Gannington was silent an instant, his lips working in a queer, inarticulate fashion; as if he were stunned momentarily by the very violence of his anger at the man's insubordination. And in the silence, I heard the sounds again: Thud! Thud! Thud! Thud! Quite distinctly now, beating, it seemed suddenly to me, right down under my feet, but deep.

"I stared down at the mould on which I was standing, with a quick, disgusting sense of the terrible all about me; then I looked at the captain, and tried to say something, without appearing frightened. I saw that he had turned again to the mound, and all the anger had gone out of his face. He had his lamp out towards the mound, and was listening. There was a further moment of absolute silence; at least, I know that I was not conscious of any sound at all, in all the world, except that extraordinary Thud! Thud! Thud! Thud! down somewhere in the huge bulk under us.

"The captain shifted his feet, with a sudden, nervous movement; and as he lifted them, the mould went plop! plop! He looked quickly at me, trying to smile, as if he were not thinking anything very much about it: 'What do you make of it, Doctor?' he said.

"'I think —' I began. But the second mate interrupted with a single word; his voice pitched a little high, in a tone that made both stare instantly at him:

"'Look!' he said, and pointed at the mound. The thing was all of a slow quiver. A strange ripple ran outward from it, along the deck, like you will see a ripple run inshore out of a calm sea. It reached a mound a little fore-side of us, which I had supposed to be the cabin-skylight; and in a moment the second mound sank nearly level with the surrounding decks, quivering floppily in a most extraordinary fashion. A sudden quick tremor took the mould right under the second mate, and he gave out a hoarse little cry, and held his arms out on each side of him, to keep his balance. The tremor in the mould spread, and Captain Gannington swayed, and spread his feet with a sudden curse of fright. The second mate jumped across to him, and caught him by the wrist:

"'The boat, Sir!' he said, saying the very thing that I had lacked the pluck to say. 'For God's sake —'

"But he never finished; for a tremendous hoarse scream cut off his words. They hove themselves round, and looked. I could see without turning. The man who had run from us, was standing in the waist of the ship, about a fathom from the starboard bulwarks. He was swaying from side to side and screaming in a dreadful fashion. He appeared to be trying to lift his feet, and the light from his swaying lantern showed an almost incredible sight. All about him the mould was in active movement. His feet had sunk out of sight. The stuff appeared to be *lapping* at his legs; and abruptly his bare flesh showed. The hideous stuff had rent his trouser-legs away, as if they were paper. He gave out a simply sickening scream, and, with a vast effort, wrenched one leg free. It was partly destroyed. The next instant he pitched face downward, and the stuff heaped itself upon him, as if it were actually alive, with a dreadful savage life. It was simply infernal. The man had gone from sight. Where he had fallen was now a writhing, elongated mound, in constant and horrible increase, as the mould appeared to move towards it in strange ripples from all sides.

"Captain Gannington and the second mate were stone silent, in amazed and incredulous horror; but I had begun to reach towards a grotesque and terrific conclusion, both helped and hindered by my professional training.

"From the men in the boat alongside, there was a loud shouting, and I saw two of their faces appear suddenly above the rail. They showed clearly a moment in the light from the lamp which the man had snatched from Mr. Selvern; for strangely enough, this lamp was standing upright and unharmed on the deck, a little way fore-side of that dreadful, elongated, growing mound, that still swayed and writhed with an incredible horror. The lamp rose and fell on the passing ripples of the mould just—for all the world—as you will see a boat rise and fall on little swells. It is of some interest to me now, psychologically, to remember how that rising and falling lantern brought home to me, more than anything, the incomprehensible, dreadful strangeness of it all.

"The men's faces disappeared, with sudden yells, as if they had slipped or been suddenly hurt; and there was a fresh uproar of shouting from the boat. The men were calling to us to come away; to come away. In the same instant, I felt my left boot drawn suddenly and forcibly downward, with a horrible painful grip. I wrenched it free, with a yell of angry fear. Forrard of us, I saw that the vile surface was all a-move, and abruptly I found myself shouting in a queer frightened voice:

"'The boat, Captain! The boat, Captain!'

"Captain Gannington stared round at me, over his right shoulder, in a peculiar, dull way, that told me he was utterly dazed with bewilderment and the incomprehensibleness of it all. I took a quick, clogged, nervous step towards him, and gripped his arm and shook it fiercely.

"'The boat!' I shouted at him. 'The boat! For God's sake, tell the men to bring the boat aft!'

"Then the mould must have drawn his feet down; for, abruptly, he bellowed fiercely with terror, his momentary apathy giving place to furious energy. His thick-set, vastly muscular body doubled and writhed with his enormous effort, and he struck out madly, dropping the lantern. He tore his feet free, something ripping as he did so. The *reality* and necessity of the situation had come upon him, brutishly real, and he was roaring to the men in the boat:

"'Bring the boat aft! Bring 'er aft! Bring 'er aft!'

"The second mate and I were shouting the same thing, madly.

"'For God's sake be smart, lads!' roared the captain, and stooped quickly for his lamp, which still burned. His feet were gripped again, and he hove them out, blaspheming breathlessly, and leaping a yard high with his effort. Then he made a run for the side, wrenching his feet free at each step. In the same instant, the second mate cried out something, and grabbed at the captain:

"'It's got hold of my feet! It's got hold of my feet!' he screamed. His feet had disappeared up to his boot-tops, and Captain Gannington caught him round the waist with his powerful left arm, gave a mighty heave, and the next instant had him free; but both his boot-soles had almost gone.

"For my part, I jumped madly from foot to foot, to avoid the plucking of the mould; and suddenly I made a run for the ship's side. But before I could get there, a queer gap came in the mould, between us and the side, at least a couple of feet wide, and how deep I don't know. It closed up in an instant, and all the mould, where the gap had been, went into a sort of flurry of horrible ripplings, so that I ran back from it; for I did not dare to put my foot upon it. Then the captain was shouting at me:

"'Aft, Doctor! Aft, Doctor! This way, Doctor! Run!' I saw then that he had passed me, and was up on the after raised portion of the poop. He had the second mate thrown like a sack, all loose and quiet, over his left shoulder; for Mr. Selvern had fainted, and his long legs flopped, limp and helpless, against the captain's massive knees as the captain ran. I saw, with a queer unconscious noting of minor details, how the torn soles of the second mate's boots flapped and jigged, as the captain staggered aft.

"'Boat ahoy! Boat ahoy! Boat ahoy!' shouted the captain; and then I was beside him, shouting also. The men were answering with loud yells of encouragement, and it was plain they were working desperately to force the boat aft, through the thick scum about the ship.

"We reached the ancient, mould-hid taffrail, and slewed about, breathlessly, in the half darkness, to see what was happening. Captain Gannington had left his lantern by the big mound, when he picked up the second mate; and as we stood gasping, we discovered suddenly that all the mould between us and the light was full of movement. Yet, the part on which we stood, for about six or eight feet forrard of us, was still firm.

"Every couple of seconds, we shouted to the men to hasten, and they kept on calling to us that they would be with us in an instant. And all the time, we watched the deck of that dreadful hulk, feeling, for my part, literally sick with mad suspense, and ready to jump overboard into that filthy scum all about us.

"Down somewhere in the huge bulk of the ship, there was all the time that extraordinary dull, ponderous Thud! Thud! Thud! Thud! growing ever louder. I seemed to feel the whole hull of the derelict beginning to quiver and thrill with each dull beat. And to me, with the grotesque and monstrous suspicion of what made that noise, it was, at once, the most dreadful and incredible sound I have ever heard.

"As we waited desperately for the boat, I scanned incessantly so much of the grey-white bulk as the lamp showed. The whole of the decks seemed to be in strange movement. Forrard of the lamp I could see, indistinctly, the moundings of the mould swaying and nodding hideously, beyond the circle of the brightest rays. Nearer, and full in the glow of the lamp, the mound which should have indicated the skylight, was swelling steadily. There were ugly purple veinings on it, and as it swelled, it seemed to me that the veinings and mottling on it were becoming plainer—rising, as though embossed upon it, like you will see the veins stand out on the body of a powerful full-blooded horse. It was most extraordinary. The mound that we had supposed to cover the companion-way had sunk flat with the surrounding mould, and I could not see that it jetted out any more of the purplish fluid.

"A quaking movement of the mould began, away forrard of the lamp, and came flurrying away aft towards us; and at the sight of that,

I climbed up on to the spongy-feeling taffrail, and yelled afresh for the boat. The men answered with a shout, which told me they were nearer, but the beastly scum was so thick that it was evidently a fight to move the boat at all. Beside me, Captain Gannington was shaking the second mate furiously, and the man stirred and began to moan. The captain shook him awake.

"'Wake up! Wake up, Mister!' he shouted.

"The second mate staggered out of the captain's arms, and collapsed suddenly, shrieking: 'My feet! Oh, God! My feet!' The captain and I lugged him off the mould, and got him into a sitting position upon the taffrail, where he kept up a continual moaning.

"'Hold 'im, Doctor,' said the captain, and whilst I did so, he ran forrard a few yards, and peered down over the starboard quarter rail. 'For God's sake, be smart, lads! Be smart! Be smart!' He shouted down to the men; and they answered him, breathless, from close at hand; yet still too far away for the boat to be any use to us on the instant.

"I was holding the moaning, half-unconscious officer, and staring forrard along the poop decks. The flurrying of the mould was coming aft, slowly and noiselessly. And then, suddenly, I saw something closer:

"'Look out, Captain!' I shouted; and even as I shouted, the mould near to him gave a sudden peculiar slobber. I had seen a ripple stealing towards him through the horrible stuff. He gave an enormous, clumsy leap, and landed near to us on the sound part of the mould, but the movement followed him. He turned and faced it, swearing fiercely. All about his feet there came abruptly little gapings, which made horrid sucking noises.

"'Come *back,* Captain!' I yelled. 'Come back, *quick!*'

"As I shouted, a ripple came at his feet—lipping at them; and he stamped insanely at it, and leaped back, his boot torn half off his foot. He swore madly with pain and anger, and jumped swiftly for the taffrail.

"'Come on, Doctor! Over we go!' he called. Then he remembered the filthy scum, and hesitated, roaring out desperately to the men to hurry. I stared down, also.

"'The second mate?' I said.

"'I'll take charge, Doctor,' said Captain Gannington, and caught hold of Mr. Selvern. As he spoke, I thought I saw something beneath us, outlined against the scum. I leaned out over the stern, and peered. There was something under the port quarter.

"'There's something down there, Captain!' I called, and pointed in the darkness.

"He stooped far over, and stared.

"'A boat, by Gum! A *boat!*' he yelled, and began to wriggle swiftly along the taffrail, dragging the second mate after him. I followed.

"'A boat it is, sure!' he exclaimed, a few moments later, and, picking up the second mate clear of the rail, he hove him down into the boat, where he fell with a crash into the bottom.

"'Over ye go, Doctor!' he yelled at me, and pulled me bodily off the rail, and dropped me after the officer. As he did so, I felt the whole of the ancient, spongy rail give a peculiar sickening quiver, and begin to wobble. I fell on to the second mate, and the captain came after, almost in the same instant; but fortunately he landed clear of us, on to the fore thwart, which broke under his weight, with a loud crack and splintering of wood.

"'Thank God!' I heard him mutter. 'Thank God! . . . I guess that was a mighty near thing to goin' to hell.'

"He struck a match, just as I got to my feet, and between us we got the second mate straightened out on one of the after thwarts. We shouted to the men in the boat, telling them where we were, and saw the light of their lantern shining round the starboard counter of the derelict. They called back to us, to tell us they were doing their best, and then, while we waited, Captain Gannington struck another match, and began to overhaul the boat we had dropped into. She was a modern, two-oared boat, and on the stern there was painted *Cyclone Glasgow*. She was in pretty fair condition, and had evidently drifted into the scum and been held by it.

"Captain Gannington struck several matches, and went forrard towards the derelict. Suddenly he called to me, and I jumped over the thwarts to him.

"'Look, Doctor,' he said; and I saw what he meant—a mass of bones, up in the bows of the boat. I stooped over them, and looked. They were the bones of at least three people, all mixed together, in an extraordinary fashion, and quite clean and dry. I had a sudden thought concerning the bones; but I said nothing; for my thought was vague, in some ways, and concerned the grotesque and incredible suggestion that had come to me, as to the cause of that ponderous, dull Thud! Thud! Thud! Thud! that beat on so infernally within the hull, and was plain to hear even now that we had got off the vessel herself. And all the while, you know, I had a sick, horrible, mental picture of that frightful wriggling mound aboard the hulk.

"As Captain Gannington struck a final match I saw something that sickened me, and the captain saw it in the same instant. The match went out, and he fumbled clumsily for another, and struck it. We saw the thing again. We had not been mistaken . . . A great lip of grey-white was protruding in over the edge of the boat—a great lappet of the mould was coming stealthily towards us; a live mass of *the very hull itself.* And suddenly Captain Gannington yelled out, in so many words, the grotesque and incredible thing I was thinking:

"'*She's alive!*'

"I never heard such a sound of *comprehension* and terror in a man's voice. The very horrified assurance of it, made actual to me the thing that, before, had only lurked in my subconscious mind. I knew he was right; I knew that the explanation, my reason and my training, both repelled and reached towards, was the true one . . . I wonder whether anyone can possibly understand our feelings in that moment . . . the unmitigable horror of it, and the *incredibleness*.

"As the light of the match burned up fully, I saw that the mass of living matter, coming towards us, was streaked and veined with purple, the veins standing out, enormously distended. The whole thing quivered continuously to each ponderous Thud! Thud! Thud! Thud! of that gargantuan organ that pulsed within the huge grey-white bulk. The flame of the match reached the captain's fingers, and there came to me a little sickly whiff of burned flesh; but he seemed unconscious of any pain. Then the flame went out, in a brief sizzle, yet at the last moment, I had seen an extraordinary raw look, become visible upon the end of that monstrous, protruding lappet. It had become dewed with a hideous, purplish sweat. And with the darkness, there came a sudden charnel-like stench.

"I heard the match-box split in Captain Gannington's hands, as he wrenched it open. Then he swore, in a queer frightened voice; for he had come to the end of his matches. He turned clumsily in the darkness, and tumbled over the nearest thwart, in his eagerness, to get to the stern of the boat, and I after him; for we knew that thing was coming towards us through the darkness, reaching over that piteous mingled heap of human bones, all jumbled together in the bows. We shouted madly to the men, and for answer saw the bows of the boat emerge dimly into view, round the starboard counter of the derelict.

"'Thank God!' I gasped out; but Captain Gannington yelled to them to show a light. Yet this they could not do, for the lamp had just been stepped on, in their desperate efforts to force the boat round to us.

"'Quick! Quick!' I shouted.

"'For God's sake be smart, men!' roared the captain; and both of us faced the darkness under the port counter, out of which we knew (but could not see) the thing was coming towards us.

"'An oar! Smart now; pass me an oar!' shouted the captain; and reached out his hands through the gloom towards the oncoming boat. I saw a figure stand up in the bows, and hold something out to us, across the intervening yards of scum. Captain Gannington swept his hands through the darkness, and encountered it.

"'I've got it! Let go there!' he said, in a quick, tense voice.

"In the same instant, the boat we were in, was pressed over suddenly to starboard by some tremendous weight. Then I heard the captain shout: 'Duck y'r head, Doctor,' and directly afterwards he swung the heavy, fourteen-foot ash oar round his head, and struck into the darkness. There came a sudden squelch, and he struck again, with a savage grunt of fierce energy. At the second blow, the boat righted, with a slow movement, and directly afterwards the other boat bumped gently into ours.

"Captain Gannington dropped the oar, and springing across to the second mate, hove him up off the thwart, and pitched him with knee and arms clear in over the bows among the men; then he shouted to me to follow, which I did, and he came after me, bringing the oar with him. We carried the second mate aft, and the captain shouted to the men to back the boat a little; then they got her bows clear of the boat we had just left, and so headed out through the scum for the open sea.

"'Where's Tom 'Arrison?' gasped one of the men, in the midst of his exertions. He happened to be Tom Harrison's particular chum; and Captain Gannington answered him briefly enough:

"'Dead! Pull! Don't talk!'

"Now, difficult as it had been to force the boat through the scum to our rescue, the difficulty to get clear seemed tenfold. After some five minutes pulling, the boat seemed hardly to have moved a fathom, if so much, and a quite dreadful fear took me afresh; which one of the panting men put suddenly into words:

"'It's got us!' he gasped out; 'same as poor Tom!' It was the man who had inquired where Harrison was.

"'Shut y'r mouth an' *pull!*' roared the captain. And so another few minutes passed. Abruptly, it seemed to me that the dull, ponderous Thud! Thud! Thud! Thud! came more plainly through the dark, and I stared intently over the stern. I sickened a little; for I could almost swear that the dark mass of the monster was actually *nearer* . . . that it was coming nearer to us through the darkness. Captain Gannington must have had the same thought; for after a brief look into the darkness, he made one jump to the stroke-oar, and began to double-bank it.

"'Get forrid under the thwarts, Doctor!' he said to me, rather breathlessly. 'Get in the bows, an' see if you can't free the stuff a bit round the bows.'

"I did as he told me, and a minute later I was in the bows of the boat, puddling the scum from side to side with the boat-hook, and trying to break up the viscid, clinging muck. A heavy almost animal-like odour rose off it, and all the air seemed full of the deadening smell. I shall never find words to tell any one on the whole horror of it all—the threat that seemed to hang in the very air around us; and, but a little astern, that incredible thing, coming, as I firmly believe, nearer, and the scum holding us like half-melted glue.

"The minutes passed in a deadly, eternal fashion, and I kept staring back astern into the darkness; but never ceasing to puddle that filthy scum, striking at it and switching it from side to side, until I sweated.

"Abruptly, Captain Gannington sang out:

"'We're gaining, lads. Pull!' And I felt the boat forge ahead perceptibly, as they gave way, with renewed hope and energy. There was soon no doubt of it; for presently that hideous Thud! Thud! Thud! Thud! had grown quite dim and vague somewhere astern, and I could no longer see the derelict! for the night had come down tremendously dark, and all the sky was thick overset with heavy clouds. As we drew nearer and nearer to the edge of the scum, the boat moved more and more freely, until suddenly we emerged with a clean, sweet, fresh sound, into the open sea.

"'Thank God!' I said aloud, and drew in the boat-hook, and made my way aft again to where Captain Gannington now sat once more at the tiller. I saw him looking anxiously up at the sky, and across to where the lights of our vessel burned, and again he would seem to listen intently; so that I found myself listening also.

"'What's that, Captain?' I said sharply; for it seemed to me that I heard a sound far astern, something between a queer whine and a low whistling. 'What's that?'

"'It's wind, Doctor,' he said, in a low voice. 'I wish to God we were aboard.'

"Then, to the men: 'Pull! Put y'r backs into it, or ye'll never put y'r teeth through good bread again!'

"The men obeyed nobly, and we reached the vessel safely, and had the boat safely stowed, before the storm came, which it did in a furious white smother out of the west. I could see it for some minutes beforehand, tearing the sea, in the gloom, into a wall of phosphorescent foam; and as it came nearer, that peculiar whining, piping sound grew louder and louder, until it was like a vast steam-whistle, rushing towards us across the sea.

"And when it did come, we got it very heavy indeed; so that the morning showed us nothing but a welter of white seas; and that grim derelict many a score of miles away in the smother, lost as utterly as our hearts could wish to lose her.

"When I came to examine the second mate's feet, I found them in a very extraordinary condition. The soles of them had the appearance of having been partly digested. I know of no other word that so exactly describes their condition; and the agony the man suffered, must have been dreadful.

"Now," concluded the doctor, "that is what I call a case in point. If we could know exactly what the old vessel had originally been loaded with, and the juxtaposition of the various articles of her cargo, plus the heat and time she had endured, plus one or two other only guessable quantities, we should have solved the chemistry of the Life-Force, gentlemen. Not necessarily the *origin*, mind you; but, at least, we should have taken a big step on the way. I've often regretted that gale, you know—in a way, that is, in a way! It was a most amazing discovery; but, at the same time, I had nothing but thankfulness to be rid of it . . . A most amazing chance. I often think of the way the monster woke out of its torpor. And that scum . . . The dead pigs caught in it . . . I fancy that was a grim kind of a net, gentlemen . . . It caught many things . . . It . . ."

The old doctor sighed and nodded.

"If I could have had her bill of lading," he said, his eyes full of regret. "If—It might have told me something to help. But, anyway . . ." He began to fill his pipe again . . . "I suppose," he ended, looking round at us gravely, "I s'pose we humans are an ungrateful lot of beggars, at the best! . . . But . . . but what a chance! What a chance—eh?"

Sredni Vashtar

Saki (H. H. Munro)

CONRADIN WAS ten years old, and the doctor had pronounced his professional opinion that the boy would not live another five years. The doctor was silky and effete, and counted for little, but his opinion was endorsed by Mrs. De Ropp, who counted for nearly everything. Mrs. De Ropp was Conradin's cousin and guardian, and in his eyes she represented those three-fifths of the world that are necessary and disagreeable and real; the other two-fifths, in perpetual antagonism to the foregoing, were summed up in himself and his imagination. One of these days Conradin supposed he would succumb to the mastering pressure of wearisome necessary things—such as illnesses and coddling restrictions and drawn-out dullness. Without his imagination, which was rampant under the spur of loneliness, he would have succumbed long ago.

Mrs. De Ropp would never, in her honestest moments, have confessed to herself that she disliked Conradin, though she might have been dimly aware that thwarting him "for his good" was a duty which she did not find particularly irksome. Conradin hated her with a desperate sincerity which he was perfectly able to mask. Such few pleasures as he could contrive for himself gained an added relish from the likelihood that they would be displeasing to his guardian, and from the realm of his imagination she was locked out—an unclean thing, which should find no entrance.

In the dull, cheerless garden, overlooked by so many windows that were ready to open with a message not to do this or that, or a reminder that medicines were due, he found little attraction. The few fruit-trees that it contained were set jealously apart from his plucking, as though they were rare specimens of their kind blooming in an arid waste; it would probably have been difficult to find a market-gardener who would have offered ten shillings for their entire yearly produce. In a forgotten corner, however, almost hidden behind a dismal shrubbery, was a disused tool-shed of respectable proportions, and within its walls Conradin found a haven, something that took on the varying aspects of a playroom and a cathedral. He had peopled it with a legion of familiar phantoms, evoked partly from fragments of history and partly from his own brain, but it also boasted two inmates of flesh and blood. In one corner lived a ragged-plumaged Houdan hen, on which the boy lavished an affection that had scarcely another outlet. Further back in the gloom stood a large hutch, divided into two compartments, one of which was fronted with close iron bars. This was the abode of a large polecat-ferret, which a friendly butcher-boy had once smuggled, cage and all, into its present quarters, in exchange for a long-secreted hoard of small silver. Conradin was dreadfully afraid of the lithe, sharp-fanged beast, but it was his most treasured possession. Its very presence in the tool-shed was a secret and fearful joy, to be kept scrupulously from the knowledge of the Woman, as he privately dubbed his cousin. And one day, out of Heaven knows what material, he spun the beast a wonderful name, and from that moment it grew into a god and a religion. The Woman indulged in religion once a week at a church near by, and took Conradin with her, but to him the church service was an alien rite in the House of Rimmon. Every Thursday, in the dim and musty silence of the tool-shed, he worshipped with mystic and elaborate ceremonial before the wooden hutch where dwelt Sredni Vashtar, the great ferret. Red flowers in their season and scarlet berries in the winter-time were offered at his shrine, for he was a god who laid some special stress on the fierce impatient side of things, as opposed to the Woman's religion, which, as far as Conradin could observe, went to great lengths in the contrary direction. And on great festivals powdered nutmeg was strewn in front of his hutch, an important feature of the offering being that the nutmeg had to be stolen. These festivals were of irregular occurrence, and were chiefly appointed to celebrate some passing event. On one occasion, when Mrs. De Ropp suffered from acute toothache for three days, Conradin kept up the festival during the entire three days, and almost succeeded in persuading himself that Sredni Vashtar was personally responsible for the toothache. If the malady had lasted for another day the supply of nutmeg would have given out.

The Houdan hen was never drawn into the cult of Sredni Vashtar. Conradin had long ago settled that she was Anabaptist. He did not pretend to have the remotest knowledge as to what an Anabaptist was, but he privately hoped that it was dashing and not very respectable. Mrs. De Ropp was the ground plan on which he based and detested all respectability.

After a while Conradin's absorption in the tool-shed began to attract the notice of his guardian. "It is not good for him to be pottering down there in all weathers," she promptly decided, and at breakfast one morning she announced that the Houdan hen had been sold and taken away overnight. With her short-sighted eyes she peered at Conradin, waiting for an outbreak of rage and sorrow, which she was ready to rebuke with a flow of excellent precepts and reasoning. But Conradin said nothing: there was nothing to be said. Something perhaps in his white set face gave her a momentary qualm, for at tea that afternoon there was toast on the table, a delicacy which she usually banned on the ground that it was bad for him; also because the making of it "gave trouble," a deadly offence in the middle-class feminine eye.

"I thought you liked toast," she exclaimed, with an injured air, observing that he did not touch it.

"Sometimes," said Conradin.

In the shed that evening there was an innovation in the worship of the hutch-god. Conradin had been wont to chant his praises; tonight he asked a boon.

"Do one thing for me, Sredni Vashtar."

The thing was not specified. As Sredni Vashtar was a god he must be supposed to know. And choking back a sob as he looked at that other empty corner, he went back to the world he so hated.

And every night, in the welcome darkness of his bedroom, and every evening in the dusk of the tool-shed, Conradin's bitter litany went up: "Do one thing for me, Sredni Vashtar."

Mrs. De Ropp noticed that the visits to the shed did not cease, and one day she made a further journey of inspection.

"What are you keeping in that locked hutch?" she asked. "I believe it's guinea-pigs. I'll have them all cleared away."

Conradin shut his lips tight, but the Woman ransacked his bedroom till she found the carefully hidden key, and forthwith marched down to the shed to complete her discovery. It was a cold afternoon, and Conradin had been bidden to keep to the house. From the furthest window of the dining-room the door of the shed could just be seen beyond the corner of the shrubbery, and there Conradin stationed himself. He saw the Woman enter, and then he imagined her opening the door of the sacred hutch and peering down with her short-sighted eyes into the thick straw bed where his god lay hidden. Perhaps she would prod at the straw in her clumsy impatience. And Conradin fervently breathed his prayer for the last time. But he knew as he prayed that he did not believe. He knew that the Woman would come out presently with that pursed smile he loathed so well on her face, and that in an hour or two the gardener would carry away his wonderful god, a god no longer, but a simple brown ferret in a hutch. And he knew that the Woman would triumph always as she triumphed now, and that he would grow ever more sickly under her pestering and domineering and superior wisdom, till one day nothing would matter much more with him, and the doctor would be proved right. And in the sting and misery of his defeat, he began to chant loudly and defiantly the hymn of his threatened idol:

Sredni Vashtar went forth,
His thoughts were red thoughts and his teeth were white.
His enemies called for peace, but he brought them death.
Sredni Vashtar the Beautiful.

And then of a sudden he stopped his chanting and drew closer to the window-pane. The door of the shed still stood ajar as it had been left, and the minutes were slipping by. They were long minutes, but they slipped by nevertheless. He watched the starlings running and flying in little parties across the lawn; he counted them over and over again, with one eye always on that swinging door. A sour-faced maid came in to lay the table for tea, and still Conradin stood and waited and watched. Hope had crept by inches into his heart, and now a look of triumph began to blaze in his eyes that had only known the wistful patience of defeat. Under his breath, with a furtive exultation, he began once again the paean of victory and devastation. And presently his eyes were rewarded: out through that doorway came a long, low, yellow-and-brown beast, with eyes a-blink at the waning daylight, and dark wet stains around the fur of jaws and throat. Conradin dropped on his knees. The great polecat-ferret made its way down to a small brook at the foot of the garden, drank for a moment, then crossed a little plank bridge and was lost to sight in the bushes. Such was the passing of Sredni Vashtar.

"Tea is ready," said the sour-faced maid; "where is the mistress?"

"She went down to the shed some time ago," said Conradin.

And while the maid went to summon her mistress to tea, Conradin fished a toasting-fork out of the sideboard drawer and proceeded to toast himself a piece of bread. And during the toasting of it and the buttering of it with much butter and the slow enjoyment of eating it, Conradin listened to the noises and silences which fell in quick spasms beyond the dining-room door. The loud foolish screaming of the maid, the answering chorus of wondering ejaculations from the kitchen region, the scuttering footsteps and hurried embassies for outside help, and then, after a lull, the scared sobbings and the shuffling tread of those who bore a heavy burden into the house.

"Whoever will break it to the poor child? I couldn't for the life of me!" exclaimed a shrill voice. And while they debated the matter among themselves, Conradin made himself another piece of toast.

The Monkey's Paw

W. W. Jacobs

I.

WITHOUT, THE night was cold and wet, but in the small parlour of Laburnam Villa the blinds were drawn and the fire burned brightly. Father and son were at chess; the former, who possessed ideas about the game involving radical changes, putting his king into such sharp and unnecessary perils that it even provoked comment from the white-haired old lady knitting placidly by the fire.

"Hark at the wind," said Mr. White, who, having seen a fatal mistake after it was too late, was amiably desirous of preventing his son from seeing it.

"I'm listening," said the latter, grimly surveying the board as he stretched out his hand. "Check."

"I should hardly think that he'd come to-night," said his father, with his hand poised over the board.

"Mate," replied the son.

"That's the worst of living so far out," bawled Mr. White, with sudden and unlooked-for violence; "of all the beastly, slushy, out-of-the-way places to live in, this is the worst. Path's a bog, and the road's a torrent. I don't know what people are thinking about. I suppose because only two houses in the road are let, they think it doesn't matter."

"Never mind, dear," said his wife, soothingly; "perhaps you'll win the next one."

Mr. White looked up sharply, just in time to intercept a knowing glance between mother and son. The words died away on his lips, and he hid a guilty grin in his thin grey beard.

"There he is," said Herbert White, as the gate banged to loudly and heavy footsteps came toward the door.

The old man rose with hospitable haste, and opening the door, was heard condoling with the new arrival. The new arrival also condoled with himself, so that Mrs. White said, "Tut, tut!" and coughed gently as her husband entered the room, followed by a tall, burly man, beady of eye and rubicund of visage.

"Sergeant-Major Morris," he said, introducing him.

The sergeant-major shook hands, and taking the proffered seat by the fire, watched contentedly while his host got out whisky and tumblers and stood a small copper kettle on the fire.

At the third glass his eyes got brighter, and he began to talk, the little family circle regarding with eager interest this visitor from distant parts, as he squared his broad shoulders in the chair, and spoke of wild scenes and doughty deeds; of wars and plagues and strange peoples.

"Twenty-one years of it," said Mr. White, nodding at his wife and son. "When he went away he was a slip of a youth in the warehouse. Now look at him."

"He don't look to have taken much harm," said Mrs. White, politely.

"I'd like to go to India myself," said the old man, "just to look around a bit, you know."

"Better where you are," said the sergeant-major, shaking his head. He put down the empty glass, and sighing softly, shook it again.

"I should like to see those old temples and fakirs and jugglers," said the old man. "What was that you started telling me the other day about a monkey's paw or something, Morris?"

"Nothing," said the soldier, hastily. "Leastways nothing worth hearing."

"Monkey's paw?" said Mrs. White curiously.

"Well, it's just a bit of what you might call magic, perhaps," said the sergeant-major off-handedly.

His three listeners leaned forward eagerly. The visitor absent-mindedly put his empty glass to his lips and then set it down again. His host filled it for him.

"To look at," said the sergeant-major, fumbling in his pocket, "it's just an ordinary little paw, dried to a mummy."

He took something out of his pocket and proffered it. Mrs. White drew back with a grimace, but her son, taking it, examined it curiously.

"And what is there special about it?" inquired Mr. White as he took it from his son, and having examined it, placed it upon the table.

"It had a spell put on it by an old fakir," said the sergeant-major, "a very holy man. He wanted to show that fate ruled people's lives, and that those who interfered with it did so to their sorrow. He put a spell on it so that three separate men could each have three wishes from it."

His manner was so impressive that his hearers were conscious that their light laughter jarred somewhat.

"Well, why don't you have three, sir?" said Herbert White cleverly.

The soldier regarded him in the way that middle age is wont to regard presumptuous youth. "I have," he said, quietly, and his blotchy face whitened.

"And did you really have the three wishes granted?" asked Mrs. White.

"I did," said the sergeant-major, and his glass tapped against his strong teeth.

"And has anybody else wished?" persisted the old lady.

"The first man had his three wishes. Yes," was the reply; "I don't know what the first two were, but the third was for death. That's how I got the paw."

His tones were so grave that a hush fell upon the group.

"If you've had your three wishes, it's no good to you now then, Morris," said the old man at last. "What do you keep it for?"

The soldier shook his head. "Fancy, I suppose," he said, slowly. "I did have some idea of selling it, but I don't think I will. It has caused enough mischief already. Besides, people won't buy. They think it's a fairy tale, some of them; and those who do think anything of it want to try it first and pay me afterward."

"If you could have another three wishes," said the old man, eyeing him keenly, "would you have them?"

"I don't know," said the other. "I don't know."

He took the paw, and dangling it between his forefinger and thumb, suddenly threw it upon the fire. White, with a slight cry, stooped down and snatched it off.

"Better let it burn," said the soldier, solemnly.

"If you don't want it, Morris," said the other, "give it to me."

"I won't," said his friend doggedly. "I threw it on the fire. If you keep it, don't blame me for what happens. Pitch it on the fire again like a sensible man."

The other shook his head and examined his new possession closely. "How do you do it?" he inquired.

"Hold it up in your right hand and wish aloud," said the sergeant-major, "but I warn you of the consequences."

"Sounds like the *Arabian Nights,*" said Mrs. White, as she rose and began to set the supper. "Don't you think you might wish for four pairs of hands for me?"

Her husband drew the talisman from his pocket, and then all three burst into laughter as the sergeant-major, with a look of alarm on his face, caught him by the arm.

"If you must wish," he said, gruffly, "wish for something sensible."

Mr. White dropped it back in his pocket, and placing chairs, motioned his friend to the table. In the business of supper the talisman was partly forgotten, and afterward the three sat listening in an enthralled fashion to a second installment of the soldier's adventures in India.

"If the tale about the monkey's paw is not more truthful than those he has been telling us," said Herbert, as the door closed behind their guest, just in time for him to catch the last train, "we shan't make much out of it."

"Did you give him anything for it, father?" inquired Mrs. White, regarding her husband closely.

"A trifle," said he, colouring slightly. "He didn't want it, but I made him take it. And he pressed me again to throw it away."

"Likely," said Herbert, with pretended horror. "Why, we're going to be rich, and famous and happy. Wish to be an emperor, father, to begin with; then you can't be henpecked."

He darted round the table, pursued by the maligned Mrs. White armed with an antimacassar.

Mr. White took the paw from his pocket and eyed it dubiously. "I don't know what to wish for, and that's a fact," he said, slowly. "It seems to me I've got all I want."

"If you only cleared the house, you'd be quite happy, wouldn't you?" said Herbert, with his hand on his shoulder. "Well, wish for two hundred pounds, then; that'll just do it."

His father, smiling shamefacedly at his own credulity, held up the talisman, as his son, with a solemn face, somewhat marred by a wink at his mother, sat down at the piano and struck a few impressive chords.

"I wish for two hundred pounds," said the old man distinctly.

A fine crash from the piano greeted the words, interrupted by a shuddering cry from the old man. His wife and son ran toward him.

"It moved," he cried, with a glance of disgust at the object as it lay on the floor. "As I wished, it twisted in my hand like a snake."

"Well, I don't see the money," said his son as he picked it up and placed it on the table, "and I bet I never shall."

"It must have been your fancy, father," said his wife, regarding him anxiously.

He shook his head. "Never mind, though; there's no harm done, but it gave me a shock all the same."

They sat down by the fire again while the two men finished their pipes. Outside, the wind was higher than ever, and the old man started nervously at the sound of a door banging upstairs. A silence unusual and depressing settled upon all three, which lasted until the old couple rose to retire for the night.

"I expect you'll find the cash tied up in a big bag in the middle of your bed," said Herbert, as he bade them good night, "and something horrible squatting up on top of the wardrobe watching you pocket your ill-gotten gains."

He sat alone in the darkness, gazing at the dying fire, and seeing faces in it. The last face was so horrible and so simian that he gazed at it with amazement.' It got so vivid that, with a little uneasy laugh, he felt on the table for a glass containing a little water to throw over it. His hand grasped the monkey's paw, and with a little shiver he wiped his hand on his coat and went up to bed.

II.

In the brightness of the wintery sun next morning as it streamed over the breakfast table he laughed at his fears. There was an air of prosaic wholesomeness about the room which it had lacked on the previous night, and the dirty, shrivelled little paw was pitched on the side-board with a carelessness which betokened no great belief in its virtues.

"I suppose all old soldiers are the same," said Mrs. White. "The idea of our listening to such nonsense! How could wishes be granted in these days? And if they could, how could two hundred pounds hurt you, father?"

"Might drop on his head from the sky," said the frivolous Herbert.

"Morris said the things happened so naturally," said his father, "that you might if you so wished attribute it to coincidence."

"Well, don't break into the money before I come back," said Herbert as he rose from the table. "I'm afraid it'll turn you into a mean, avaricious man, and we will have to disown you."

His mother laughed, and following him to the door, watched him down the road; and returning to the breakfast table, was very happy at the expense of her husband's credulity. All of which did not prevent her from scurrying to the door at the postman's knock, nor prevent her from referring somewhat shortly to retired sergeant-majors of bibulous habits when she found that the post brought a tailor's bill.

"Herbert will have some more of his funny remarks, I expect, when he comes home," she said, as they sat at dinner.

"I dare say," said Mr. White, pouring himself out some beer; "but for all that, the thing moved in my hand; that I'll swear to."

"You thought it did," said the old lady soothingly.

"I say it did," replied the other. "There was no thought about it; I had just—What's the matter?"

His wife made no reply. She was watching the mysterious movements of a man outside, who, peering in an undecided fashion at the house, appeared to be trying to make up his mind to enter. In mental connection with the two hundred pounds, she noticed that the stranger was well dressed, and wore a silk hat of glossy newness. Three times he paused at the gate, and then walked on again. The fourth time he stood with his hand upon it, and then with a sudden resolution flung it open and walked up the path. Mrs. White at the same moment placed her hands behind her, and hurriedly unfastening the strings on her apron, put that useful article of apparel beneath the cushion of her chair.

She brought the stranger, who seemed ill at ease, into the room. He gazed at her furtively, and listened in a preoccupied fashion as the old lady apologized for the appearance of the room, and her husband's coat, a garment which he usually reserved for the garden. She then waited as patiently as her sex would permit, for him to broach his business, but he was at first strangely silent.

"I was asked to call," he said at last, and stooped and picked a piece of cotton from his trousers. "I come from Maw and Meggins."

The old lady started. "Is anything the matter?" she asked breathlessly. "Has anything happened to Herbert? What is it? What is it?"

Her husband interposed. "There, there, mother," he said hastily. "Sit down, and don't jump to conclusions. You've not brought bad news, I'm sure, sir"; and he eyed the other wistfully.

"I'm sorry—" began the visitor.

"Is he hurt?" demanded the mother wildly.

The visitor bowed in assent. "Badly hurt," he said quietly, "but he is not in any pain."

"Oh, thank God!" said the old woman, clasping her hands. "Thank God for that! Thank—"

She broke off suddenly as the sinister meaning of the assurance dawned upon her, and she saw the awful confirmation of her fears in the other's averted face. She caught her breath, and turning to her slower-witted husband, laid her trembling old hand upon his. There was a long silence.

"He was caught in the machinery," said the visitor at length in a low voice.

"Caught in the machinery," repeated Mr. White, in a dazed fashion, "yes."

He sat staring blankly out at the window, and taking his wife's hand between his own, pressed it as he had been wont to do in their old courting days nearly forty years before.

"He was the only one left to us," he said, turning gently to the visitor. "It is hard."

The other coughed, and rising, walked slowly to the window.

"The firm wished me to convey their sincere sympathy with you in your great loss," he said, without looking round. "I beg that you will understand I am only their servant and merely obeying orders."

There was no reply; the old woman's face was white, her eyes staring, and her breath inaudible; on the husband's face was a look such as his friend the sergeant might have carried into his first action.

"I was to say that Maw and Meggins disclaim all responsibility," continued the other. "They admit no liability at all, but in consideration of your son's services, they wish to present you with a certain sum as compensation."

Mr. White dropped his wife's hand, and rising to his feet, gazed with a look of horror at his visitor. His dry lips shaped the words, "How much?"

"Two hundred pounds," was the answer.

Unconscious of his wife's shriek, the old man smiled faintly, put out his hands like a sightless man, and dropped, a senseless heap, to the floor.

III.

In the huge new cemetery, some two miles distant, the old people buried their dead, and came back to the house steeped in shadow and silence. It was all over so quickly that at first they could hardly realise it, and remained in a state of expectation as though of something else to happen—something else which was to lighten this load, too heavy for old hearts to bear.

But the days passed, and expectation gave place to resignation—the hopeless resignation of the old, sometimes miscalled apathy. Sometimes they hardly exchanged a word, for now they had nothing to talk about, and their days were long to weariness.

It was about a week after, that the old man, waking suddenly in the night, stretched out his hand and found himself alone. The room was in darkness, and the sound of subdued weeping came from the window. He raised himself in bed and listened.

"Come back," he said, tenderly. "You will be cold."

"It is colder for my son," said the old woman, and wept afresh.

The sound of her sobs died away on his ears. The bed was warm, and his eyes heavy with sleep. He dozed fitfully, and then slept until a sudden wild cry from his wife awoke him with a start.

"*The paw!*" she cried wildly. "The monkey's paw!"

He started up in alarm. "Where? Where is it? What's the matter?"

She came stumbling across the room toward him. "I want it," she said quietly. "You've not destroyed it?"

"It's in the parlour, on the bracket," he replied, marvelling. "Why?"

She cried and laughed together, and bending over, kissed his cheek.

"I only just thought of it," she said hysterically. "Why didn't I think of it before? Why didn't *you* think of it?"

"Think of what?" he questioned.

"The other two wishes," she replied rapidly. "We've only had one."

"Was not that enough?" he demanded fiercely.

"No," she cried triumphantly; "we'll have one more. Go down and get it quickly, and wish our boy alive again."

The man sat up in bed and flung the bedclothes from his quaking limbs. "Good God, you are mad!" he cried, aghast.

"Get it," she panted; "get it quickly, and wish—Oh, my boy, my boy!"

Her husband struck a match and lit the candle. "Get back to bed," he said unsteadily. "You don't know what you are saying."

"We had the first wish granted," said the old woman feverishly; "why not the second?"

"A coincidence," stammered the old man.

"Go and get it and wish," cried his wife, quivering with excitement.

The old man turned and regarded her, and his voice shook. "He has been dead ten days, and besides he—I would not tell you else, but—I could only recognize him by his clothing. If he was too terrible for you to see then, how now?"

"Bring him back," cried the old woman, and dragged him toward the door. "Do you think I fear the child I have nursed?"

He went down in the darkness, and felt his way to the parlour, and then to the mantelpiece. The talisman was in its place, and a horrible fear that the unspoken wish might bring his mutilated son before him ere he could escape from the room seized upon him, and he caught his breath as he found that he had lost the direction of the door. His brow cold with sweat, he felt his way round the table, and groped along the wall until he found himself in the small passage with the unwholesome thing in his hand.

Even his wife's face seemed changed as he entered the room. It was white and expectant, and to his fears seemed to have an unnatural look upon it. He was afraid of her.

"*Wish!*" she cried, in a strong voice.

"It is foolish and wicked," he faltered.

"*Wish!*" repeated his wife.

He raised his hand. "I wish my son alive again."

The talisman fell to the floor, and he regarded it fearfully. Then he sank trembling into a chair as the old woman, with burning eyes, walked to the window and raised the blind.

He sat until he was chilled with the cold, glancing occasionally at the figure of the old woman peering through the window. The candle-end, which had burned below the rim of the china candle-stick, was throwing pulsating shadows on the ceiling and walls, until, with a flicker larger than the rest it expired. The old man, with an unspeakable sense of relief at the failure of the talisman, crept back to his bed, and a minute or two afterward the old woman came silently and apathetically beside him.

Neither spoke, but lay silently listening to the ticking of the clock. A stair creaked, and a squeaky mouse scurried noisily through the wall. The darkness was oppressive, and after lying for some time screwing up his courage, he took the box of matches, and striking one, went downstairs for a candle.

At the foot of the stairs the match went out, and he paused to strike another; and at the same moment a knock, so quiet and stealthy as to be scarcely audible, sounded on the front door.

The matches fell from his hand and spilled in the passage. He stood motionless, his breath suspended until the knock was repeated. Then he turned and fled swiftly back to his room, and closed the door behind him. A third knock sounded through the house.

"*What's that?*" cried the old woman, starting up.

"A rat," said the old man in shaking tones—"a rat. It passed me on the stairs."

His wife sat up in bed listening. A loud knock resounded through the house.

"It's Herbert!" she screamed. "It's Herbert!"

She ran to the door, but her husband was before her, and catching her by the arm, held her tightly.

"What are you going to do?" he whispered hoarsely.

"It's my boy; it's Herbert!" she cried, struggling mechanically. "I forgot it was two miles away. What are you holding me for? Let go. I must open the door.

"For God's sake don't let it in," cried the old man, trembling.

"You're afraid of your own son," she cried, struggling. "Let me go. I'm coming, Herbert; I'm coming."

There was another knock, and another. The old woman with a

sudden wrench broke free and ran from the room. Her husband followed to the landing, and called after her appealingly as she hurried downstairs. He heard the chain rattle back and the bottom bolt drawn slowly and stiffly from the socket. Then the old woman's voice strained and panting.

"The bolt," she cried, loudly. "Come down. I can't reach it."

But her husband was on his hands and knees groping wildly on the floor in search of the paw. If he could only find it before the thing outside got in. A perfect fusillade of knocks reverberated through the house, and he heard the scraping of a chair as his wife put it down in the passage against the door. He heard the creaking of the bolt as it came slowly back, and at the same moment he found the monkey's paw, and frantically breathed his third and last wish.

The knocking ceased suddenly, although the echoes of it were still in the house. He heard the chair drawn back, and the door opened. A cold wind rushed up the staircase, and a long loud wail of disappointment and misery from his wife gave him courage to run down to her side, and then to the gate beyond. The street lamp flickering opposite shone on a quiet and deserted road.

The Willows

Algernon Blackwood

After leaving Vienna, and long before you come to Buda-Pesth, the Danube enters a region of singular loneliness and desolation, where its waters spread away on all sides regardless of a main channel, and the country becomes a swamp for miles upon miles, covered by a vast sea of low willow bushes. On the big maps this deserted area is painted in a fluffy blue, growing fainter in color as it leaves the banks, and across it may be seen in large straggling letters the word *Sümpfe*, meaning marshes.

In high flood this great acreage of sand, shingle-beds, and willow-grown islands is almost topped by the water, but in normal seasons the bushes bend and rustle in the free winds, showing their silver leaves to the sunshine in an ever-moving plain of bewildering beauty. These willows never attain to the dignity of trees; they have no rigid trunks; they remain humble bushes, with rounded tops and soft outline, swaying on slender stems that answer to the least pressure of the wind; supple as grasses, and so continually shifting that they somehow give the impression that the entire plain is moving and *alive*. For the wind sends waves rising and falling over the whole surface, waves of leaves instead of waves of water, green swells like the sea, too, until the branches turn and lift, and then silvery white as their under-side turns to the sun.

Happy to slip beyond the control of the stern banks, the Danube here wanders about at will among the intricate network of channels intersecting the islands everywhere with broad avenues down which the waters pour with a shouting sound; making whirlpools, eddies, and foaming rapids; tearing at the sandy banks; carrying away masses of shore and willow-clumps; and forming new islands innumerable which shift daily in size and shape and possess at best an impermanent life, since the flood-time obliterates their very existence.

Properly speaking, this fascinating part of the river's life begins soon after leaving Pressburg, and we, in our Canadian canoe, with gipsy tent and frying-pan on board, reached it on the crest of a rising flood about mid-July. That very same morning, when the sky was reddening before sunrise, we had slipped swiftly through still-sleeping Vienna, leaving it a couple of hours later a mere patch of smoke against the blue hills of the Wienerwald on the horizon; we had breakfasted below Fischerarmend under a grove of birch trees roaring in the wind; and had then swept on the tearing current past Orth, Hamburg, Petronell (the old Roman Carnuntum of Marcus Aurelius), and so under the frowning heights of Theben on a spur of the Carpathians, where the March steals in quietly from the left and the frontier is crossed between Austria and Hungary.

Racing along at twelve kilometers an hour soon took us well into Hungary, and the muddy waters—sure sign of flood—sent us aground on many a shingle-bed, and twisted us like a cork in many a sudden belching whirlpool before the towers of Pressburg (Hungarian, Poszóny) showed against the sky; and then the canoe, leaping like a spirited horse, flew at top speed under the grey walls, negotiated safely the sunken chain of the Fliegende Brücke ferry, turned the corner sharply to the left, and plunged on yellow foam into the wilderness of islands, sand-banks, and swamp-land beyond—the land of the willows.

The change came suddenly, as when a series of bioscope pictures snaps down on the streets of a town and shifts without warning into the scenery of lake and forest. We entered the land of desolation on wings, and in less than half an hour there was neither boat nor fishing-hut nor red roof, nor any single sign of human habitation and civilization within sight. The sense of remoteness from the world of human kind, the utter isolation, the fascination of this singular world of willows, winds, and waters, instantly laid its spell upon us both, so that we allowed laughingly to one another that we ought by rights to have held some special kind of passport to admit us, and that we had, somewhat audaciously, come without asking leave into a separate little kingdom of wonder and magic—a kingdom that was reserved for the use of others who had a right to it, with everywhere unwritten warnings to trespassers for those who had the imagination to discover them.

Though still early in the afternoon, the ceaseless buffetings of a most tempestuous wind made us feel weary, and we at once began casting about for a suitable camping-ground for the night. But the bewildering character of the islands made landing difficult; the swirling flood carried us in-shore and then swept us out again; the willow branches tore our hands as we seized them to stop the canoe, and we pulled many a yard of sandy bank into the water before at length we shot with a great sideways blow from the wind into a backwater and managed to beach the bows in a cloud of spray. Then we lay panting and laughing after our exertions on hot yellow sand, sheltered from the wind, and in the full blaze of a scorching sun, a cloudless blue sky above, and an immense army of dancing, shouting willow bushes, closing in from all sides, shining with spray and clapping their thousand little hands as though to applaud the success of our efforts.

"What a river!" I said to my companion, thinking of all the way we had travelled from the source in the Black Forest, and how we had often been obliged to wade and push in the upper shallows at the beginning of June.

"Won't stand much nonsense now, will it?" he said, pulling the canoe a little farther into safety up the sand, and then composing himself for a nap.

I lay by his side, happy and peaceful in the bath of the elements—water, wind, sand, and the great fire of the sun—thinking of the long journey that lay behind us, and of the great stretch before us to the Black Sea, and how lucky I was to have such a delightful and charming travelling companion as my friend, the Swede.

We had made many similar journeys together, but the Danube, more than any other river I knew, impressed us from the very beginning with its *aliveness*. From its tiny bubbling entry into the world among the pinewood gardens of Donaueschingen, until this moment when it began to play the great river-game of losing itself among the deserted swamps, unobserved, unrestrained, it had seemed to us like following the growth of some living creature. Sleepy at first, but later developing violent desires as it became conscious of its deep soul, it rolled, like some huge fluid being, through all the countries we had passed, holding our little craft on its mighty shoulders, playing roughly with us sometimes, yet always friendly and well-meaning, till at length we had come inevitably to regard it as a Great Personage.

How, indeed, could it be otherwise, since it told us so much of its secret life? At night we heard it singing to the moon as we lay in our tent, uttering that odd sibilant note peculiar to itself and said to be caused by the rapid tearing of the pebbles along its bed, so great is its hurrying speed. We knew, too, the voice of its gurgling whirlpools, suddenly bubbling up on a surface previously quite calm; the roar of its shallows and swift rapids; its constant steady thundering below all mere surface sounds; and that ceaseless tearing of its icy waters at the banks. How it stood up and shouted when the rains fell flat upon its face! And how its laughter roared out when the wind blew upstream and tried to stop its growing speed! We knew all its sounds and voices, its tumblings and foamings, its unnecessary splashing against the bridges; that self-conscious chatter when there were hills to look on; the affected dignity of its speech when it passed through the little towns, far too important to laugh; and all these faint, sweet whisperings when the sun caught it fairly in some slow curve and poured down upon it till the steam rose.

It was full of tricks, too, in its early life before the great world knew it. There were places in the upper reaches among the Swabian forests, when yet the first whispers of its destiny had not reached it, where it elected to disappear through holes in the ground, to appear again on the other side of the porous limestone hills and start a new river with another name; leaving, too, so little water in its own bed that we had to climb out and wade and push the canoe through miles of shallows.

And a chief pleasure, in those early days of its irresponsible youth, was to lie low, like Brer Fox, just before the little turbulent tributaries came to join it from the Alps, and to refuse to acknowledge them when in, but to run for miles side by side, the dividing line well marked, the very levels different, the Danube utterly declining to recognize the newcomer. Below Passau, however, it gave up this particular trick, for there the Inn comes in with a thundering power impossible to ignore, and so pushes and incommodes the parent river that there is hardly room for them in the long twisting gorge that follows, and the Danube is shoved this way and that against the cliffs, and forced to hurry itself with great waves and much dashing to and fro in order to get through in time. And during the fight our canoe slipped down from its shoulder to its breast, and had the time of its life among the struggling waves. But the Inn taught the old river a lesson, and after Passau it no longer pretended to ignore new arrivals.

This was many days back, of course, and since then we had come to know other aspects of the great creature, and across the Bavarian wheat plain of Straubing she wandered so slowly under the blazing June sun that we could well imagine only the surface inches were water, while below there moved, concealed as by a silken mantle, a whole army of Undines, passing silently and unseen down to the sea, and very leisurely too, lest they be discovered.

Much, too, we forgave her because of her friendliness to the birds and animals that haunted the shores. Cormorants lined the banks in lonely places in rows like short black palings; grey crows crowded the shingle-beds; storks stood fishing in the vistas of shallower water that opened up between the islands, and hawks, swans, and marsh birds of all sorts filled the air with glinting wings and singing, petulant cries. It was impossible to feel annoyed with the river's vagaries after seeing a deer leap with a splash into the water at sunrise and swim past the bows of the canoe; and often we saw fawns peering at us from the underbrush, or looked straight into the brown eyes of a stag as we charged full tilt round a corner and entered another reach of the river.

Foxes, too, everywhere haunted the banks, tripping daintily among the driftwood and disappearing so suddenly that it was impossible to see how they managed it.

But now, after leaving Pressburg, everything changed a little, and the Danube became more serious. It ceased trifling. It was halfway to the Black Sea, within scenting distance almost of other, stranger countries where no tricks would be permitted or understood. It became suddenly grown-up, and claimed our respect and even our awe. It broke out into three arms, for one thing, that only met again a hundred kilometers farther down, and for a canoe there were no indications which one was intended to be followed.

"If you take a side channel," said the Hungarian officer we met in the Pressburg shop while buying provisions, "you may find yourselves, when the flood subsides, forty miles from anywhere, high and dry, and you may easily starve. There are no people, no farms, no fishermen. I warn you not to continue. The river, too, is still rising, and this wind will increase."

The rising river did not alarm us in the least, but the matter of being left high and dry by a sudden subsidence of the waters might be serious, and we had consequently laid in an extra stock of provisions. For the rest, the officer's prophecy held true, and the wind, blowing down a perfectly clear sky, increased steadily till it reached the dignity of a westerly gale.

It was earlier than usual when we camped, for the sun was a good hour or two from the horizon, and leaving my friend still asleep on the hot sand, I wandered about in desultory examination of our hotel. The island, I found, was less than an acre in extent, a mere sandy bank standing some two or three feet above the level of the river. The far end, pointing into the sunset, was covered with flying spray which the tremendous wind drove off the crests of the broken waves. It was triangular in shape, with the apex upstream.

I stood there for several minutes, watching the impetuous crimson flood bearing down with a shouting roar, dashing in waves against the bank as though to sweep it bodily away, and then swirling by in two foaming streams on either side. The ground seemed to shake with the shock and rush, while the furious movement of the willow bushes as the wind poured over them increased the curious illusion that the island itself actually moved. Above, for a mile or two, I could see the great river descending upon me: it was like looking up the slope of a sliding hill, white with foam, and leaping up everywhere to show itself to the sun.

The rest of the island was too thickly grown with willows to make walking pleasant, but I made the tour, nevertheless. From the lower end the light, of course, changed, and the river looked dark and angry. Only the backs of the flying waves were visible, streaked with foam, and pushed forcibly by the great puffs of wind that fell upon them from behind. For a short mile it was visible, pouring in and out among the islands, and then disappearing with a huge sweep into the willows, which closed about it like a herd of monstrous antediluvian creatures crowding down to drink. They made me think of gigantic sponge-like growths that sucked the river up into themselves. They caused it to vanish from sight. They herded there together in such overpowering numbers.

Altogether it was an impressive scene, with its utter loneliness, its bizarre suggestion; and as I gazed, long and curiously, a singular emotion began to stir somewhere in the depths of me. Midway in my delight of the wild beauty, there crept unbidden and unexplained, a curious feeling of disquietude, almost of alarm.

A rising river, perhaps, always suggests something of the ominous: many of the little islands I saw before me would probably have been swept away by the morning; this resistless, thundering flood of water touched the sense of awe. Yet I was aware that my uneasiness lay deeper far than the emotions of awe and wonder. It was not that I felt. Nor had it directly to do with the power of the driving wind—this shouting hurricane that might almost carry up a few acres of willows into the air and scatter them like so much chaff over the landscape. The wind was simply enjoying itself, for nothing rose out of the flat landscape to stop it, and I was conscious of sharing its great game with a kind of pleasurable excitement. Yet this novel emotion had nothing to do with the wind. Indeed, so vague was the sense of distress I experienced, that it was impossible to trace it to its source and deal with it accordingly, though I was aware somehow that it had to do with my realization of our utter insignificance before this unrestrained power of the elements about me. The huge-grown river had something to do with it too—a vague, unpleasant idea that we had somehow trifled with these great elemental forces in whose power we lay helpless every hour of the day and night. For here, indeed, they were gigantically at play together, and the sight appealed to the imagination.

But my emotion, so far as I could understand it, seemed to attach itself more particularly to the willow bushes, to these acres and acres of willows, crowding, so thickly growing there, swarming everywhere the eye could reach, pressing upon the river as though to suffocate it, standing in dense array mile after mile beneath the sky, watching, waiting, listening. And, apart quite from the elements, the willows connected themselves subtly with my malaise, attacking the mind insidiously somehow by reason of their vast numbers, and contriving in some way or other to represent to the imagination a new and mighty power, a power, moreover, not altogether friendly to us.

Great revelations of nature, of course, never fail to impress in one way or another, and I was no stranger to moods of the kind. Mountains overawe and oceans terrify, while the mystery of great forests exercises a spell peculiarly its own. But all these, at one point or another, somewhere link on intimately with human life and human experience. They stir comprehensible, even if alarming, emotions. They tend on the whole to exalt.

With this multitude of willows, however, it was something far different, I felt. Some essence emanated from them that besieged the heart. A sense of awe awakened, true, but of awe touched somewhere by a vague terror. Their serried ranks, growing everywhere darker about me as the shadows deepened, moving furiously yet softly in the wind, woke in me the curious and unwelcome suggestion that we had trespassed here upon the borders of an alien world, a world where we were intruders, a world where we were not wanted or invited to remain—where we ran grave risks perhaps!

The feeling, however, though it refused to yield its meaning entirely to analysis, did not at the time trouble me by passing into menace. Yet it never left me quite, even during the very practical business of putting up the tent in a hurricane of wind and building a fire for the stew-pot. It remained, just enough to bother and perplex, and to rob a most delightful camping-ground of a good portion of its charm. To my companion, however, I said nothing, for he was a man I considered devoid of imagination. In the first place, I could never have explained to him what I meant, and in the second, he would have laughed stupidly at me if I had.

There was a slight depression in the centre of the island, and here we pitched the tent. The surrounding willows broke the wind a bit.

"A poor camp," observed the imperturbable Swede when at last the tent stood upright; "no stones and precious little firewood. I'm for moving on early to-morrow—eh? This sand won't hold anything."

But the experience of a collapsing tent at midnight had taught us many devices, and we made the cosy gipsy house as safe as possible, and then set about collecting a store of wood to last till bed-time. Willow bushes drop no branches, and driftwood was our only source of supply. We hunted the shores pretty thoroughly. Everywhere the banks were crumbling as the rising flood tore at them and carried away great portions with a splash and a gurgle.

"The island's much smaller than when we landed," said the accurate Swede. "It won't last long at this rate. We'd better drag the canoe close to the tent, and be ready to start at a moment's notice. *I* shall sleep in my clothes."

He was a little distance off, climbing along the bank, and I heard his rather jolly laugh as he spoke.

"By Jove!" I heard him call, a moment later, and turned to see what had caused his exclamation. But for the moment he was hidden by the willows, and I could not find him.

"What in the world's this?" I heard him cry again, and this time his voice had become serious.

I ran up quickly and joined him on the bank. He was looking over the river, pointing at something in the water.

"Good Heavens, it's a man's body!" he cried excitedly. "Look!"

A black thing, turning over and over in the foaming waves, swept rapidly past. It kept disappearing and coming up to the surface again. It was about twenty feet from the shore, and just as it was opposite to where we stood it lurched round and looked straight at us. We saw its eyes reflecting the sunset, and gleaming an odd yellow as the body turned over. Then it gave a swift, gulping plunge, and dived out of sight in a flash.

"An otter, by gad!" we exclaimed in the same breath, laughing.

It *was* an otter, alive, and out on the hunt; yet it had looked exactly like the body of a drowned man turning helplessly in the current. Far below it came to the surface once again, and we saw its black skin, wet and shining in the sunlight.

Then, too, just as we turned back, our arms full of driftwood, another thing happened to recall us to the river bank. This time it really was a man, and what was more, a man in a boat. Now a small boat on the Danube was an unusual sight at any time, but here in this deserted region, and at flood time, it was so unexpected as to constitute a real event. We stood and stared.

Whether it was due to the slanting sunlight, or the refraction from the wonderfully illumined water, I cannot say, but, whatever the cause, I found it difficult to focus my sight properly upon the flying apparition. It seemed, however, to be a man standing upright in a sort of flat-bottomed boat, steering with a long oar, and being carried down the opposite shore at a tremendous pace. He apparently was looking across in our direction, but the distance was too great and the light too uncertain for us to make out very plainly what he was about. It seemed to me that he was gesticulating and making signs at us. His voice came across the water to us shouting something furiously, but the wind drowned it so that no single word was audible. There was something curious about the whole appearance—man, boat, signs, voice—that made an impression on me out of all proportion to its cause.

"He's crossing himself!" I cried. "Look, he's making the sign of the Cross!"

"I believe you're right," the Swede said, shading his eyes with his hand and watching the man out of sight. He seemed to be gone in a moment, melting away down there into the sea of willows where the sun caught them in the bend of the river and turned them into a great crimson wall of beauty. Mist, too, had begun to rise, so that the air was hazy.

"But what in the world is he doing at nightfall on this flooded river?" I said, half to myself. "Where is he going at such a time, and what did he mean by his signs and shouting? D'you think he wished to warn us about something?"

"He saw our smoke, and thought we were spirits probably," laughed my companion. "These Hungarians believe in all sorts of rubbish: you remember the shopwoman at Pressburg warning us that no one ever landed here because it belonged to some sort of beings outside man's world! I suppose they believe in fairies and elementals, possibly demons too. That peasant in the boat saw people on the islands for the first time in his life," he added, after a slight pause, "and it scared him, that's all."

The Swede's tone of voice was not convincing, and his manner lacked something that was usually there. I noted the change instantly while he talked, though without being able to label it precisely.

"If they had enough imagination," I laughed loudly—I remember trying to make as much *noise* as I could—"they might well people a place like this with the old gods of antiquity. The Romans must have haunted all this region more or less with their shrines and sacred groves and elemental deities."

The subject dropped and we returned to our stew-pot, for my friend was not given to imaginative conversation as a rule. Moreover, just then I remember feeling distinctly glad that he was not imaginative; his stolid, practical nature suddenly seemed to me welcome and comforting. It was an admirable temperament, I felt: he could steer down rapids like a red Indian, shoot dangerous bridges and whirlpools better than any white man I ever saw in a canoe. He was a grand fellow for an adventurous trip, a tower of strength when untoward things happened. I looked at his strong face and light curly hair as he staggered along under his pile of driftwood (twice the size of mine!), and I experienced a feeling of relief. Yes, I was distinctly glad just then that the Swede was—what he was, and that he never made remarks that suggested more than they said.

"The river's still rising, though," he added, as if following out some thoughts of his own, and dropping his load with a gasp. "This island will be under water in two days if it goes on."

"I wish the *wind* would go down," I said. "I don't care a fig for the river."

The flood, indeed, had no terrors for us; we could get off at ten minutes' notice, and the more water the better we liked it. It meant an increasing current and the obliteration of the treacherous shingle-beds that so often threatened to tear the bottom out of our canoe.

Contrary to our expectations, the wind did not go down with the sun. It seemed to increase with the darkness; howling overhead and shaking the willows round us like straws. Curious sounds accompanied it sometimes, like the explosion of heavy guns, and it fell upon the water and the island in great flat blows of immense power. It made me think of the sounds a planet must make, could we only hear it, driving along through space.

But the sky kept wholly clear of clouds, and soon after supper the full moon rose up in the east and covered the river and the plain of shouting willows with a light like the day.

We lay on the sandy patch beside the fire, smoking, listening to the noises of the night round us, and talking happily of the journey we had already made, and of our plans ahead. The map lay spread in the door of the tent, but the high wind made it hard to study, and presently we lowered the curtain and extinguished the lantern. The firelight was enough to smoke and see each other's faces by, and the sparks flew about overhead like fireworks. A few yards beyond, the river gurgled and hissed, and from time to time a heavy splash announced the falling away of further portions of the bank.

Our talk, I noticed, had to do with the far-away scenes and incidents of our first camps in the Black Forest, or of other subjects altogether remote from the present setting, for neither of us spoke of the actual moment more than was necessary—almost as though we had agreed tacitly to avoid discussion of the camp and its incidents. Neither the otter nor the boatman, for instance, received the honour of a single mention, though ordinarily these would have furnished discussion for the greater part of the evening. They were, of course, distinct events in such a place.

The scarcity of wood made it a business to keep the fire going, for the wind, that drove the smoke in our faces wherever we sat, helped at the same time to make a forced draught. We took it in turn to make foraging expeditions into the darkness, and the quantity the Swede brought back always made me feel that he took an absurdly long time finding it; for the fact was I did not care much about being left alone, and yet it always seemed to be my turn to grub about among the bushes or scramble along the slippery banks in the moonlight. The long day's battle with wind and water—such wind and such water!—had tired us both, and an early bed was the obvious programme. Yet neither of us made the move for the tent. We lay there, tending the fire, talking in desultory fashion, peering about us into the dense willow bushes, and listening to the thunder of wind and river. The loneliness of the place had entered our very bones, and silence seemed natural, for after a bit the sound of our voices became a trifle unreal and forced; whispering would have been the fitting mode of communication, I felt, and the human voice, always rather absurd amid the roar of the elements, now carried with it something almost illegitimate. It was like talking out loud in church, or in some place where it was not lawful, perhaps not quite *safe*, to be overheard.

The eeriness of this lonely island, set among a million willows, swept by a hurricane, and surrounded by hurrying deep waters, touched us both, I fancy. Untrodden by man, almost unknown to man, it lay there beneath the moon, remote from human influence, on the frontier of another world, an alien world, a world tenanted by willows only and the souls of willows. And we, in our rashness, had dared to invade it, even to make use of it! Something more than the power of its mystery stirred in me as I lay on the sand, feet to fire, and peered up through the leaves at the stars. For the last time I rose to get firewood.

"When this has burnt up," I said firmly, "I shall turn in," and my companion watched me lazily as I moved off into the surrounding shadows.

For an unimaginative man I thought he seemed unusually receptive that night, unusually open to suggestion of things other than sensory. He too was touched by the beauty and loneliness of the place. I was not altogether pleased, I remember, to recognise this slight change in him, and instead of immediately collecting sticks, I made my way to the far point of the island where the moonlight on plain and river could be seen to better advantage. The desire to be alone had come suddenly upon me; my former dread returned in force; there was a vague feeling in me I wished to face and probe to the bottom.

When I reached the point of sand jutting out among the waves, the spell of the place descended upon me with a positive shock. No mere "scenery" could have produced such an effect. There was something more here, something to alarm.

I gazed across the waste of wild waters; I watched the whispering willows; I heard the ceaseless beating of the tireless wind; and, one and all, each in its own way, stirred in me this sensation of a strange distress. But the *willows* especially: for ever they went on chattering and talking among themselves, laughing a little, shrilly crying out, sometimes sighing—but what it was they made so much to-do about belonged to the secret life of the great plain they inhabited. And it was utterly alien to the world I knew, or to that of the wild yet kindly elements. They made me think of a host of beings from another plane of life, another evolution altogether, perhaps, all discussing a mystery known only to themselves. I watched them moving busily together, oddly shaking their big bushy heads, twirling their myriad leaves even when there was no wind. They moved of their own will as though alive, and they touched, by some incalculable method, my own keen sense of the *horrible*.

There they stood in the moonlight, like a vast army surrounding our camp, shaking their innumerable silver spears defiantly, formed all ready for an attack.

The psychology of places, for some imaginations at least, is very vivid; for the wanderer, especially, camps have their "note" either of welcome or rejection. At first it may not always be apparent, because the busy preparations of tent and cooking prevent, but with the first pause—after supper usually—it comes and announces itself. And the note of this willow-camp now became unmistakably plain to me: we were interlopers, trespassers; we were not welcomed. The sense of unfamiliarity grew upon me as I stood there watching. We touched the frontier of a region where our presence was resented. For a night's lodging we might perhaps be tolerated; but for a prolonged and inquisitive stay—No! by all the gods of the trees and the wilderness, no! We were the first human influences upon this island, and we were not wanted. *The willows were against us*.

Strange thoughts like these, bizarre fancies, borne I know not whence, found lodgment in my mind as I stood listening. What, I thought, if, after all, these crouching willows proved to be alive; if suddenly they should rise up, like a swarm of living creatures, marshalled by the gods whose territory we had invaded, sweep towards us off the vast swamps, booming overhead in the night—and then *settle down!* As I looked it was so easy to imagine they actually moved, crept nearer, retreated a little, huddled together in masses, hostile, waiting for the great wind that should finally start them a-running. I could have sworn their aspect changed a little, and their ranks deepened and pressed more closely together.

The melancholy shrill cry of a night-bird sounded overhead, and suddenly I nearly lost my balance as the piece of bank I stood upon fell with a great splash into the river, undermined by the flood. I stepped back just in time, and went on hunting for firewood again, half laughing at the odd fancies that crowded so thickly into my mind and cast their spell upon me. I recall the Swede's remark about moving on next day, and I was just thinking that I fully agreed with him, when I turned with a start and saw the subject of my thoughts standing immediately in front of me. He was quite close. The roar of the elements had covered his approach.

"You've been gone so long," he shouted above the wind, "I thought something must have happened to you."

But there was that in his tone, and a certain look in his face as well, that conveyed to me more than his actual words, and in a flash I understood the real reason for his coming. It was because the spell of the place had entered his soul too, and he did not like being alone.

"River still rising," he cried, pointing to the flood in the moonlight, "and the wind's simply awful."

He always said the same things, but it was the cry for companionship that gave the real importance to his words.

"Lucky," I cried back, "our tent's in the hollow. I think it'll hold all right." I added something about the difficulty of finding wood, in order to explain my absence, but the wind caught my words and flung them across the river, so that he did not hear, but just looked at me through the branches, nodding his head.

"Lucky if we get away without disaster!" he shouted, or words to that effect; and I remember feeling half angry with him for putting the thought into words, for it was exactly what I felt myself. There was disaster impending somewhere, and the sense of presentiment lay unpleasantly upon me.

We went back to the fire and made a final blaze, poking it up with our feet. We took a last look round. But for the wind the heat would have been unpleasant. I put this thought into words, and I remember my friend's reply struck me oddly: that he would rather have the heat, the ordinary July weather, than this "diabolical wind."

Everything was snug for the night; the canoe lying turned over beside the tent, with both yellow paddles beneath her; the provision sack hanging from a willow-stem, and the washed-up dishes removed to a safe distance from the fire, all ready for the morning meal.

We smothered the embers of the fire with sand, and then turned in. The flap of the tent door was up, and I saw the branches and the stars and the white moonlight. The shaking willows and the heavy buffetings of the wind against our taut little house were the last things I remembered as sleep came down and covered all with its soft and delicious forgetfulness.

Suddenly I found myself lying awake, peering from my sandy mattress through the door of the tent. I looked at my watch pinned against the canvas, and saw by the bright moonlight that it was past twelve o'clock—the threshold of a new day—and I had therefore slept a couple of hours. The Swede was asleep still beside me; the wind howled as before; something plucked at my heart and made me feel afraid. There was a sense of disturbance in my immediate neighborhood.

I sat up quickly and looked out. The trees were swaying violently to and fro as the gusts smote them, but our little bit of green canvas lay snugly safe in the hollow, for the wind passed over it without meeting enough resistance to make it vicious. The feeling of disquietude did not pass, however, and I crawled quietly out of the tent to see if our belongings were safe. I moved carefully so as not to waken my companion. A curious excitement was on me.

I was half-way out, kneeling on all fours, when my eye first took in that the tops of the bushes opposite, with their moving tracery of leaves, made shapes against the sky. I sat back on my haunches and stared. It was incredible, surely, but there, opposite and slightly above me, were shapes of some indeterminate sort among the willows, and as the branches swayed in the wind they seemed to group themselves about these shapes, forming a series of monstrous outlines that shifted rapidly beneath the moon. Close, about fifty feet in front of me, I saw these things.

My first instinct was to waken my companion, that he too might see them, but something made me hesitate—the sudden realisation, probably, that I should not welcome corroboration; and meanwhile I crouched there staring in amazement with smarting eyes. I was wide awake. I remember saying to myself that I was *not* dreaming.

They first became properly visible, these huge figures, just within the tops of the bushes—immense bronze-coloured, moving, and wholly independent of the swaying of the branches. I saw them plainly and noted, now I came to examine them more calmly, that they were very much larger than human, and indeed that something in their appearance proclaimed them to be *not human* at all. Certainly they were not merely the moving tracery of the branches against the moonlight. They shifted independently. They rose upwards in a continuous stream from earth to sky, vanishing utterly as soon as they reached the dark of the sky. They were interlaced one with another, making a great column, and I saw their limbs and huge bodies melting in and out of each other, forming this serpentine line that bent and swayed and twisted spirally with the contortions of the wind-tossed trees. They were nude, fluid shapes, passing up the bushes, *within* the leaves almost—rising up in a living column into the heavens. Their faces I never could see. Unceasingly they poured upwards, swaying in great bending curves, with a hue of dull bronze upon their skins.

I stared, trying to force every atom of vision from my eyes. For a long time I thought they *must* every moment disappear and resolve themselves into the movements of the branches and prove to be an optical illusion. I searched everywhere for a proof of reality, when all the while I understood quite well that the standard of reality had changed. For the longer I looked the more certain I became that these figures were real and living, though perhaps not according to the standards that the camera and the biologist would insist upon.

Far from feeling fear, I was possessed with a sense of awe and wonder such as I have never known. I seemed to be gazing at the personified elemental forces of this haunted and primeval region. Our intrusion had stirred the powers of the place into activity. It was we who were the cause of the disturbance, and my brain filled to bursting with stories and legends of the spirits and deities of places that have been acknowledged and worshiped by men in all ages of the world's history. But, before I could arrive at any possible explanation, something impelled me to go farther out, and I crept forward on to the sand and stood upright. I felt the ground still warm under my bare feet; the wind tore at my hair and face; and the sound of the river burst upon my ears with a sudden roar. These things, I knew, were real, and proved that my senses were acting normally. Yet the figures still rose from earth to heaven, silent, majestically, in a great spiral of grace and strength that overwhelmed me at length with a genuine deep emotion of worship. I felt that I must fall down and worship—absolutely worship.

Perhaps in another minute I might have done so, when a gust of wind swept against me with such force that it blew me sideways, and I nearly stumbled and fell. It seemed to shake the dream violently out of me. At least it gave me another point of view somehow. The figures still remained, still ascended into heaven from the heart of the night, but my reason at last began to assert itself. It must be a subjective experience, I argued—none the less real for that, but still subjective. The moonlight and the branches combined to work out these pictures upon the mirror of my imagination, and for some reason I projected them outwards and made them appear objective. I knew this must be the case, of course. I was the subject of a vivid and interesting hallucination. I took courage, and began to move forward across the open patches of sand. By Jove, though, was it all hallucination? Was it merely subjective? Did not my reason argue in the old futile way from the little standard of the known?

I only know that great column of figures ascended darkly into the sky for what seemed a very long period of time, and with a very complete measure of reality as most men are accustomed to gauge reality. Then suddenly they were gone!

And, once they were gone and the immediate wonder of their great presence had passed, fear came down upon me with a cold rush. The esoteric meaning of this lonely and haunted region suddenly flamed up within me, and I began to tremble dreadfully. I took a quick look round—a look of horror that came near to panic—calculating vainly ways of escape; and then, realising how helpless I was to achieve anything really effective, I crept back silently into the tent and lay down again upon my sandy mattress, first lowering the door-curtain to shut out the sight of the willows in the moonlight, and then burying my head as deeply as possible beneath the blankets to deaden the sound of the terrifying wind.

As though further to convince me that I had not been dreaming, I remember that it was a long time before I fell again into a troubled and restless sleep; and even then only the upper crust of me slept, and underneath there was something that never quite lost consciousness, but lay alert and on the watch.

But this second time I jumped up with a genuine start of terror. It was neither the wind nor the river that woke me, but the slow approach of something that caused the sleeping portion of me to grow smaller and smaller till at last it vanished altogether, and I found myself sitting bolt upright—listening.

Outside there was a sound of multitudinous little patterings. They had been coming, I was aware, for a long time, and in my sleep they had first become audible. I sat there nervously wide awake as though I had not slept at all. It seemed to me that my breathing came with difficulty, and that there was a great weight upon the surface of my body. In spite of the hot night, I felt clammy with cold and shivered. Something surely was pressing steadily against the sides of the tent and weighing down upon it from above. Was it the body of the wind? Was this the pattering rain, the dripping of the leaves? The spray blown from the river by the wind and gathering in big drops? I thought quickly of a dozen things.

Then suddenly the explanation leaped into my mind: a bough from the poplar, the only large tree on the island, had fallen with the wind. Still half caught by the other branches, it would fall with the next gust and crush us, and meanwhile its leaves brushed and tapped upon the tight canvas surface of the tent. I raised the loose flap and rushed out, calling to the Swede to follow.

But when I got out and stood upright I saw that the tent was free. There was no hanging bough; there was no rain or spray; nothing approached.

A cold, grey light filtered down through the bushes and lay on the faintly gleaming sand. Stars still crowded the sky directly overhead, and the wind howled magnificently, but the fire no longer gave out any glow, and I saw the east reddening in streaks through the trees.

Several hours must have passed since I stood there before, watching the ascending figures, and the memory of it now came back to me horribly, like an evil dream. Oh, how tired it made me feel, that ceaseless raging wind! Yet, though the deep lassitude of a sleepless night was on me, my nerves were tingling with the activity of an equally tireless apprehension, and all idea of repose was out of the question. The river I saw had risen further. Its thunder filled the air, and a fine spray made itself felt through my thin sleeping shirt.

Yet nowhere did I discover the slightest evidences of anything to cause alarm. This deep, prolonged disturbance in my heart remained wholly unaccounted for.

My companion had not stirred when I called him, and there was no need to waken him now. I looked about me carefully, noting everything: the turned-over canoe; the yellow paddles—two of them, I'm certain; the provision sack and the extra lantern hanging together from the tree; and, crowding everywhere about me, enveloping all, the willows, those endless, shaking willows. A bird uttered its morning cry, and a string of duck passed with whirring flight overhead in the twilight. The sand whirled, dry and stinging, about my bare feet in the wind.

I walked round the tent and then went out a little way into the bush, so that I could see across the river to the farther landscape, and the same profound yet indefinable emotion of distress seized upon me again as I saw the interminable sea of bushes stretching to the horizon, looking ghostly and unreal in the wan light of dawn. I walked softly here and there, still puzzling over that odd sound of infinite pattering, and of that pressure upon the tent that had wakened me. It *must* have been the wind, I reflected—the wind beating upon the loose, hot sand, driving the dry particles smartly against the taut canvas—the wind dropping heavily upon our fragile roof.

Yet all the time my nervousness and malaise increased appreciably.

I crossed over to the farther shore and noted how the coastline had altered in the night, and what masses of sand the river had torn away. I dipped my hands and feet into the cool torrent, and bathed my forehead. Already there was a glow of sunrise in the sky and the exquisite freshness of coming day. On my way back I passed purposely beneath the very bushes where I had seen the column of figures rising into the air, and midway among the clumps I suddenly found myself overtaken by a sense of vast terror. From the shadows a large figure went swiftly by. Someone passed me, as sure as ever man did . . .

It was a great staggering blow from the wind that helped me forward again, and once out in the more open space, the sense of terror diminished strangely. The winds were about and walking, I remember saying to myself; for the winds often move like great presences under the trees. And altogether the fear that hovered about me was such an unknown and immense kind of fear, so unlike anything I had ever felt before, that it woke a sense of awe and wonder in me that did much to counteract its worst effects; and when I reached a high point in the middle of the island from which I could see the wide stretch of river, crimson in the sunrise, the whole magical beauty of it all was so overpowering that a sort of wild yearning woke in me and almost brought a cry up into the throat.

But this cry found no expression, for as my eyes wandered from the plain beyond to the island round me and noted our little tent half hidden among the willows, a dreadful discovery leaped out at me, compared to which my terror of the walking winds seemed as nothing at all.

For a change, I thought, had somehow come about in the arrangement of the landscape. It was not that my point of vantage gave me a different view, but that an alteration had apparently been effected in the relation of the tent to the willows, and of the willows to the tent. Surely the bushes now crowded much closer—unnecessarily, unpleasantly close. *They had moved nearer.*

Creeping with silent feet over the shifting sands, drawing imperceptibly nearer by soft, unhurried movements, the willows had come closer during the night. But had the wind moved them, or had they moved of themselves? I recalled the sound of infinite small patterings and the pressure upon the tent and upon my own heart that caused me to wake in terror. I swayed for a moment in the wind like a tree, finding it hard to keep my upright position on the sandy hillock. There was a suggestion here of personal agency, of deliberate intention, of aggressive hostility, and it terrified me into a sort of rigidity.

Then the reaction followed quickly. The idea was so bizarre, so absurd, that I felt inclined to laugh. But the laughter came no more readily than the cry, for the knowledge that my mind was so receptive to such dangerous imaginings brought the additional terror that it was through our minds and not through our physical bodies that the attack would come, and was coming.

The wind buffeted me about, and, very quickly it seemed, the sun came up over the horizon, for it was after four o'clock, and I must have stood on that little pinnacle of sand longer than I knew, afraid to come down at close quarters with the willows. I returned quietly, creepily, to the tent, first taking another exhaustive look round and—yes, I confess it—making a few measurements. I paced out on the warm sand the distances between the willows and the tent, making a note of the shortest distance particularly.

I crawled stealthily into my blankets. My companion, to all appearances, still slept soundly, and I was glad that this was so. Provided my experiences were not corroborated, I could find strength somehow to deny them, perhaps. With the daylight I could persuade myself that it was all a subjective hallucination, a fantasy of the night, a projection of the excited imagination.

Nothing further came to disturb me, and I fell asleep almost at once, utterly exhausted, yet still in dread of hearing again that weird sound of multitudinous pattering, or of feeling the pressure upon my heart that had made it difficult to breathe.

The sun was high in the heavens when my companion woke me from a heavy sleep and announced that the porridge was cooked and there was just time to bathe. The grateful smell of frizzling bacon entered the tent door.

"River still rising," he said, "and several islands out in midstream have disappeared altogether. Our own island's much smaller."

"Any wood left?" I asked sleepily.

"The wood and the island will finish to-morrow in a dead heat," he laughed, "but there's enough to last us till then."

I plunged in from the point of the island, which had indeed altered a lot in size and shape during the night, and was swept down in a moment to the landing-place opposite the tent. The water was icy, and the banks flew by like the country from an express train. Bathing under such conditions was an exhilarating operation, and the terror of the night seemed cleansed out of me by a process of evaporation in the brain. The sun was blazing hot; not a cloud showed itself anywhere; the wind, however, had not abated one little jot.

Quite suddenly then the implied meaning of the Swede's words flashed across me, showing that he no longer wished to leave posthaste, and had changed his mind. "Enough to last till to-morrow"—he assumed we should stay on the island another night. It struck me as odd. The night before he was so positive the other way. How had the change come about?

Great crumblings of the banks occurred at breakfast, with heavy splashings and clouds of spray which the wind brought into our frying-pan, and my fellow-traveller talked incessantly about the difficulty the Vienna-Pesth steamers must have to find the channel in flood. But the state of his mind interested and impressed me far more than the state of the river or the difficulties of the steamers. He had changed somehow since the evening before. His manner was different—a trifle excited, a trifle shy, with a sort of suspicion about his voice and gestures. I hardly know how to describe it now in cold blood, but at the time I remember being quite certain of one thing—that he had become frightened.

He ate very little breakfast, and for once omitted to smoke his pipe. He had the map spread open beside him, and kept studying its markings.

"We'd better get off sharp in an hour," I said presently, feeling for an opening that must bring him indirectly to a partial confession at any rate. And his answer puzzled me uncomfortably: "Rather! If they'll let us."

"Who'll let us? The elements?" I asked quickly, with affected indifference.

"The powers of this awful place, whoever they are," he replied, keeping his eyes on the map. "The gods are here, if they are anywhere at all in the world."

"The elements are always the true immortals," I replied, laughing as naturally as I could manage, yet knowing quite well that my face reflected my true feelings when he looked up gravely at me and spoke across the smoke:

"We shall be fortunate if we get away without further disaster."

This was exactly what I had dreaded, and I screwed myself up to the point of the direct question. It was like agreeing to allow the dentist to extract the tooth; it *had* to come anyhow in the long run, and the rest was all pretence.

"Further disaster! Why, what's happened?"

"For one thing—the steering paddle's gone," he said quietly.

"The steering paddle gone!" I repeated, greatly excited, for this was our rudder, and the Danube in flood without a rudder was suicide. "But what—"

"And there's a tear in the bottom of the canoe," he added, with a genuine little tremor in his voice.

I continued staring at him, able only to repeat the words in his face somewhat foolishly. There, in the heat of the sun, and on this burning sand, I was aware of a freezing atmosphere descending round us. I got up to follow him, for he merely nodded his head gravely and led the way towards the tent a few yards on the other side of the fireplace. The canoe still lay there as I had last seen her in the night, ribs uppermost, the paddles, or rather, *the* paddle, on the sand beside her.

"There's only one," he said, stooping to pick it up. "And here's the rent in the base-board."

It was on the tip of my tongue to tell him that I had clearly noticed *two* paddles a few hours before, but a second impulse made me think better of it, and I said nothing. I approached to see.

There was a long, finely-made tear in the bottom of the canoe where a little slither of wood had been neatly taken clean out; it looked as if the tooth of a sharp rock or snag had eaten down her length, and investigation showed that the hole went through. Had we launched out in her without observing it we must inevitably have foundered. At first the water would have made the wood swell so as to close the hole, but once out in mid-stream the water must have poured in, and the canoe, never more than two inches above the surface, would have filled and sunk very rapidly.

"There, you see, an attempt to prepare a victim for the sacrifice," I heard him saying, more to himself than to me, "two victims rather," he added as he bent over and ran his fingers along the slit.

I began to whistle—a thing I always do unconsciously when utterly nonplussed—and purposely paid no attention to his words. I was determined to consider them foolish.

"It wasn't there last night," he said presently, straightening up from his examination and looking anywhere but at me.

"We must have scratched her in landing, of course," I stopped whistling to say, "The stones are very sharp—"

I stopped abruptly, for at that moment he turned round and met my eye squarely. I knew just as well as he did how impossible my explanation was. There were no stones, to begin with.

"And then there's this to explain too," he added quietly, handing me the paddle and pointing to the blade.

A new and curious emotion spread freezingly over me as I took and examined it. The blade was scraped down all over, beautifully scraped, as though someone had sandpapered it with care, making it so thin that the first vigorous stroke must have snapped it off at the elbow.

"One of us walked in his sleep and did this thing," I said feebly, "or—or it has been filed by the constant stream of sand particles blown against it by the wind, perhaps."

"Ah," said the Swede, turning away, laughing a little, "you can explain everything!"

"The same wind that caught the steering paddle and flung it so near the bank that it fell in with the next lump that crumbled," I called out after him, absolutely determined to find an explanation for everything he showed me.

"I see," he shouted back, turning his head to look at me before disappearing among the willow bushes.

Once alone with these perplexing evidences of personal agency, I think my first thought took the form of "One of us must have done this thing, and it certainly was not I." But my second thought decided how impossible it was to suppose, under all the circumstances, that either of us had done it. That my companion, the trusted friend of a dozen similar expeditions, could have knowingly had a hand in it, was a suggestion not to be entertained for a moment. Equally absurd seemed the explanation that this imperturbable and densely practical nature had suddenly become insane and was busied with insane purposes.

Yet the fact remained that what disturbed me most, and kept my fear actively alive even in this blaze of sunshine and wild beauty, was the clear certainty that some curious alteration had come about in his *mind*—that he was nervous, timid, suspicious, aware of goings on he did not speak about, watching a series of secret and hitherto unmentionable events—waiting, in a word, for a climax that he expected, and, I thought, expected very soon. This grew up in my mind intuitively—I hardly knew how.

I made a hurried examination of the tent and its surroundings, but the measurements of the night remained the same. There were deep hollows formed in the sand I now noticed for the first time, basin-shaped and of various depths and sizes, varying from that of a tea-cup to a large bowl. The wind, no doubt, was responsible for these miniature craters, just as it was for lifting the paddle and tossing it towards the water. The rent in the canoe was the only thing that seemed quite inexplicable; and, after all, it *was* conceivable that a sharp point had caught it when we landed. The examination I made of the shore did not assist this theory, but all the same I clung to it with that diminishing portion of my intelligence which I called my "reason." An explanation of some kind was an absolute necessity, just as some working explanation of the universe is necessary—however absurd—to the happiness of every individual who seeks to do his duty in the world and face the problems of life. The simile seemed to me at the time an exact parallel.

I at once set the pitch melting, and presently the Swede joined me at the work, though under the best conditions in the world the canoe could not be safe for travelling till the following day. I drew his attention casually to the hollows in the sand.

"Yes," he said, "I know. They're all over the island. But *you* can explain them, no doubt!"

"Wind, of course," I answered without hesitation. "Have you never watched those little whirlwinds in the street that twist and twirl everything into a circle? This sand's loose enough to yield, that's all."

He made no reply, and we worked on in silence for a bit. I watched him surreptitiously all the time, and I had an idea he was watching me. He seemed, too, to be always listening attentively to something I could not hear, or perhaps for something that he expected to hear, for he kept turning about and staring into the bushes, and up into the sky, and out across the water where it was visible through the openings among the willows. Sometimes he even put his hand to his ear and held it there for several minutes. He said nothing to me, however, about it, and I asked no questions. And meanwhile, as he mended that torn canoe with the skill and address of a red Indian, I was glad to notice his absorption in the work, for there was a vague dread in my heart that he would speak of the changed aspect of the willows. And, if he had noticed *that*, my imagination could no longer be held a sufficient explanation of it.

At length, after a long pause, he began to talk.

"Queer thing," he added in a hurried sort of voice, as though he wanted to say something and get it over. "Queer thing, I mean, about that otter last night."

I had expected something so totally different that he caught me with surprise, and I looked up sharply.

"Shows how lonely this place is. Otters are awfully shy things—"

"I don't mean that, of course," he interrupted. "I mean—do you think—did you think it really *was* an otter?"

"What else, in the name of Heaven, what else?"

"You know, I saw it before you did, and at first it seemed—so *much* bigger than an otter."

"The sunset as you looked up-stream magnified it, or something," I replied.

He looked at me absently a moment, as though his mind were busy with other thoughts.

"It had such extraordinary yellow eyes," he went on half to himself.

"That was the sun too," I laughed, a trifle boisterously. "I suppose you'll wonder next if that fellow in the boat—"

I suddenly decided not to finish the sentence. He was in the act again of listening, turning his head to the wind, and something in the expression of his face made me halt. The subject dropped, and we went on with our caulking. Apparently he had not noticed my unfinished sentence. Five minutes later, however, he looked at me across the canoe, the smoking pitch in his hand, his face grave.

"I *did* rather wonder, if you want to know," he said slowly, "what that thing in the boat was. I remember thinking at the time it was not a man. The whole business seemed to rise quite suddenly out of the water."

I laughed again boisterously in his face, but this time there was impatience and a strain of anger too, in my feeling.

"Look here now," I cried, "this place is quite queer enough without going out of our way to imagine things! That boat was an ordinary boat, and the man in it was an ordinary man, and they were both going down-stream as fast as they could lick. And that otter was an otter, so don't let's play the fool about it!"

He looked steadily at me with the same grave expression. He was not in the least annoyed. I took courage from his silence.

"And, for Heaven's sake," I went on, "don't keep pretending you hear things, because it only gives me the jumps, and there's nothing to hear but the river and this cursed old thundering wind."

"You *fool!*" he answered in a low, shocked voice, "you utter fool. That's just the way all victims talk. As if you didn't understand just as well as I do!" he sneered with scorn in his voice, and a sort of resignation. "The best thing you can do is to keep quiet and try to hold your mind as firm as possible. This feeble attempt at self-deception only makes the truth harder when you're forced to meet it."

My little effort was over, and I found nothing more to say, for I knew quite well his words were true, and that *I* was the fool, not *he*. Up to a certain stage in the adventure he kept ahead of me easily, and I think I felt annoyed to be out of it, to be thus proved less psychic, less sensitive than himself to these extraordinary happenings, and half ignorant all the time of what was going on under my very nose. *He knew* from the very beginning, apparently. But at the moment I wholly missed the point of his words about the necessity of there being a victim, and that we ourselves were destined to satisfy the want. I dropped all pretence thenceforward, but thenceforward likewise my fear increased steadily to the climax.

"But you're quite right about one thing," he added, before the subject passed, "and that is that we're wiser not to talk about it, or even to think about it, because what one *thinks* finds expression in words, and what one says, happens."

That afternoon, while the canoe dried and hardened, we spent trying to fish, testing the leak, collecting wood, and watching the enormous flood of rising water. Masses of driftwood swept near our shores sometimes, and we fished for them with long willow branches. The island grew perceptibly smaller as the banks were torn away with great gulps and splashes. The weather kept brilliantly fine till about four o'clock, and then for the first time for three days the wind showed signs of abating. Clouds began to gather in the south-west, spreading thence slowly over the sky.

This lessening of the wind came as a great relief, for the incessant roaring, banging, and thundering had irritated our nerves. Yet the silence that came about five o'clock with its sudden cessation was in a manner quite as oppressive. The booming of the river had everything its own way then: it filled the air with deep murmurs, more musical than the wind noises, but infinitely more monotonous. The wind held many notes, rising, falling, always beating out some sort of great elemental tune; whereas the river's song lay between three notes at most—dull pedal notes, that held a lugubrious quality foreign to the wind, and somehow seemed to me, in my then nervous state, to sound wonderfully well the music of doom.

It was extraordinary, too, how the withdrawal suddenly of bright sunlight took everything out of the landscape that made for cheerfulness; and since this particular landscape had already managed to convey the suggestion of something sinister, the change of course was all the more unwelcome and noticeable. For me, I know, the darkening outlook became distinctly more alarming, and I found myself more than once calculating how soon after sunset the full moon would get up in the east, and whether the gathering clouds would greatly interfere with her lighting of the little island.

With this general hush of the wind—though it still indulged in occasional brief gusts—the river seemed to me to grow blacker, the willows to stand more densely together. The latter, too, kept up a sort of independent movement of their own, rustling among themselves when no wind stirred, and shaking oddly from the roots upwards. When common objects in this way become charged with the suggestion of horror, they stimulate the imagination far more than things of unusual appearance; and these bushes, crowding huddled about us, assumed for me in the darkness a bizarre *grotesquerie* of appearance that lent to them somehow the aspect of purposeful and living creatures. Their very ordinariness, I felt, masked what was malignant and hostile to us. The forces of the region drew nearer with the coming of night. They were focusing upon our island, and more particularly upon ourselves. For thus, somehow, in the terms of the imagination, did my really indescribable sensations in this extraordinary place present themselves.

I had slept a good deal in the early afternoon, and had thus recovered somewhat from the exhaustion of a disturbed night, but this only served apparently to render me more susceptible than before to the obsessing spell of the haunting. I fought against it, laughing at my feelings as absurd and childish, with very obvious physiological explanations, yet, in spite of every effort, they gained in strength upon me so that I dreaded the night as a child lost in a forest must dread the approach of darkness.

The canoe we had carefully covered with a waterproof sheet during the day, and the one remaining paddle had been securely tied by the Swede to the base of a tree, lest the wind should rob us of that too. From five o'clock onwards I busied myself with the stew-pot and preparations for dinner, it being my turn to cook that night. We had potatoes, onions, bits of bacon fat to add flavour, and a general thick residue from former stews at the bottom of the pot; with black bread broken up into it the result was most excellent, and it was followed by a stew of plums with sugar and a brew of strong tea with dried milk. A good pile of wood lay close at hand, and the absence of wind made my duties easy. My companion sat lazily watching me, dividing his attentions between cleaning his pipe and giving useless advice—an admitted privilege of the off-duty man. He had been very quiet all the afternoon, engaged in re-caulking the canoe, strengthening the tent ropes, and fishing for driftwood while I slept. No more talk about undesirable things had passed between us, and I think his only remarks had to do with the gradual destruction of the island, which he declared was now fully a third smaller than when we first landed.

The pot had just begun to bubble when I heard his voice calling to me from the bank, where he had wandered away without my noticing. I ran up.

"Come and listen," he said, "and see what you make of it." He held his hand cupwise to his ear, as so often before.

"*Now* do you hear anything?" he asked, watching me curiously.

We stood there, listening attentively together. At first I heard only the deep note of the water and the hissings rising from its turbulent surface. The willows, for once, were motionless and silent. Then a sound began to reach my ears faintly, a peculiar sound—something like the humming of a distant gong. It seemed to come across to us in the darkness from the waste of swamps and willows opposite. It was repeated at regular intervals, but it was certainly neither the sound of a bell nor the hooting of a distant steamer. I can liken it to nothing so much as to the sound of an immense gong, suspended far up in the sky, repeating incessantly its muffled metallic note, soft and musical, as it was repeatedly struck. My heart quickened as I listened.

"I've heard it all day," said my companion. "While you slept this afternoon it came all round the island. I hunted it down, but could never get near enough to see—to localise it correctly. Sometimes it was overhead, and sometimes it seemed under the water. Once or twice, too, I could have sworn it was not outside at all, but *within myself*—you know—the way a sound in the fourth dimension is supposed to come."

I was too much puzzled to pay much attention to his words. I listened carefully, striving to associate it with any known familiar sound I could think of, but without success. It changed in direction, too, coming nearer, and then sinking utterly away into remote distance. I cannot say that it was ominous in quality, because to me it seemed distinctly musical, yet I must admit it set going a distressing feeling that made me wish I had never heard it.

"The wind blowing in those sand-funnels," I said, determined to find an explanation, "or the bushes rubbing together after the storm perhaps."

"It comes off the whole swamp," my friend answered. "It comes from everywhere at once." He ignored my explanations. "It comes from the willow bushes somehow—"

"But now the wind has dropped," I objected "The willows can hardly make a noise by themselves, can they?"

His answer frightened me, first because I had dreaded it, and secondly, because I knew intuitively it was true.

"It is *because* the wind has dropped we now hear it. It was drowned before. It is the cry, I believe of the—"

I dashed back to my fire, warned by a sound of bubbling that the stew was in danger, but determined at the same time to escape further conversation. I was resolute, if possible, to avoid the exchanging of views. I dreaded, too, that he would begin again about the gods, or the elemental forces, or something else disquieting, and I wanted to keep myself well in hand for what might happen later. There was another night to be faced before we escaped from this distressing place, and there was no knowing yet what it might bring forth.

"Come and cut up bread for the pot," I called to him, vigorously stirring the appetising mixture. That stew-pot held sanity for us both, and the thought made me laugh.

He came over slowly and took the provision sack from the tree, fumbling in its mysterious depths, and then emptying the entire contents upon the ground-sheet at his feet.

"Hurry up!" I cried; "it's boiling."

The Swede burst out into a roar of laughter that startled me. It was forced laughter, not artificial exactly, but mirthless.

"There's nothing here!" he shouted, holding his sides.

"Bread, I mean."

"It's gone. There is no bread. They've taken it!"

I dropped the long spoon and ran up. Everything the sack had contained lay upon the ground-sheet, but there was no loaf.

The whole dead weight of my growing fear fell upon me and shook me. Then I burst out laughing too. It was the only thing to do: and the sound of my own laughter also made me understand his. The strain of psychical pressure caused it—this explosion of unnatural laughter in both of us; it was an effort of repressed forces to seek relief; it was a temporary safety-valve. And with both of us it ceased quite suddenly.

"How criminally stupid of me!" I cried, still determined to be consistent and find an explanation. "I clean forgot to buy a loaf at Pressburg. That chattering woman put everything out of my head, and I must have left it lying on the counter or—"

"The oatmeal, too, is much less than it was this morning," the Swede interrupted.

Why in the world need he draw attention to it? I thought angrily.

"There's enough for to-morrow," I said, stirring vigorously, "and we can get lots more at Komorn or Gran. In twenty-four hours we shall be miles from here."

"I hope so—to God," he muttered, putting the things back into the sack, "unless we're claimed first as victims for the sacrifice," he added with a foolish laugh. He dragged the sack into the tent, for safety's sake, I suppose, and I heard him mumbling on to himself, but so indistinctly that it seemed quite natural for me to ignore his words.

Our meal was beyond question a gloomy one, and we ate it almost in silence, avoiding one another's eyes, and keeping the fire bright. Then we washed up and prepared for the night, and, once smoking, our minds unoccupied with any definite duties, the apprehension I had felt all day long became more and more acute. It was not then active fear, I think, but the very vagueness of its origin distressed me far more than if I had been able to ticket and face it squarely. The curious sound I have likened to the note of a gong became now almost incessant, and filled the stillness of the night with a faint, continuous ringing rather than a series of distinct notes. At one time it was behind and at another time in front of us. Sometimes I fancied it came from the bushes on our left, and then again from the clumps on our right. More often it hovered directly overhead like the whirring of wings. It was really everywhere at once, behind, in front, at our sides and over our heads, completely surrounding us. The sound really defies description. But nothing within my knowledge is like that ceaseless muffled humming rising off the deserted world of swamps and willows.

We sat smoking in comparative silence, the strain growing every minute greater. The worst feature of the situation seemed to me that we did not know what to expect, and could therefore make no sort of preparation by way of defense. We could anticipate nothing. My explanations made in the sunshine, moreover, now came to haunt me with their foolish and wholly unsatisfactory nature, and it was more and more clear to me that some kind of plain talk with my companion was inevitable, whether I liked it or not. After all, we had to spend the night together, and to sleep in the same tent side by side. I saw that I could not get along much longer without the support of his mind, and for that, of course, plain talk was imperative. As long as possible, however, I postponed this little climax, and tried to ignore or laugh at the occasional sentences he flung into the emptiness.

Some of these sentences, moreover, were confoundedly disquieting to me, coming as they did to corroborate much that I felt myself: corroboration, too—which made it so much more convincing—from a totally different point of view. He composed such curious sentences, and hurled them at me in such an inconsequential sort of way, as though his main line of thought was secret to himself, and these fragments were the bits he found it impossible to digest. He got rid of them by uttering them. Speech relieved him. It was like being sick.

"There are things about us, I'm sure, that make for disorder, disintegration, destruction, *our* destruction," he said once, while the fire blazed between us. "We've strayed out of a safe line somewhere."

And another time, when the gong sounds had come nearer, ringing much louder than before, and directly over our heads, he said, as though talking to himself:

"I don't think a gramophone would show any record of that. The sound doesn't come to me by the ears at all. The vibrations reach me in another manner altogether, and seem to be within me, which is precisely how a fourth dimensional sound might be supposed to make itself heard."

I purposely made no reply to this, but I sat up a little closer to the fire and peered about me into the darkness. The clouds were massed all over the sky and no trace of moonlight came through. Very still, too, everything was, so that the river and the frogs had things all their own way.

"It has that about it," he went on, "which is utterly out of common experience. It is *unknown*. Only one thing describes it really: it is a non-human sound; I mean a sound outside humanity."

Having rid himself of this indigestible morsel, he lay quiet for a time; but he had so admirably expressed my own feeling that it was a relief to have the thought out, and to have confined it by the limitation of words from dangerous wandering to and fro in the mind.

The solitude of that Danube camping-place, can I ever forget it? The feeling of being utterly alone on an empty planet! My thoughts ran incessantly upon cities and the haunts of men. I would have given my soul, as the saying is, for the "feel" of those Bavarian villages we had passed through by the score; for the normal, human commonplaces: peasants drinking beer, tables beneath the trees, hot sunshine, and a ruined castle on the rocks behind the red-roofed church. Even the tourists would have been welcome.

Yet what I felt of dread was no ordinary ghostly fear. It was infinitely greater, stranger, and seemed to arise from some dim ancestral sense of terror more profoundly disturbing than anything I had known or dreamed of. We had "strayed," as the Swede put it, into some region or some set of conditions where the risks were great, yet unintelligible to us; where the frontiers of some unknown world lay close about us. It was a spot held by the dwellers in some outer space, a sort of peep-hole whence they could spy upon the earth, themselves unseen, a point where the veil between had worn a little thin. As the final result of too long a sojourn here, we should be carried over the border and deprived of what we called "our lives," yet by mental, not physical, processes. In that sense, as he said, we should be the victims of our adventure—a sacrifice.

It took us in different fashion, each according to the measure of his sensitiveness and powers of resistance. I translated it vaguely into a personification of the mightily disturbed elements, investing them with the horror of a deliberate and malefic purpose, resentful of our audacious intrusion into their breeding-place; whereas my friend threw it into the unoriginal form at first of a trespass on some ancient shrine, some place where the old gods still held sway, where the emotional forces of former worshippers still clung, and the ancestral portion of him yielded to the old pagan spell.

At any rate, here was a place unpolluted by men, kept clean by the winds from coarsening human influences, a place where spiritual agencies were within reach and aggressive. Never, before or since, have I been so attacked by indescribable suggestions of a "beyond region," of another scheme of life, another evolution not parallel to the human. And in the end our minds would succumb under the weight of the awful spell, and we should be drawn across the frontier into *their* world.

Small things testified to this amazing influence of the place, and now in the silence round the fire they allowed themselves to be noted by the mind. The very atmosphere had proved itself a magnifying medium to distort every indication: the otter rolling in the current, the hurrying boatman making signs, the shifting willows, one and all had been robbed of its natural character, and revealed in something of its other aspect—as it existed across the border in that other region. And this changed aspect I felt was new not merely to me, but to the race. The whole experience whose verge we touched was unknown to humanity at all. It was a new order of experience, and in the true sense of the word *unearthly*.

"It's the deliberate, calculating purpose that reduces one's courage to zero," the Swede said suddenly, as if he had been actually following my thoughts. "Otherwise imagination might count for much. But the paddle, the canoe, the lessening food—"

"Haven't I explained all that once?" I interrupted viciously.

"You have," he answered dryly; "you have indeed."

He made other remarks too, as usual, about what he called the "plain determination to provide a victim"; but, having now arranged my thoughts better, I recognised that this was simply the cry of his frightened soul against the knowledge that he was being attacked in a vital part, and that he would be somehow taken or destroyed. The situation called for a courage and calmness of reasoning that neither of us could compass, and I have never before been so clearly conscious of two persons in me—the one that explained everything, and the other that laughed at such foolish explanations, yet was horribly afraid.

Meanwhile, in the pitchy night the fire died down and the wood pile grew small. Neither of us moved to replenish the stock, and the darkness consequently came up very close to our faces. A few feet beyond the circle of firelight it was inky black. Occasionally a stray puff of wind set the willows shivering about us, but apart from this not very welcome sound a deep and depressing silence reigned, broken only by the gurgling of the river and the humming in the air overhead.

We both missed, I think, the shouting company of the winds.

At length, at a moment when a stray puff prolonged itself as though the wind were about to rise again, I reached the point for me of saturation, the point where it was absolutely necessary to find relief in plain speech, or else to betray myself by some hysterical extravagance that must have been far worse in its effect upon both of us. I kicked the fire into a blaze, and turned to my companion abruptly. He looked up with a start.

"I can't disguise it any longer," I said; "I don't like this place, and the darkness, and the noises, and the awful feelings I get. There's something here that beats me utterly. I'm in a blue funk, and that's the plain truth. If the other shore was—different, I swear I'd be inclined to swim for it!"

The Swede's face turned very white beneath the deep tan of sun and wind. He stared straight at me and answered quietly, but his voice betrayed his huge excitement by its unnatural calmness. For the moment, at any rate, he was the strong man of the two. He was more phlegmatic, for one thing.

"It's not a physical condition we can escape from by running away," he replied, in the tone of a doctor diagnosing some grave disease; "we must sit tight and wait. There are forces close here that could kill a herd of elephants in a second as easily as you or I could squash a fly. Our only chance is to keep perfectly still. Our insignificance perhaps may save us."

I put a dozen questions into my expression of face, but found no words. It was precisely like listening to an accurate description of a disease whose symptoms had puzzled me.

"I mean that so far, although aware of our disturbing presence, they have not *found* us—not 'located' us, as the Americans say," he went on. "They're blundering about like men hunting for a leak of gas. The paddle and canoe and provisions prove that. I think they *feel* us, but cannot actually see us. We must keep our minds quiet—it's our minds they feel. We must control our thoughts, or it's all up with us."

"Death you mean?" I stammered, icy with the horror of his suggestion.

"Worse—by far," he said. "Death, according to one's belief, means either annihilation or release from the limitations of the senses, but it involves no change of character. *You* don't suddenly alter just because the body's gone. But this means a radical alteration, a complete change, a horrible loss of oneself by substitution—far worse than death, and not even annihilation. We happen to have camped in a spot where their region touches ours, where the veil between has worn thin"—horrors! he was using my very own phrase, my actual words—"so that they are aware of our being in their neighborhood."

"But *who* are aware?" I asked.

I forgot the shaking of the willows in the windless calm, the humming overhead, everything except that I was waiting for an answer that I dreaded more than I can possibly explain.

He lowered his voice at once to reply, leaning forward a little over the fire, an indefinable change in his face that made me avoid his eyes and look down upon the ground.

"All my life," he said, "I have been strangely, vividly conscious of another region—not far removed from our own world in one sense, yet wholly different in kind—where great things go on unceasingly, where immense and terrible personalities hurry by, intent on vast purposes compared to which earthly affairs, the rise and fall of nations, the destinies of empires, the fate of armies and continents, are all as dust in the balance; vast purposes, I mean, that deal directly with the soul, and not indirectly with mere expressions of the soul—"

"I suggest just now—" I began, seeking to stop him, feeling as though I was face to face with a madman. But he instantly overbore me with his torrent that *had* to come.

"You think," he said, "it is the spirits of the elements, and I thought perhaps it was the old gods. But I tell you now it is—*neither*. These would be comprehensible entities, for they have relations with men, depending upon them for worship or sacrifice, whereas these beings who are now about us have absolutely nothing to do with mankind, and it is mere chance that their space happens just at this spot to touch our own."

The mere conception, which his words somehow made so convincing, as I listened to them there in the dark stillness of that lonely island, set me shaking a little all over. I found it impossible to control my movements.

"And what do you propose?" I began again.

"A sacrifice, a victim, might save us by distracting them until we could get away," he went on, "just as the wolves stop to devour the dogs and give the sleigh another start. But—I see no chance of any other victim now."

I stared blankly at him. The gleam in his eyes was dreadful. Presently he continued.

"It's the willows, of course. The willows *mask* the others, but the others are feeling about for us. If we let our minds betray our fear, we're lost, lost utterly." He looked at me with an expression so calm, so determined, so sincere, that I no longer had any doubts as to his sanity. He was as sane as any man ever was. "If we can hold out through the night," he added, "we may get off in the daylight unnoticed, or rather, *undiscovered*."

"But you really think a sacrifice would—"

That gong-like humming came down very close over our heads as I spoke, but it was my friend's scared face that really stopped my mouth.

"Hush!" he whispered, holding up his hand. "Do not mention them more than you can help. Do not refer to them *by name*. To name is to reveal: it is the inevitable clue, and our only hope lies in ignoring them, in order that they may ignore us."

"Even in thought?" He was extraordinarily agitated.

"Especially in thought. Our thoughts make spirals in their world. We must keep them *out of our minds* at all costs if possible."

I raked the fire together to prevent the darkness having everything its own way. I never longed for the sun as I longed for it then in the awful blackness of that summer night.

"Were you awake all last night?" he went on suddenly.

"I slept badly a little after dawn," I replied evasively, trying to follow his instructions, which I knew instinctively were true, "but the wind, of course—"

"I know. But the wind won't account for all the noises."

"Then you heard it too?"

"The multiplying countless little footsteps I heard," he said, adding, after a moment's hesitation, "and that other sound—"

"You mean above the tent, and the pressing down upon us of something tremendous, gigantic?"

He nodded significantly.

"It was like the beginning of a sort of inner suffocation?" I said.

"Partly, yes. It seemed to me that the weight of the atmosphere had been altered—had increased enormously, so that we should be crushed."

"And *that*," I went on, determined to have it all out, pointing upwards where the gong-like note hummed ceaselessly, rising and falling like wind. "What do you make of that?"

"It's *their* sound," he whispered gravely. "It's the sound of their world, the humming in their region. The division here is so thin that it leaks through somehow. But, if you listen carefully, you'll find it's not above so much as around us. It's in the willows. It's the willows themselves humming, because here the willows have been made symbols of the forces that are against us."

I could not follow exactly what he meant by this, yet the thought and idea in my mind were beyond question the thought and idea in his. I realised what he realised, only with less power of analysis than his. It was on the tip of my tongue to tell him at last about my hallucination of the ascending figures and the moving bushes, when he suddenly thrust his face again close into mine across the firelight and began to speak in a very earnest whisper. He amazed me by his calmness and pluck, his apparent control of the situation. This man I had for years deemed unimaginative, stolid!

"Now listen," he said. "The only thing for us to do is to go on as though nothing had happened, follow our usual habits, go to bed, and so forth; pretend we feel nothing and notice nothing. It is a question wholly of the mind, and the less we think about them the better our chance of escape. Above all, don't *think*, for what you think happens!"

"All right," I managed to reply, simply breathless with his words and the strangeness of it all; "all right, I'll try, but tell me one thing more first. Tell me what you make of those hollows in the ground all about us, those sand-funnels?"

"No!" he cried, forgetting to whisper in his excitement. "I dare not, simply dare not, put the thought into words. If you have not guessed I am glad. Don't try to. *They* have put it into my mind; try your hardest to prevent their putting it into yours."

He sank his voice again to a whisper before he finished, and I did not press him to explain. There was already just about as much horror in me as I could hold. The conversation came to an end, and we smoked our pipes busily in silence.

Then something happened, something unimportant apparently, as the way is when the nerves are in a very great state of tension, and this small thing for a brief space gave me an entirely different point of view. I chanced to look down at my sand-shoe—the sort we used for the canoe—and something to do with the hole at the toe suddenly recalled to me the London shop where I had bought them, the difficulty the man had in fitting me, and other details of the uninteresting but practical operation. At once, in its train, followed a wholesome view of the modern sceptical world I was accustomed to move in at home. I thought of roast beef and ale, motor-cars, policemen, brass bands, and a dozen other things that proclaimed the soul of ordinariness or utility. The effect was immediate and astonishing even to myself. Psychologically, I suppose, it was simply a sudden and violent reaction after the strain of living in an atmosphere of things that to the normal consciousness must seem impossible and incredible. But, whatever the cause, it momentarily lifted the spell from my heart, and left me for the short space of a minute feeling free and utterly unafraid. I looked up at my friend opposite.

"You damned old pagan!" I cried, laughing aloud in his face. "You imaginative idiot! You superstitious idolator! You—"

I stopped in the middle, seized anew by the old horror. I tried to smother the sound of my voice as something sacrilegious. The Swede, of course, heard it too—the strange cry overhead in the darkness—and that sudden drop in the air as though something had come nearer.

He had turned ashen white under the tan. He stood bolt upright in front of the fire, stiff as a rod, staring at me.

"After that," he said in a sort of helpless, frantic way, "we must go! We can't stay now; we must strike camp this very instant and go on—down the river."

He was talking, I saw, quite wildly, his words dictated by abject terror—the terror he had resisted so long, but which had caught him at last.

"In the dark?" I exclaimed, shaking with fear after my hysterical outburst, but still realising our position better than he did. "Sheer madness! The river's in flood, and we've only got a single paddle. Besides, we only go deeper into their country! There's nothing ahead for fifty miles but willows, willows, willows!"

He sat down again in a state of semi-collapse. The positions, by one of those kaleidoscopic changes nature loves, were suddenly reversed, and the control of our forces passed over into my hands. His mind at last had reached the point where it was beginning to weaken.

"What on earth possessed you to do such a thing?" he whispered, with the awe of genuine terror in his voice and face.

I crossed round to his side of the fire. I took both his hands in mine, kneeling down beside him and looking straight into his frightened eyes.

"We'll make one more blaze," I said firmly, "and then turn in for the night. At sunrise we'll be off full speed for Komorn. Now, pull yourself together a bit, and remember your own advice about *not thinking fear!*"

He said no more, and I saw that he would agree and obey. In some measure, too, it was a sort of relief to get up and make an excursion into the darkness for more wood. We kept close together, almost touching, groping among the bushes and along the bank. The humming overhead never ceased, but seemed to me to grow louder as we increased our distance from the fire. It was shivery work!

We were grubbing away in the middle of a thickish clump of willows where some driftwood from a former flood had caught high among the branches, when my body was seized in a grip that made me half drop upon the sand. It was the Swede. He had fallen against me, and was clutching me for support. I heard his breath coming and going in short gasps.

"Look! By my soul!" he whispered, and for the first time in my experience I knew what it was to hear tears of terror in a human voice. He was pointing to the fire, some fifty feet away. I followed the direction of his finger, and I swear my heart missed a beat.

There, in front of the dim glow, *something was moving.*

I saw it through a veil that hung before my eyes like the gauze drop-curtain used at the back of a theater—hazily a little. It was neither a human figure nor an animal. To me it gave the strange impression of being as large as several animals grouped together, like horses, two or three, moving slowly. The Swede, too, got a similar result, though expressing it differently, for he thought it was shaped and sized like a clump of willow bushes, rounded at the top, and moving all over upon its surface—"coiling upon itself like smoke," he said afterwards.

"I watched it settle downwards through the bushes," he sobbed at me. "Look, by God! It's coming this way! Oh, oh!"—he gave a kind of whistling cry. "*They've found us.*"

I gave one terrified glance, which just enabled me to see that the shadowy form was swinging towards us through the bushes, and then I collapsed backwards with a crash into the branches. These failed, of course, to support my weight, so that with the Swede on the top of me we fell in a struggling heap upon the sand. I really hardly knew what was happening. I was conscious only of a sort of enveloping sensation of icy fear that plucked the nerves out of their fleshly covering, twisted them this way and that, and replaced them quivering. My eyes were tightly shut; something in my throat choked me; a feeling that my consciousness was expanding, extending out into space, swiftly gave way to another feeling that I was losing it altogether, and about to die.

An acute spasm of pain passed through me, and I was aware that the Swede had hold of me in such a way that he hurt me abominably. It was the way he caught at me in falling.

But it was the pain, he declared afterwards, that saved me: it caused me to *forget them* and think of something else at the very instant when they were about to find me. It concealed my mind from them at the moment of discovery, yet just in time to evade their terrible seizing of me. He himself, he says, actually swooned at the same moment, and that was what saved him.

I only know that at a later date, how long or short is impossible to say, I found myself scrambling up out of the slippery network of willow branches, and saw my companion standing in front of me holding out a hand to assist me. I stared at him in a dazed way, rubbing the arm he had twisted for me. Nothing came to me to say, somehow.

"I lost consciousness for a moment or two," I heard him say. "That's what saved me. It made me stop thinking about them."

"You nearly broke my arm in two," I said, uttering my only connected thought at the moment. A numbness came over me.

"That's what saved *you!*" he replied. "Between us, we've managed to set them off on a false tack somewhere. The humming has ceased. It's gone—for the moment at any rate!"

A wave of hysterical laughter seized me again, and this time spread to my friend too—great healing gusts of shaking laughter that brought a tremendous sense of relief in their train. We made our way back to the fire and put the wood on so that it blazed at once. Then we saw that the tent had fallen over and lay in a tangled heap upon the ground.

We picked it up, and during the process tripped more than once and caught our feet in sand.

"It's those sand-funnels," exclaimed the Swede, when the tent was up again and the firelight lit up the ground for several yards about us. "And look at the size of them!"

All round the tent and about the fireplace where we had seen the moving shadows there were deep funnel-shaped hollows in the sand, exactly similar to the ones we had already found over the island, only far bigger and deeper, beautifully formed, and wide enough in some instances to admit the whole of my foot and leg.

Neither of us said a word. We both knew that sleep was the safest thing we could do, and to bed we went accordingly without further delay, having first thrown sand on the fire and taken the provision sack and the paddle inside the tent with us. The canoe, too, we propped in such a way at the end of the tent that our feet touched it, and the least motion would disturb and wake us.

In case of emergency, too, we again went to bed in our clothes, ready for a sudden start.

It was my firm intention to lie awake all night and watch, but the exhaustion of nerves and body decreed otherwise, and sleep after a while came over me with a welcome blanket of oblivion. The fact that my companion also slept quickened its approach. At first he fidgeted and constantly sat up, asking me if I "heard this" or "heard that." He tossed about on his cork mattress, and said the tent was moving and the river had risen over the point of the island; but each time I went out to look I returned with the report that all was well, and finally he grew calmer and lay still. Then at length his breathing became regular and I heard unmistakable sounds of snoring—the first and only time in my life when snoring has been a welcome and calming influence.

This, I remember, was the last thought in my mind before dozing off.

A difficulty in breathing woke me, and I found the blanket over my face. But something else besides the blanket was pressing upon me, and my first thought was that my companion had rolled off his mattress on to my own in his sleep. I called to him and sat up, and at the same moment it came to me that the tent was *surrounded*. That sound of multitudinous soft pattering was again audible outside, filling the night with horror.

I called again to him, louder than before. He did not answer, but I missed the sound of his snoring and also noticed that the flap of the tent door was down. This was the unpardonable sin. I crawled out in the darkness to hook it back securely, and it was then for the first time I realized positively that the Swede was not there. He had gone.

I dashed out in a mad run, seized by a dreadful agitation, and the moment I was out I plunged into a sort of torrent of humming that surrounded me completely and came out of every quarter of the heavens at once. It was that same familiar humming—gone mad! A swarm of great invisible bees might have been about me in the air. The sound seemed to thicken the very atmosphere, and I felt that my lungs worked with difficulty.

But my friend was in danger, and I could not hesitate.

The dawn was just about to break, and a faint whitish light spread upwards over the clouds from a thin strip of clear horizon. No wind stirred. I could just make out the bushes and river beyond, and the pale sandy patches. In my excitement I ran frantically to and fro about the island, calling him by name, shouting at the top of my voice the first words that came into my head. But the willows smothered my voice, and the humming muffled it, so that the sound only traveled a few feet round me. I plunged among the bushes, tripping headlong, tumbling over roots, and scraping my face as I tore this way and that among the preventing branches.

Then, quite unexpectedly, I came out upon the island's point and saw a dark figure outlined between the water and the sky. It was the Swede. And already he had one foot in the river! A moment more and he would have taken the plunge.

I threw myself upon him, flinging my arms about his waist and dragging him shorewards with all my strength. Of course he struggled furiously, making a noise all the time just like that cursed humming, and using the most outlandish phrases in his anger about "going *inside* to Them," and "taking the way of the water and the wind," and God only knows what more besides, that I tried in vain to recall afterwards, but which turned me sick with horror and amazement as I listened. But in the end I managed to get him into the comparative safety of the tent, and flung him breathless and cursing upon the mattress where I held him until the fit had passed.

I think the suddenness with which it all went and he grew calm, coinciding as it did with the equally abrupt cessation of the humming and pattering outside—I think this was almost the strangest part of the whole business perhaps. For he just opened his eyes and turned his tired face up to me so that the dawn threw a pale light upon it through the doorway, and said, for all the world just like a frightened child:

"My life, old man—it's my life I owe you. But it's all over now anyhow. They've found a victim in our place!"

Then he dropped back upon his blankets and went to sleep literally under my eyes. He simply collapsed, and began to snore again as healthily as though nothing had happened and he had never tried to offer his own life as a sacrifice by drowning. And when the sunlight woke him three hours later—hours of ceaseless vigil for me—it became so clear to me that he remembered absolutely nothing of what he had attempted to do, that I deemed it wise to hold my peace and ask no dangerous questions.

He woke naturally and easily, as I have said, when the sun was already high in a windless hot sky, and he at once got up and set about the preparation of the fire for breakfast. I followed him anxiously at bathing, but he did not attempt to plunge in, merely dipping his head and making some remark about the extra coldness of the water.

"River's falling at last," he said, "and I'm glad of it."

"The humming has stopped too," I said.

He looked up at me quietly with his normal expression. Evidently he remembered everything except his own attempt at suicide.

"Everything has stopped," he said, "because—"

He hesitated. But I knew some reference to that remark he had made just before he fainted was in his mind, and I was determined to know it.

"Because 'They've found another victim'?" I said, forcing a little laugh.

"Exactly," he answered, "exactly! I feel as positive of it as though—as though—I feel quite safe again, I mean," he finished.

He began to look curiously about him. The sunlight lay in hot patches on the sand. There was no wind. The willows were motionless. He slowly rose to his feet.

"Come," he said; "I think if we look, we shall find it."

He started off on a run, and I followed him. He kept to the banks, poking with a stick among the sandy bays and caves and little backwaters, myself always close on his heels.

"Ah!" he exclaimed presently, "ah!"

The tone of his voice somehow brought back to me a vivid sense of the horror of the last twenty-four hours, and I hurried up to join him. He was pointing with his stick at a large black object that lay half in the water and half on the sand. It appeared to be caught by some twisted willow roots so that the river could not sweep it away. A few hours before the spot must have been under water.

"See," he said quietly, "the victim that made our escape possible!"

And when I peered across his shoulder I saw that his stick rested on the body of a man. He turned it over. It was the corpse of a peasant, and the face was hidden in the sand. Clearly the man had been drowned but a few hours before, and his body must have been swept down upon our island somewhere about the hour of the dawn—*at the very time the fit had passed*.

"We must give it a decent burial, you know."

"I suppose so," I replied. I shuddered a little in spite of myself, for there was something about the appearance of that poor drowned man that turned me cold.

The Swede glanced up sharply at me, an undecipherable expression on his face, and began clambering down the bank. I followed him more leisurely. The current, I noticed, had torn away much of the clothing from the body, so that the neck and part of the chest lay bare.

Half-way down the bank my companion suddenly stopped and held up his hand in warning; but either my foot slipped, or I had gained too much momentum to bring myself quickly to a halt, for I bumped into him and sent him forward with a sort of leap to save himself. We tumbled together on to the hard sand so that our feet splashed into the water. And, before anything could be done, we had collided a little heavily against the corpse.

The Swede uttered a sharp cry. And I sprang back as if I had been shot.

At the moment we touched the body there arose from its surface the loud sound of humming—the sound of several hummings—which passed with a vast commotion as of winged things in the air about us and disappeared upwards into the sky, growing fainter and fainter till they finally ceased in the distance. It was exactly as though we had disturbed some living yet invisible creatures at work.

My companion clutched me, and I think I clutched him, but before either of us had time properly to recover from the unexpected shock, we saw that a movement of the current was turning the corpse round so that it became released from the grip of the willow roots. A moment later it had turned completely over, the dead face uppermost, staring at the sky. It lay on the edge of the main stream. In another moment it would be swept away.

The Swede started to save it, shouting again something I did not catch about a "proper burial"—and then abruptly dropped upon his knees on the sand and covered his eyes with his hands. I was beside him in an instant.

I saw what he had seen.

For just as the body swung round to the current the face and the exposed chest turned full towards us, and showed plainly how the skin and flesh were indented with small hollows, beautifully formed, and exactly similar in shape and kind to the sand-funnels that we had found all over the island.

"Their mark!" I heard my companion mutter under his breath. "Their awful mark!"

And when I turned my eyes again from his ghastly face to the river, the current had done its work, and the body had been swept away into mid-stream and was already beyond our reach and almost out of sight, turning over and over on the waves like an otter.

A Tale of Three Who Were Blind*

Izumi Kyōka

1

"ONE MOMENT . . . you, sir."

At the voice, a chill shot down Sakagami's back—though not as at a voice he remembered and disliked. From the foot of the hill he had seen them creeping down toward him from Yotsuya, appearing and disappearing, floating up and falling back again, in the mist that huddled in motionless spirals halfway up the slope. He could hardly hear the sound of their feet; and then, as they passed, that voice.

They were nothing to him, and yet he knew that something must happen before he would be allowed to pass. They would call him, they would stop him—he was strangely sure that somehow he must hear a voice. It might be as when a traveler hears the cry of a raven or the scream of a night heron and cannot be sure, even if he is quite alone, that the call has been at him; but Sakagami knew that he would have to hear that unpleasant, that odious voice.

Three blind ones in single file.

In the center was a woman, perhaps in her middle years, white throated, thick haired, her shoulders thin and slight. The long sleeves, falling down from her folded arms, were of a darkness that seemed to sink through to the thin breasts beneath, and their trailing edges gave way to a like darkness in the obi. Was the slapping from her sandals?—but the long skirt brushed the ground and hid her feet.

The man in front wore a limp, loose garment, grey perhaps, in the darkness almost like the night mist itself spun and woven. His brimless cap shot into the air, a veritable miter. His gaunt body swayed as he drew near—and passed.

The other man, slender and of no more than medium height, clung to the woman as if he meant to hide in the shadow of her hair.

---

*Translated by Edward Seidensticker

Though Sakagami had had no clear view of any of them, the third had been the most obscure of all.

And yet Sakagami knew immediately that he had been stopped by this shadowy one.

"Are you speaking to me?" Sakagami looked back. His shoulders were hunched in the sudden chill, and his answer was like a curse flung at a barking dog.

"I am speaking to you." The voice was low. It was indeed the slight man in the rear. He seemed to straighten up as he spoke to Sakagami, who was two or three paces up the hill from him. He held his staff at an angle, an oar with which to row his way through the mist.

The other two—the long head in front; and the high Japanese coiffure (Sakagami could not be sure what style), like a wig on an actor's wig stand, suspended upside-down—stood diagonally down the slope with their backs to their companion.

Sakagami turned on his heels to stare at the man.

"And what do you want?"

"I should like to talk to you." Whether he was very sure of himself, or out of breath, his slowness seemed wrong in the cold of the late winter night.

2

"What is it?"

Coming toward him in the mist, they had seemed like two grave markers, a tall one and a low one, blown in by a last gust of the autumn winds from some cemetery on the moors, the dead tufts of grass white in the earth still clinging to their bases.

But his tone became more gentle as he saw that the three, groping their way along this shabby, deserted street as through the caves on the Musashino Plain, were only three blind ones who made their living by massaging and who had set out together, who would blow the flutes that were the sign of their trade, as thin and high in the winter night as the sound of a mosquito in January, and who would presently disappear behind the lantern of a poor rooming house.

"I have little to say. But I should like to know where you are going. Where? Where? Where?" There was a touch of derision in the nasal tone. His head cocked to one side, the man looked up at Sakagami. He raised his hand as if to scratch his ear, and tapped at the head of the staff.

"It makes no difference," said Sakagami testily. He was going to meet a woman who had been forbidden to see him. "Does it matter where I'm going?"

"It does. I am sorry, sir, but it does." There was a strength in the voice that kept Sakagami fixed to the spot.

"And why?" Sakagami turned and started down toward the man; but he pulled back as the mist clutched at his face.

"It is late." The voice was suddenly strong. The head bowed heavily toward the earth.

Long Head, in front, turned slowly to face the bank above the road.

The woman seemed to sink into the earth as she sat down disconsolately on her heels. The tip of her staff was white against the dark hair.

Seeing that the three meant to stay, Sakagami resigned himself to being delayed; but at the thought of what lay ahead his chest rose and fell violently, as if poison were being forced in through his mouth. A rising, a rush of blood, and a collapse with an angry tremor of the flesh.

Banks rose on both sides like mountain slopes. Against the sky, over the bank toward which Long Head faced, one or two barracks-style houses stood like tea huts on a mountain pass, tight and dark. Not a sliver of light escaped from them. On the bank, dead grass, blanketed by the mist as by a frost.

On the side of the road where the three had stopped, the bank had slid away, exposing the roots of trees and the retaining stakes. Trees sent up their skeleton forms above. Here and there the mist clung to the branches like dirty moonlight. There were no stars. The bottom of a defile in Yotsuya, like the bottom of a mountain ravine, at one o'clock in the morning.

Only the racing in the chest. "Is it wrong to be so late?" The words themselves seemed to be weighted down by the heavy air.

"You were certain to say that." The man slapped the back of the hand that held the staff. "It is wrong, very wrong indeed."

"I am not to go on then?" Perhaps this oracle could tell him something of the meeting that was to come.

"If you will go on, whatever I say, let that be the end of it. But I must stop you for a moment. I alone—or that gentleman too."

Long Head coughed faintly as the other brought his staff upright.

3

"And what if I have to go?" Sakagami's breath came faster. "What if my father is dying, or a friend is ill? How can you know? You speak as though I were doing something wrong."

The man bent his head as though to rub his cheek against the staff, and laughed unpleasantly. "I know where you are going. And that gentleman says I must speak. . . . Shall I tell you? It will be no trouble. And you will tell me I am right. You go to meet a woman."

Sakagami did not answer.

"She has duties and ties. There are obstacles and complications. But you have pushed and slashed, and broken down fences and walls. . . . You have pressed her with an urgency that would tear her very breast open, and she will meet you at the risk of her life. You are on your way to meet her. I knew from your footsteps as you came up, and met us, and passed. I knew a man rushing along, out of his senses.

"Dew falls, frost falls. The moon clouds over, the stars are dark. In the wide skies too there are shadows. The shadows are gentle. But the breast is blocked and the breath is tight. See the lightning and the thunderclap after the darkness.

"In the heart of man, nothing is strange.

"I think as you do, I put myself in your place, and everything is clear, even to a blind man, as clear as this hand itself." The man brought his hand up to cover his face.

Sakagami could see in the dim light that the other two were nodding deeply, as if on a signal.

"You are fortunetellers, are you? I was in a hurry, and perhaps I was rude." Sakagami heaved a sigh. "She left home barefoot. . . . It is some distance from here, but she is waiting in the woods alone. She cannot move until I come.

"I had a telephone call from her just now, so short that it was no more than a signal, and I hardly know what I am about. Can I help going? Do you say I shouldn't go?"

"I thought as much. . . . No, you were right to admit everything like a man. It will be sad for both of you. But how very dangerous." The man clutched his staff to his chest with both hands, and stood in silence for a moment. "I shall ask you a question. Along this bank where we are gathered there is a row of gaslights. How many of them are lighted, and how many are dark? Tell me, please. Tell me." He nodded as he spoke, and his head fell to his chest.

Sakagami followed the line from the bottom of the hill behind the three. It was not the first time he had taken this road. Below the cliff, on one side, the gaslights stood at intervals of about two yards, put up by a nearby movie theatre for the safety of passers-by.

The lamps were white and cold as frost needles. The glass chambers, like windows in the face of the cliff, were dark as far as his eye reached. They drank at the mist and sucked it in, and at intervals spewed out an ashen breath.

Like a devil's death mask shaped from cotton wadding, the mist clung to the nearest lamp and became a great earth spider, sending out horrible threads on that ashen breath, into the sky and down to the ground. Was that why the mist seemed to clutch so at the face?

4

"They will all be out," the man said as Sakagami looked up and down the row.

"They are all out." The darkness of the night closed in more tightly.

"They will all be out. And now, you will see that one lamp up the hill from here is still burning. You see it? How many lamps away is it?"

"I see it." There was one feeble, wavering flame, about to float off on the mist. "But I can't tell you how many lamps away it is."

"Not far away. When the traveler sees a night crane in the pines along a lonely road, it is always in the fifth pine away. . . . The lamp will be the fifth up the hill from you.

"If I am wrong, that gentleman will tell me so. He says nothing. I am right. Count them for yourself, count them for yourself. One . . ." He tapped twice with his staff.

"One."

"Two." Tap, tap, tap.

"Three. Four. Five. It is the fifth."

"As I said."

"But why?"

"You see us, and this bank, and these dark lamps, all because of that one light. But for it, you would not see me if I were to pinch your nose."

He did indeed see the dim figures by the light of that one lamp. By that faint light, even the row of dark lamps down the slope sent out an occasional flicker of light—and Sakagami stood dim and uncertain in the breathing mist.

"What does it mean?"

"And can you see nothing under the fifth lamp, the lamp that is burning?"

"I beg your pardon?" Sakagami's voice shook.

"And can you see nothing?"

"Nothing."

"Nothing?"

"Not a thing."

"That is not as it should be. If you will but go up and look, you will see. It is for that that I have stopped you. Listen, if you will."

He twisted and bent forward a little, and rattled his staff in the stones that lay at the base of a gas lamp. The sound was drunk up in the mist.

"Let me make the point clear: The gaslight under which we stand—it has moved not one step ahead of us and not one step behind us since I stopped you—is the nineteenth in the row from the bottom of the hill.

"If I am wrong, the master there will correct me.

"Three years ago, on a different night indeed, but in this same November, at this same hour, this happened to me too.

"I was not then the blind man you see now."

He turned squarely toward Sakagami, but his head was still bowed.

"I was going to meet a woman as you are, and I was climbing this hill.

"But I passed only one blind man. That is the whole of the difference."

Long Head faced squarely down the hill away from Sakagami, and started to walk off—and was still again.

5

And the woman: still sitting on her heels, she turned to hear the story. The knee of her kimono and the obi at her waist were folded one against the other. Her throat was white.

The man's voice was firm. "He called me from behind, as I called you, and, at the nineteenth lamp, the fifth below the lighted lamp, he said to me what I have said to you.

"I have but repeated it.

"And why should I not go to meet the woman, I retorted as you did. He answered. . . ."

Sakagami somehow knew that "he" was Long Head here.

"'There is a strange creature under the fifth lamp ahead, the lamp that is still lighted. . . . A demon that takes the shadows of men, snatches them, devours them.

"'He sucks at a shadow, and the man grows thin; licks the shadow with his tongue, and the man languishes; tramps on the shadow, and the man is ill; snuffs it quite away, and the man dies.

"'The demon is always about, in the sunlight and the moonlight, to suck, to lick, to trample, and in time the man dies. Terrible though that is, it is more terrible when, under just such a light as we have here, he opens his mouth . . .'"

The blind man's gaping mouth.

"'. . . and swallows the shadow. That is all. The man dies. You are not to pass by here again.'

"That is what he said.

"But I was young and hotheaded. What was he talking about? I retorted. In the first place, what sort of monster was it? He did not smile. 'Very well, very well, I shall tell you. It is like a lizard with a fez. It is like a white dog spread-eagled, and on its head a biretta.'

"Seeing was quicker than hearing, I said. Let the thing have my shadow—I had believed nothing. I climbed to that fifth light, kicking up the gravel as I went. I found nothing there.

"The blind man, scraping at the gravel with his staff, sprang up the hill after me. 'Have you gone mad? You are too brave for your own good. It is no use talking to one who believes nothing I say, but the demon will not be after your shadow for a time.

"'He has long been after the shadow of the woman, the woman you are going to meet. I tell her through you to be forever careful, not for a moment to be off her guard.'

"That is what he said."

6

"And why should he be giving advice—did he know the woman, I asked. 'A housewife in my block saw her just this evening. They were at the bath together. The skin like snow, patted and rounded—one wondered why it did not melt in the stream. Over it, scarlet satin, and a pale yellow sash—scarlet that seemed to glide and flow from the breasts. A kimono for good autumn weather, a latticework of indigo and dark-blue stripes. A black damask obi, and a scarlet cord. An azure ribbon to bind the hair. An ear, faint through hair aglow like falling dew. And the rich swell of the neck and shoulders. Woman though she was, the housewife I speak of stood fascinated. She moved around to the front, and stared at the back, and peered at the naked form in the mirror. And she described everything to me, down to the mole on the white skin at the base of the left breast.'

"'It will be this woman you are going to see.'

"That is what he said."

Sakagami was trembling. Not only because the faint image of the woman, now looking away, came to him as that of the woman being described—the same kimono, the same obi.

But because of the woman he was going to meet tonight. He expected her to have on *that* obi, and *that* kimono—but what if she should have on the everyday black obi and the latticed kimono that had so become a part of his life?

His blood ran cold, and an instant later he flushed.

"'Am I right? The kimono, the obi, the scarlet beneath . . . am I right about the woman you are going to meet?' It made no difference about the black damask, or about the indigo and blue, or about the white skin. But imagine, if you will, how it was to be told even of the mole on the breast.

"It was as though I could see before my eyes—fearsome thing—the figure lying naked, the kimono open, here in this Yotsuya Valley.

"The demon, said the blind man, was after the woman, to lick her shadow, to suck at it, to take it, to trample it, to devour it. 'Tell her, if you please, that she is to be careful.' But I was not listening. I flew off in a dark cloud. I was not to be stopped by iron gate or stone door, and I went to meet that small, defenseless woman.

"I had seen a demon that would take her shadow, would suck at her shadow, would lick at her shadow. I had seen it in the light of the gas lamp.

"The woman's house was very near here.

"'It will be after you day and night. You are not looking well, your shadow is thin already. Watch for it.' That, sir, is what I said.

"An unhappy woman, whom labor and anguish had already so devastated that her obi, however tightly bound, could not be tight enough—into the head of this unhappy woman I drove my words as with a hammer.

"In my anger that she had shown herself naked to another. She fell upon my knee, and in a voice that trembled asked whom I had met and what I had heard along the way. Look to your own conscience—I said; and I did not tell her I had heard the story from a blind man.

"A tragic mistake. It was the blind man himself who clung to the woman like her very shadow. It was the blind man himself who might have been taken for a lizard in the gaslight, who hovered about the back fence, the well, the hedge, face livid, eyes red, lips pale and tight, waiting for the woman to come in or go out.

"Had she known it was the blind man, she would not have been so haunted by the story."

7

"Thereafter I saw the woman less often.

"She seemed to avoid me.

"I thought of killing her and myself; but presently, as I heard the details, I learned that she was avoiding everyone. She had a strange longing to be hidden.

"And finally, like the splittailed cat who has taken the shape of a beautiful woman, she came to hate the light of the sun. Whether it was night or day, she closed the doors and the shutters, and lay hidden behind two and three screens.

"I forced my way through, and saw her. Her very kimono seemed moldering and musty, and she only knelt looking at the floor, so slight and wraithlike that it seemed she must quite disappear.

"I raised her face. The eyes were destroyed. I beg your pardon? No, the woman's eyes, both the woman's eyes.

"I heard her story. She had not been able even for an instant to take her eyes from her shadow.

"If she went into the kitchen it was on the window, if she went to the veranda it was on the doorstep or behind her on the door, the wall, the screen.

"And wherever the shadow was, there was the demon, to suck at it, to lick, trample, rub, embrace, cover.

"In the light of the moon, the light of the sun, the light of the lamp, the faint light of the snow or of trees in blossom, there was always that shadow. And with the shadow: discomfort, revulsion—terror and loathing.

"Finally, darkness. But even when she could not see the palm of her own hand, there was the shadow. When all the lights were out.

"In the alcove, on the lintel, on the ceiling, on the doorframe, the floor, now here and now there—the shape of a lizard with something slapped down on its head, weirdly white, the body long, the legs writhing—now clinging, now curling into a ball, now crawling along stretched out its full length.

"She would scream when she saw it, and it would flit away—how quickly! But a moment later it would come creeping back again.

"She tried desperately not to see. But she saw because she had eyes. Lying back on her pillow, her hair pulled tightly back, she dropped medicine into her eyes, and was blind.

"Darkness, over the heart too. I took her hand, and for the first time told her that I had heard the story of the demon who eats shadows from a certain blind man halfway up the hill. I told her how old he seemed to be, and described his appearance, and the woman gasped as though her eyes had suddenly been opened, and began weeping bitterly.

"Frustrated in love, the blind man had put his curse on her.

"I clutched at the flesh of my face and wept tears of anger, chagrin, vexation—and finally of pity. I determined that I would be with her, and with this hand I drove a needle into both my eyes.

"A bond from one life lasts through three. Enlightenment has come to us, and penitence, and release from the appetites of the world. We take our staffs, that blind man with us, and, ashamed of the daylight, go out into the night.

"We have met you along the way.

"I have troubled you; but as our sleeves brushed in the mist, I knew, and I spoke to you. It is for you to take my advice or throw it away.

"I have nothing more to say. If you will, I shall leave you."

Forlorn and graceful, the woman rose to her feet. Her weeping had sounded below the narrative.

Led by Long Head, the three of them groped their way down the hill. Three staffs, three phantoms in the fading gaslight.

The bit of silk pressed to the eyes by that white hand as the woman had arisen seemed to linger on, a scarlet butterfly cutting its way in and out of the mist.

The Damned Thing

Ambrose Bierce

1

One Does Not Always Eat What Is on the Table

BY THE LIGHT of a tallow candle which had been placed on one end of a rough table a man was reading something written in a book. It was an old account book, greatly worn; and the writing was not, apparently, very legible, for the man sometimes held the page close to the flame of the candle to get a stronger light on it. The shadow of the book would then throw into obscurity a half of the room, darkening a number of faces and figures; for besides the reader, eight other men were present. Seven of them sat against the rough log walls, silent, motionless, and the room being small, not very far from the table. By extending an arm any one of them could have touched the eighth man, who lay on the table, face upward, partly covered by a sheet, his arms at his sides. He was dead.

The man with the book was not reading aloud, and no one spoke; all seemed to be waiting for something to occur; the dead man only was without expectation. From the blank darkness outside came in, through the aperture that served for a window, all the ever unfamiliar noises of night in the wilderness—the long nameless note of a distant coyote; the stilly pulsing thrill of tireless insects in trees; strange cries of night birds, so different from those of the birds of day; the drone of great blundering beetles, and all that mysterious chorus of small sounds that seem always to have been but half heard when they have suddenly ceased, as if conscious of an indiscretion. But nothing of all this was noted in that company; its members were not overmuch addicted to idle interest in matters of no practical importance; that was obvious in every line of their rugged faces—obvious even in the dim light of the single candle. They were evidently men of the vicinity—farmers and woodsmen.

The person reading was a trifle different; one would have said of him that he was of the world, worldly, albeit there was that in his attire which attested a certain fellowship with the organisms of his environment. His coat would hardly have passed muster in San Francisco; his foot-gear was not of urban origin, and the hat that lay by him on the floor (he was the only one uncovered) was such that if one had considered it as an article of mere personal adornment he would have missed its meaning. In countenance the man was rather prepossessing, with just a hint of sternness; though that he may have assumed or cultivated, as appropriate to one in authority. For he was a coroner. It was by virtue of his office that he had possession of the book in which he was reading; it had been found among the dead man's effects—in his cabin, where the inquest was now taking place.

When the coroner had finished reading he put the book into his breast pocket. At that moment the door was pushed open and a young man entered. He, clearly, was not of mountain birth and breeding: he was clad as those who dwell in cities. His clothing was dusty, however, as from travel. He had, in fact, been riding hard to attend the inquest.

The coroner nodded; no one else greeted him.

"We have waited for you," said the coroner. "It is necessary to have done with this business to-night."

The young man smiled. "I am sorry to have kept you," he said. "I went away, not to evade your summons, but to post to my newspaper an account of what I suppose I am called back to relate."

The coroner smiled.

"The account that you posted to your newspaper," he said, "differs, probably, from that which you will give here under oath."

"That," replied the other, rather hotly and with a visible flush, "is as you please. I used manifold paper and have a copy of what I sent. It was not written as news, for it is incredible, but as fiction. It may go as a part of my testimony under oath."

"But you say it is incredible."

"That is nothing to you, sir, if I also swear that it is true."

The coroner was silent for a time, his eyes upon the floor. The men about the sides of the cabin talked in whispers, but seldom withdrew their gaze from the face of the corpse. Presently the coroner lifted his eyes and said: "We will resume the inquest."

The men removed their hats. The witness was sworn.

"What is your name?" the coroner asked.

"William Harker."

"Age?"

"Twenty-seven."

"You knew the deceased, Hugh Morgan?"

"Yes."

"You were with him when he died?"

"Near him."

"How did that happen—your presence, I mean?"

"I was visiting him at this place to shoot and fish. A part of my purpose, however, was to study him and his odd, solitary way of life. He seemed a good model for a character in fiction. I sometimes write stories."

"I sometimes read them."

"Thank you."

"Stories in general—not yours."

Some of the jurors laughed. Against a sombre background humor shows high lights. Soldiers in the intervals of battle laugh easily, and a jest in the death chamber conquers by surprise.

"Relate the circumstances of this man's death," said the coroner. "You may use any notes or memoranda that you please."

The witness understood. Pulling a manuscript from his breast pocket he held it near the candle and turning the leaves until he found the passage that he wanted began to read.

2

What May Happen in a Field of Wild Oats

". . . The sun had hardly risen when we left the house. We were looking for quail, each with a shotgun, but we had only one dog. Morgan said that our best ground was beyond a certain ridge that he pointed out, and we crossed it by a trail through the *chaparral*. On the other side was comparatively level ground, thickly covered with wild oats. As we emerged from the *chaparral* Morgan was but a few yards in advance. Suddenly we heard, at a little distance to our right and partly in front, a noise as of some animal thrashing about in the bushes, which we could see were violently agitated.

"'We've started a deer,' I said. 'I wish we had brought a rifle.'

"Morgan, who had stopped and was intently watching the agitated *chaparral,* said nothing, but had cocked both barrels of his gun and was holding it in readiness to aim. I thought him a trifle excited, which surprised me, for he had a reputation for exceptional coolness, even in moments of sudden and imminent peril.

"'Oh, come,' I said. 'You are not going to fill up a deer with quail-shot, are you?'

"Still he did not reply; but catching sight of his face as he turned it slightly toward me I was struck by the intensity of his look. Then I understood that we had serious business in hand and my first conjecture was that we had 'jumped' a grizzly. I advanced to Morgan's side, cocking my piece as I moved.

"The bushes were now quiet and the sounds had ceased, but Morgan was as attentive to the place as before.

"'What is it? What the devil is it?' I asked.

"'That Damned Thing!' he replied, without turning his head. His voice was husky and unnatural. He trembled visibly.

"I was about to speak further, when I observed the wild oats near the place of the disturbance moving in the most inexplicable way. I can hardly describe it. It seemed as if stirred by a streak of wind, which not only bent it, but pressed it down—crushed it so that it did not rise; and this movement was slowly prolonging itself directly toward us.

"Nothing that I had ever seen had affected me so strangely as this unfamiliar and unaccountable phenomenon, yet I am unable to recall any sense of fear. I remember—and tell it here because, singularly enough, I recollected it then—that once in looking carelessly out of an open window I momentarily mistook a small tree close at hand for one of a group of larger trees at a little distance away. It looked the same size as the others, but being more distinctly and sharply defined in mass and detail seemed out of harmony with them. It was a mere falsification of the law of aërial perspective, but it startled, almost terrified me. We so rely upon the orderly operation of familiar natural laws that any seeming suspension of them is noted as a menace to our safety, a warning of unthinkable calamity. So now the apparently causeless movement of the herbage and the slow, undeviating approach of the line of disturbance were distinctly disquieting. My companion appeared actually frightened, and I could hardly credit my senses when I saw him suddenly throw his gun to his shoulder and fire both barrels at the agitated grain! Before the smoke of the discharge had cleared away I heard a loud savage cry—a scream like that of a wild animal—and flinging his gun upon the ground Morgan sprang away and ran swiftly from the spot. At the same instant I was thrown violently to the ground by the impact of something unseen in the smoke—some soft, heavy substance that seemed thrown against me with great force.

"Before I could get upon my feet and recover my gun, which seemed to have been struck from my hands, I heard Morgan crying out as if in mortal agony, and mingling with his cries were such hoarse, savage sounds as one hears from fighting dogs. Inexpressibly terrified, I struggled to my feet and looked in the direction of Morgan's retreat; and may Heaven in mercy spare me from another sight like that! At a distance of less than thirty yards was my friend, down upon one knee, his head thrown back at a frightful angle, hatless, his long hair in disorder and his whole body in violent movement from side to side, backward and forward. His right arm was lifted and seemed to lack the hand—at least, I could see none. The other arm was invisible. At times, as my memory now reports this extraordinary scene, I could discern but a part of his body; it was as if he had been partly blotted out—I cannot otherwise express it—then a shifting of his position would bring it all into view again.

"All this must have occurred within a few seconds, yet in that time Morgan assumed all the postures of a determined wrestler vanquished by superior weight and strength. I saw nothing but him and not always distinctly. During the entire incident his shouts and curses were heard, as if through an enveloping uproar of such sounds of rage and fury as I had never heard from the throat of man or brute!

"For a moment only I stood irresolute, then throwing down my gun I ran forward to my friend's assistance. I had a vague belief that he was suffering from a fit, or some form of convulsion. Before I could reach his side he was down and quiet. All sounds had ceased, but with a feeling of such terror as even these awful events had not inspired I now saw again the mysterious movement of the wild oats, prolonging itself from the trampled area about the prostrate man toward the edge of a wood. It was only when it had reached the wood that I was able to withdraw my eyes and look at my companion. He was dead."

3

A Man Though Naked May Be in Rags

The coroner rose from his seat and stood beside the dead man. Lifting an edge of the sheet he pulled it away, exposing the entire body, altogether naked and showing in the candle-light a clay-like yellow. It had, however, broad maculations of bluish black, obviously caused by extravasated blood from contusions. The chest and sides looked as if they had been beaten with a bludgeon. There were dreadful lacerations; the skin was torn in strips and shreds.

The coroner moved round to the end of the table and undid a silk handkerchief which had been passed under the chin and knotted on the top of the head. When the handkerchief was drawn away it exposed what had been the throat. Some of the jurors who had risen to get a better view repented their curiosity and turned away their faces. Witness Harker went to the open window and leaned out across the sill, faint and sick. Dropping the handkerchief upon the dead man's neck the coroner stepped to an angle of the room and from a pile of clothing produced one garment after another, each of which he held up a moment for inspection. All were torn, and stiff with blood. The jurors did not make a closer inspection. They seemed rather uninterested. They had, in truth, seen all this before; the only thing that was new to them being Harker's testimony.

"Gentlemen," the coroner said, "we have no more evidence, I think. Your duty has been already explained to you; if there is nothing you wish to ask you may go outside and consider your verdict."

The foreman rose—a tall, bearded man of sixty, coarsely clad.

"I shall like to ask one question, Mr. Coroner," he said. "What asylum did this yer last witness escape from?"

"Mr. Harker," said the coroner gravely and tranquilly, "from what asylum did you last escape?"

Harker flushed crimson again, but said nothing, and the seven jurors rose and solemnly filed out of the cabin.

"If you have done insulting me, sir," said Harker, as soon as he and the officer were left alone with the dead man, "I suppose I am at liberty to go?"

"Yes."

Harker started to leave, but paused, with his hand on the door latch. The habit of his profession was strong in him—stronger than his sense of personal dignity. He turned about and said:

"The book you have there—I recognize it as Morgan's diary. You seemed greatly interested in it; you read in it while I was testifying. May I see it? The public would like—"

"The book will cut no figure in this matter," replied the official, slipping it into his coat pocket; "all the entries in it were made before the writer's death."

As Harker passed out of the house the jury reëntered and stood about the table, on which the now covered corpse showed under the sheet with sharp definition. The foreman seated himself near the candle, produced from his breast pocket a pencil and scrap of paper and wrote rather laboriously the following verdict, which with various degrees of effort all signed:

"We, the jury, do find that the remains come to their death at the hands of a mountain lion, but some of us thinks, all the same, they had fits."

4

An Explanation from the Tomb

In the diary of the late Hugh Morgan are certain interesting entries having, possibly, a scientific value as suggestions. At the inquest upon his body the book was not put in evidence; possibly the coroner thought it not worth while to confuse the jury. The date of the first of the entries mentioned cannot be ascertained; the upper part of the leaf is torn away; the part of the entry remaining follows:

". . . would run in a half-circle, keeping his head turned always toward the centre, and again he would stand still, barking furiously. At last he ran away into the brush as fast as he could go. I thought at first that he had gone mad, but on returning to the house found no other alteration in his manner than what was obviously due to fear of punishment.

"Can a dog see with his nose? Do odours impress some cerebral centre with images of the thing that emitted them? . . .

"Sept. 2.—Looking at the stars last night as they rose above the crest of the ridge east of the house, I observed them successively disappear—from left to right. Each was eclipsed but an instant, and only a few at the same time, but along the entire length of the ridge all that were within a degree or two of the crest were blotted out. It was as if something had passed along between me and them; but I could not see it, and the stars were not thick enough to define its outline. Ugh! don't like this." . . .

Several weeks' entries are missing, three leaves being torn from the book.

"Sept. 27.—It has been about here again—I find evidences of its presence every day. I watched again all last night in the same cover, gun in hand, double-charged with buckshot. In the morning the fresh footprints were there, as before. Yet I would have sworn that I did not sleep—indeed, I hardly sleep at all. It is terrible, insupportable! If these amazing experiences are real I shall go mad; if they are fanciful I am mad already.

"Oct. 3.—I shall not go—it shall not drive me away. No, this is *my* house, *my* land. God hates a coward. . . .

"Oct. 5.—I can stand it no longer; I have invited Harker to pass a few weeks with me—he has a level head. I can judge from his manner if he thinks me mad.

"Oct. 7.—I have the solution of the mystery; it came to me last night—suddenly, as by revelation. How simple—how terribly simple!

"There are sounds we cannot hear. At either end of the scale are notes that stir no chord of that imperfect instrument, the human ear. They are too high or too grave. I have observed a flock of blackbirds occupying an entire tree-top—the tops of several trees—and all in full song. Suddenly—in a moment—at absolutely the same instant—all spring into the air and fly away. How? They could not all see one another—whole tree-tops intervened. At no point could a leader have been visible to all. There must have been a signal of warning or command, high and shrill above the din, but by me unheard. I have observed, too, the same simultaneous flight when all were silent, among not only blackbirds, but other birds—quail, for example, widely separated by bushes—even on opposite sides of a hill.

"It is known to seamen that a school of whales basking or sporting on the surface of the ocean, miles apart, with the convexity of the earth between, will sometimes dive at the same instant—all gone out of sight in a moment. The signal has been sounded—too grave for the ear of the sailor at the masthead and his comrades on the deck—who nevertheless feel its vibrations in the ship as the stones of a cathedral are stirred by the bass of the organ.

"As with sounds, so with colors. At each end of the solar spectrum the chemist can detect the presence of what are known as 'actinic' rays. They represent colors—integral colors in the composition of light—which we are unable to discern. The human eye is an imperfect instrument; its range is but a few octaves of the real 'chromatic scale.' I am not mad; there are colors that we cannot see.

"And, God help me! the Damned Thing is of such a color!"

The White People

Arthur Machen

Prologue

"SORCERY AND SANCTITY," said Ambrose, "these are the only realities. Each is an ecstasy, a withdrawal from the common life."

Cotgrave listened, interested. He had been brought by a friend to this mouldering house in a northern suburb, through an old garden to the room where Ambrose the recluse dozed and dreamed over his books.

"Yes," he went on, "magic is justified of her children. There are many, I think, who eat dry crusts and drink water, with a joy infinitely sharper than anything within the experience of the 'practical' epicure."

"You are speaking of the saints?"

"Yes, and of the sinners, too. I think you are falling into the very general error of confining the spiritual world to the supremely good; but the supremely wicked, necessarily, have their portion in it. The merely carnal, sensual man can no more be a great sinner than he can be a great saint. Most of us are just indifferent, mixed-up creatures; we muddle through the world without realizing the meaning and the inner sense of things, and, consequently, our wickedness and our goodness are alike second-rate, unimportant."

"And you think the great sinner, then, will be an ascetic, as well as the great saint?"

"Great people of all kinds forsake the imperfect copies and go to the perfect originals. I have no doubt but that many of the very highest among the saints have never done a 'good action' (using the words in their ordinary sense). And, on the other hand, there have been those who have sounded the very depths of sin, who all their lives have never done an 'ill deed.'"

He went out of the room for a moment, and Cotgrave, in high delight, turned to his friend and thanked him for the introduction.

"He's grand," he said. "I never saw that kind of lunatic before."

Ambrose returned with more whisky and helped the two men in a liberal manner. He abused the teetotal sect with ferocity, as he handed the seltzer, and pouring out a glass of water for himself, was about to resume his monologue, when Cotgrave broke in—

"I can't stand it, you know," he said, "your paradoxes are too monstrous. A man may be a great sinner and yet never do anything sinful! Come!"

"You're quite wrong," said Ambrose. "I never make paradoxes; I wish I could. I merely said that a man may have an exquisite taste in Romanée Conti, and yet never have even smelt four ale. That's all, and it's more like a truism than a paradox, isn't it? Your surprise at my remark is due to the fact that you haven't realized what sin is. Oh, yes, there is a sort of connexion between Sin with the capital letter, and actions which are commonly called sinful: with murder, theft, adultery, and so forth. Much the same connexion that there is between the A, B, C and fine literature. But I believe that the misconception—it is all but universal—arises in great measure from our looking at the matter through social spectacles. We think that a man who does evil to *us* and to his neighbours must be very evil. So he is, from a social standpoint; but can't you realize that Evil in its essence is a lonely thing, a passion of the solitary, individual soul? Really, the average murderer, *qua* murderer, is not by any means a sinner in the true sense of the word. He is simply a wild beast that we have to get rid of to save our own necks from his knife. I should class him rather with tigers than with sinners."

"It seems a little strange."

"I think not. The murderer murders not from positive qualities, but from negative ones; he lacks something which non-murderers possess. Evil, of course, is wholly positive—only it is on the wrong side. You may believe me that sin in its proper sense is very rare; it is probable that there have been far fewer sinners than saints. Yes, your standpoint is all very well for practical, social purposes; we are naturally inclined to think that a person who is very disagreeable to us must be a very great sinner! It is very disagreeable to have one's pocket picked, and we pronounce the thief to be a very great sinner. In truth, he is merely an undeveloped man. He cannot be a saint, of course; but he may be, and often is, an infinitely better creature than thousands who have never broken a single commandment. He is a great nuisance to *us,* I admit, and we very properly lock him up if we catch him; but between his troublesome and unsocial action and evil—Oh, the connexion is of the weakest."

It was getting very late. The man who had brought Cotgrave had probably heard all this before, since he assisted with a bland and judicious smile, but Cotgrave began to think that his "lunatic" was turning into a sage.

"Do you know," he said, "you interest me immensely? You think, then, that we do not understand the real nature of evil?"

"No, I don't think we do. We over-estimate it and we under-estimate it. We take the very numerous infractions of our social 'bye-laws'—the very necessary and very proper regulations which keep the human company together—and we get frightened at the prevalence of 'sin' and 'evil.' But this is really nonsense. Take theft, for example. Have you any *horror* at the thought of Robin Hood, of the Highland caterans of the seventeenth century, of the moss-troopers, of the company promoters of our day?

"Then, on the other hand, we underrate evil. We attach such an enormous importance to the 'sin' of meddling with our pockets (and our wives) that we have quite forgotten the awfulness of real sin."

"And what is sin?" said Cotgrave.

"I think I must reply to your question by another. What would your feelings be, seriously, if your cat or your dog began to talk to you, and to dispute with you in human accents? You would be overwhelmed with horror. I am sure of it. And if the roses in your garden sang a weird song, you would go mad. And suppose the stones in the road began to swell and grow before your eyes, and if the pebble that you noticed at night had shot out stony blossoms in the morning?

"Well, these examples may give you some notion of what sin really is."

"Look here," said the third man, hitherto placid, "you two seem pretty well wound up. But I'm going home. I've missed my tram, and I shall have to walk."

Ambrose and Cotgrave seemed to settle down more profoundly when the other had gone out into the early misty morning and the pale light of the lamps.

"You astonish me," said Cotgrave. "I had never thought of that. If that is really so, one must turn everything upside down. Then the essence of sin really is—"

"In the taking of heaven by storm, it seems to me," said Ambrose. "It appears to me that it is simply an attempt to penetrate into another and higher sphere in a forbidden manner. You can understand why it is so rare. There are few, indeed, who wish to penetrate into other spheres, higher or lower, in ways allowed or forbidden. Men, in the mass, are amply content with life as they find it. Therefore there are few saints, and sinners (in the proper sense) are fewer still, and men of genius, who partake sometimes of each character are rare also. Yes; on the whole, it is, perhaps, harder to be a great sinner than a great saint."

"There is something profoundly unnatural about sin? Is that what you mean?"

"Exactly. Holiness requires as great, or almost as great, an effort; but holiness works on lines that *were* natural once; it is an effort to recover the ecstasy that was before the Fall. But sin is an effort to gain the ecstasy and the knowledge that pertain alone to angels, and in making this effort man becomes a demon. I told you that the mere murderer is not *therefore* a sinner; that is true, but the sinner is sometimes a murderer. Gilles de Rais is an instance. So you see that while the good and the evil are unnatural to man as he now is—to man the social, civilized being—evil is unnatural in a much deeper sense than good. The saint endeavours to recover a gift which he has lost; the sinner tries to obtain something which was never his. In brief, he repeats the Fall."

"But are you a Catholic?" said Cotgrave.

"Yes; I am a member of the persecuted Anglican Church."

"Then, how about those texts which seem to reckon as sin that which you would set down as a mere trivial dereliction?"

"Yes; but in one place the word 'sorcerers' comes in the same sentence, doesn't it? That seems to me to give the key-note. Consider: can you imagine for a moment that a false statement which saves an innocent man's life is a sin? No; very good, then, it is not the mere liar who is excluded by those words; it is, above all, the 'sorcerers' who use the material life, who use the failings incidental to material life as instruments to obtain their infinitely wicked ends. And let me tell you this: our higher senses are so blunted, we are so drenched with materialism, that we should probably fail to recognize real wickedness if we encountered it."

"But shouldn't we experience a certain horror—a terror such as you hinted we would experience if a rose tree sang—in the mere presence of an evil man?"

"We should if we were natural: children and women feel this horror you speak of, even animals experience it. But with most of us convention and civilization and education have blinded and deafened and obscured the natural reason. No, sometimes we may recognize evil by its hatred of the good—one doesn't need much penetration to guess at the influence which dictated, quite unconsciously, the 'Blackwood' review of Keats—but this is purely incidental; and, as a rule, I suspect that the Hierarchs of Tophet pass quite unnoticed, or, perhaps, in certain cases, as good but mistaken men."

"But you used the word 'unconscious' just now, of Keats' reviewers. Is wickedness ever unconscious?"

"Always. It must be so. It is like holiness and genius in this as in other points; it is a certain rapture or ecstasy of the soul; a transcendent effort to surpass the ordinary bounds. So, surpassing these, it surpasses also the understanding, the faculty that takes note of that which comes before it. No, a man may be infinitely and horribly wicked and never suspect it. But I tell you, evil in this, its certain and true sense, is rare, and I think it is growing rarer."

"I am trying to get hold of it all," said Cotgrave. "From what you say, I gather that the true evil differs generically from that which we call evil?"

"Quite so. There is, no doubt, an analogy between the two; a resemblance such as enables us to use, quite legitimately, such terms as the 'foot of the mountain' and the 'leg of the table.' And, sometimes, of course, the two speak, as it were, in the same language. The rough miner, or 'puddler,' the untrained, undeveloped 'tiger-man,' heated by a quart or two above his usual measure, comes home and kicks his irritating and injudicious wife to death. He is a murderer. And Gilles de Rais was a murderer. But you see the gulf that separates the two? The 'word,' if I may so speak, is accidentally the same in each case, but the 'meaning' is utterly different. It is flagrant 'Hobson Jobson' to confuse the two, or rather, it is as if one supposed that Juggernaut and the Argonauts had something to do etymologically with one another. And no doubt the same weak likeness, or analogy, runs between all the 'social' sins and the real spiritual sins, and in some cases, perhaps, the lesser may be 'schoolmaster' to lead one on to the greater—from the shadow to the reality. If you are anything of a theologian, you will see the importance of all this."

"I am sorry to say," remarked Cotgrave, "that I have devoted very little of my time to theology. Indeed, I have often wondered on what grounds theologians have claimed the title of Science of Sciences for their favourite study; since the 'theological' books I have looked into have always seemed to me to be concerned with feeble and obvious pieties, or with the kings of Israel and Judah. I do not care to hear about those kings."

Ambrose grinned.

"We must try to avoid theological discussion," he said. "I perceive that you would be a bitter disputant. But perhaps the 'dates of the kings' have as much to do with theology as the hobnails of the murderous puddler with evil."

"Then, to return to our main subject, you think that sin is an esoteric, occult thing?"

"Yes. It is the infernal miracle as holiness is the supernal. Now and then it is raised to such a pitch that we entirely fail to suspect its existence; it is like the note of the great pedal pipes of the organ, which is so deep that we cannot hear it. In other cases it may lead to the lunatic asylum, or to still stranger issues. But you must never confuse it with mere social misdoing. Remember how the Apostle, speaking of the 'other side,' distinguishes between 'charitable' actions and charity. And as one may give all one's goods to the poor, and yet lack charity; so, remember, one may avoid every crime and yet be a sinner."

"Your psychology is very strange to me," said Cotgrave, "but I confess I like it, and I suppose that one might fairly deduce from your premisses the conclusion that the real sinner might very possibly strike the observer as a harmless personage enough?"

"Certainly; because the true evil has nothing to do with social life or social laws, or if it has, only incidentally and accidentally. It is a lonely passion of the soul—or a passion of the lonely soul—whichever you like. If, by chance, we understand it, and grasp its full significance, then, indeed, it will fill us with horror and with awe. But this emotion is widely distinguished from the fear and the disgust with which we regard the ordinary criminal, since this latter is largely or entirely founded on the regard which we have for our own skins or purses. We hate a murderer, because we know that we should hate to be murdered, or to have any one that we like murdered. So, on the 'other side,' we venerate the saints, but we don't 'like' them as we like our friends. Can you persuade yourself that you would have 'enjoyed' St. Paul's company? Do you think that you and I would have 'got on' with Sir Galahad?

"So with the sinners, as with the saints. If you met a very evil man, and recognized his evil; he would, no doubt, fill you with horror and awe; but there is no reason why you should 'dislike' him. On the contrary, it is quite possible that if you could succeed in putting the sin out of your mind you might find the sinner capital company, and in a little while you might have to reason yourself back into horror. Still, how awful it is. If the roses and the lilies suddenly sang on this coming morning; if the furniture began to move in procession, as in De Maupassant's tale!"

"I am glad you have come back to that comparison," said Cotgrave, "because I wanted to ask you what it is that corresponds in humanity to these imaginary feats of inanimate things. In a word—what is sin? You have given me, I know, an abstract definition, but I should like a concrete example."

"I told you it was very rare," said Ambrose, who appeared willing to avoid the giving of a direct answer. "The materialism of the age, which has done a good deal to suppress sanctity, has done perhaps more to suppress evil. We find the earth so very comfortable that we have no inclination either for ascents or descents. It would seem as if the scholar who decided to 'specialize' in Tophet, would be reduced to purely antiquarian researches. No palæontologist could show you a *live* pterodactyl."

"And yet you, I think, have 'specialized,' and I believe that your researches have descended to our modern times."

"You are really interested, I see. Well, I confess that I have dabbled a little, and if you like I can show you something that bears on the very curious subject we have been discussing."

Ambrose took a candle and went away to a far, dim corner of the room. Cotgrave saw him open a venerable bureau that stood there, and from some secret recess he drew out a parcel, and came back to the window where they had been sitting.

Ambrose undid a wrapping of paper, and produced a green book.

"You will take care of it?" he said. "Don't leave it lying about. It is one of the choicer pieces in my collection, and I should be very sorry if it were lost."

He fondled the faded binding.

"I knew the girl who wrote this," he said. "When you read it, you will see how it illustrates the talk we have had to-night. There is a sequel, too, but I won't talk of that.

"There was an odd article in one of the reviews some months ago," he began again, with the air of a man who changes the subject. "It was written by a doctor—Dr. Coryn, I think, was the name. He says that a lady, watching her little girl playing at the drawing-room window, suddenly saw the heavy sash give way and fall on the child's fingers. The lady fainted, I think, but at any rate the doctor was summoned, and when he had dressed the child's wounded and maimed fingers he was summoned to the mother. She was groaning with pain, and it was found that three fingers of her hand, corresponding with those that had been injured on the child's hand, were swollen and inflamed, and later, in the doctor's language, purulent sloughing set in."

Ambrose still handled delicately the green volume.

"Well, here it is," he said at last, parting with difficulty, it seemed, from his treasure.

"You will bring it back as soon as you have read it," he said, as they went out into the hall, into the old garden, faint with the odour of white lilies.

There was a broad red band in the east as Cotgrave turned to go, and from the high ground where he stood he saw that awful spectacle of London in a dream.

The Green Book

The morocco binding of the book was faded, and the colour had grown faint, but there were no stains nor bruises nor marks of usage. The book looked as if it had been bought "on a visit to London" some seventy or eighty years ago, and had somehow been forgotten and suffered to lie away out of sight. There was an old, delicate, lingering odour about it, such an odour as sometimes haunts an ancient piece of furniture for a century or more. The end-papers, inside the binding, were oddly decorated with coloured patterns and faded gold. It looked small, but the paper was fine, and there were many leaves, closely covered with minute, painfully formed characters.

I found this book (the manuscript began) in a drawer in the old bureau that stands on the landing. It was a very rainy day and I could not go out, so in the afternoon I got a candle and rummaged in the bureau. Nearly all the drawers were full of old dresses, but one of the small ones looked empty, and I found this book hidden right at the back. I wanted a book like this, so I took it to write in. It is full of secrets. I have a great many other books of secrets I have written, hidden in a safe place, and I am going to write here many of the old secrets and some new ones; but there are some I shall not put down at all. I must not write down the real names of the days and months which I found out a year ago, nor the way to make the Aklo letters, or the Chian language, or the great beautiful Circles, nor the Mao Games, nor the chief songs. I may write something about all these things but not the way to do them, for peculiar reasons. And I must not say who the Nymphs are, or the Dôls, or Jeelo, or what voolas mean. All these are most secret secrets, and I am glad when I remember what they are, and how many wonderful languages I know, but there are some things that I call the secrets of the secrets of the secrets that I dare not think of unless I am quite alone, and then I shut my eyes, and put my hands over them and whisper the word, and the Alala comes. I only do this at night in my room or in certain woods that I know, but I must not describe them, as they are secret woods. Then there are the Ceremonies, which are all of them important, but some are more delightful than others—there are the White Ceremonies, and the Green Ceremonies, and the Scarlet Ceremonies. The Scarlet Ceremonies are the best, but there is only one place where they can be performed properly, though there is a very nice imitation which I have done in other places. Besides these, I have the dances, and the Comedy, and I have done the Comedy sometimes when the others were looking, and they didn't understand anything about it. I was very little when I first knew about these things.

When I was very small, and mother was alive, I can remember remembering things before that, only it has all got confused. But I remember when I was five or six I heard them talking about me when they thought I was not noticing. They were saying how queer I was a year or two before, and how nurse had called my mother to come and listen to me talking all to myself, and I was saying words that nobody could understand. I was speaking the Xu language, but I only remember a very few of the words, as it was about the little white faces that used to look at me when I was lying in my cradle. They used to talk to me, and I learnt their language and talked to them in it about some great white place where they lived, where the trees and the grass were all white, and there were white hills as high up as the moon, and a cold wind. I have often dreamed of it afterwards, but the faces went away when I was very little. But a wonderful thing happened when I was about five. My nurse was carrying me on her shoulder; there was a field of yellow corn, and we went through it, it was very hot. Then we came to a path through a wood, and a tall man came after us, and went with us till we came to a place where there was a deep pool, and it was very dark and shady. Nurse put me down on the soft moss under a tree, and she said: "She can't get to the pond now." So they left me there, and I sat quite still and watched, and out of the water and out of the wood came two wonderful white people, and they began to play and dance and sing. They were a kind of creamy white like the old ivory figure in the drawing-room; one was a beautiful lady with kind dark eyes, and a grave face, and long black hair, and she smiled such a strange sad smile at the other, who laughed and came to her. They played together, and danced round and round the pool, and they sang a song till I fell asleep. Nurse woke me up when she came back, and she was looking something like the lady had looked, so I told her all about it, and asked her why she looked like that. At first she cried, and then she looked very frightened, and turned quite pale. She put me down on the grass and stared at me, and I could see she was shaking all over. Then she said I had been dreaming, but I knew I hadn't. Then she made me promise not to say a word about it to anybody, and if I did I should be thrown into the black pit. I was not frightened at all, though nurse was, and I never forgot about it, because when I shut my eyes and it was quite quiet, and I was all alone, I could see them again, very faint and far away, but very splendid; and little bits of the song they sang came into my head, but I couldn't sing it.

I was thirteen, nearly fourteen, when I had a very singular adventure, so strange that the day on which it happened is always called the White Day. My mother had been dead for more than a year, and in the morning I had lessons, but they let me go out for walks in the afternoon. And this afternoon I walked a new way, and a little brook led me into a new country, but I tore my frock getting through many bushes, and beneath the low branches of trees, and up thorny thickets on the hills, and by dark woods full of creeping thorns. And it was a long, long way. It seemed as if I was going on for ever and ever, and I had to creep by a place like a tunnel where a brook must have been, but all the water had dried up, and the floor was rocky, and the bushes had grown overhead till they met, so that it was quite dark. And I went on and on through that dark place; it was a long, long way. And I came to a hill that I never saw before. I was in a dismal thicket full of black twisted boughs that tore me as I went through them, and I cried out because I was smarting all over, and then I found that I was climbing, and I went up and up a long way, till at last the thicket stopped and I came out crying just under the top of a big bare place, where there were ugly grey stones lying all about on the grass, and here and there a little twisted, stunted tree came out from under a stone, like a snake. And I went up, right to the top, a long way. I never saw such big ugly stones before; they came out of the earth some of them, and some looked as if they had been rolled to where they were, and they went on and on as far as I could see, a long, long way. I looked out from them and saw the country, but it was strange. It was winter time, and there were black terrible woods hanging from the hills all round; it was like seeing a large room hung with black curtains, and the shape of the trees seemed quite different from any I had ever seen before. I was afraid. Then beyond the woods there were other hills round in a great ring, but I had never seen any of them; it all looked black, and everything had a voor over it. It was all so still and silent, and the sky was heavy and grey and sad, like a wicked voorish dome in Deep Dendo. I went on into the dreadful rocks. There were hundreds and hundreds of them. Some were like horrid-grinning men; I could see their faces as if they would jump at me out of the stone, and catch hold of me, and drag me with them back into the rock, so that I should always be there. And there were other rocks that were like animals, creeping, horrible animals, putting out their tongues, and others were like words that I could not say, and others like dead people lying on the grass. I went on among them, though they frightened me, and my heart was full of wicked songs that they put into it; and I wanted to make faces and twist myself about in the way they did, and I went on and on a long way till at last I liked the rocks, and they didn't frighten me any more. I sang the songs I thought of; songs full of words that must not be spoken or written down. Then I made faces like the faces on the rocks, and I twisted myself about like the twisted ones, and I lay down flat on the ground like the dead ones, and I went up to one that was grinning, and put my arms round him and hugged him. And so I went on and on through the rocks till I came to a round mound in the middle of them. It was higher than a mound, it was nearly as high as our house, and it was like a great basin turned upside down, all smooth and round and green, with one stone, like a post, sticking up at the top. I climbed up the sides, but they were so steep I had to stop or I should have rolled all the way down again, and I should have knocked against the stones at the bottom, and perhaps been killed. But I wanted to get up to the very top of the big round mound, so I lay down flat on my face, and took hold of the grass with my hands and drew myself up, bit by bit, till I was at the top. Then I sat down on the stone in the middle, and looked all round about. I felt I had come such a long, long way, just as if I were a hundred miles from home, or in some other country, or in one of the strange places I had read about in the *Tales of the Genie* and the *Arabian Nights,* or as if I had gone across the sea, far away, for years and I had found another world that nobody had ever seen or heard of before, or as if I had somehow flown through the sky and fallen on one of the stars I had read about where everything is dead and cold and grey, and there is no air, and the wind doesn't blow. I sat on the stone and looked all round and down and round about me. It was just as if I was sitting on a tower in the middle of a great empty town, because I could see nothing all around but the grey rocks on the ground. I couldn't make out their shapes any more, but I could see them on and on for a long way, and I looked at them, and they seemed as if they had been arranged into patterns, and shapes, and figures. I knew they couldn't be, because I had seen a lot of them coming right out of the earth, joined to the deep rocks below, so I looked again, but still I saw nothing but circles, and small circles inside big ones, and pyramids, and domes, and spires, and they seemed all to go round and round the place where I was sitting, and the more I looked, the more I saw great big rings of rocks, getting bigger and bigger, and I stared so long that it felt as if they were all moving and turning, like a great wheel, and I was turning, too, in the middle. I got quite dizzy and queer in the head, and everything began to be hazy and not clear, and I saw little sparks of blue light, and the stones looked as if they were springing and dancing and twisting as they went round and round and round. I was frightened again, and I cried out loud, and jumped up from the stone I was sitting on, and fell down. When I got up I was so glad they all looked still, and I sat down on the top and slid down the mound, and went on again. I danced as I went in the peculiar way the rocks had danced when I got giddy, and I was so glad I could do it quite well, and I danced and danced along, and sang extraordinary songs that came into my head. At last I came to the edge of that great flat hill, and there were no more rocks, and the way went again through a dark thicket in a hollow. It was just as bad as the other one I went through climbing up, but I didn't mind this one, because

I was so glad I had seen those singular dances and could imitate them. I went down, creeping through the bushes, and a tall nettle stung me on my leg, and made me burn, but I didn't mind it, and I tingled with the boughs and the thorns, but I only laughed and sang. Then I got out of the thicket into a close valley, a little secret place like a dark passage that nobody ever knows of, because it was so narrow and deep and the woods were so thick round it. There is a steep bank with trees hanging over it, and there the ferns keep green all through the winter, when they are dead and brown upon the hill, and the ferns there have a sweet, rich smell like what oozes out of fir trees. There was a little stream of water running down this valley, so small that I could easily step across it. I drank the water with my hand, and it tasted like bright, yellow wine, and it sparkled and bubbled as it ran down over beautiful red and yellow stones, so that it seemed alive and all colours at once. I drank it, and I drank more with my hand, but I couldn't drink enough, so I lay down and bent my head and sucked the water up with my lips. It tasted much better, drinking it that way, and a ripple would come up to my mouth and give me a kiss, and I laughed, and drank again, and pretended there was a nymph, like the one in the old picture at home, who lived in the water and was kissing me. So I bent low down to the water, and put my lips softly to it, and whispered to the nymph that I would come again. I felt sure it would not be common water, I was so glad when I got up and went on; and I danced again and went up and up the valley, under hanging hills. And when I came to the top, the ground rose up in front of me, tall and steep as a wall, and there was nothing but the green wall and the sky. I thought of "for ever and for ever, world without end, Amen"; and I thought I must have really found the end of the world, because it was like the end of everything, as if there could be nothing at all beyond, except the kingdom of Voor, where the light goes when it is put out, and the water goes when the sun takes it away. I began to think of all the long, long way I had journeyed, how I had found a brook and followed it, and followed it on, and gone through bushes and thorny thickets, and dark woods full of creeping thorns. Then I had crept up a tunnel under trees, and climbed a thicket, and seen all the grey rocks, and sat in the middle of them when they turned round, and then I had gone on through the grey rocks and come down the hill through the stinging thicket and up the dark valley, all a long, long way. I wondered how I should get home again, if I could ever find the way, and if my home was there any more, or if it were turned and everybody in it into grey rocks, as in the *Arabian Nights.* So I sat down on the grass and thought what I should do next. I was tired, and my feet were hot with walking, and as I looked about I saw there was a wonderful well just under the high, steep wall of grass. All the ground round it was covered with bright, green, dripping moss; there was every kind of moss there, moss like beautiful little ferns, and like palms and fir trees, and it was all green as jewellery, and drops of water hung on it like diamonds. And in the middle was the great well, deep and shining and beautiful, so clear it looked as if I could touch the red sand at the bottom, but it was far below. I stood by it and looked in, as if I were looking in a glass. At the bottom of the well, in the middle of it, the red grains of sand were moving and stirring all the time, and I saw how the water bubbled up, but at the top it was quite smooth, and full and brimming. It was a great well, large like a bath, and with the shining, glittering green moss about it, it looked like a great white jewel, with green jewels all round. My feet were so hot and tired that I took off my boots and stockings, and let my feet down into the water, and the water was soft and cold, and when I got up I wasn't tired any more, and I felt I must go on, farther and farther, and see what was on the other side of the wall. I climbed up it very slowly, going sideways all the time, and when I got to the top and looked over, I was in the queerest country I had seen, stranger even than the hill of the grey rocks. It looked as if earth-children had been playing there with their spades, as it was all hills and hollows, and castles and walls made of earth and covered with grass. There were two mounds like big beehives, round and great and solemn, and then hollow basins, and then a steep mounting wall like the ones I saw once by the seaside where the big guns and the soldiers were. I nearly fell into one of the round hollows, it went away from under my feet so suddenly, and I ran fast down the side and stood at the bottom and looked up. It was strange and solemn to look up. There was nothing but the grey, heavy sky and the sides of the hollow; everything else had gone away, and the hollow was the whole world, and I thought that at night it must be full of ghosts and moving shadows and pale things when the moon shone down to the bottom at the dead of the night, and the wind wailed up above. It was so strange and solemn and lonely, like a hollow temple of dead heathen gods. It reminded me of a tale my nurse had told me when I was quite little; it was the same nurse that took me into the wood where I saw the beautiful white people. And I remembered how nurse had told me the story one winter night, when the wind was beating the trees against the wall, and crying and moaning in the nursery chimney. She said there was, somewhere or other, a hollow pit, just like the one I was standing in, everybody was afraid to go into it or near it, it was such a bad place. But once upon a time there was a poor girl who said she would go into the hollow pit, and everybody tried to stop her, but she would go.

And she went down into the pit and came back laughing, and said there was nothing there at all, except green grass and red stones, and white stones and yellow flowers. And soon after people saw she had the most beautiful emerald earrings, and they asked how she got them, as she and her mother were quite poor. But she laughed, and said her earrings were not made of emeralds at all, but only of green grass. Then, one day, she wore on her breast the reddest ruby that any one had ever seen, and it was as big as a hen's egg, and glowed and sparkled like a hot burning coal of fire. And they asked how she got it, as she and her mother were quite poor. But she laughed, and said it was not a ruby at all, but only a red stone. Then one day she wore round her neck the loveliest necklace that any one had ever seen, much finer than the queen's finest, and it was made of great bright diamonds, hundreds of them, and they shone like all the stars on a night in June. So they asked her how she got it, as she and her mother were quite poor. But she laughed, and said they were not diamonds at all, but only white stones. And one day she went to the court, and she wore on her head a crown of pure angel-gold, so nurse said, and it shone like the sun, and it was much more splendid than the crown the king was wearing himself, and in her ears she wore the emeralds, and the big ruby was the brooch on her breast, and the great diamond necklace was sparkling on her neck. And the king and queen thought she was some great princess from a long way off, and got down from their thrones and went to meet her, but somebody told the king and queen who she was, and that she was quite poor. So the king asked why she wore a gold crown, and how she got it, as she and her mother were so poor. And she laughed, and said it wasn't a gold crown at all, but only some yellow flowers she had put in her hair. And the king thought it was very strange, and said she should stay at the court, and they would see what would happen next. And she was so lovely that everybody said that her eyes were greener than the emeralds, that her lips were redder than the ruby, that her skin was whiter than the diamonds, and that her hair was brighter than the golden crown. So the king's son said he would marry her, and the king said he might. And the bishop married them, and there was a great supper, and afterwards the king's son went to his wife's room. But just when he had his hand on the door, he saw a tall, black man, with a dreadful face, standing in front of the door, and a voice said—

Venture not upon your life,
This is mine own wedded wife.

Then the king's son fell down on the ground in a fit. And they came and tried to get into the room, but they couldn't, and they hacked at the door with hatchets, but the wood had turned hard as iron, and at last everybody ran away, they were so frightened at the screaming and laughing and shrieking and crying that came out of the room. But next day they went in, and found there was nothing in the room but thick black smoke, because the black man had come and taken her away. And on the bed there were two knots of faded grass and a red stone, and some white stones, and some faded yellow flowers. I remembered this tale of nurse's while I was standing at the bottom of the deep hollow; it was so strange and solitary there, and I felt afraid. I could not see any stones or flowers, but I was afraid of bringing them away without knowing, and I thought I would do a charm that came into my head to keep the black man away. So I stood right in the very middle of the hollow, and I made sure that I had none of those things on me, and then I walked round the place, and touched my eyes, and my lips, and my hair in a peculiar manner, and whispered some queer words that nurse taught me to keep bad things away. Then I felt safe and climbed up out of the hollow, and went on through all those mounds and hollows and walls, till I came to the end, which was high above all the rest, and I could see that all the different shapes of the earth were arranged in patterns, something like the grey rocks, only the pattern was different. It was getting late, and the air was indistinct, but it looked from where I was standing something like two great figures of people lying on the grass. And I went on, and at last I found a certain wood, which is too secret to be described, and nobody knows of the passage into it, which I found out in a very curious manner, by seeing some little animal run into the wood through it. So I went in after the animal by a very narrow dark way, under thorns and bushes, and it was almost dark when I came to a kind of open place in the middle. And there I saw the most wonderful sight I have ever seen, but it was only for a minute, as I ran away directly, and crept out of the wood by the passage I had come by, and ran and ran as fast as ever I could, because I was afraid, what I had seen was so wonderful and so strange and beautiful. But I wanted to get home and think of it, and I did not know what might not happen if I stayed by the wood. I was hot all over and trembling, and my heart was beating, and strange cries that I could not help came from me as I ran from the wood. I was glad that a great white moon came up from over a round hill and showed me the way, so I went back through the mounds and hollows and down the close valley, and up through the thicket over the place of the grey rocks, and so at last I got home again. My father was busy in his study, and the servants had not told about my not coming home, though they were frightened, and wondered what they ought to do, so I told them I had lost my way, but I did not let them find out the real way I had been. I went to bed and lay awake all through the night, thinking of what I had seen. When I came out of the narrow way, and it looked all shining, though the air was dark, it seemed so certain, and all the way home I was quite sure that I had seen it, and I wanted to be alone in my room, and be glad over it all to myself, and shut my eyes and pretend it was there, and do all the things I would have done if I had not been so afraid. But when I shut my eyes the sight would not come, and I began to think about my adventures all over again, and I remembered how dusky and queer it was at the end, and I was afraid it must be all a mistake, because it seemed impossible it could happen. It seemed like one of nurse's tales, which I didn't really believe in, though I was frightened at the bottom of the hollow; and the stories she told me when I was little came back into my head, and I wondered whether it was really there what I thought I had seen, or whether any of her tales could have happened a long time ago. It was so queer; I lay awake there in my room at the back of the house, and the moon was shining on the other side towards the river, so the bright light did not fall upon the wall. And the house was quite still. I had heard my father come upstairs, and just after the clock struck twelve, and after the house was still and empty, as if there was nobody alive in it. And though it was all dark and indistinct in my room, a pale glimmering kind of light shone in through the white blind, and once I got up and looked out, and there was a great black shadow of the house covering the garden, looking like a prison where men are hanged; and then beyond it was all white; and the wood shone white with black gulfs between the trees. It was still and clear, and there were no clouds in the sky. I wanted to think of what I had seen but I couldn't, and I began to think of all the tales that nurse had told me so long ago that I thought I had forgotten, but they all came back, and mixed up with the thickets and the grey rocks and the hollows in the earth and the secret wood, till I hardly knew what was new and what was old, or whether it was not all dreaming. And then I remembered that hot summer afternoon, so long ago, when nurse left me by myself in the shade, and the white people came out of the water and out of the wood, and played, and danced, and sang, and I began to fancy that nurse told me about something like it before I saw them, only I couldn't recollect exactly what she told me. Then I wondered whether she had been the white lady, as I remembered she was just as white and beautiful, and had the same dark eyes and black hair; and sometimes she smiled and looked like the lady had looked, when she was telling me some of her stories, beginning with "Once on a time," or "In the time of the fairies." But I thought she couldn't be the lady, as she seemed to have gone a different way into the wood, and I didn't think the man who came after us could be the other, or I couldn't have seen that wonderful secret in the secret wood. I thought of the moon: but it was afterwards when I was in the middle of the wild land, where the earth was made into the shape of great figures, and it was all walls, and mysterious hollows, and smooth round mounds, that I saw the great white moon come up over a round hill. I was wondering about all these things, till at last I got quite frightened, because I was afraid something had happened to me, and I remembered nurse's tale of the poor girl who went into the hollow pit, and was carried away at last by the black man. I knew I had gone into a hollow pit too, and perhaps it was the same, and I had done something dreadful. So I did the charm over again, and touched my eyes and my lips and my hair in a peculiar manner, and said the old words from the fairy language, so that I might be sure I had not been carried away. I tried again to see the secret wood, and to creep up the passage and see what I had seen there, but somehow I couldn't, and I kept on thinking of nurse's stories. There was one I remembered about a young man who once upon a time went hunting, and all the day he and his hounds hunted everywhere, and they crossed the rivers and went into all the woods, and went round the marshes, but they couldn't find anything at all, and they hunted all day till the sun sank down and began to set behind the mountain. And the young man was angry because he couldn't find anything, and he was going to turn back, when just as the sun touched the mountain, he saw come out of a brake in front of him a beautiful white stag. And he cheered to his hounds, but they whined and would not follow, and he cheered to his horse, but it shivered and stood stock still, and the young man jumped off the horse and left the hounds and began to follow the white stag all alone. And soon it was quite dark, and the sky was black, without a single star shining in it, and the stag went away into the darkness. And though the man had brought his gun with him he never shot at the stag, because he wanted to catch it, and he was afraid he would lose it in the night. But he never lost it once, though the sky was so black and the air was so dark, and the stag went on and on till the young man didn't know a bit where he was. And they went through enormous woods where the air was full of whispers and a pale, dead light came out from the rotten trunks that were lying on the ground, and just as the man thought he had lost the stag, he would see it all white and shining in front of him, and he would run fast to catch it, but the stag always ran faster, so he did not catch it. And they went through the enormous woods, and they swam across rivers, and they waded through black marshes where the ground bubbled, and the air was full of will-o'-the-wisps, and the stag fled away down into rocky narrow valleys, where the air was like the smell of a vault, and the man went after it. And they went over the great mountains, and the man heard the wind come down from the sky, and the stag went on and the man went after. At last the sun rose and the young man found he was in a country that he had never seen before; it was a beautiful valley with a bright stream running through it, and a great, big round hill in the middle. And the stag went down the valley, towards the hill, and it seemed to be getting tired and went slower and slower, and though the man was tired, too, he began to run faster, and he was sure he would catch the stag at last. But just as they got to the bottom of the hill, and the man stretched out his hand to catch the stag, it vanished into the earth, and the man began to cry; he was so sorry that he had lost it after all his long hunting. But as he was crying he saw there was a door in the hill, just in front of him, and he went in, and it was quite dark, but he went on, as he thought he would find the white stag. And all of a sudden it got light, and there was the sky, and the sun shining, and birds singing in the trees, and there was a beautiful fountain. And by the fountain a lovely lady was sitting, who was the queen of the fairies, and she told the man that she had changed herself into a stag to bring him there because she loved him so much. Then she brought out a great gold cup, covered with jewels, from her fairy palace, and she offered him wine in the cup to drink. And he drank, and the more he drank the more he longed to drink, because the wine was enchanted. So he kissed the lovely lady, and she became his wife, and he stayed all that day and all that night in the hill where she lived, and when he woke he found he was lying on the ground, close to where he had seen the stag first, and his horse was there and his hounds were there waiting, and he looked up, and the sun sank behind the mountain. And he went home and lived a long time, but he would never kiss any other lady because he had kissed the queen of the fairies, and he would never drink common wine any more, because he had drunk enchanted wine. And sometimes nurse told me tales that she had heard from her great-grandmother, who was very old, and lived in a cottage on the mountain all alone, and most of these tales were about a hill where people used to meet at night long ago, and they used to play all sorts of strange games and do queer things that nurse told me of, but I couldn't understand, and now, she said, everybody but her great-grandmother had forgotten all about it, and nobody knew where the hill was, not even her great-grandmother. But she told me one very strange story about the hill, and I trembled when I remembered it. She said that people always went there in summer, when it was very hot, and they had to dance a good deal. It would be all dark at first, and there were trees there, which made it much darker, and people would come, one by one, from all directions, by a secret path which nobody else knew, and two persons would keep the gate, and every one as they came up had to give a very curious sign, which nurse showed me as well as she could, but she said she couldn't show me properly. And all kinds of people would come; there would be gentle folks and village folks, and some old people and boys and girls, and quite small children, who sat and watched. And it would all be dark as they came in, except in one corner where some one was burning something that smelt strong and sweet, and made them laugh, and there one would see a glaring of coals, and the smoke mounting up red. So they would all come in, and when the last had come there was no door any more, so that no one else could get in, even if they knew there was anything beyond. And once a gentleman who was a stranger and had ridden a long way, lost his path at night, and his horse took him into the very middle of the wild country, where everything was upside down, and there were dreadful marshes and great stones everywhere, and holes underfoot, and the trees looked like gibbet-posts, because they had great black arms that stretched out across the way. And this strange gentleman was very frightened, and his horse began to shiver all over, and at last it stopped and wouldn't go any farther, and the gentleman got down and tried to lead the horse, but it wouldn't move, and it was all covered with a sweat, like death. So the gentleman went on all alone, going farther and farther into the wild country, till at last he came to a dark place, where he heard shouting and singing and crying, like nothing he had ever heard before. It all sounded quite close to him, but he couldn't get in, and so he began to call, and while he was calling, something came behind him, and in a minute his mouth and arms and legs were all bound up, and he fell into a swoon. And when he came to himself, he was lying by the roadside, just where he had first lost his way, under a blasted oak with a black trunk, and his horse was tied beside him. So he rode on to the town and told the people there what had happened, and some of them were amazed; but others knew. So when once everybody had come, there was no door at all for anybody else to pass in by. And when they were all inside, round in a ring, touching each other, some one began to sing in the darkness, and some one else would make a noise like thunder with a thing they had on purpose, and on still nights people would hear the thundering noise far, far away beyond the wild land, and some of them, who thought they knew what it was, used to make a sign on their breasts when they woke up in their beds at dead of night and heard that terrible deep noise, like thunder on the mountains. And the noise and the singing would go on and on for a long time, and the people who were in a ring swayed a little to and fro; and the song was in an old, old language that nobody knows now, and the tune was queer. Nurse said her great-grandmother had known some one who remembered a little of it, when she was quite a little girl, and nurse tried to sing some of it to me, and it was so strange a tune that I turned all cold and my flesh crept as if I had put my hand on something dead. Sometimes it was a man that sang and sometimes it was a woman, and sometimes the one who sang it did it so well that two or three of the people who were there fell to the ground shrieking and tearing with their hands. The singing went on, and the people in the ring kept swaying to and fro for a long time, and at last the moon would rise over a place they called the Tole Deol, and came up and showed them swinging and swaying from side to side, with the sweet thick smoke curling up from the burning coals, and floating in circles all around them. Then they had their supper. A boy and a girl brought it to them; the boy carried a great cup of wine, and the girl carried a cake of bread, and they passed the bread and the wine round and round, but they tasted quite different from common bread and common wine, and changed everybody that tasted them. Then they all rose up and danced, and secret things were brought out of some hiding place, and they played extraordinary games, and danced round and round and round in the moonlight, and sometimes people would suddenly disappear and never be heard of afterwards, and nobody knew what had happened to them. And they drank more of that curious wine, and they made images and worshipped them, and nurse showed me how the images were made one day when we were out for a walk, and we passed by a place where there was a lot of wet clay. So nurse asked me if I would like to know what those things were like that they made on the hill, and I said yes. Then she asked me if I would promise never to tell a living soul a word about it, and if I did I was to be thrown into the black pit with the dead people, and I said I wouldn't tell anybody, and she said the same thing again and again, and I promised. So she took my wooden spade and dug a big lump of clay and put it in my tin bucket, and told me to say if any one met us that I was going to make pies when I went home. Then we went on a little way till we came to a little brake growing right down into the road, and nurse stopped, and looked up the road and down it, and then peeped through the hedge into the field on the other side, and then she said, "Quick!" and we ran into the brake, and crept in and out among the bushes till we had gone a good way from the road. Then we sat down under a bush, and I wanted so much to know what nurse was going to make with the clay, but before she would begin she made me promise again not to say a word about it, and she went again and peeped through the bushes on every side, though the lane was so small and deep that hardly anybody ever went there. So we sat down, and nurse took the clay out of the bucket, and began to knead it with her hands, and do queer things with it, and turn it about. And she hid it under a big dock-leaf for a minute or two and then she brought it out again, and then she stood up and sat down, and walked round the clay in a peculiar manner, and all the time she was softly singing a sort of rhyme, and her face got very red. Then she sat down again, and took the clay in her hands and began to shape it into a doll, but not like the dolls I have at home, and she made the queerest doll I had ever seen, all out of the wet clay, and hid it under a bush to get dry and hard, and all the time she was making it she was singing these rhymes to herself, and her face got redder and redder. So we left the doll there, hidden away in the bushes where nobody would ever find it. And a few days later we went the same walk, and when we came to that narrow, dark part of the lane where the brake runs down to the bank, nurse made me promise all over again, and she looked about, just as she had done before, and we crept into the bushes till we got to the green place where the little clay man was hidden. I remember it all so well, though I was only eight, and it is eight years ago now as I am writing it down, but the sky was a deep violet blue, and in the middle of the brake where we were sitting there was a great elder tree covered with blossoms, and on the other side there was a clump of meadowsweet, and when I think of that day the smell of the meadowsweet and elder blossom seems to fill the room, and if I shut my eyes I can see the glaring sky, with little clouds very white floating across it, and nurse who went away long ago sitting opposite me and looking like the beautiful white lady in the wood. So we sat down and nurse took out the clay doll from the secret place where she had hidden it, and she said we must "pay our respects," and she would show me what to do, and I must watch her all the time. So she did all sorts of queer things with the little clay man, and I noticed she was all streaming with perspiration, though we had walked so slowly, and then she told me to "pay my respects," and I did everything she did because I liked her, and it was such an odd game. And she said that if one loved very much, the clay man was very good, if one did certain things with it, and if one hated very much, it was just as good, only one had to do different things, and we played with it a long time, and pretended all sorts of things. Nurse said her great-grandmother had told her all about these images, but what we did was no harm at all, only a game. But she told me a story about these images that frightened me very much, and that was what I remembered that night when I was lying awake in my room in the pale, empty darkness, thinking of what I had seen and the secret wood. Nurse said there was once a young lady of the high gentry, who lived in a great castle. And she was so beautiful that all the gentlemen wanted to marry her, because she was the loveliest lady that anybody had ever seen, and she was kind to everybody, and everybody thought she was very good. But though she was polite to all the gentlemen who wished to marry her, she put them off, and said she couldn't make up her mind, and she wasn't sure she wanted to marry anybody at all. And her father, who was a very great lord, was angry, though he was so fond of her, and he asked her why she wouldn't choose a bachelor out of all the handsome young men who came to the castle. But she only said she didn't love any of them very much, and she must wait, and if they pestered her, she said she would go and be a nun in a nunnery. So all the gentlemen said they would go away and wait for a year and a day, and when a year and a day were gone, they would come back again and ask her to say which one she would marry. So the day was appointed and they all went away; and the lady had promised that in a year and a day it would be her wedding day with one of them. But the truth was, that she was the queen of the people who danced on the hill on summer nights, and on the proper nights she would lock the door of her room, and she and her maid would steal out of the castle by a secret passage that only they knew of, and go away up to the hill in the wild land. And she knew more of the secret things than any one else, and more than any one knew before or after, because she would not tell anybody the most secret secrets. She knew how to do all the awful things, how to destroy young men, and how to put a curse on people, and other things that I could not understand. And her real name was the Lady Avelin, but the dancing people called her Cassap, which meant somebody very wise, in the old language. And she was whiter than any of them and taller, and her eyes shone in the dark like burning rubies; and she could sing songs that none of the others could sing, and when she sang they all fell down on their faces and worshipped her. And she could do what they called the shib-show, which was a very wonderful enchantment. She would tell the great lord, her father, that she wanted to go into the woods to gather flowers, so he let her go, and she and her maid went into the woods where nobody came, and the maid would keep watch. Then the lady would lie down under the trees and begin to sing a particular song, and she stretched out her arms, and from every part of the wood great serpents would come, hissing and gliding in and out among the trees, and shooting out their forked tongues as they crawled up to the lady. And they all came to her, and twisted round her, round her body, and her arms, and her neck, till she was covered with writhing serpents, and there was only her head to be seen. And she whispered to them, and she sang to them, and they writhed round and round, faster and faster, till she told them to go. And they all went away directly, back to their holes, and on the lady's breast there would be a most curious, beautiful stone, shaped something like an egg, and coloured dark blue and yellow, and red, and green, marked like a serpent's scales. It was called a glame stone, and with it one could do all sorts of wonderful things, and nurse said her great-grandmother had seen a glame stone with her own eyes, and it was for all the world shiny and scaly like a snake. And the lady could do a lot of other things as well, but she was quite fixed that she would not be married. And there were a great many gentlemen who wanted to marry her, but there were five of them who were chief, and their names were Sir Simon, Sir John, Sir Oliver, Sir Richard, and Sir Rowland. All the others believed she spoke the truth, and that she would choose one of them to be her man when a year and a day was done; it was only Sir Simon, who was very crafty, who thought she was deceiving them all, and he vowed he would watch and try if he could find out anything. And though he was very wise he was very young, and he had a smooth, soft face like a girl's, and he pretended, as the rest did, that he would not come to the castle for a year and a day, and he said he was going away beyond the sea to foreign parts. But he really only went a very little way, and came back dressed like a servant girl, and so he got a place in the castle to wash the dishes. And he waited and watched, and he listened and said nothing, and he hid in dark places, and woke up at night and looked out, and he heard things and he saw things that he thought were very strange. And he was so sly that he told the girl that waited on the lady that he was really a young man, and that he had dressed up as a girl because he loved her so very much and wanted to be in the same house with her, and the girl was so pleased that she told him many things, and he was more than ever certain that the Lady Avelin was deceiving him and the others. And he was so clever, and told the servant so many lies, that one night he managed to hide in the Lady Avelin's room behind the curtains. And he stayed quite still and never moved, and at last the lady came. And she bent down under the bed, and raised up a stone, and there was a hollow place underneath, and out of it she took a waxen image, just like the clay one that I and nurse had made in the brake. And all the time her eyes were burning like rubies. And she took the little wax doll up in her arms and held it to her breast, and she whispered and she murmured, and she took it up and she laid it down again, and she held it high, and she held it low, and she laid it down again. And she said, "Happy is he that begat the bishop, that ordered the clerk, that married the man, that had the wife, that fashioned the hive, that harboured the bee, that gathered the wax that my own true love was made of." And she brought out of a closet a great jar of wine, and she poured some of the wine into the bowl, and she laid her mannikin very gently in the wine, and washed it in the wine all over. Then she went to a cupboard and took a small round cake and laid it on the image's mouth, and then she bore it softly and covered it up. And Sir Simon, who was watching all the time, though he was terribly frightened, saw the lady bend down and stretch out her arms and whisper and sing, and then Sir Simon saw beside her a handsome young man, who kissed her on the lips. And they drank wine out of the golden bowl together, and they ate the cake together. But when the sun rose there was only the little wax doll, and the lady hid it again under the bed in the hollow place. So Sir Simon knew quite well what the lady was, and he waited and he watched, till the time she had said was nearly over, and in a week the year and a day would be done. And one night, when he was watching behind the curtains in her room, he saw her making more wax dolls. And she made five, and hid them away. And the next night she took one out, and held it up, and filled the golden bowl with water, and took the doll by the neck and held it under the water. Then she said—

Sir Dickon, Sir Dickon, your day is done,
You shall be drowned in the water wan.

And the next day news came to the castle that Sir Richard had been drowned at the ford. And at night she took another doll and tied a violet cord round its neck and hung it up on a nail. Then she said—

Sir Rowland, your life has ended its span,
High on a tree I see you hang.

And the next day news came to the castle that Sir Rowland had been hanged by robbers in the wood. And at night she took another doll, and drove her bodkin right into its heart. Then she said—

Sir Noll, Sir Noll, so cease your life,
Your heart piercèd with the knife.

And the next day news came to the castle that Sir Oliver had fought in a tavern, and a stranger had stabbed him to the heart. And at night she took another doll, and held it to a fire of charcoal till it was melted. Then she said—

Sir John, return, and turn to clay,
In fire of fever you waste away.

And the next day news came to the castle that Sir John had died in a burning fever. So then Sir Simon went out of the castle and mounted his horse and rode away to the bishop and told him everything. And the bishop sent his men, and they took the Lady Avelin, and everything she had done was found out. So on the day after the year and a day, when she was to have been married, they carried her through the town in her smock, and they tied her to a great stake in the market-place, and burned her alive before the bishop with her wax image hung round her neck. And people said the wax man screamed in the burning of the flames. And I thought of this story again and again as I was lying awake in my bed, and I seemed to see the Lady Avelin in the market-place, with the yellow flames eating up her beautiful white body. And I thought of it so much that I seemed to get into the story myself, and I fancied I was the lady, and that they were coming to take me to be burnt with fire, with all the people in the town looking at me. And I wondered whether she cared, after all the strange things she had done, and whether it hurt very much to be burned at the stake. I tried again and again to forget nurse's stories, and to remember the secret I had seen that afternoon, and what was in the secret wood, but I could only see the dark and a glimmering in the dark, and then it went away, and I only saw myself running, and then a great moon came up white over a dark round hill. Then all the old stories came back again, and the queer rhymes that nurse used to sing to me; and there was one beginning "Halsy cumsy Helen musty," that she used to sing very softly when she wanted me to go to sleep. And I began to sing it to myself inside of my head, and I went to sleep.

The next morning I was very tired and sleepy, and could hardly do my lessons, and I was very glad when they were over and I had had my dinner, as I wanted to go out and be alone. It was a warm day, and I went to a nice turfy hill by the river, and sat down on my mother's old shawl that I had brought with me on purpose. The sky was grey, like the day before, but there was a kind of white gleam behind it, and from where I was sitting I could look down on the town, and it was all still and quiet and white, like a picture. I remembered that it was on that hill that nurse taught me to play an old game called "Troy Town," in which one had to dance, and wind in and out on a pattern in the grass, and then when one had danced and turned long enough the other person asks you questions, and you can't help answering whether you want to or not, and whatever you are told to do you feel you have to do it. Nurse said there used to be a lot of games like that that some people knew of, and there was one by which people could be turned into anything you liked, and an old man her great-grandmother had seen had known a girl who had been turned into a large snake. And there was another very ancient game of dancing and winding and turning, by which you could take a person out of himself and hide him away as long as you liked, and his body went walking about quite empty, without any sense in it. But I came to that hill because I wanted to think of what had happened the day before, and of the secret of the wood. From the place where I was sitting I could see beyond the town, into the opening I had found, where a little brook had led me into an unknown country. And I pretended I was following the brook over again, and I went all the way in my mind, and at last I found the wood, and crept into it under the bushes, and then in the dusk I saw something that made me feel as if I were filled with fire, as if I wanted to dance and sing and fly up into the air, because I was changed and wonderful. But what I saw was not changed at all, and had not grown old, and I wondered again and again how such things could happen, and whether nurse's stories were really true, because in the daytime in the open air everything seemed quite different from what it was at night, when I was frightened, and thought I was to be burned alive. I once told my father one of her little tales, which was about a ghost, and asked him if it was true, and he told me it was not true at all, and that only common, ignorant people believed in such rubbish. He was very angry with nurse for telling me the story, and scolded her, and after that I promised her I would never whisper a word of what she told me, and if I did I should be bitten by the great black snake that lived in the pool in the wood. And all alone on the hill I wondered what was true. I had seen something very amazing and very lovely, and I knew a story, and if I had really seen it, and not made it up out of the dark, and the black bough, and the bright shining that was mounting up to the sky from over the great round hill, but had really seen it in truth, then there were all kinds of wonderful and lovely and terrible things to think of, so I longed and trembled, and I burned and got cold. And I looked down on the town, so quiet and still, like a little white picture, and I thought over and over if it could be true. I was a long time before I could make up my mind to anything; there was such a strange fluttering at my heart that seemed to whisper to me all the time that I had not made it up out of my head, and yet it seemed quite impossible, and I knew my father and everybody would say it was dreadful rubbish. I never dreamed of telling him or anybody else a word about it, because I knew it would be of no use, and I should only get laughed at or scolded, so for a long time I was very quiet, and went about thinking and wondering; and at night I used to dream of amazing things, and sometimes I woke up in the early morning and held out my arms with a cry. And I was frightened, too, because there were dangers, and some awful thing would happen to me, unless I took great care, if the story were true. These old tales were always in my head, night and morning, and I went over them and told them to myself over and over again, and went for walks in the places where nurse had told them to me; and when I sat in the nursery by the fire in the evenings I used to fancy nurse was sitting in the other chair, and telling me some wonderful story in a low voice, for fear anybody should be listening. But she used to like best to tell me about things when we were right out in the country, far from the house, because she said she was telling me such secrets, and walls have ears. And if it was something more than ever secret, we had to hide in brakes or woods; and I used to think it was such fun creeping along a hedge, and going very softly, and then we would get behind the bushes or run into the wood all of a sudden, when we were sure that none was watching us; so we knew that we had our secrets quite all to ourselves, and nobody else at all knew anything about them. Now and then, when we had hidden ourselves as I have described, she used to show me all sorts of odd things. One day, I remember, we were in a hazel brake, overlooking the brook, and we were so snug and warm, as though it was April; the sun was quite hot, and the leaves were just coming out. Nurse said she would show me something funny that would make me laugh, and then she showed me, as she said, how one could turn a whole house upside down, without anybody being able to find out, and the pots and pans would jump about, and the china would be broken, and the chairs would tumble over of themselves. I tried it one day in the kitchen, and I found I could do it quite well, and a whole row of plates on the dresser fell off it, and cook's little work-table tilted up and turned right over "before her eyes," as she said, but she was so frightened and turned so white that I didn't do it again, as I liked her. And afterwards, in the hazel copse, when she had shown me how to make things tumble about, she showed me how to make rapping noises, and I learnt how to do that, too. Then she taught me rhymes to say on certain occasions, and peculiar marks to make on other occasions, and other things that her great-grandmother had taught her when she was a little girl herself. And these were all the things I was thinking about in those days after the strange walk when I thought I had seen a great secret, and I wished nurse were there for me to ask her about it, but she had gone away more than two years before, and nobody seemed to know what had become of her, or where she had gone. But I shall always remember those days if I live to be quite old, because all the time I felt so strange, wondering and doubting, and feeling quite sure at one time, and making up my mind, and then I would feel quite sure that such things couldn't happen really, and it began all over again. But I took great care not to do certain things that might be very dangerous. So I waited and wondered for a long time, and though I was not sure at all, I never dared to try to find out. But one day I became sure that all that nurse said was quite true, and I was all alone when I found it out. I trembled all over with joy and terror, and as fast as I could I ran into one of the old brakes where we used to go—it was the one by the lane, where nurse made the little clay man—and I ran into it, and I crept into it; and when I came to the place where the elder was, I covered up my face with my hands and lay down flat on the grass, and I stayed there for two hours without moving, whispering to myself delicious, terrible things, and saying some words over and over again. It was all true and wonderful and splendid, and when I remembered the story I knew and thought of what I had really seen, I got hot and I got cold, and the air seemed full of scent, and flowers, and singing. And first I wanted to make a little clay man, like the one nurse had made so long ago, and I had to invent plans and stratagems, and to look about, and to think of things beforehand, because nobody must dream on anything that I was doing or going to do, and I was too old to carry clay about in a tin bucket. At last I thought of a plan, and I brought the wet clay to the brake, and did everything that nurse had done, only I made a much finer image than the one she had made; and when it was finished I did everything that I could imagine and much more than she did, because it was the likeness of something far better. And a few days later, when I had done my lessons early, I went for the second time by the way of the little brook that had led me into a strange country. And I followed the brook, and went through the bushes, and beneath the low branches of trees, and up thorny thickets on the hill, and by dark woods full of creeping thorns, a long, long way. Then I crept through the dark tunnel where the brook had been and the ground was stony, till at last I came to the thicket that climbed up the hill, and though the leaves were coming out upon the trees, everything looked almost as black as it was on the first day that I went there. And the thicket was just the same, and I went up slowly till I came out on the big bare hill, and began to walk among the wonderful rocks. I saw the terrible voor again on everything, for though the sky was brighter, the ring of wild hills all around was still dark, and the hanging woods looked dark and dreadful, and the strange rocks were as grey as ever; and when I looked down on them from the great mound, sitting on the stone, I saw all their amazing circles and rounds within rounds, and I had to sit quite still and watch them as they began to turn about me, and each stone danced in its place, and they seemed to go round and round in a great whirl, as if one were in the middle of all the stars and heard them rushing through the air. So I went down among the rocks to dance with them and to sing extraordinary songs; and I went down through the other thicket, and drank from the bright stream in the close and secret valley, putting my lips down to the bubbling water; and then I went on till I came to the deep, brimming well among the glittering moss, and I sat down. I looked before me into the secret darkness of the valley, and behind me was the great high wall of grass, and all around me there were the hanging woods that made the valley such a secret place. I knew there was nobody here at all besides myself, and that no one could see me. So I took off my boots and stockings, and let my feet down into the water, saying the words that I knew. And it was not cold at all, as I expected, but warm and very pleasant, and when my feet were in it I felt as if they were in silk, or as if the nymph were kissing them. So when I had done, I said the other words and made the signs, and then I dried my feet with a towel I had brought on purpose, and put on my stockings and boots. Then I climbed up the steep wall, and went into the place where there are the hollows, and the two beautiful mounds, and the round ridges of land, and all the strange shapes. I did not go down into the hollow this time, but I turned at the end, and made out the figures quite plainly, as it was lighter, and I had remembered the story I had quite forgotten before, and in the story the two figures are called Adam and Eve, and only those who know the story understand what they mean. So I went on and on till I came to the secret wood which must not be described, and I crept into it by the way I had found. And when I had gone about halfway I stopped, and turned round, and got ready, and I bound the handkerchief tightly round my eyes, and made quite sure that I could not see at all, not a twig, nor the end of a leaf, nor the light of the sky, as it was an old red silk handkerchief with large yellow spots, that went round twice and covered my eyes, so that I could see nothing. Then I began to go on, step by step, very slowly. My heart beat faster and faster, and something rose in my throat that choked me and made me want to cry out, but I shut my lips, and went on. Boughs caught in my hair as I went, and great thorns tore me; but I went on to the end of the path. Then I stopped, and held out my arms and bowed, and I went round the first time, feeling with my hands, and there was nothing. I went round the second time, feeling with my hands, and there was nothing. Then I went round the third time, feeling with my hands, and the story was all true, and I wished that the years were gone by, and that I had not so long a time to wait before I was happy for ever and ever.

Nurse must have been a prophet like those we read of in the Bible. Everything that she said began to come true, and since then other things that she told me of have happened. That was how I came to know that her stories were true and that I had not made up the secret myself out of my own head. But there was another thing that happened that day. I went a second time to the secret place. It was at the deep brimming well, and when I was standing on the moss I bent over and looked in, and then I knew who the white lady was that I had seen come out of the water in the wood long ago when I was quite little. And I trembled all over, because that told me other things. Then I remembered how sometime after I had seen the white people in the wood, nurse asked me more about them, and I told her all over again, and she listened, and said nothing for a long, long time, and at last she said, "You will see her again." So I understood what had happened and what was to happen. And I understood about the nymphs; how I might meet them in all kinds of places, and they would always help me, and I must always look for them, and find them in all sorts of strange shapes and appearances. And without the nymphs I could never have found the secret, and without them none of the other things could happen. Nurse had told me all about them long ago, but she called them by another name, and I did not know what she meant, or what her tales of them were about, only that they were very queer. And there were two kinds, the bright and the dark, and both were very lovely and very wonderful, and some people saw only one kind, and some only the other, but some saw them both. But usually the dark appeared first, and the bright ones came afterwards, and there were extraordinary tales about them. It was a day or two after I had come home from the secret place that I first really knew the nymphs. Nurse had shown me how to call them, and I had tried, but I did not know what she meant, and so I thought it was all nonsense. But I made up my mind I would try again, so I went to the wood where the pool was, where I saw the white people, and I tried again. The dark nymph, Alanna, came, and she turned the pool of water into a pool of fire. . . .

Epilogue

"That's a very queer story," said Cotgrave, handing back the green book to the recluse, Ambrose. "I see the drift of a good deal, but there are many things that I do not grasp at all. On the last page, for example, what does she mean by 'nymphs'?"

"Well, I think there are references throughout the manuscript to certain 'processes' which have been handed down by tradition from age to age. Some of these processes are just beginning to come within the purview of science, which has arrived at them—or rather at the steps which lead to them—by quite different paths. I have interpreted the reference to 'nymphs' as a reference to one of these processes."

"And you believe that there are such things?"

"Oh, I think so. Yes, I believe I could give you convincing evidence on that point. I am afraid you have neglected the study of alchemy. It is a pity, for the symbolism, at all events, is very beautiful, and moreover if you were acquainted with certain books on the subject, I could recall to your mind phrases which might explain a good deal in the manuscript that you have been reading."

"Yes; but I want to know whether you seriously think that there is any foundation of fact beneath these fancies. Is it not all a department of poetry; a curious dream which man has indulged himself?"

"I can only say that it is no doubt better for the great mass of people to dismiss it all as a dream. But if you ask my veritable belief—that goes quite the other way. No; I should not say belief, but rather knowledge. I may tell you that I have known cases in which men have stumbled quite by accident on certain of these 'processes,' and have been astonished by wholly unexpected results. In the cases I am thinking of there could have been no possibility of 'suggestion' or subconscious action of any kind. One might as well suppose a schoolboy 'suggesting' the existence of Æschylus to himself, while he plods mechanically through the declensions.

"But you have noticed the obscurity," Ambrose went on, "and in this particular case it must have been dictated by instinct, since the writer never thought that her manuscripts would fall into other hands. But the practice is universal, and for most excellent reasons. Powerful and sovereign medicines, which are, of necessity, virulent poisons also, are kept in a locked cabinet. The child may find the key by chance, and drink herself dead; but in most cases the search is educational, and the phials contain precious elixirs for him who has patiently fashioned the key for himself."

"You do not care to go into details?"

"No, frankly, I do not. No, you must remain unconvinced. But you saw how the manuscript illustrates the talk we had last week?"

"Is this girl still alive?"

"No. I was one of those who found her. I knew the father well; he was a lawyer, and had always left her very much to herself. He thought of nothing but deeds and leases, and the news came to him as an awful surprise. She was missing one morning; I suppose it was about a year after she had written what you have read. The servants were called, and they told things, and put the only natural interpretation on them—a perfectly erroneous one.

"They discovered that green book somewhere in her room, and I found her in the place that she described with so much dread, lying on the ground before the image."

"It was an image?"

"Yes; it was hidden by the thorns and the thick undergrowth that had surrounded it. It was a wild, lonely country; but you know what it was like by her description, though of course you will understand that the colours have been heightened. A child's imagination always makes the heights higher and the depths deeper than they really are; and she had, unfortunately for herself, something more than imagination. One might say, perhaps, that the picture in her mind which she succeeded in a measure in putting into words, was the scene as it would have appeared to an imaginative artist. But it is a strange, desolate land."

"And she was dead?"

"Yes. She had poisoned herself—in time. No; there was not a word to be said against her in the ordinary sense. You may recollect a story I told you the other night about a lady who saw her child's fingers crushed by a window?"

"And what was this statue?"

"Well, it was of Roman workmanship, of a stone that with the centuries had not blackened, but had become white and luminous. The thicket had grown up about it and concealed it, and in the Middle Ages the followers of a very old tradition had known how to use it for their own purposes. In fact it had been incorporated into the monstrous mythology of the Sabbath. You will have noted that those to whom a sight of that shining whiteness had been vouchsafed by chance, or rather, perhaps, by apparent chance, were required to blindfold themselves on their second approach. That is very significant."

"And is it there still?"

"I sent for tools, and we hammered it into dust and fragments."

"The persistence of tradition never surprises me," Ambrose went on after a pause. "I could name many an English parish where such traditions as that girl had listened to in her childhood are still existent in occult but unabated vigour. No, for me, it is the 'story' not the 'sequel,' which is strange and awful, for I have always believed that wonder is of the soul."

Dracula's Guest

Bram Stoker

Preface

WHEN WE started for our drive the sun was shining brightly on Munich, and the air was full of the joyousness of early summer. Just as we were about to depart, Herr Delbrück (the *maître d'hôtel* of the Quatre Saisons, where I was staying) came down, bareheaded, to the carriage and, after wishing me a pleasant drive, said to the coachman, still holding his hand on the handle of the carriage door: "Remember you are back by nightfall. The sky looks bright but there is a shiver in the north wind that says there may be a sudden storm. But I am sure you will not be late," here he smiled, and added, "for you know what night it is."

Johann answered with an emphatic, "Ja, mein Herr," and, touching his hat, drove off quickly. When we had cleared the town, I said, after signalling to him to stop: "Tell me, Johann, what is tonight?"

He crossed himself, as he answered laconically: "Walpurgis nacht." Then he took out his watch, a great, old-fashioned German silver thing as big as a turnip, and looked at it, with his eyebrows gathered together and a little impatient shrug of his shoulders. I realised that this was his way of respectfully protesting against the unnecessary delay, and sank back in the carriage, merely motioning him to proceed. He started off rapidly, as if to make up for lost time. Every now and then the horses seemed to throw up their heads and sniff the air suspiciously. On such occasions I often looked round in alarm. The road was pretty bleak, for we were traversing a sort of high, wind-swept plateau. As we drove, I saw a road that looked but seldom used, and which seemed to dip through a little, winding valley. It looked so inviting that, even at the risk of offending him, I called Johann to stop—and when he had pulled up, I told him I would like to drive down that road. He made all sorts of excuses, and frequently crossed himself as he spoke. This somewhat piqued my curiosity, so I asked him various questions. He answered fencingly, and repeatedly looked at his watch in protest.

Finally I said: "Well, Johann, I want to go down this road. I shall not ask you to come unless you like; but tell me why you do not like to go, that is all I ask." For answer he seemed to throw himself off the box, so quickly did he reach the ground. Then he stretched out his hands appealingly to me, and implored me not to go. There was just enough of English mixed with the German for me to understand the drift of his talk. He seemed always just about to tell me something—the very idea of which evidently frightened him; but each time he pulled himself up, saying, as he crossed himself: "Walpurgis nacht!"

I tried to argue with him, but it was difficult to argue with a man when I did not know his language. The advantage certainly rested with him, for although he began to speak in English, of a very crude and broken kind, he always got excited and broke into his native tongue—and every time he did so, he looked at his watch. Then the horses became restless and sniffed the air. At this he grew very pale, and, looking around in a frightened way, he suddenly jumped forward, took them by the bridles and led them on some twenty feet. I followed, and asked why he had done this. For answer he crossed himself, pointed to the spot we had left and drew his carriage in the direction of the other road, indicating a cross, and said, first in German, then in English: "Buried him—him what killed themselves."

I remembered the old custom of burying suicides at crossroads: "Ah! I see, a suicide. How interesting!" But for the life of me I could not make out why the horses were frightened.

Whilst we were talking, we heard a sort of sound between a yelp and a bark. It was far away; but the horses got very restless, and it took Johann all his time to quiet them. He was pale, and said, "It sounds like a wolf—but yet there are no wolves here now."

"No?" I said, questioning him; "isn't it long since the wolves were so near the city?"

"Long, long," he answered, "in the spring and summer; but with the snow the wolves have been here not so long."

Whilst he was petting the horses and trying to quiet them, dark clouds drifted rapidly across the sky. The sunshine passed away, and a breath of cold wind seemed to drift past us. It was only a breath, however, and more in the nature of a warning than a fact, for the sun came out brightly again. Johann looked under his lifted hand at the horizon and said: "The storm of snow, he comes before long time." Then he looked at his watch again, and, straightway holding his reins firmly—for the horses were still pawing the ground restlessly and shaking their heads—he climbed to his box as though the time had come for proceeding on our journey.

I felt a little obstinate and did not at once get into the carriage.

"Tell me," I said, "about this place where the road leads," and I pointed down.

Again he crossed himself and mumbled a prayer, before he answered, "It is unholy."

"What is unholy?" I enquired.

"The village."

"Then there is a village?"

"No, no. No one lives there hundreds of years." My curiosity was piqued, "But you said there was a village."

"There was."

"Where is it now?"

Whereupon he burst out into a long story in German and English, so mixed up that I could not quite understand exactly what he said, but roughly I gathered that long ago, hundreds of years, men had died there and been buried in their graves; and sounds were heard under the clay, and when the graves were opened, men and women were found rosy with life, and their mouths red with blood. And so, in haste to save their lives (aye, and their souls!—and here he crossed himself) those who were left fled away to other places, where the living lived, and the dead were dead and not—not something. He was evidently afraid to speak the last words. As he proceeded with his narration, he grew more and more excited. It seemed as if his imagination had got hold of him, and he ended in a perfect paroxysm of fear—white-faced, perspiring, trembling and looking round him, as if expecting that some dreadful presence would manifest itself there in the bright sunshine on the open plain. Finally, in an agony of desperation, he cried: "Walpurgis nacht!" and pointed to the carriage for me to get in. All my English blood rose at this, and, standing back, I said: "You are afraid, Johann—you are afraid. Go home; I shall return alone; the walk will do me good." The carriage door was open. I took from the seat my oak walking-stick—which I always carry on my holiday excursions—and closed the door, pointing back to Munich, and said, "Go home, Johann—Walpurgis nacht doesn't concern Englishmen."

The horses were now more restive than ever, and Johann was trying to hold them in while excitedly imploring me not to do anything so foolish. I pitied the poor fellow, he was deeply in earnest; but all the same I could not help laughing. His English was quite gone now. In his anxiety he had forgotten that his only means of making me understand was to talk my language, so he jabbered away in his native German. It began to be a little tedious. After giving the direction, "Home!" I turned to go down the crossroad into the valley.

With a despairing gesture, Johann turned his horses towards Munich. I leaned on my stick and looked after him. He went slowly along the road for a while; then there came over the crest of the hill a man tall and thin. I could see so much in the distance. When he drew near the horses, they began to jump and kick about, then to scream with terror. Johann could not hold them in; they bolted down the road, running away madly. I watched them out of sight, then looked for the stranger, but I found that he, too, was gone.

With a light heart I turned down the side road through the deepening valley to which Johann had objected. There was not the slightest reason, that I could see, for his objection; and I dare say I tramped for a couple of hours without thinking of time or distance, and certainly without seeing a person or a house. So far as the place was concerned, it was desolation itself. But I did not notice this particularly till, on turning a bend in the road, I came upon a scattered fringe of wood; then I recognised that I had been impressed unconsciously by the desolation of the region through which I had passed.

I sat down to rest myself, and began to look around. It struck me that it was considerably colder than it had been at the commencement of my walk—a sort of sighing sound seemed to be around me, with, now and then, high overhead, a sort of muffled roar. Looking upwards I noticed that great thick clouds were drifting rapidly across the sky from north to south at a great height. There were signs of coming storm in some lofty stratum of the air. I was a little chilly, and, thinking that it was the sitting still after the exercise of walking, I resumed my journey.

The ground I passed over was now much more picturesque. There were no striking objects that the eye might single out; but in all there was a charm of beauty. I took little heed of time and it was only when the deepening twilight forced itself upon me that I began to think of how I should find my way home. The brightness of the day had gone. The air was cold, and the drifting of clouds high overhead was more marked. They were accompanied by a sort of far-away rushing sound, through which seemed to come at intervals that mysterious cry which the driver had said came from a wolf. For a while I hesitated. I had said I would see the deserted village, so on I went, and presently came on a wide stretch of open country, shut in by hills all around. Their sides were covered with trees which spread down to the plain, dotting, in clumps, the gentler slopes and hollows which showed here and there. I followed with my eye the winding of the road, and saw that it curved close to one of the densest of these clumps and was lost behind it.

As I looked there came a cold shiver in the air, and the snow began to fall. I thought of the miles and miles of bleak country I had passed, and then hurried on to seek the shelter of the wood in front. Darker and darker grew the sky, and faster and heavier fell the snow, till the earth before and around me was a glistening white carpet, the further edge of which was lost in misty vagueness. The road was here but crude, and when on the level its boundaries were not so marked as when it passed through the cuttings; and in a little while I found that I must have strayed from it, for I missed underfoot the hard surface, and my feet sank deeper in the grass and moss. Then the wind grew stronger and blew with ever increasing force, till I was fain to run before it. The air became icy-cold, and in spite of my exercise I began to suffer. The snow was now falling so thickly and whirling around me in such rapid eddies that I could hardly keep my eyes open. Every now and then the heavens were torn asunder by vivid lightning, and in the flashes I could see ahead of me a great mass of trees, chiefly yew and cypress all heavily coated with snow.

I was soon amongst the shelter of the trees, and there, in comparative silence, I could hear the rush of the wind high overhead. Presently the blackness of the storm had become merged in the darkness of the night. By and by the storm seemed to be passing away: it now only came in fierce bursts or blasts. At such moments the weird sound of the wolf appeared to be echoed by many similar sounds around me.

Now and again, through the black mass of drifting cloud, came a straggling ray of moonlight, which lit up the expanse, and showed me that I was at the edge of a dense mass of cypress and yew trees. As the snow had ceased to fall, I walked out from the shelter and began to investigate more closely. It appeared to me that, amongst so many old foundations as I had passed, there might be still standing a house in which, though in ruins, I could find some sort of shelter for a while. As I skirted the edge of the copse, I found that a low wall encircled it, and following this I presently found an opening. Here the cypresses formed an alley leading up to a square mass of some kind of building. Just as I caught sight of this, however, the drifting clouds obscured the moon, and I passed up the path in darkness. The wind must have grown colder, for I felt myself shiver as I walked; but there was hope of shelter, and I groped my way blindly on.

I stopped, for there was a sudden stillness. The storm had passed; and, perhaps in sympathy with nature's silence, my heart seemed to cease to beat. But this was only momentarily; for suddenly the moonlight broke through the clouds, showing me that I was in a graveyard, and that the square object before me was a great massive tomb of marble, as white as the snow that lay on and all around it. With the moonlight there came a fierce sigh of the storm, which appeared to resume its course with a long, low howl, as of many dogs or wolves. I was awed and shocked, and felt the cold perceptibly grow upon me till it seemed to grip me by the heart. Then while the flood of moonlight still fell on the marble tomb, the storm gave further evidence of renewing, as though it was returning on its track. Impelled by some sort of fascination, I approached the sepulchre to see what it was, and why such a thing stood alone in such a place. I walked around it, and read, over the Doric door, in German:

COUNTESS DOLINGEN OF GRATZ
IN STYRIA
SOUGHT AND FOUND DEATH
1801

On the top of the tomb, seemingly driven through the solid marble—for the structure was composed of a few vast blocks of stone—was a great iron spike or stake. On going to the back I saw, graven in great Russian letters:

THE DEAD TRAVEL FAST

There was something so weird and uncanny about the whole thing that it gave me a turn and made me feel quite faint. I began to wish, for the first time, that I had taken Johann's advice. Here a thought struck me, which came under almost mysterious circumstances and with a terrible shock. This was Walpurgis Night!

Walpurgis Night, when, according to the belief of millions of people, the devil was abroad—when the graves were opened and the dead came forth and walked. When all evil things of earth and air and water held revel. This very place the driver had specially shunned. This was the depopulated village of centuries ago. This was where the suicide lay; and this was the place where I was alone—unmanned, shivering with cold in a shroud of snow with a wild storm gathering again upon me! It took all my philosophy, all the religion I had been taught, all my courage, not to collapse in a paroxysm of fright.

And now a perfect tornado burst upon me. The ground shook as though thousands of horses thundered across it; and this time the storm bore on its icy wings, not snow, but great hailstones which drove with such violence that they might have come from the thongs of Balearic slingers—hailstones that beat down leaf and branch and made the shelter of the cypresses of no more avail than if their stems were standing-corn. At the first I had rushed to the nearest tree; but I was soon fain to leave it and seek the only spot that seemed to afford refuge, the deep Doric doorway of the marble tomb. There, crouching against the massive bronze door, I gained a certain amount of protection from the beating of the hailstones, for now they only drove against me as they ricocheted from the ground and the side of the marble.

As I leaned against the door, it moved slightly and opened inwards. The shelter of even a tomb was welcome in that pitiless tempest, and

I was about to enter it when there came a flash of forked-lightning that lit up the whole expanse of the heavens. In the instant, as I am a living man, I saw, as my eyes were turned into the darkness of the tomb, a beautiful woman, with rounded cheeks and red lips, seemingly sleeping on a bier. As the thunder broke overhead, I was grasped as by the hand of a giant and hurled out into the storm. The whole thing was so sudden that, before I could realise the shock, moral as well as physical, I found the hailstones beating me down. At the same time I had a strange, dominating feeling that I was not alone. I looked towards the tomb. Just then there came another blinding flash, which seemed to strike the iron stake that surmounted the tomb and to pour through to the earth, blasting and crumbling the marble, as in a burst of flame. The dead woman rose for a moment of agony, while she was lapped in the flame, and her bitter scream of pain was drowned in the thundercrash. The last thing I heard was this mingling of dreadful sound, as again I was seized in the giant-grasp and dragged away, while the hailstones beat on me, and the air around seemed reverberant with the howling of wolves. The last sight that I remembered was a vague, white, moving mass, as if all the graves around me had sent out the phantoms of their sheeted-dead, and that they were closing in on me through the white cloudiness of the driving hail.

Gradually there came a sort of vague beginning of consciousness; then a sense of weariness that was dreadful. For a time I remembered nothing; but slowly my senses returned. My feet seemed positively racked with pain, yet I could not move them. They seemed to be numbed. There was an icy feeling at the back of my neck and all down my spine, and my ears, like my feet, were dead, yet in torment; but there was in my breast a sense of warmth which was, by comparison, delicious. It was as a nightmare—a physical nightmare, if one may use such an expression; for some heavy weight on my chest made it difficult for me to breathe.

This period of semi-lethargy seemed to remain a long time, and as it faded away I must have slept or swooned. Then came a sort of loathing, like the first stage of sea-sickness, and a wild desire to be free from something—I knew not what. A vast stillness enveloped me, as though all the world were asleep or dead—only broken by the low panting as of some animal close to me. I felt a warm rasping at my throat, then came a consciousness of the awful truth, which chilled me to the heart and sent the blood surging up through my brain. Some great animal was lying on me and now licking my throat. I feared to stir, for some instinct of prudence bade me lie still; but the brute seemed to realise that there was now some change in me, for it raised its head. Through my eyelashes I saw above me the two great flaming eyes of a gigantic wolf. Its sharp white teeth gleamed in the gaping red mouth, and I could feel its hot breath fierce and acrid upon me.

For another spell of time I remembered no more. Then I became conscious of a low growl, followed by a yelp, renewed again and again. Then, seemingly very far away, I heard a "Holloa! holloa!" as of many voices calling in unison. Cautiously I raised my head and looked in the direction whence the sound came; but the cemetery blocked my view. The wolf still continued to yelp in a strange way, and a red glare began to move round the grove of cypresses, as though following the sound. As the voices drew closer, the wolf yelped faster and louder. I feared to make either sound or motion. Nearer came the red glow, over the white pall which stretched into the darkness around me. Then all at once from beyond the trees there came at a trot a troop of horsemen bearing torches. The wolf rose from my breast and made for the cemetery. I saw one of the horsemen (soldiers by their caps and their long military cloaks) raise his carbine and take aim. A companion knocked up his arm, and I heard the ball whizz over my head. He had evidently taken my body for that of the wolf. Another sighted the animal as it slunk away, and a shot followed. Then, at a gallop, the troop rode forward—some towards me, others following the wolf as it disappeared amongst the snow-clad cypresses.

As they drew nearer I tried to move, but was powerless, although I could see and hear all that went on around me. Two or three of the soldiers jumped from their horses and knelt beside me. One of them raised my head, and placed his hand over my heart.

"Good news, comrades!" he cried. "His heart still beats!"

Then some brandy was poured down my throat; it put vigour into me, and I was able to open my eyes fully and look around. Lights and shadows were moving among the trees, and I heard men call to one another. They drew together, uttering frightened exclamations; and the lights flashed as the others came pouring out of the cemetery pell-mell, like men possessed. When the farther ones came close to us, those who were around me asked them eagerly: "Well, have you found him?"

The reply rang out hurriedly: "No! no! Come away quick, quick! This is no place to stay, and on this of all nights!"

"What was it?" was the question, asked in all manner of keys. The answer came variously and all indefinitely as though the men were moved by some common impulse to speak, yet were restrained by some common fear from giving their thoughts.

"It—it—indeed!" gibbered one, whose wits had plainly given out for the moment.

"A wolf—and yet not a wolf!" another put in shudderingly.

"No use trying for him without the sacred bullet," a third remarked in a more ordinary manner.

"Serve us right for coming out on this night! Truly we have earned our thousand marks!" were the ejaculations of a fourth.

"There was blood on the broken marble," another said after a pause—"the lightning never brought that there. And for him—is he safe? Look at his throat! See, comrades, the wolf has been lying on him and keeping his blood warm."

The officer looked at my throat and replied: "He is all right; the skin is not pierced. What does it all mean? We should never have found him but for the yelping of the wolf."

"What became of it?" asked the man who was holding up my head, and who seemed the least panic-stricken of the party, for his hands were steady and without tremor. On his sleeve was the chevron of a petty officer.

"It went to its home," answered the man, whose long face was pallid, and who actually shook with terror as he glanced around him fearfully. "There are graves enough there in which it may lie. Come, comrades—come quickly! Let us leave this cursed spot."

The officer raised me to a sitting posture, as he uttered a word of command; then several men placed me upon a horse. He sprang to the saddle behind me, took me in his arms, gave the word to advance; and, turning our faces away from the cypresses, we rode away in swift, military order.

As yet my tongue refused its office, and I was perforce silent. I must have fallen asleep; for the next thing I remembered was finding myself standing up, supported by a soldier on each side of me. It was almost broad daylight, and to the north a red streak of sunlight was reflected, like a path of blood, over the waste of snow. The officer was telling the men to say nothing of what they had seen, except that they found an English stranger, guarded by a large dog.

"Dog! that was no dog," cut in the man who had exhibited such fear. "I think I know a wolf when I see one."

The young officer answered calmly: "I said a dog."

"Dog!" reiterated the other ironically. It was evident that his courage was rising with the sun; and, pointing to me, he said, "Look at his throat. Is that the work of a dog, master?"

Instinctively I raised my hand to my throat, and as I touched it I cried out in pain. The men crowded round to look, some stooping down from their saddles; and again there came the calm voice of the young officer: "A dog, as I said. If aught else were said we should only be laughed at."

I was then mounted behind a trooper, and we rode on into the suburbs of Munich. Here we came across a stray carriage, into which I was lifted, and it was driven off to the Quatre Saisons—the young officer accompanying me, whilst a trooper followed with his horse, and the others rode off to their barracks.

When we arrived, Herr Delbrück rushed so quickly down the steps to meet me that it was apparent he had been watching within. Taking me by both hands he solicitously led me in. The officer saluted me and was turning to withdraw, when I recognised his purpose, and insisted that he should come to my rooms. Over a glass of wine I warmly thanked him and his brave comrades for saving me. He replied simply that he was more than glad, and that Herr Delbrück had at the first taken steps to make all the searching party pleased; at which ambiguous utterance the *maître d'hôtel* smiled, while the officer pleaded duty and withdrew.

"But Herr Delbrück," I enquired, "how and why was it that the soldiers searched for me?"

He shrugged his shoulders, as if in depreciation of his own deed, as he replied: "I was so fortunate as to obtain leave from the commander of the regiment in which I served, to ask for volunteers."

"But how did you know I was lost?" I asked.

"The driver came hither with the remains of his carriage, which had been upset when the horses ran away."

"But surely you would not send a search-party of soldiers merely on this account?"

"Oh, no!" he answered; "but even before the coachman arrived, I had this telegram from the boyar whose guest you are," and he took from his pocket a telegram which he handed to me, and I read:

Bistritz

> Be careful of my guest—his safety is most precious to me. Should aught happen to him, or if he be missed, spare nothing to find him and ensure his safety. He is English and therefore adventurous. There are often dangers from snow and wolves and night. Lose not a moment if you suspect harm to him. I answer your zeal with my fortune.

DRACULA

As I held the telegram in my hand, the room seemed to whirl around me; and, if the attentive *maître d'hôtel* had not caught me, I think I should have fallen. There was something so strange in all this, something so weird and impossible to imagine, that there grew on me a sense of my being in some way the sport of opposite forces—the mere vague idea of which seemed in a way to paralyse me. I was certainly under some form of mysterious protection. From a distant country had come, in the very nick of time, a message that took me out of the danger of the snow-sleep and the jaws of the wolf.

The Facts in the Case of M. Valdemar

Edgar Allan Poe

OF COURSE I shall not pretend to consider it any matter for wonder, that the extraordinary case of M. Valdemar has excited discussion. It would have been a miracle had it not—especially under the circumstances. Through the desire of all parties concerned, to keep the affair from the public, at least for the present, or until we had further opportunities for investigation—through our endeavours to effect this—a garbled or exaggerated account made its way into society, and became the source of many unpleasant misrepresentations, and, very naturally, of a great deal of disbelief.

It is now rendered necessary that I give the *facts*—as far as I comprehend them myself. They are, succinctly, these:

My attention, for the last three years, had been repeatedly drawn to the subject of Mesmerism; and, about nine months ago, it occurred to me, quite suddenly, that in the series of experiments made hitherto, there had been a very remarkable and most unaccountable omission: —no person had as yet been mesmerized *in articulo mortis*. It remained to be seen, first, whether, in such condition, there existed in the patient any susceptibility to the magnetic influence; secondly, whether, if any existed, it was impaired or increased by the condition; thirdly, to what extent, or for how long a period, the encroachments of Death might be arrested by the process. There were other points to be ascertained, but these most excited my curiosity—the last one especially, from the immensely important character of its consequences.

In looking around me for some subject by whose means I might test these particulars, I was brought to think of my friend, M. Ernest Valdemar, the well-known compiler of the *Bibliotheca Forensica*, and author (under the *nom de plume* of Issachar Marx) of the Polish versions of *Wallenstein* and *Gargantua*. M. Valdemar, who has resided principally at Haarlem, N.Y., since the year 1839, is (or was) particularly noticeable for the extreme spareness of his person—his lower limbs much resembling those of John Randolph; and, also, for the whiteness of his whiskers, in violent contrast to the blackness of his hair—the latter, in consequence, being very generally mistaken for a wig. His temperament was markedly nervous, and rendered him a good subject for mesmeric experiment. On two or three occasions I had put him to sleep with little difficulty, but was disappointed in other results which his peculiar constitution had naturally led me to anticipate. His will was at no period positively, or thoroughly, under my control, and in regard to *clairvoyance,* I could accomplish with him nothing to be relied upon. I always attributed my failure at these points to the disordered state of his health. For some months previous to my becoming acquainted with him, his physicians had declared him in a confirmed phthisis. It was his custom, indeed, to speak calmly of his approaching dissolution, as of a matter neither to be avoided nor regretted.

When the ideas to which I have alluded first occurred to me, it was of course very natural that I should think of M. Valdemar. I knew the steady philosophy of the man too well to apprehend any scruples from *him*; and he had no relatives in America who would be likely to interfere. I spoke to him frankly upon the subject; and, to my surprise, his interest seemed vividly excited. I say to my surprise; for, although he had always yielded his person freely to my experiments, he had never before given me any tokens of sympathy with what I did. His disease was of that character which would admit of exact calculation in respect to the epoch of its termination in death; and it was finally arranged between us that he would send for me about twenty-four hours before the period announced by his physicians as that of his decease.

It is now rather more than seven months since I received, from M. Valdemar himself, the subjoined note:

My Dear P—,

You may as well come now. D— and F— are agreed that I cannot hold out beyond tomorrow midnight; and I think they have hit the time very nearly.

VALDEMAR

I received this note within half an hour after it was written, and in fifteen minutes more I was in the dying man's chamber. I had not seen him for ten days, and was appalled by the fearful alteration which the brief interval had wrought in him. His face wore a leaden hue; the eyes were utterly lustreless; and the emaciation was so extreme that the skin had been broken through by the cheek-bones. His expectoration was excessive. The pulse was barely perceptible. He retained, nevertheless, in a very remarkable manner, both his mental power and a certain degree of physical strength. He spoke with distinctness—took some palliative medicines without aid—and, when I entered the room, was occupied in pencilling memoranda in a pocket-book. He was propped up in the bed by pillows. Doctors D— and F— were in attendance.

After pressing Valdemar's hand, I took these gentlemen aside, and obtained from them a minute account of the patient's condition. The left lung had been for eighteen months in a semi-osseous or cartilaginous state, and was, of course, entirely useless for all purposes of vitality. The right, in its upper portion, was also partially, if not thoroughly, ossified, while the lower region was merely a mass of purulent tubercles, running one into another. Several extensive perforations existed; and, at one point, permanent adhesion to the ribs had taken place. These appearances in the right lobe were of comparatively recent date. The ossification had proceeded with very unusual rapidity; no sign of it had been discovered a month before, and the adhesion had only been observed during the three previous days. Independently of the phthisis, the patient was suspected of aneurism of the aorta; but on this point the osseous symptoms rendered an exact diagnosis impossible. It was the opinion of both physicians that M. Valdemar would die about midnight on the morrow (Sunday). It was then seven o'clock on Saturday evening.

On quitting the invalid's bedside to hold conversation with myself, Doctors D— and F— had bidden him a final farewell. It had not been their intention to return; but, at my request, they agreed to look in upon the patient about ten the next night.

When they had gone, I spoke freely with M. Valdemar on the subject of his approaching dissolution, as well as, more particularly, of the experiment proposed. He still professed himself quite willing and even anxious to have it made, and urged me to commence it at once. A male and a female nurse were in attendance; but I did not feel myself altogether at liberty to engage in a task of this character with no more reliable witnesses than these people, in case of sudden accident, might prove. I therefore postponed operations until about eight the next night, when the arrival of a medical student with whom I had some acquaintance, (Mr. Theodore L—l), relieved me from further embarrassment. It had been my design, originally, to wait for the physicians; but I was induced to proceed, first by the urgent entreaties of M. Valdemar, and secondly, by my conviction that I had not a moment to lose, as he was evidently sinking fast.

Mr. L—l was so kind as to accede to my desire that he would take notes of all that occurred; and it is from his memoranda that what I now have to relate is, for the most part, either condensed or copied *verbatim*.

It wanted about five minutes of eight when, taking the patient's hand, I begged him to state, as distinctly as he could, to Mr. L—l, whether he (M. Valdemar) was entirely willing that I should make the experiment of mesmerizing him in his then condition.

He replied feebly, yet quite audibly, "Yes, I wish to be mesmerized"—adding immediately afterwards, "I fear you have deferred it too long."

While he spoke thus, I commenced the passes which I had already found most effectual in subduing him. He was evidently influenced with the first lateral stroke of my hand across his forehead; but although I exerted all my powers, no farther perceptible effect was induced until some minutes after ten o'clock, when Doctors D— and F— called, according to appointment. I explained to them, in a few words, what I designed, and as they opposed no objection, saying that the patient was already in the death agony, I proceeded without hesitation—exchanging, however, the lateral passes for downward ones, and directing my gaze entirely into the right eye of the sufferer.

By this time his pulse was imperceptible and his breathing was stertorous, and at intervals of half a minute.

This condition was nearly unaltered for a quarter of an hour. At the expiration of this period, however, a natural although a very deep sigh escaped the bosom of the dying man, and the stertorous breathing ceased—that is to say, its stertorousness was no longer apparent; the intervals were undiminished. The patient's extremities were of an icy coldness.

At five minutes before eleven I perceived unequivocal signs of the mesmeric influence. The glassy roll of the eye was changed for that expression of uneasy *inward* examination which is never seen except in cases of sleep-waking, and which it is quite impossible to mistake. With a few rapid lateral passes I made the lids quiver, as in incipient sleep, and with a few more I closed them altogether. I was not satisfied, however, with this, but continued the manipulation vigorously, and with the fullest exertion of the will, until I had completely stiffened the limbs of the slumberer, after placing them in a seemingly easy position. The legs were at full length; the arms were nearly so, and reposed on the bed at a moderate distance from the loins. The head was very slightly elevated.

When I had accomplished this, it was fully midnight, and I requested the gentlemen present to examine M. Valdemar's condition. After a few experiments, they admitted him to be in an unusually perfect state of mesmeric trance. The curiosity of both the physicians was greatly excited. Dr. D— resolved at once to remain with the patient all night, while Dr. F— took leave with a promise to return at daybreak. Mr. L—l and the nurse remained.

We left M. Valdemar entirely undisturbed until about three o'clock in the morning, when I approached him and found him in precisely the same condition as when Dr. F— went away—that is to say, he lay in the same position; the pulse was imperceptible; the breathing was gentle (scarcely noticeable, unless through the application of a mirror to the lips); the eyes were closed naturally; and the limbs were as rigid and as cold as marble. Still, the general appearance was certainly not that of death.

As I approached M. Valdemar I made a kind of half effort to influence his right arm into pursuit of my own, as I passed the latter gently to and fro above his person. In such experiments with this patient I had never perfectly succeeded before, and assuredly I had little thought of succeeding now; but to my astonishment, his arm very readily, although feebly, followed every direction I assigned it with mine. I determined to hazard a few words of conversation.

"M. Valdemar," I said, "are you asleep?" He made no answer, but I perceived a tremor about the lips, and was thus induced to repeat the question, again and again. At its third repetition, his whole frame was agitated by a very slight shivering; the eyelids unclosed themselves so far as to display a white line of the ball; the lips moved sluggishly, and from between them, in a barely audible whisper, issued the words:

"Yes; asleep now. Do not wake me—let me die so!"

I here felt the limbs and found them as rigid as ever. The right arm, as before, obeyed the direction of my hand. I questioned the sleep-waker again:

"Do you still feel pain in the breast, M. Valdemar?"

The answer now was immediate, but even less audible than before:

"No pain—I am dying."

I did not think it advisable to disturb him further just then, and nothing more was said or done until the arrival of Dr. F—, who came a little before sunrise, and expressed unbounded astonishment at finding the patient still alive. After feeling the pulse and applying a mirror to the lips, he requested me to speak to the sleep-waker again. I did so, saying:

"M. Valdemar, do you still sleep?"

As before, some minutes elapsed ere a reply was made; and during the interval the dying man seemed to be collecting his energies to speak. At my fourth repetition of the question, he said very faintly, almost inaudibly:

"Yes; still asleep—dying."

It was now the opinion, or rather the wish, of the physicians that M. Valdemar should be suffered to remain undisturbed in his present apparently tranquil condition, until death should supervene—and this, it was generally agreed, must now take place within a few minutes. I concluded, however, to speak to him once more, and merely repeated my previous question.

While I spoke, there came a marked change over the countenance of the sleep-waker. The eyes rolled themselves slowly open, the pupils disappearing upwardly; the skin generally assumed a cadaverous hue, resembling not so much parchment as white paper; and the circular hectic spots which, hitherto, had been strongly defined in the centre of each cheek, *went out* at once. I use this expression, because the suddenness of their departure put me in mind of nothing so much as the extinguishment of a candle by a puff of the breath. The upper lip, at the same time, writhed itself away from the teeth, which it had previously covered completely; while the lower jaw fell with an audible jerk, leaving the mouth widely extended, and disclosing in full view the swollen and blackened tongue. I presume that no member of the party then present had been unaccustomed to death-bed horrors; but so hideous beyond conception was the appearance of M. Valdemar at this moment that there was a general shrinking back from the region of the bed.

I now feel that I have reached a point of this narrative at which every reader will be startled into positive disbelief. It is my business, however, simply to proceed.

There was no longer the faintest sign of vitality in M. Valdemar; and concluding him to be dead, we were consigning him to the charge of the nurses, when a strong vibratory motion was observable in the tongue. This continued for perhaps a minute. At the expiration of this period, there issued from the distended and motionless jaws a voice—such as it would be madness in me to attempt describing. There are, indeed, two or three epithets which might be considered as applicable to it in parts; I might say, for example, that the sound was harsh, and broken, and hollow; but the hideous whole is indescribable, for the simple reason that no similar sounds have ever jarred upon the ear of humanity. There were two particulars, nevertheless, which I thought then, and still think, might fairly be stated as characteristic of the intonation—as well adapted to convey some idea of its unearthly peculiarity. In the first place, the voice seemed to reach our ears—at least mine—from a vast distance, or from some deep cavern within the earth. In the second place, it impressed me (I fear, indeed, that it will be impossible to make myself comprehended) as gelatinous or glutinous matters impress the sense of touch.

I have spoken both of "sound" and of "voice." I mean to say that the sound was one of distinct—of even wonderfully, thrillingly distinct—syllabification. M. Valdemar *spoke*—obviously in reply to the question I had propounded to him a few minutes before. I had asked him, it will be remembered, if he still slept. He now said:

"Yes; no; I *have been* sleeping—and now—now—*I am dead.*"

No person present even affected to deny, or attempted to repress, the unutterable, shuddering horror which these few words, thus uttered, were so well calculated to convey. Mr. L—l (the student) swooned. The nurses immediately left the chamber, and could not be induced to return. My own impressions I would not pretend to render intelligible to the reader. For nearly an hour, we busied ourselves, silently—without the utterance of a word—in endeavours to revive Mr. L—l. When he came to himself, we addressed ourselves again to an investigation of M. Valdemar's condition.

It remained in all respects as I have last described it, with the exception that the mirror no longer afforded evidence of respiration. An attempt to draw blood from the arm failed. I should mention, too, that this limb was no further subject to my will. I endeavored in vain to make it follow the direction of my hand. The only real indication, indeed, of the mesmeric influence was now found in the vibratory movement of the tongue whenever I addressed M. Valdemar a question. He seemed to be making an effort to reply, but had no longer sufficient volition. To queries put to him by any other person than myself he seemed utterly insensible—although I endeavored to place each member of the company in mesmeric *rapport* with him. I believe that I have now related all that is necessary to an understanding of the sleep-waker's state at this epoch. Other nurses were procured; and at ten o'clock I left the house in company with the two physicians and Mr. L—l.

In the afternoon we all called again to see the patient. His condition remained precisely the same. We had now some discussion as the propriety and feasibility of awakening him; but we had little difficulty in agreeing that no good purpose would be served by so doing. It was evident that, so far, death (or what is usually termed death) had been arrested by the mesmeric process. It seemed clear to us all that to awaken M. Valdemar would be merely to insure his instant, or at least his speedy dissolution.

From this period until the close of last week—*an interval of nearly seven months*—we continued to make daily calls at M. Valdemar's house, accompanied now and then by medical and other friends. All this time the sleep-waker remained *exactly* as I have last described him. The nurses' attentions were continual.

It was on Friday last that we finally resolved to make the experiment of awakening, or attempting to awaken him; and it is the (perhaps) unfortunate result of this latter experiment which has given rise to so much discussion in private circles—to so much of what I cannot help thinking unwarranted popular feeling.

For the purpose of relieving M. Valdemar from the mesmeric trance, I made use of the customary passes. These, for a time, were unsuccessful. The first indication of revival was afforded by a partial descent of the iris. It was observed, as especially remarkable, that this lowering of the pupil was accompanied by the profuse outflowing of a yellowish ichor (from beneath the lids) of a pungent and highly offensive odor.

It was now suggested that I should attempt to influence the patient's arm, as heretofore. I made the attempt and failed. Dr. F— then intimated a desire to have me put a question. I did so, as follows:

"M. Valdemar, can you explain to us what are your feelings or wishes now?"

There was an instant return of the hectic circles on the cheeks; the tongue quivered, or rather rolled violently in the mouth (although the jaws and lips remained rigid as before); and at length the same hideous voice which I have already described broke forth:

"For God's sake!—quick!—quick!—put me to sleep—or, quick!—waken me!—quick! *I say to you that I am dead!*"

I was thoroughly unnerved, and for an instant remained undecided what to do. At first I made an endeavor to re-compose the patient; but, failing in this through total abeyance of the will, I retraced my steps and as earnestly struggled to awaken him. In this attempt I soon saw that I should be successful—or at least I soon fancied that my success would be complete—and I am sure that all in the room were prepared to see the patient awaken.

For what really occurred, however, it is quite impossible that any human being could have been prepared.

As I rapidly made the mesmeric passes, amid ejaculations of "dead! dead!" absolutely *bursting* from the tongue and not from the lips of the sufferer, his whole frame at once—within the space of a single minute, or even less, shrunk—crumbled—absolutely *rotted* away beneath my hands. Upon the bed, before that whole company, there lay a nearly liquid mass of loathsome—of detestable putridity.

The Lottery

Shirley Jackson

THE MORNING of June 27th was clear and sunny, with the fresh warmth of a full-summer day; the flowers were blossoming profusely and the grass was richly green. The people of the village began to gather in the square, between the post office and the bank, around ten o'clock; in some towns there were so many people that the lottery took two days and had to be started on June 26th, but in this village, where there were only about three hundred people, the whole lottery took less than two hours, so it could begin at ten o'clock in the morning and still be through in time to allow the villagers to get home for noon dinner.

The children assembled first, of course. School was recently over for the summer, and the feeling of liberty sat uneasily on most of them; they tended to gather together quietly for a while before they broke into boisterous play, and their talk was still of the classroom and the teacher, of books and reprimands. Bobby Martin had already stuffed his pockets full of stones, and the other boys soon followed his example, selecting the smoothest and roundest stones: Bobby and Harry Jones and Dickie Delacroix—the villagers pronounced this name "Dellacroy"—eventually made a great pile of stones in one corner of the square and guarded it against the raids of the other boys. The girls stood aside, talking among themselves, looking over their shoulders at the boys, and the very small children rolled in the dust or clung to the hands of their older brothers or sisters.

Soon the men began to gather, surveying their own children, speaking of planting and rain, tractors and taxes. They stood together, away from the pile of stones in the corner, and their jokes were quiet and they smiled rather than laughed. The women, wearing faded house dresses and sweaters, came shortly after their menfolk. They greeted one another and exchanged bits of gossip as they went to join their husbands. Soon the women, standing by their husbands, began to call to their children, and the children came reluctantly, having to be called four or five times. Bobby Martin ducked under his mother's grasping hand and ran, laughing, back to the pile of stones. His father spoke up sharply, and Bobby came quickly and took his place between his father and his oldest brother.

The lottery was conducted—as were the square dances, the teen club, the Halloween program—by Mr. Summers, who had time and energy to devote to civic activities. He was a round-faced, jovial man and he ran the coal business, and people were sorry for him, because he had no children and his wife was a scold. When he arrived in the square, carrying the black wooden box, there was a murmur of conversation among the villagers, and he waved and called, "Little late today, folks." The postmaster, Mr. Graves, followed him, carrying a three-legged stool, and the stool was put in the center of the square and Mr. Summers set the black box down on it. The villagers kept their distance, leaving a space between themselves and the stool, and when Mr. Summers said, "Some of you fellows want to give me a hand?" there was a hesitation before two men, Mr. Martin and his oldest son, Baxter, came forward to hold the box steady on the stool while Mr. Summers stirred up the papers inside it.

The original paraphernalia for the lottery had been lost long ago, and the black box now resting on the stool had been put into use even before Old Man Warner, the oldest man in town, was born. Mr. Summers spoke frequently to the villagers about making a new box, but no one liked to upset even as much tradition as was represented by the black box. There was a story that the present box had been made with some pieces of the box that had preceded it, the one that had been constructed when the first people settled down to make a village here. Every year, after the lottery, Mr. Summers began talking again about a new box, but every year the subject was allowed to fade off without anything's being done. The black box grew shabbier each year: by now it was no longer completely black but splintered badly along one side to show the original wood color, and in some places faded or stained.

Mr. Martin and his oldest son, Baxter, held the black box securely on the stool until Mr. Summers had stirred the papers thoroughly with his hand. Because so much of the ritual had been forgotten or discarded, Mr. Summers had been successful in having slips of paper substituted for the chips of wood that had been used for generations. Chips of wood, Mr. Summers had argued, had been all very well when the village was tiny, but now that the population was more than three hundred and likely to keep on growing, it was necessary to use something that would fit more easily into the black box. The night before the lottery, Mr. Summers and Mr. Graves made up the slips of paper and put them in the box, and it was then taken to the safe of Mr. Summers' coal company and locked up until Mr. Summers was ready to take it to the square next morning. The rest of the year, the box was put away, sometimes one place, sometimes another; it had spent one year in Mr. Graves's barn and another year underfoot in the post office, and sometimes it was set on a shelf in the Martin grocery and left there.

There was a great deal of fussing to be done before Mr. Summers declared the lottery open. There were the lists to make up—of heads of families, heads of households in each family, members of each household in each family. There was the proper swearing-in of Mr. Summers by the postmaster, as the official of the lottery; at one time, some people remembered, there had been a recital of some sort, performed by the official of the lottery, a perfunctory, tuneless chant that had been rattled off duly each year; some people believed that the official of the lottery used to stand just so when he said or sang it, others believed that he was supposed to walk among the people, but years and years ago this part of the ritual had been allowed to lapse. There had been, also, a ritual salute, which the official of the lottery had had to use in addressing each person who came up to draw from the box, but this also had changed with time, until now it was felt necessary only for the official to speak to each person approaching. Mr. Summers was very good at all this; in his clean white shirt and blue jeans, with one hand resting carelessly on the black box, he seemed very proper and important as he talked interminably to Mr. Graves and the Martins.

Just as Mr. Summers finally left off talking and turned to the assembled villagers, Mrs. Hutchinson came hurriedly along the path to the square, her sweater thrown over her shoulders, and slid into place in the back of the crowd. "Clean forgot what day it was," she said to Mrs. Delacroix, who stood next to her, and they both laughed softly. "Thought my old man was out back stacking wood," Mrs. Hutchinson went on. "And then I looked out the window and the kids was gone, and then I remembered it was twenty-seventh and came a-running." She dried her hands on her apron, and Mrs. Delacroix said, "You're in time, though. They're still talking away up there."

Mrs. Hutchinson craned her neck to see through the crowd and found her husband and children standing near the front. She tapped Mrs. Delacroix on the arm as a farewell and began to make her way through the crowd. The people separated good-humoredly to let her through: two or three people said, in voices just loud enough to be heard across the crowd, "Here comes your Missus, Hutchinson," and "Bill, she made it after all." Mrs. Hutchinson reached her husband, and Mr. Summers, who had been waiting, said cheerfully, "Thought we were going to have to get on without you, Tessie." Mrs. Hutchinson said, grinning, "Wouldn't have me leave m'dishes in the sink, now, would you, Joe?," and soft laughter ran through the crowd as the people stirred back into position after Mrs. Hutchinson's arrival.

"Well, now," Mr. Summers said soberly, "guess we better get started, get this over with, so's we can go back to work. Anybody ain't here?"

"Dunbar," several people said. "Dunbar. Dunbar."

Mr. Summers consulted his list. "Clyde Dunbar," he said. "That's right. He's broke his leg, hasn't he? Who's drawing for him?"

"Me, I guess," a woman said, and Mr. Summers turned to look at her. "Wife draws for her husband," Mr. Summers said. "Don't you have a grown boy to do it for you, Janey?" Although Mr. Summers and everyone else in the village knew the answer perfectly well, it was the business of the official of the lottery to ask such questions formally. Mr. Summers waited with an expression of polite interest while Mrs. Dunbar answered.

"Horace's not but sixteen yet," Mrs. Dunbar said regretfully. "Guess I gotta fill in for the old man this year."

"Right," Mr. Summers said. He made a note on the list he was holding. Then he asked, "Watson's boy drawing this year?"

A tall boy in the crowd raised his hand. "Here," he said. "I'm drawing for my mother and me." He blinked his eyes nervously and ducked his head as several voices in the crowd said things like "Good fellow, Jack," and "Glad to see your mother's got a man to do it."

"Well," Mr. Summers said, "guess that's everyone. Old Man Warner make it?"

"Here," a voice said, and Mr. Summers nodded.

A sudden hush fell on the crowd as Mr. Summers cleared his throat and looked at the list. "All ready?" he called. "Now, I'll read the names—heads of families first—and the men come up and take a paper out of the box. Keep the paper folded in your hand without looking at it until everyone has had a turn. Everything clear?"

The people had done it so many times that they only half listened to the directions: most of them were quiet, wetting their lips, not looking around. Then Mr. Summers raised one hand high and said, "Adams." A man disengaged himself from the crowd and came forward. "Hi, Steve," Mr. Summers said, and Mr. Adams said, "Hi, Joe." They grinned at one another humorlessly and nervously. Then Mr. Adams reached into the black box and took out a folded paper. He held it firmly by one corner as he turned and went hastily back to his place in the crowd, where he stood a little apart from his family, not looking down at his hand.

"Allen," Mr. Summers said. "Anderson . . . Bentham."

"Seems like there's no time at all between lotteries anymore," Mrs. Delacroix said to Mrs. Graves in the back row.

"Seems like we got through with the last one only last week."

"Time sure goes fast," Mrs. Graves said.

"Clark . . . Delacroix."

"There goes my old man," Mrs. Delacroix said. She held her breath while her husband went forward.

"Dunbar," Mr. Summers said, and Mrs. Dunbar went steadily to the box while one of the women said, "Go on, Janey," and another said, "There she goes."

"We're next," Mrs. Graves said. She watched while Mr. Graves came around from the side of the box, greeted Mr. Summers gravely, and selected a slip of paper from the box. By now, all through the crowd there were men holding the small folded papers in their large hands, turning them over and over nervously. Mrs. Dunbar and her two sons stood together, Mrs. Dunbar holding the slip of paper.

"Harburt . . . Hutchinson."

"Get up there, Bill," Mrs. Hutchinson said, and the people near her laughed.

"Jones."

"They do say," Mr. Adams said to Old Man Warner, who stood next to him, "that over in the north village they're talking of giving up the lottery."

Old Man Warner snorted. "Pack of crazy fools," he said. "Listening to the young folks, nothing's good enough for them. Next thing you know, they'll be wanting to go back to living in caves, nobody work anymore, live that way for a while. Used to be a saying about 'Lottery in June, corn be heavy soon.' First thing you know, we'd all be eating stewed chickweed and acorns. There's always been a lottery," he added petulantly. "Bad enough to see young Joe Summers up there joking with everybody."

"Some places have already quit lotteries," Mrs. Adams said.

"Nothing but trouble in that," Old Man Warner said stoutly. "Pack of young fools."

"Martin." And Bobby Martin watched his father go forward. "Overdyke . . . Percy."

"I wish they'd hurry," Mrs. Dunbar said to her older son. "I wish they'd hurry."

"They're almost through," her son said.

"You get ready to run tell Dad," Mrs. Dunbar said.

Mr. Summers called his own name and then stepped forward precisely and selected a slip from the box. Then he called, "Warner."

"Seventy-seventh year I been in the lottery," Old Man Warner said as he went through the crowd. "Seventy-seventh time."

"Watson." The tall boy came awkwardly through the crowd. Someone said, "Don't be nervous, Jack," and Mr. Summers said, "Take your time, son."

"Zanini."

After that, there was a long pause, a breathless pause, until Mr. Summers, holding his slip of paper in the air, said, "All right, fellows." For a minute, no one moved, and then all the slips of paper were opened. Suddenly, all the women began to speak at once, saying, "Who is it?" "Who's got it?" "Is it the Dunbars?" "Is it the Watsons?" Then the voices began to say, "It's Hutchinson. It's Bill." "Bill Hutchinson's got it."

"Go tell your father," Mrs. Dunbar said to her older son.

People began to look around to see the Hutchinsons. Bill Hutchinson was standing quiet, staring down at the paper in his hand. Suddenly, Tessie Hutchinson shouted to Mr. Summers, "You didn't give him time enough to take any paper he wanted. I saw you. It wasn't fair!"

"Be a good sport, Tessie," Mrs. Delacroix called, and Mrs. Graves said, "All of us took the same chance."

"Shut up, Tessie," Bill Hutchinson said.

"Well, everyone," Mr. Summers said, "that was done pretty fast, and now we've got to be hurrying a little more to get done in time." He consulted his next list. "Bill," he said, "you draw for the Hutchinson family. You got any other households in the Hutchinsons?"

"There's Don and Eva," Mrs. Hutchinson yelled. "Make them take their chance!"

"Daughters draw with their husbands' families, Tessie," Mr. Summers said gently. "You know that as well as anyone else."

"It wasn't fair," Tessie said.

"I guess not, Joe," Bill Hutchinson said regretfully. "My daughter draws with her husband's family; that's only fair. And I've got no other family except the kids."

"Then, as far as drawing for families is concerned, it's you," Mr. Summers said in explanation, "and as far as drawing for households is concerned, that's you, too. Right?"

"Right," Bill Hutchinson said.

"How many kids, Bill?" Mr. Summers asked formally.

"Three," Bill Hutchinson said.

"There's Bill Jr., and Nancy, and little Dave. And Tessie and me."

"All right, then," Mr. Summers said. "Harry, you got their tickets back?"

Mr. Graves nodded and held up the slips of paper. "Put them in the box, then," Mr. Summers directed. "Take Bill's and put it in."

"I think we ought to start over," Mrs. Hutchinson said, as quietly as she could. "I tell you it wasn't fair. You didn't give him time enough to choose. Everybody saw that."

Mr. Graves had selected the five slips and put them in the box, and he dropped all the papers but those onto the ground, where the breeze caught them and lifted them off.

"Listen, everybody," Mrs. Hutchinson was saying to the people around her.

"Ready, Bill?" Mr. Summers asked, and Bill Hutchinson, with one quick glance around at his wife and children, nodded.

"Remember," Mr. Summers said, "take the slips and keep them folded until each person has taken one. Harry, you help little Dave." Mr. Graves took the hand of the little boy, who came willingly with him up to the box. "Take a paper out of the box, Davy," Mr. Summers said. Davy put his hand into the box and laughed. "Take just one paper," Mr. Summers said. "Harry, you hold it for him." Mr. Graves took the child's hand and removed the folded paper from the tight fist and held it while little Dave stood next to him and looked up at him wonderingly.

"Nancy next," Mr. Summers said. Nancy was twelve, and her school friends breathed heavily as she went forward switching her skirt, and took a slip daintily from the box. "Bill Jr.," Mr. Summers said, and Billy, his face red and his feet overlarge, near knocked the box over as he got a paper out. "Tessie," Mr. Summers said. She hesitated for a minute, looking around defiantly, and then set her lips and went up to the box. She snatched a paper out and held it behind her.

"Bill," Mr. Summers said, and Bill Hutchinson reached into the box and felt around, bringing his hand out at last with the slip of paper in it.

The crowd was quiet. A girl whispered, "I hope it's not Nancy," and the sound of the whisper reached the edges of the crowd.

"It's not the way it used to be," Old Man Warner said clearly. "People ain't the way they used to be."

"All right," Mr. Summers said. "Open the papers. Harry, you open little Dave's."

Mr. Graves opened the slip of paper and there was a general sigh through the crowd as he held it up and everyone could see that it was blank. Nancy and Bill Jr. opened theirs at the same time, and both beamed and laughed, turning around to the crowd and holding their slips of paper above their heads.

"Tessie," Mr. Summers said. There was a pause, and then Mr. Summers looked at Bill Hutchinson, and Bill unfolded his paper and showed it. It was blank.

"It's Tessie," Mr. Summers said, and his voice was hushed. "Show us her paper, Bill."

Bill Hutchinson went over to his wife and forced the slip of paper out of her hand. It had a black spot on it, the black spot Mr. Summers had made the night before with the heavy pencil in the coal company office. Bill Hutchinson held it up, and there was a stir in the crowd.

"All right, folks," Mr. Summers said. "Let's finish quickly."

Although the villagers had forgotten the ritual and lost the original black box, they still remembered to use stones. The pile of stones the boys had made earlier was ready; there were stones on the ground with the blowing scraps of paper that had come out of the box. Delacroix selected a stone so large she had to pick it up with both hands and turned to Mrs. Dunbar. "Come on," she said. "Hurry up."

Mrs. Dunbar had small stones in both hands, and she said, gasping for breath, "I can't run at all. You'll have to go ahead and I'll catch up with you."

The children had stones already. And someone gave little Davy Hutchinson a few pebbles.

Tessie Hutchinson was in the center of a cleared space by now, and she held her hands out desperately as the villagers moved in on her. "It isn't fair," she said. A stone hit her on the side of the head. Old Man Warner was saying, "Come on, come on, everyone." Steve Adams was in the front of the crowd of villagers, with Mrs. Graves beside him.

"It isn't fair, it isn't right," Mrs. Hutchinson screamed, and then they were upon her.

The Beast with Five Fingers

W. F. Harvey

THE STORY, I suppose, begins with Adrian Borlsover, whom I met when I was a little boy and he an old man. My father had called to appeal for a subscription, and I was with him. Before we left, Mr. Borlsover laid his right hand in blessing on my head. I shall never forget the awe in which I gazed up at his face and realised for the first time that eyes might be dark and beautiful and shining, and yet not able to see.

For Adrian Borlsover was blind.

He was an extraordinary man, who came of an eccentric stock. Borlsover sons for some reason always seemed to marry very ordinary women; which perhaps accounted for the fact that no Borlsover had been a genius, and only one Borlsover had been mad. But they were great champions of little causes, generous patrons of odd sciences, founders of querulous sects, trustworthy guides to the bypath meadows of erudition.

Adrian was an authority on the fertilisation of orchids. He had held at one time the family living at Borlsover Conyers, until a congenital weakness of the lungs obliged him to seek a less rigorous climate in the sunny southcoast watering-place where I had seen him. Occasionally he would relieve one or other of the local clergy. My father described him as a fine preacher, who gave long and inspiring sermons from what many men would have considered unprofitable texts. "An excellent proof," he would add, "of the truth of the doctrine of direct verbal inspiration."

Adrian Borlsover was exceedingly clever with his hands. His penmanship was exquisite. He illustrated all his scientific papers, made his own woodcuts, and carved the reredos that is at present the chief feature of interest in the church at Borlsover Conyers. He had an exceedingly clever knack in cutting silhouettes for young ladies and paper pigs and cows for little children, and made more than one complicated wind-instrument of his own devising.

When he was fifty years old Adrian Borlsover lost his sight. In a wonderfully short time he adapted himself to the new conditions of life. He quickly learnt to read Braille. So marvellous indeed was his sense of touch that he was still able to maintain his interest in botany. The mere passing of his long supple fingers over a flower was sufficient means for its identification, though occasionally he would use his lips. I have found several letters of his among my father's correspondence; in no case was there anything to show that he was afflicted with blindness and this in spite of the fact that he exercised undue economy in the spacing of lines. Towards the close of his life Adrian Borlsover was credited with powers of touch that seemed almost uncanny. It has been said that he could tell at once the colour of a ribbon placed between his fingers. My father would neither confirm nor deny the story.

Adrian Borlsover was a bachelor. His elder brother, Charles, had married late in life, leaving one son, Eustace, who lived in the gloomy Georgian mansion at Borlsover Conyers, where he could work undisturbed in collecting material for his great book on heredity.

Like his uncle, he was a remarkable man. The Borlsovers had always been born naturalists, but Eustace possessed in a special degree the power of systematising his knowledge. He had received his university education in Germany; and then, after post-graduate work in Vienna and Naples, had travelled for four years in South America and the East, getting together a huge store of material for a new study into the processes of variation.

He lived alone at Borlsover Conyers with Saunders, his secretary, a man who bore a somewhat dubious reputation in the district, but whose powers as a mathematician, combined with his business abilities, were invaluable to Eustace.

Uncle and nephew saw little of each other. The visits of Eustace were confined to a week in the summer or autumn—tedious weeks, that dragged almost as slowly as the bath-chair in which the old man was drawn along the sunny seafront. In their way the two men were fond of each other, though their intimacy would, doubtless, have been greater, had they shared the same religious views. Adrian held to the old-fashioned evangelical dogmas of his early manhood; his nephew for many years had been thinking of embracing Buddhism. Both men possessed, too, the reticence the Borlsovers had always shown, and which their enemies sometimes called hypocrisy. With Adrian it was a reticence as to the things he had left undone; but with Eustace it seemed that the curtain which he was so careful to leave undrawn hid something more than a half-empty chamber.

Two years before his death, Adrian Borlsover developed, unknown to himself, the not uncommon power of automatic writing. Eustace made the discovery by accident. Adrian was sitting reading in bed, the forefinger of his left hand tracing the Braille characters, when his nephew noticed that a pencil the old man held in his right hand was moving slowly along the opposite page. He had left his seat in the window and sat down beside the bed. The right hand continued to move, and now he could see plainly that they were letters and words which it was forming.

"Adrian Borlsover," wrote the hand, "Eustace Borlsover, Charles Borlsover, Francis Borlsover, Sigismund Borlsover, Adrian Borlsover, Eustace Borlsover, Saville Borlsover. B for Borlsover. Honesty is the Best Policy. Beautiful Belinda Borlsover."

"What curious nonsense!" said Eustace to himself.

"King George ascended the throne in 1760," wrote the hand. "Crowd, a noun of multitude; a collection of individuals. Adrian Borlsover, Eustace Borlsover."

"It seems to me," said his uncle, closing the book, "that you had much better make the most of the afternoon sunshine and take your walk now."

"I think perhaps I will," Eustace answered as he picked up the volume. "I won't go far, and when I come back I can read to you those articles in *Nature* about which we were speaking."

He went along the promenade, but stopped at the first shelter, and, seating himself in the corner best protected from the wind, he examined the book at leisure. Nearly every page was scored with a meaningless jumble of pencil-marks; rows of capital letters, short words, long words, complete sentences, copy-book tags. The whole thing, in fact, had the appearance of a copy-book, and, on a more careful scrutiny, Eustace thought that there was ample evidence to show that the handwriting at the beginning of the book, good though it was, was not nearly so good as the handwriting at the end.

He left his uncle at the end of October with a promise to return early in December. It seemed to him quite clear that the old man's power of automatic writing was developing rapidly, and for the first time he looked forward to a visit that would combine duty with interest.

But on his return he was at first disappointed. His uncle, he thought, looked older. He was listless, too, preferring others to read to him and dictating nearly all his letters. Not until the day before he left had Eustace an opportunity of observing Adrian Borlsover's new-found faculty.

The old man, propped up in bed with pillows, had sunk into a light sleep. His two hands lay on the coverlet, his left hand tightly clasping his right. Eustace took an empty manuscript book and placed a pencil within reach of the fingers of the right hand. They snatched at it eagerly, then dropped the pencil to loose the left hand from its restraining grasp.

"Perhaps to prevent interference I had better hold that hand," said Eustace to himself, as he watched the pencil. Almost immediately it began to write.

"Blundering Borlsovers, unnecessarily unnatural, extraordinarily eccentric, culpably curious."

"Who are you?" asked Eustace in a low voice.

"Never you mind," wrote the hand of Adrian.

"Is it my uncle who is writing?"

"O my prophetic soul, mine uncle!"

"Is it anyone I know?"

"Silly Eustace, you'll see me very soon."

"When shall I see you?"

"When poor old Adrian's dead."

"Where shall I see you?"

"Where shall you not?"

Instead of speaking his next question, Eustace wrote it. "What is the time?"

The fingers dropped the pencil and moved three or four times across the paper. Then, picking up the pencil, they wrote: "Ten minutes before four. Put your book away, Eustace. Adrian mustn't find us working at this sort of thing. He doesn't know what to make of it, and I won't have poor old Adrian disturbed. Au revoir!"

Adrian Borlsover awoke with a start.

"I've been dreaming again," he said; "such queer dreams of leaguered cities and forgotten towns. You were mixed up in this one, Eustace, though I can't remember how. Eustace, I want to warn you. Don't walk in doubtful paths. Choose your friends well. Your poor grandfather . . ."

A fit of coughing put an end to what he was saying, but Eustace saw that the hand was still writing. He managed unnoticed to draw the book away. "I'll light the gas," he said, "and ring for tea." On the other side of the bedcurtain he saw the last sentence that had been written.

"It's too late, Adrian," it said. "We're friends already, aren't we, Eustace Borlsover?"

On the following day Eustace left. He thought his uncle looked ill when he said goodbye, and the old man spoke despondently of the failure his life had been.

"Nonsense, uncle," said his nephew. "You have got over your difficulties in a way not one in a hundred thousand would have done. Everyone marvels at your splendid perseverance in teaching your hand to take the place of your lost sight. To me it's been a revelation of the possibilities of education."

"Education," said his uncle dreamily, as if the word had started a new train of thought. "Education is good so long as you know to whom and for what purpose you give it. But with the lower orders of men, the base and more sordid spirits, I have grave doubts as to its results. Well, goodbye, Eustace; I may not see you again. You are a true Borlsover, with all the Borlsover faults. Marry, Eustace. Marry some good, sensible girl. And if by any chance I don't see you again, my will is at my solicitors. I've not left you any legacy, because I know you're well provided for; but I thought you might like to have my books. Oh, and there's just another thing. You know, before the end, people often lose control over themselves and make absurd requests. Don't pay any attention to them, Eustace. Goodbye!" and he held out his hand. Eustace took it. It remained in his a fraction of a second longer than he had expected and gripped him with a virility that was surprising. There was, too, in its touch a subtle sense of intimacy.

"Why, uncle," he said, "I shall see you alive and well for many long years to come."

Two months later Adrian Borlsover died.

Eustace Borlsover was in Naples at the time. He read the obituary notice in the *Morning Post* on the day announced for the funeral.

"Poor old fellow!" he said. "I wonder whether I shall find room for all his books."

The question occurred to him again with greater force when, three days later, he found himself standing in the library at Borlsover Conyers, a huge room built for use and not for beauty in the year of Waterloo by a Borlsover who was an ardent admirer of the great Napoleon. It was arranged on the plan of many college libraries, with tall projecting bookcases forming deep recesses of dusty silence, fit graves for the old hates of forgotten controversy, the dead passions of forgotten lives. At the end of the room, behind the bust of some unknown eighteenth-century divine, an ugly iron corkscrew stair led to a shelf-lined gallery. Nearly every shelf was full.

"I must talk to Saunders about it," said Eustace. "I suppose that we shall have to have the billiard-room fitted up with bookcases."

The two men met for the first time after many weeks in the dining-room that evening.

"Hallo!" said Eustace, standing before the fire with his hands in his pockets. "How goes the world, Saunders? Why these dress togs?" He himself was wearing an old shooting-jacket. He did not believe in mourning, as he had told his uncle on his last visit; and, though he usually went in for quiet-coloured ties, he wore this evening one of an ugly red, in order to shock Morton the butler, and to make them thrash out the whole question of mourning for themselves in the servants' hall. Eustace was a true Borlsover. "The world," said Saunders, "goes the same as usual, confoundedly slow. The dress togs are accounted for by an invitation from Captain Lockwood to bridge."

"How are you getting there?"

"There's something the matter with the car, so I've told Jackson to drive me round in the dogcart. Any objection?"

"Oh dear me, no! We've had all things in common for far too many years for me to raise objections at this hour of the day."

You'll find your correspondence in the library," went on Saunders. "Most of it I've seen to. There are a few private letters I haven't opened. There's also a box with a rat or something inside it that came by the evening post. Very likely it's the six-toed beast Terry was sending us to cross with the four-toed albino. I didn't look because I didn't want to mess up my things; but I should gather from the way it's jumping about that it's pretty hungry."

"Oh, I'll see to it," said Eustace, "while you and the captain earn an honest penny."

Dinner over and Saunders gone, Eustace went into the library. Though the fire had been lit, the room was by no means cheerful.

"We'll have all the lights on, at any rate," he said, as he turned the switches. "And, Morton," he added, when the butler brought the coffee, "get me a screwdriver or something to undo this box. Whatever the animal is, he's kicking up the deuce of a row. What is it? Why are you dawdling?"

"If you please, sir, when the postman brought it, he told me that they'd bored the holes in the lid at the post office. There were no breathing holes in the lid, sir, and they didn't want the animal to die. That is all, sir."

"It's culpably careless of the man, whoever he was," said Eustace, as he removed the screws, "packing an animal like this in a wooden box with no means of getting air. Confound it all! I meant to ask Morton to bring me a cage to put it in. Now I suppose I shall have to get one myself."

He placed a heavy book on the lid from which the screws had been removed, and went into the billiard-room. As he came back into the library with an empty cage in his hand, he heard the sound of something falling, and then of something scuttling along the floor.

"Bother it! The beast's got out. How in the world am I to find it again in this library?"

To search for it did indeed seem hopeless. He tried to follow the sound of the scuttling in one of the recesses, where the animal seemed to be running behind the books in the shelves; but it was impossible to locate it. Eustace resolved to go on quietly reading. Very likely the animal might gain confidence and show itself. Saunders seemed to have dealt in his usual methodical manner with most of the correspondence. There were still the private letters.

What was that? Two sharp clicks and the lights in the hideous candelabras that hung from the ceiling suddenly went out.

"I wonder if something has gone wrong with the fuse," said Eustace, as he went to the switches by the door. Then he stopped. There was a noise at the other end of the room, as if something was crawling up the iron corkscrew stair. "If it's gone into the gallery," he said, "well and good." He hastily turned on the lights, crossed the room, and climbed up the stair. But he could see nothing. His grandfather had placed a little gate at the top of the stair, so that children could run and romp in the gallery without fear of accident. This Eustace closed, and, having considerably narrowed the circle of his search, returned to his desk by the fire.

How gloomy the library was! There was no sense of intimacy about the room. The few busts that an eighteenth-century Borlsover had brought back from the Grand Tour might have been in keeping in the old library. Here they seemed out of place. They made the room feel cold in spite of the heavy red damask curtains and great gilt cornices.

With a crash two heavy books fell from the gallery to the floor; then, as Borlsover looked, another and yet another.

"Very well. You'll starve for this, my beauty!" he said. "We'll do some little experiments on the metabolism of rats deprived of water. Go on! Chuck them down! I think I've got the upper hand!" He turned once more to his correspondence. One letter was from the family solicitor. It spoke of his uncle's death, and of the valuable collection of books that had been left to him in the will.

> There was one request [he read] which certainly came as a surprise to me. As you know, Mr. Adrian Borlsover had left instructions that his body was to be buried in as simple a manner as possible at Eastbourne. He expressed a desire that there should be neither wreaths nor flowers of any kind, and hoped that his friends and relatives would not consider it necessary to wear mourning. The day before his death we received a letter cancelling these instructions. He wished the body to be embalmed (he gave us the address of the man we were to employ—

Pennifer, Ludgate Hill), with orders that his right hand should be sent to you, stating that it was at your special request. The other arrangements about the funeral remained unaltered.

"Good Lord," said Eustace, "what in the world was the old boy driving at? And what in the name of all that's holy is that?"

Someone was in the gallery. Someone had pulled the cord attached to one of the blinds, and it had rolled up with a snap. Someone must be in the gallery, for a second blind did the same. Someone must be walking round the gallery, for one after the other the blinds sprang up, letting in the moonlight.

"I haven't got to the bottom of this yet," said Eustace, "but I will do, before the night is very much older," and he hurried up the corkscrew stair. He had just got to the top, when the lights went out a second time, and he heard again the scuttling along the floor. Quickly he stole on tiptoe in the dim moonshine in the direction of the noise, feeling, as he went, for one of the switches. His fingers touched the metal knob at last. He turned on the electric light.

About ten yards in front of him, crawling along the floor, was a man's hand. Eustace stared at it in utter amazement. It was moving quickly in the manner of a geometer caterpillar, the fingers humped up one moment, flattened out the next; the thumb appeared to give a crablike motion to the whole. While he was looking, too surprised to stir, the hand disappeared round the corner.

Eustace ran forward. He no longer saw it, but he could hear it as it squeezed its way behind the books on one of the shelves. A heavy volume had been displaced. There was a gap in the row of books, where it had got in. In his fear lest it should escape him again, he seized the first book that came to his hand and plugged it into the hole. Then, emptying two shelves of their contents, he took the wooden boards and propped them up in front to make his barrier doubly sure.

"I wish Saunders was back," he said; "one can't tackle this sort of thing alone." It was after eleven, and there seemed little likelihood of Saunders returning before twelve. He did not dare to leave the shelf unwatched even to run downstairs to ring the bell. Morton, the butler, often used to come round about eleven to see that the windows were fastened, but he might not come tonight. Eustace was thoroughly unstrung. At last he heard steps down below.

"Morton!" he shouted. "Morton!"

"Sir?"

"Has Mr. Saunders got back yet?"

"Not yet, sir."

"Well, bring me some brandy, and hurry up about it. I'm up in the gallery, you duffer."

Morton fetched the brandy.

"Thanks," said Eustace, as he emptied the glass. "Don't go to bed yet, Morton. There are a lot of books that have fallen down by accident. Bring them up and put them back in their shelves."

Morton had never seen Borlsover in so talkative a mood as on that night. "Here," said Eustace, when the books had been put back and dusted, "you might hold up these boards for me, Morton. That beast in the box got out, and I've been chasing it all over the place."

"I think I can hear it clawing at the books, sir. They're not valuable, I hope? I think that's the carriage, sir; I'll go and call Mr. Saunders."

It seemed to Eustace that he was away for five minutes but it could hardly have been more than one when he returned with Saunders. "All right, Morton, you can go now. I'm up here, Saunders."

"What's all the row?" asked Saunders, as he lounged forward with his hands in his pockets. The luck had been with him all the evening. He was completely satisfied, both with himself and with Captain Lockwood's taste in wines. "What's the matter? You look to me to be in an absolutely blue funk."

"That old devil of an uncle of mine," began Eustace—"Oh, I can't explain it all. It's his hand that's been playing Old Harry all the evening. But I've got it cornered behind these books. You've got to help me to catch it."

"What's up with you, Eustace? What's the game?"

"It's no game, you silly idiot! If you don't believe me, take out one of those books and put your hand in and feel."

"All right," said Saunders; "but wait till I've rolled up my sleeves. The accumulated dust of centuries, eh?" He took off his coat, knelt down, and thrust his arm along the shelf.

"There's something there right enough," he said. "It's got a funny, stumpy end to it, whatever it is, and nips like a crab. Ah! no, you don't!" He pulled his hand out in a flash. "Shove in a book quickly. Now it can't get out."

"What was it?" asked Eustace.

"Something that wanted very much to get hold of me. I felt what seemed like a thumb and forefinger. Give me some brandy."

"How are we to get it out of there? What about a landing-net?"

"No good. It would be too smart for us. I tell you, Saunders, it can cover the ground far faster than I can walk. But I think I see how we can manage it. The two books at the end of the shelf are big ones that go right back against the wall. The others are very thin. I'll take out one at a time, and you slide the rest along, until we have it squashed between the end two."

It certainly seemed to be the best plan. One by one as they took out the books, the space behind grew smaller and smaller. There was something in it that was certainly very much alive. Once they caught sight of fingers feeling for a way of escape. At last they had it pressed between the two big books.

"There's muscle there, if there isn't warm flesh and blood," said Saunders, as he held them together. "It seems to be a hand right enough, too. I suppose this is a sort of infectious hallucination. I've read about such cases before."

"Infectious fiddlesticks!" said Eustace, his face white with anger; "bring the thing downstairs. We'll get it back into the box."

It was not altogether easy, but they were successful at last. "Drive in the screws," said Eustace, "we won't run any risks. Put the box in this old desk of mine. There's nothing in it that I want. Here's the key. Thank goodness there's nothing wrong with the lock."

"Quite a lively evening," said Saunders. "Now let's hear more about your uncle."

They sat up together until early morning. Saunders had no desire for sleep. Eustace was trying to explain and forget; to conceal from himself a fear that he had never felt before—the fear of walking alone down the long corridor to his bedroom.

"Whatever it was," said Eustace to Saunders on the following morning, "I propose that we drop the subject. There's nothing to keep us here for the next ten days. We'll motor up to the Lakes and get some climbing."

"And see nobody all day, and sit bored to death with each other every night. Not for me, thanks. Why not run up to town? Run's the exact word in this case, isn't it? We're both in such a blessed funk. Pull yourself together, Eustace, and let's have another look at the hand."

"As you like," said Eustace; "there's the key."

They went into the library and opened the desk. The box was as they had left it on the previous night.

"What are you waiting for?" asked Eustace.

"I am waiting for you to volunteer to open the lid. However, since you seem to funk it, allow me. There doesn't seem to be the likelihood of any rumpus this morning at all events." He opened the lid and picked out the hand.

"Cold?" asked Eustace.

"Tepid. A bit below blood heat by the feel. Soft and supple too. If it's the embalming, it's a sort of embalming I've never seen before. Is it your uncle's hand?"

"Oh, yes, it's his all right," said Eustace. "I should know those long thin fingers anywhere. Put it back in the box, Saunders. Never mind about the screws. I'll lock the desk, so that there'll be no chance of its getting out. We'll compromise by motoring up to town for a week. If we can get off soon after lunch, we ought to be at Grantham or Stamford by night."

"Right," said Saunders, "and tomorrow—oh, well, by tomorrow we shall have forgotten all about this beastly thing."

If, when the morrow came, they had not forgotten, it was certainly true that at the end of the week they were able to tell a very vivid ghost-story at the little supper Eustace gave on Hallowe'en.

"You don't want us to believe that it's true, Mr. Borlsover? How perfectly awful!"

"I'll take my oath on it, and so would Saunders here, wouldn't you, old chap?"

"Any number of oaths," said Saunders. "It was a long, thin hand, you know, and it gripped me just like that."

"Don't, Mr. Saunders! Don't! How perfectly horrid! Now tell us another one, do! Only a really creepy one, please."

"Here's a pretty mess!" said Eustace on the following day, as he threw a letter across the table to Saunders. It's your affair, though. Mrs. Merritt, if I understand it, gives a month's notice."

"Oh, that's quite absurd on Mrs. Merritt's part," replied Saunders. "She doesn't know what she's talking about. Let's see what she says.

DEAR SIR—This is to let you know that I must give you a month's notice as from Tuesday, the 13th. For a long time I've felt the place too big for me; but when Jane Parfit and Emma Laidlaw go off with scarcely as much as an "If you please," after frightening the wits out of the other girls, so that they can't turn out a room by themselves or walk alone down the stairs for fear of treading on half-frozen toads or hearing it run along the passages at night, all I can say is that it's no place for me. So I must ask you, Mr. Borlsover, sir, to find a new housekeeper, that has no objection to large and lonely houses, which some people do say—not that I believe them for a minute, my poor mother always having been a Wesleyan—are haunted.

Yours faithfully,
ELIZABETH MERRITT

PS—I should be obliged if you would give my respects to Mr. Saunders. I hope that he won't run any risks with his cold."

"Saunders," said Eustace, "you've always had a wonderful way with you in dealing with servants. You mustn't let poor old Merritt go."

"Of course she shan't go," said Saunders. "She's probably only angling for a rise in salary. I'll write to her this morning."

"No. There's nothing like a personal interview. We've had enough of town. We'll go back tomorrow, and you must work your cold for all it's worth. Don't forget that it's got on to the chest, and will require weeks of feeding up and nursing."

"All right; I think I can manage Mrs. Merritt."

But Mrs. Merritt was more obstinate than he had thought. She was very sorry to hear of Mr. Saunders's cold, and how he lay awake all night in London coughing; very sorry indeed. She'd change his room for him gladly and get the south room aired, and wouldn't he have a hot basin of bread and milk last thing at night? But she was afraid that she would have to leave at the end of the month.

"Try her with an increase of salary," was the advice of Eustace.

It was no use. Mrs. Merritt was obdurate, though she knew of a Mrs. Goddard, who had been housekeeper to Lord Gargrave, who might be glad to come at the salary mentioned.

"What's the matter with the servants, Morton?" asked Eustace that evening, when he brought the coffee into the library. "What's all this about Mrs. Merritt wanting to leave?"

"If you please, sir, I was going to mention it myself. I have a confession to make, sir. When I found your note, asking me to open that desk and take out the box with the rat, I broke the lock, as you told me, and was glad to do it, because I could hear the animal in the box making a great noise, and I thought it wanted food. So I took out the box, sir, and got a cage, and was going to transfer it, when the animal got away."

"What in the world are you talking about? I never wrote any such note."

"Excuse me, sir; it was the note I picked up here on the floor the day you and Mr. Saunders left. I have it in my pocket now."

It certainly seemed to be in Eustace's handwriting. It was written in pencil and began somewhat abruptly.

"*Get a hammer, Morton,*" he read, "*or some tool and break open the lock in the old desk in the library. Take out the box that is inside. You need not do anything else. The lid is already open. Eustace Borlsover.*"

"And you opened the desk?"

"Yes, sir; and, as I was getting the cage ready, the animal hopped out."

"What animal?"

"The animal inside the box, sir."

"What did it look like?"

"Well, sir, I couldn't tell you," said Morton, nervously. "My back was turned, and it was halfway down the room when I looked up."

"What was its colour?" asked Saunders. "Black?"

"Oh, no, sir; a greyish white. It crept along in a very funny way, sir. I don't think it had a tail."

"What did you do then?"

"I tried to catch it; but it was no use. So I set the rat-traps and kept the library shut. Then that girl, Emma Laidlaw, left the door open when she was cleaning, and I think it must have escaped."

"And you think it is the animal that's been frightening the maids?"

"Well, no, sir, not quite. They said it was—you'll excuse me, sir—a hand that they saw. Emma trod on it once at the bottom of the stairs. She thought then it was a half-frozen toad, only white. And then Parfit was washing up the dishes in the scullery. She wasn't thinking about anything in particular. It was close on dusk. She took her hands out of the water and was drying them absent-minded-like on the roller towel, when she found she was drying someone else's hand as well, only colder than hers."

"What nonsense!" exclaimed Saunders.

"Exactly, sir; that's what I told her, but we couldn't get her to stop."

"You don't believe all this?" said Eustace, turning suddenly towards the butler.

"Me, sir? Oh, no, sir! I've not seen anything."

"Nor heard anything?"

"Well, sir, if you must know the bells do ring at odd times, and there's nobody there when we go; and when we go round to draw the blinds of a night, as often as not somebody's been there before us. But, as I says to Mrs. Merritt, a young monkey might do wonderful things, and we all know that Mr. Borlsover has had some strange animals about the place."

"Very well, Morton, that will do."

"What do you make of it?" asked Saunders, when they were alone. "I mean of the letter he said you wrote."

"Oh, that's simple enough," said Eustace. "See the paper it's written on? I stopped using that paper years ago, but there were a few odd sheets and envelopes left in the old desk. We never fastened up the lid of the box before locking it in. The hand got out, found a pencil, wrote this note, and shoved it through the crack on to the floor, where Morton found it. That's plain as daylight."

"But the hand couldn't write!"

"Couldn't it? You've not seen it do the things I've seen." And he told Saunders more of what had happened at Eastbourne.

"Well," said Saunders, "in that case we have at least an explanation of the legacy. It was the hand which wrote, unknown to your uncle, that letter to your solicitor bequeathing itself to you. Your uncle had no more to do with that request than I. In fact, it would seem that he had some idea of this automatic writing and feared it."

"Then if it's not my uncle, what is it?"

"I suppose some people might say that a disembodied spirit had got your uncle to educate and prepare a little body for it. Now it's got into that little body and is off on its own."

"Well, what are we to do?"

"We'll keep our eyes open," said Saunders, "and try to catch it. If we can't do that, we shall have to wait till the bally clockwork runs down. After all, if it's flesh and blood, it can't live for ever."

For two days nothing happened. Then Saunders saw it sliding down the banister in the hall. He was taken unawares and lost a full second before he started in pursuit, only to find that the thing had escaped him. Three days later, Eustace, writing alone in the library at night, saw it sitting on an open book at the other end of the room. The fingers crept over the page, as if it were reading, but before he had time to get up from his seat, it had taken the alarm, and was pulling itself up the curtains. Eustace watched it grimly, as it hung on to the cornice with three fingers and flicked thumb and forefinger at him in an expression of scornful derision.

"I know what I'll do," he said. "If I only get it into the open, I'll set the dogs on to it."

He spoke to Saunders of the suggestion.

"It's a jolly good idea," he said; "only we won't wait till we find it out of doors. We'll get the dogs. There are the two terriers and the under-keeper's Irish mongrel that's on to rats like a flash. Your spaniel has not got spirit enough for this sort of game."

They brought the dogs into the house, and the keeper's Irish mongrel chewed up the slippers, and the terriers tripped up Morton, as he waited at table; but all three were welcome. Even false security is better than no security at all.

For a fortnight nothing happened. Then the hand was caught, not by the dogs, but by Mrs. Merritt's grey parrot. The bird was in the habit of periodically removing the pins that kept his seed- and water-tins in place, and then escaping through the holes in the side of his cage. When once at liberty, Peter would show no inclination to return, and would often be about the house for days. Now, after six consecutive weeks of captivity, Peter had again discovered a new way of unloosing his bolts and was at large, exploring the tapestried forests of the curtains and singing songs in praise of liberty from cornice and picture-rail.

"It's no use your trying to catch him," said Eustace to Mrs. Merritt, as she came into the study one afternoon towards dusk with a stepladder. "You'd much better leave Peter alone. Starve him into surrender, Mrs. Merritt: and don't leave bananas and seed about for him to peck at when he fancies he's hungry. You're far too soft-hearted!"

"Well, sir, I see he's right out of reach now on that picture-rail; so, if you wouldn't mind closing the door, sir, when you leave the room, I'll bring his cage in tonight and put some meat inside it. He's that fond of meat, though it does make him pull out his feathers to suck the quills. They say that if you cook—"

"Never mind, Mrs. Merritt," said Eustace, who was busy writing; "that will do; I'll keep an eye on the bird."

For a short time there was silence in the room.

"Scratch poor Peter," said the bird. "Scratch poor old Peter!"

"Be quiet, you beastly bird!"

"Poor old Peter! Scratch poor Peter; do!"

"I'm more likely to wring your neck, if I get hold of you." He looked up at the picture-rail, and there was the hand, holding on to a hook with three fingers, and slowly scratching the head of the parrot with the fourth. Eustace ran to the bell and pressed it hard; then across to the window, which he closed with a bang. Frightened by the noise, the parrot shook its wings preparatory to flight, and, as it did so, the fingers of the hand got hold of it by the throat. There was a shrill scream from Peter, as he fluttered across the room, wheeling round in circles that ever descended, borne down under the weight that clung to him. The bird dropped at last quite suddenly, and Eustace saw fingers and feathers rolled into an inextricable mass on the floor. The struggle abruptly ceased, as finger and thumb squeezed the neck; the bird's eyes rolled up to show the whites, and there was a faint, half-choked gurgle. But, before the fingers had time to loose their hold, Eustace had them in his own.

"Send Mr. Saunders here at once," he said to the maid who came in answer to the bell. "Tell him I want him immediately."

Then he went with the hand to the fire. There was a ragged gash across the back, where the bird's beak had torn it, but no blood oozed from the wound. He noted with disgust that the nails had grown long and discoloured.

"I'll burn the beastly thing," he said. But he could not burn it. He tried to throw it into the flames, but his own hands, as if impelled by some old primitive feeling, would not let him. And so Saunders found him, pale and irresolute, with the hand still clasped tightly in his fingers.

"I've got it at last," he said, in a tone of triumph.

"Good, let's have a look at it."

"Not when it's loose. Get me some nails and a hammer and a board of some sort."

"Can you hold it all right?"

"Yes, the thing's quite limp; tired out with throttling poor old Peter, I should say."

"And now," said Saunders, when he returned with the things, "what are we going to do?"

"Drive a nail through it first, so that it can't get away. Then we can take our time over examining it."

"Do it yourself," said Saunders. "I don't mind helping you with guinea-pigs occasionally, when there's something to be learned, partly because I don't fear a guinea-pig's revenge. This thing's different."

"Oh, my aunt!" Eustace giggled hysterically, "look at it now." For the hand was writhing in agonised contortions, squirming and wriggling upon the nail like a worm upon the hook.

"Well," said Saunders, "you've done it now. I'll leave you to examine it."

"Don't go, in heaven's name! Cover it up, man; cover it up! Shove a cloth over it! Here!" and he pulled off the antimacassar from the back of a chair and wrapped the board in it. "Now get the keys from my pocket and open the safe. Chuck the other things out. Oh, Lord, it's getting itself into frightful knots! Open it quick!" He threw the thing in and banged the door.

"We'll keep it there till it dies," he said. "May I burn in hell, if I ever open the door of that safe again."

Mrs. Merritt departed at the end of the month. Her successor, Mrs. Handyside, certainly was more successful in the management of the servants. Early in her rule she declared that she would stand no nonsense, and gossip soon withered and died.

"I shouldn't be surprised if Eustace married one of these days," said Saunders. "Well, I'm in no hurry for such an event! I know him far too well for the future Mrs. Borlsover to like me. It will be the same old story again; a long friendship slowly made—marriage—and a long friendship quickly forgotten."

But Eustace did not follow the advice of his uncle and marry. Old habits crept over and covered his new experience. He was, if anything, less morose, and showed a greater inclination to take his natural part in country society.

Then came the burglary. The men, it was said, broke into the house by way of the conservatory. It was really little more than an attempt, for they only succeeded in carrying away a few pieces of plate from the pantry. The safe in the study was certainly found open and empty, but, as Mr. Borlsover informed the police inspector, he had kept nothing of value in it during the last six months.

"Then you're lucky in getting off so easily, sir," the man replied. "By the way they have gone about their business, I should say they were experienced cracksmen. They must have caught the alarm when they were just beginning their evening's work."

"Yes," said Eustace, "I suppose I am lucky."

"I've no doubt," said the inspector, "that we shall be able to trace the men. I've said that they must have been old hands at the game. The way they got in and opened the safe shows that. But there's one little thing that puzzles me. One of them was careless enough not to wear gloves, and I'm bothered if I know what he was trying to do. I've traced his fingermarks on the new varnish on the window-sashes in every one of the downstairs rooms. They are very distinctive ones too."

"Right or left hand, or both?" asked Eustace.

"Oh, right every time. That's the funny thing. He must have been a foolhardy fellow, and I rather think it was him that wrote that." He took out a slip of paper from his pocket. "That's what he wrote, sir: *I've got out, Eustace Borlsover, but I'll be back before long.* Some jailbird just escaped, I suppose. It will make it all the easier for us to trace him. Do you know the writing, sir?"

"No," said Eustace. "It's not the writing of anyone I know."

"I'm not going to stay here any longer," said Eustace to Saunders at luncheon. "I've got on far better during the last six months than I expected, but I'm not going to run the risk of seeing that thing again. I shall go up to town this afternoon. Get Morton to put my things together, and join me with the car at Brighton on the day after tomorrow. And bring the proofs of those two papers with you. We'll run over them together."

"How long are you going to be away?"

"I can't say for certain, but be prepared to stay for some time. We've stuck to work pretty closely through the summer, and I for one need a holiday. I'll engage the rooms at Brighton. You'll find it best to break the journey at Hitchin. I'll wire to you there at the Crown to tell you the Brighton address."

The house he chose at Brighton was in a terrace. He had been there before. It was kept by his old college gyp, a man of discreet silence, who was admirably partnered by an excellent cook. The rooms were on the first floor; the two bedrooms were at the back, and opened out of each other. "Mr. Saunders can have the smaller one, though it is the only one with a fireplace," he said. "I'll stick to the larger of the two, since it's got a bathroom adjoining. I wonder what time he'll arrive with the car."

Saunders came about seven, cold and cross and dirty. "We'll light the fire in the dining-room," said Eustace, "and get Prince to unpack some of the things while we are at dinner. What were the roads like?"

"Rotten. Swimming with mud, and a beastly cold wind against us all day. And this is July. Dear old England!"

"Yes," said Eustace, "I think we might do worse than leave old England for a few months."

They turned in soon after twelve.

"You oughtn't to feel cold, Saunders," said Eustace, "when you can afford to sport a great fur-lined coat like this. You do yourself very well, all things considered. Look at those gloves, for instance. Who could possibly feel cold when wearing them?"

"They are far too clumsy, though, for driving. Try them on and see"—and he tossed them through the door on to Eustace's bed and went on with his unpacking. A minute later he heard a shrill cry of terror. "Oh, Lord," he heard, "it's in the glove! Quick, Saunders, quick!" Then came a smacking thud. Eustace had thrown it from him. "I've chucked it into the bathroom," he gasped; "it's hit the wall and fallen into the bath. Come now, if you want to help." Saunders, with a lighted candle in his hand, looked over the edge of the bath. There it was, old and maimed, dumb and blind, with a ragged hole in the middle, crawling, staggering, trying to creep up the slippery sides, only to fall back helpless.

"Stay there," said Saunders. "I'll empty a collar-box or something, and we'll jam it in. It can't get out while I'm away."

"Yes, it can," shouted Eustace. "It's getting out now; it's climbing up the plug-chain. No, you brute, you filthy brute, you don't! Come back, Saunders; it's getting away from me. I can't hold it; it's all slippery. Curse its claws! Shut the window, you idiot! It's got out." There was the sound of something dropping on to the hard flagstones below, and Eustace fell back fainting.

For a fortnight he was ill.

"I don't know what to make of it," the doctor said to Saunders. "I can only suppose that Mr. Borlsover has suffered some great emotional shock. You had better let me send someone to help you nurse him. And by all means indulge that whim of his never to be left alone in the dark. I would keep a light burning all night, if I were you. But he must have more fresh air. It's perfectly absurd, this hatred of open windows."

Eustace would have no one with him but Saunders.

"I don't want the other man," he said. "They'd smuggle it in somehow. I know they would."

"Don't worry about it, old chap. This sort of thing can't go on indefinitely. You know I saw it this time as well as you. It wasn't half so active. It won't go on living much longer, especially after that fall. I heard it hit the flags myself. As soon as you're a bit stronger, we'll leave this place, not bag and baggage, but with only the clothes on our backs, so that it won't be able to hide anywhere. We'll escape it that way. We won't give any address, and we won't have any parcels sent after us. Cheer up, Eustace! You'll be well enough to leave in a day or two. The doctor says I can take you out in a chair tomorrow."

"What have I done?" asked Eustace. "Why does it come after me? I'm no worse than other men. I'm no worse than you, Saunders; you know I'm not. It was you who was at the bottom of that dirty business in San Diego, and that was fifteen years ago."

"It's not that, of course," said Saunders. "We are in the twentieth century, and even the parsons have dropped the idea of your old sins finding you out. Before you caught the hand in the library, it was filled with pure malevolence—to you and all mankind. After you spiked it through with that nail, it naturally forgot about other people and concentrated its attention on you. It was shut up in that safe, you know, for nearly six months. That gives plenty of time for thinking of revenge."

Eustace Borlsover would not leave his room, but he thought there might be something in Saunders's suggestion of a sudden departure from Brighton. He began rapidly to regain his strength.

"We'll go on the 1st of September," he said.

The evening of the 31st of August was oppressively warm. Though at midday the windows had been wide open, they had been shut an hour or so before dusk. Mrs. Prince had long since ceased to wonder at the strange habits of the gentlemen on the first floor. Soon after their arrival she had been told to take down the heavy window curtains in the two bedrooms, and day by day the rooms had seemed to grow more bare. Nothing was left lying about.

"Mr. Borlsover doesn't like to have any place where dirt can collect," Saunders had said as an excuse. "He likes to see into all the corners of the room."

"Couldn't I open the window just a little?" he said to Eustace that evening. "We're simpy roasting in here, you know."

"No, leave well alone. We're not a couple of boarding-school misses fresh from a course of hygiene lectures. Get the chessboard out."

They sat down and played. At ten o'clock Mrs. Prince came to the door with a note. "I am sorry I didn't bring it before," she said, "but it was left in the letterbox."

"Open it, Saunders, and see if it wants answering."

"It was very brief. There was neither address nor signature. *Will eleven o'clock tonight be suitable for our last appointment?*

"Who is it from?" asked Borlsover.

"It was meant for me," said Saunders. "There's no answer, Mrs. Prince," and he put the paper into his pocket. "A dunning letter from a tailor; I suppose he must have got wind of our leaving."

It was a clever lie, and Eustace asked no more questions. They went on with their game.

On the landing outside Saunders could hear the grandfather clock whispering the seconds, blurting out the quarter-hours.

"Check," said Eustace. The clock struck eleven. At the same time there was a gentle knocking on the door; it seemed to come from the bottom panel.

"Who's there?" asked Eustace.

There was no answer.

"Mrs. Prince, is that you?"

"She is up above," said Saunders; "I can hear her walking about the room."

"Then lock the door; bolt it too. Your move, Saunders."

While Saunders sat with his eyes on the chessboard, Eustace walked over to the window and examined the fastenings. He did the same in Saunders's room and the bathroom. There were no doors between the three rooms, or he would have shut and locked them too.

"Now, Saunders," he said, "don't stay all night over your move. I've had time to smoke one cigarette already. It's bad to keep an invalid waiting. There's only one possible thing for you to do. What was that?"

"The ivy blowing against the window. There, it's your move now, Eustace."

"It wasn't the ivy, you idiot! It was someone tapping at the window," and he pulled up the blind. On the outer side of the window, clinging to the sash, was the hand.

"What is that it's holding?"

"It's a pocketknife. It's going to try to open the window by pushing back the fastener with the blade."

"Well, let it try," said Eustace. "Those fasteners screw down; they can't be opened that way. Anyhow, we'll close the shutters. It's your move, Saunders. I've played."

But Saunders found it impossible to fix his attention on the game. He could not understand Eustace, who seemed all at once to have lost his fear. "What do you say to some wine?" he asked. "You seem to be taking things coolly, but I don't mind confessing that I'm in a blessed funk."

"You've no need to be. There's nothing supernatural about that hand, Saunders. I mean, it seems to be governed by the laws of time and space. It's not the sort of thing that vanishes into thin air or slides through oaken doors. And since that's so, I defy it to get in here. We'll leave the place in the morning. I for one have bottomed the depths of fear. Fill your glass, man! The windows are all shuttered; the door is locked and bolted. Pledge me my Uncle Adrian! Drink, man! What are you waiting for?"

Saunders was standing with his glass half raised. 'It can get in," he said hoarsely; "it can get in! We've forgotten. There's the fireplace in my bedroom. It will come down the chimney."

"Quick!" said Eustace, as he rushed into the other room; "we haven't a minute to lose. What can we do? Light the fire, Saunders. Give me a match, quick!"

"They must be all in the other room. I'll get them."

"Hurry, man, for goodness' sake! Look in the bookcase! Look in the bathroom! Here, come and stand here; I'll look!"

"Be quick!" shouted Saunders. "I can hear something!"

"Then plug a sheet from your bed up the chimney. No, here's a match!" He had found one, at last, that had slipped into a crack in the floor.

"Is the fire laid? Good, but it may not burn. I know—the oil from that old reading-lamp and this cotton-wool. Now the match, quick! Pull the sheet away, you fool! We don't want it now."

There was a great roar from the grate, as the flames shot up. Saunders had been a fraction of a second too late with the sheet. The oil had fallen on to it. It, too, was burning.

"The whole place will be on fire!" cried Eustace, as he tried to beat out the flames with a blanket. "It's no good! I can't manage it. You must open the door, Saunders, and get help."

Saunders ran to the door and fumbled with the bolts. The key was stiff in the lock. "Hurry," shouted Eustace, "or the heat will be too much for me." The key turned in the lock at last. For half a second Saunders stopped to look back. Afterwards he could never be quite sure as to what he had seen, but at the time he thought that something black and charred was creeping slowly, very slowly, from the mass of flames towards Eustace Borlsover. For a moment he thought of returning to his friend; but the noise and the smell of the burning sent him running down the passage, crying: "Fire! Fire!" He rushed to the telephone to summon help, and then back to the bathroom—he should have thought of that before—for water. As he burst into the bedroom there came a scream of terror which ended suddenly, and then the sound of a heavy fall.

This is the story which I heard on successive Saturday evenings from the senior mathematical master at a second-rate suburban school. For Saunders has had to earn a living in a way which other men might reckon less congenial than his old manner of life. I had mentioned by chance the name of Adrian Borlsover, and wondered at the time why he changed the conversation with such unusual abruptness. A week later Saunders began to tell me something of his own history; sordid enough, though shielded with a reserve I could well understand, for it had to cover not only his failings, but those of a dead friend. Of the final tragedy he was at first especially loath to speak; and it was only gradually that I was able to piece together the narrative of the preceding pages. Saunders was reluctant to draw any conclusions. At one time he thought that the fingered beast had been animated by the spirit of Sigismund Borlsover, a sinister eighteenth-century ancestor, who, according to legend, built and worshipped in the ugly pagan temple that overlooked the lake. At another time, Saunders believed the spirit to belong to a man whom Eustace had once employed as a laboratory assistant—"A black-haired, spiteful little brute," he said, "who died cursing his doctor because the fellow couldn't help him to live to settle some paltry score with Borlsover."

From the point of view of direct contemporary evidence, Saunders's story is practically uncorroborated. All the letters mentioned in the narrative were destroyed, with the exception of the last note which Eustace received, or rather, which he would have received, had not Saunders intercepted it. That I have seen myself. The handwriting was thin and shaky, the handwriting of an old man. I remember the Greek "e" was used in "appointment." A little thing that amused me at the time was that Saunders seemed to keep the note pressed between the pages of his Bible.

I had seen Adrian Borlsover once. Saunders I learnt to know well. It was by chance, however, and not by design, that I met a third person of the story—Morton, the butler. Saunders and I were walking in the Zoological Gardens one Sunday afternoon, when he called my attention to an old man who was standing before the door of the Reptile House.

"Why, Morton," he said, clapping him on the back, "how is the world treating you?"

"Poorly, Mr. Saunders," said the old fellow, though his face lighted up at the greeting. "The winters drag terribly nowadays. There don't seem to be no summers or springs."

"You haven't found what you were looking for, I suppose?"

"No, sir, not yet; but I shall some day. I always told them that Mr. Borlsover kept some queer animals."

"And what is he looking for?" I asked, when we had parted from him.

"A beast with five fingers," said Saunders. "This afternoon, since he has been in the Reptile House, I suppose it will be a reptile with the hand. Next week it will be a monkey with practically no body. The poor old chap is a born materialist."

The Colour Out of Space

H. P. Lovecraft

WEST OF ARKHAM the hills rise wild, and there are valleys with deep woods that no axe has ever cut. There are dark narrow glens where the trees slope fantastically, and where thin brooklets trickle without ever having caught the glint of sunlight. On the gentler slopes there are farms, ancient and rocky, with squat, moss-coated cottages brooding eternally over old New England secrets in the lee of great ledges; but these are all vacant now, the wide chimneys crumbling and the shingled sides bulging perilously beneath low gambrel roofs.

The old folk have gone away, and foreigners do not like to live there. French-Canadians have tried it, Italians have tried it, and the Poles have come and departed. It is not because of anything that can be seen or heard or handled, but because of something that is imagined. The place is not good for the imagination, and does not bring restful dreams at night. It must be this which keeps the foreigners away, for old Ammi Pierce has never told them of anything he recalls from the strange days. Ammi, whose head has been a little queer for years, is the only one who still remains, or who ever talks of the strange days; and he dares to do this because his house is so near the open fields and the travelled roads around Arkham.

There was once a road over the hills and through the valleys, that ran straight where the blasted heath is now; but people ceased to use it and a new road was laid curving far toward the south. Traces of the old one can still be found amidst the weeds of a returning wilderness, and some of them will doubtless linger even when half the hollows are flooded for the new reservoir. Then the dark woods will be cut down and the blasted heath will slumber far below blue waters whose surface will mirror the sky and ripple in the sun. And the secrets of the strange days will be one with the deep's secrets; one with the hidden lore of old ocean, and all the mystery of primal earth.

When I went into the hills and vales to survey for the new reservoir they told me the place was evil. They told me this in Arkham, and because that is a very old town full of witch legends I thought the evil must be something which grandams had whispered to children through centuries. The name "blasted heath" seemed to me very odd and theatrical, and I wondered how it had come into the folklore of a Puritan people. Then I saw that dark westward tangle of glens and slopes for myself, and ceased to wonder at anything besides its own elder mystery. It was morning when I saw it, but shadow lurked always there. The trees grew too thickly, and their trunks were too big for any healthy New England wood. There was too much silence in the dim alleys between them, and the floor was too soft with the dank moss and mattings of infinite years of decay.

In the open spaces, mostly along the line of the old road, there were little hillside farms; sometimes with all the buildings standing, sometimes with only one or two, and sometimes with only a lone chimney or fast-filling cellar. Weeds and briers reigned, and furtive wild things rustled in the undergrowth. Upon everything was a haze of restlessness and oppression; a touch of the unreal and the grotesque, as if some vital element of perspective or chiaroscuro were awry. I did not wonder that the foreigners would not stay, for this was no region to sleep in. It was too much like a landscape of Salvator Rosa; too much like some forbidden woodcut in a tale of terror.

But even all this was not so bad as the blasted heath. I knew it the moment I came upon it at the bottom of a spacious valley; for no other name could fit such a thing, or any other thing fit such a name. It was as if the poet had coined the phrase from having seen this one particular region. It must, I thought as I viewed it, be the outcome of a fire; but why had nothing new ever grown over those five acres of grey desolation that sprawled open to the sky like a great spot eaten by acid in the woods and fields? It lay largely to the north of the ancient road line, but encroached a little on the other side. I felt an odd reluctance about approaching, and did so at last only because my business took me through and past it. There was no vegetation of any kind on that broad expanse, but only a fine grey dust or ash which no wind seemed ever to blow about. The trees near it were sickly and stunted, and many dead trunks stood or lay rotting at the rim. As I walked hurriedly by I saw the tumbled bricks and stones of an old chimney and cellar on my right, and the yawning black maw of an abandoned well whose stagnant vapours played strange tricks with the hues of the sunlight. Even the long, dark woodland climb beyond seemed welcome in contrast, and I marvelled no more at the frightened whispers of Arkham people. There had been no house or ruin near; even in the old days the place must have been lonely and remote. And at twilight, dreading to repass that ominous spot, I walked circuitously back to the town by the curving road on the south. I vaguely wished some clouds would gather, for an odd timidity about the deep skyey voids above had crept into my soul.

In the evening I asked old people in Arkham about the blasted heath, and what was meant by that phrase "strange days" which so many evasively muttered. I could not, however, get any good answers except that all the mystery was much more recent than I had dreamed. It was not a matter of old legendry at all, but something within the lifetime of those who spoke. It had happened in the 'eighties, and a family had disappeared or was killed. Speakers would not be exact; and because they all told me to pay no attention to old Ammi Pierce's crazy tales, I sought him out the next morning, having heard that he lived alone in the ancient tottering cottage where the trees first begin to get thick. It was a fearsomely archaic place, and had begun to exude the faint miasmal odour which clings about houses that have stood too long. Only with persistent knocking could I rouse the aged man, and when he shuffled timidly to the door I could tell he was not glad to see me. He was not so feeble as I had expected; but his eyes drooped in a curious way, and his unkempt clothing and white beard made him seem very worn and dismal. Not knowing just how he could best be launched on his tales, I feigned a matter of business; told him of my surveying, and asked vague questions about the district. He was far brighter and more educated than I had been led to think, and before I knew it had grasped quite as much of the subject as any man I had talked with in Arkham. He was not like other rustics I had known in the sections where reservoirs were to be. From him there were no protests at the miles of old wood and farmland to be blotted out, though perhaps there would have been had not his home lain outside the bounds of the future lake. Relief was all that he showed; relief at the doom of the dark ancient valleys through which he had roamed all his life. They were better under water now—better under water since the strange days. And with this opening his husky voice sank low, while his body leaned forward and his right forefinger began to point shakily and impressively.

It was then that I heard the story, and as the rambling voice scraped and whispered on I shivered again and again despite the summer day. Often I had to recall the speaker from ramblings, piece out scientific points which he knew only by a fading parrot memory of professors' talk, or bridge over gaps, where his sense of logic and continuity broke down. When he was done I did not wonder that his mind had snapped a trifle, or that the folk of Arkham would not speak much of the blasted heath. I hurried back before sunset to my hotel, unwilling to have the stars come out above me in the open; and the next day returned to Boston to give up my position. I could not go into that dim chaos of old forest and slope again, or face another time that grey blasted heath where the black well yawned deep beside the tumbled bricks and stones. The reservoir will soon be built now, and all those elder secrets will be safe forever under watery fathoms. But even then I do not believe I would like to visit that country by night—at least, not when the sinister stars are out; and nothing could bribe me to drink the new city water of Arkham.

It all began, old Ammi said, with the meteorite. Before that time there had been no wild legends at all since the witch trials, and even then these western woods were not feared half so much as the small island in the Miskatonic where the devil held court beside a curious stone altar older than the Indians. These were not haunted woods, and their fantastic dusk was never terrible till the strange days. Then there had come that white noontide cloud, that string of explosions in the air, and that pillar of smoke from the valley far in the wood. And by night all Arkham had heard of the great rock that fell out of the sky and bedded itself in the ground beside the well at the Nahum Gardner place. That was the house which had stood where the blasted heath was to come—the trim white Nahum Gardner house amidst its fertile gardens and orchards.

Nahum had come to town to tell people about the stone, and dropped in at Ammi Pierce's on the way. Ammi was forty then, and all the queer things were fixed very strongly in his mind. He and his wife had gone with the three professors from Miskatonic University who hastened out the next morning to see the weird visitor from unknown stellar space, and had wondered why Nahum had called it so large the day before. It had shrunk, Nahum said as he pointed out the big brownish mound above the ripped earth and charred grass near the archaic well-sweep in his front yard; but the wise men answered that stones do not shrink. Its heat lingered persistently, and Nahum declared it had glowed faintly in the night. The professors tried it with a geologist's hammer and found it was oddly soft. It was, in truth, so soft as to be almost plastic; and they gouged rather than chipped a specimen to take back to the college for testing. They took it in an old pail borrowed from Nahum's kitchen, for even the small piece refused to grow cool. On the trip back they stopped at Ammi's to rest, and seemed thoughtful when Mrs. Pierce remarked that the fragment was growing smaller and burning the bottom of the pail. Truly, it was not large, but perhaps they had taken less than they thought.

The day after that—all this was in June of '82—the professors had trooped out again in a great excitement. As they passed Ammi's they told him what queer things the specimen had done, and how it had faded wholly away when they put it in a glass beaker. The beaker had gone, too, and the wise men talked of the strange stone's affinity for silicon. It had acted quite unbelievably in that well-ordered laboratory; doing nothing at all and showing no occluded gases when heated on charcoal, being wholly negative in the borax bead, and soon proving itself absolutely non-volatile at any producible temperature, including that of the oxy-hydrogen blowpipe. On an anvil it appeared highly malleable, and in the dark its luminosity was very marked. Stubbornly refusing to grow cool, it soon had the college in a state of real excitement; and when upon heating before the spectroscope it displayed shining bands unlike any known colours of the normal spectrum there was much breathless talk of new elements, bizarre optical properties, and other things which puzzled men of science are wont to say when faced by the unknown.

Hot as it was, they tested it in a crucible with all the proper reagents. Water did nothing. Hydrochloric acid was the same. Nitric acid and even aqua regia merely hissed and spattered against its torrid invulnerability. Ammi had difficulty in recalling all these things, but recognised some solvents as I mentioned them in the usual order of use. There were ammonia and caustic soda, alcohol and ether, nauseous carbon disulphide and a dozen others; but although the weight grew steadily less as time passed, and the fragment seemed to be slightly cooling, there was no change in the solvents to show that they had attacked the substance at all. It was a metal, though, beyond a doubt. It was magnetic, for one thing; and after its immersion in the acid solvents there seemed to be faint traces of the Widmannstätten figures found on meteoric iron. When the cooling had grown very considerable, the testing was carried on in glass; and it was in a glass beaker that they left all the chips made of the original fragment during the work. The next morning both chips and beaker were gone without trace, and only a charred spot marked the place on the wooden shelf where they had been.

All this the professors told Ammi as they paused at his door, and once more he went with them to see the stony messenger from the stars, though this time his wife did not accompany him. It had now most certainly shrunk, and even the sober professors could not doubt the truth of what they saw. All around the dwindling brown lump near the well was a vacant space, except where the earth had caved in; and whereas it had been a good seven feet across the day before, it was now scarcely five. It was still hot, and the sages studied its surface curiously as they detached another and larger piece with hammer and chisel. They gouged deeply this time, and as they pried away the smaller mass they saw that the core of the thing was not quite homogeneous.

They had uncovered what seemed to be the side of a large coloured globule embedded in the substance. The colour, which resembled some of the bands in the meteor's strange spectrum, was almost impossible to describe; and it was only by analogy that they called it colour at all. Its texture was glossy, and upon tapping it appeared to promise both brittleness and hollowness. One of the professors gave it a smart blow with a hammer, and it burst with a nervous little pop. Nothing was emitted, and all trace of the thing vanished with the puncturing. It left behind a hollow spherical space about three inches across, and all thought it probable that others would be discovered as the enclosing substance wasted away.

Conjecture was vain; so after a futile attempt to find additional globules by drilling, the seekers left again with their new specimen—which proved, however, as baffling in the laboratory as its predecessor had been. Aside from being almost plastic, having heat, magnetism, and slight luminosity, cooling slightly in powerful acids, possessing an unknown spectrum, wasting away in air, and attacking silicon compounds with mutual destruction as a result, it presented no identifying features whatsoever; and at the end of the tests the college scientists were forced to own that they could not place it. It was nothing of this earth, but a piece of the great outside; and as such dowered with outside properties and obedient to outside laws.

That night there was a thunderstorm, and when the professors went out to Nahum's the next day they met with a bitter disappointment. The stone, magnetic as it had been, must have had some peculiar electrical property; for it had "drawn the lightning," as Nahum said, with a singular persistence. Six times within an hour the farmer saw the lightning strike the furrow in the front yard, and when the storm was over nothing remained but a ragged pit by the ancient well-sweep, half-choked with caved-in earth. Digging had borne no fruit, and the scientists verified the fact of the utter vanishment. The failure was total; so that nothing was left to do but go back to the laboratory and test again the disappearing fragment left carefully cased in lead. That fragment lasted a week, at the end of which nothing of value had been learned of it. When it had gone, no residue was left behind, and in time the professors felt scarcely sure they had indeed seen with waking eyes that cryptic vestige of the fathomless gulfs outside; that lone, weird message from other universes and other realms of matter, force, and entity.

As was natural, the Arkham papers made much of the incident with its collegiate sponsoring, and sent reporters to talk with Nahum Gardner and his family. At least one Boston daily also sent a scribe, and Nahum quickly became a kind of local celebrity. He was a lean, genial person of about fifty, living with his wife and three sons on the pleasant farmstead in the valley. He and Ammi exchanged visits frequently, as did their wives; and Ammi had nothing but praise for him after all these years. He seemed slightly proud of the notice his place had attracted, and talked often of the meteorite in the succeeding weeks. That July and August were hot, and Nahum worked hard at his haying in the ten-acre pasture across Chapman's Brook; his rattling wain wearing deep ruts in the shadowy lanes between. The labour tired him more than it had in other years, and he felt that age was beginning to tell on him.

Then fell the time of fruit and harvest. The pears and apples slowly ripened, and Nahum vowed that his orchards were prospering as never before. The fruit was growing to phenomenal size and unwonted gloss, and in such abundance that extra barrels were ordered to handle the future crop. But with the ripening came sore disappointment; for of all that gorgeous array of specious lusciousness not one single jot was fit to eat. Into the fine flavour of the pears and apples had crept a stealthy bitterness and sickishness, so that even the smallest of bites induced a lasting disgust. It was the same with the melons and tomatoes, and Nahum sadly saw that his entire crop was lost. Quick to connect events, he declared that the meteorite had poisoned the soil, and thanked heaven that most of the other crops were in the upland lot along the road.

Winter came early, and was very cold. Ammi saw Nahum less often than usual, and observed that he had begun to look worried. The rest of his family, too, seemed to have grown taciturn; and were far from steady in their churchgoing or their attendance at the various social events of the countryside. For this reserve or melancholy no cause could be found, though all the household confessed now and then to poorer health and a feeling of vague disquiet. Nahum himself gave the most definite statement of anyone when he said he was disturbed about certain footprints in the snow. They were the usual winter prints of red squirrels, white rabbits, and foxes, but the brooding farmer professed to see something not quite right about their nature and arrangement. He was never specific, but appeared to think that they were not as characteristic of the anatomy and habits of squirrels and rabbits and foxes as they ought to be. Ammi listened without interest to this talk until one night when he drove past Nahum's house in his sleigh on the way back from Clark's Corners. There had been a moon, and a rabbit had run across the road, and the leaps of the rabbit were longer than either Ammi or his horse liked. The latter, indeed, had almost run away when brought up by a firm rein. Thereafter Ammi gave Nahum's tales more respect, and wondered why the

Gardner dogs seemed so cowed and quivering every morning. They had, it developed, nearly lost the spirit to bark.

In February the McGregor boys from Meadow Hill were out shooting woodchucks, and not far from the Gardner place bagged a very peculiar specimen. The proportions of its body seemed slightly altered in a queer way impossible to describe, while its face had taken on an expression which no one ever saw in a woodchuck before. The boys were genuinely frightened, and threw the thing away at once, so that only their grotesque tales of it ever reached the people of the countryside. But the shying of the horses near Nahum's house had now become an acknowledged thing, and all the basis for a cycle of whispered legend was fast taking form.

People vowed that the snow melted faster around Nahum's than it did anywhere else, and early in March there was an awed discussion in Potter's general store in Clark's Corners. Stephen Rice had driven past Gardner's in the morning, and had noticed the skunk-cabbages coming up through the mud by the woods across the road. Never were things of such size seen before, and they held strange colours that could not be put into any words. Their shapes were monstrous, and the horse had snorted at an odour which struck Stephen as wholly unprecedented. That afternoon several persons drove past to see the abnormal growth, and all agreed that plants of that kind ought never to sprout in a healthy world. The bad fruit of the fall before was freely mentioned, and it went from mouth to mouth that there was poison in Nahum's ground. Of course it was the meteorite; and remembering how strange the men from the college had found that stone to be, several farmers spoke about the matter to them.

One day they paid Nahum a visit; but having no love of wild tales and folklore were very conservative in what they inferred. The plants were certainly odd, but all skunk-cabbages are more or less odd in shape and odour and hue. Perhaps some mineral element from the stone had entered the soil, but it would soon be washed away. And as for the footprints and frightened horses—of course this was mere country talk which such a phenomenon as the aërolite would be certain to start. There was really nothing for serious men to do in cases of wild gossip, for superstitious rustics will say and believe anything. And so all through the strange days the professors stayed away in contempt. Only one of them, when given two phials of dust for analysis in a police job over a year and a half later, recalled that the queer colour of that skunk-cabbage had been very like one of the anomalous bands of light shown by the meteor fragment in the college spectroscope, and like the brittle globule found imbedded in the stone from the abyss. The samples in this analysis case gave the same odd bands at first, though later they lost the property.

The trees budded prematurely around Nahum's, and at night they swayed ominously in the wind. Nahum's second son Thaddeus, a lad of fifteen, swore that they swayed also when there was no wind; but even the gossips would not credit this. Certainly, however, restlessness was in the air. The entire Gardner family developed the habit of stealthy listening, though not for any sound which they could consciously name. The listening was, indeed, rather a product of moments when consciousness seemed half to slip away. Unfortunately such moments increased week by week, till it became common speech that "something was wrong with all Nahum's folks." When the early saxifrage came out it had another strange colour; not quite like that of the skunk-cabbage, but plainly related and equally unknown to anyone who saw it. Nahum took some blossoms to Arkham and showed them to the editor of the *Gazette,* but that dignitary did no more than write a humorous article about them, in which the dark fears of rustics were held up to polite ridicule. It was a mistake of Nahum's to tell a stolid city man about the way the great, overgrown mourning-cloak butterflies behaved in connexion with these saxifrages.

April brought a kind of madness to the country folk, and began that disuse of the road past Nahum's which led to its ultimate abandonment. It was the vegetation. All the orchard trees blossomed forth in strange colours, and through the stony soil of the yard and adjacent pasturage there sprang up a bizarre growth which only a botanist could connect with the proper flora of the region. No sane wholesome colours were anywhere to be seen except in the green grass and leafage; but everywhere those hectic and prismatic variants of some diseased, underlying primary tone without a place among the known tints of earth. The Dutchman's breeches became a thing of sinister menace, and the bloodroots grew insolent in their chromatic perversion. Ammi and the Gardners thought that most of the colours had a sort of haunting familiarity, and decided that they reminded one of the brittle globule in the meteor. Nahum ploughed and sowed the ten-acre pasture and the upland lot, but did nothing with the land around the house. He knew it would be of no use, and hoped that the summer's strange growths would draw all the poison from the soil. He was prepared for almost anything now, and had grown used to the sense of something near him waiting to be heard. The shunning of his house by neighbors told on him, of course; but it told on his wife more. The boys were better off, being at school each day; but they could not help being frightened by the gossip. Thaddeus, an especially sensitive youth, suffered the most.

In May the insects came, and Nahum's place became a nightmare of buzzing and crawling. Most of the creatures seemed not quite usual in their aspects and motions, and their nocturnal habits contradicted all former experience. The Gardners took to watching at night—watching in all directions at random for something . . . they could not tell what. It was then that they owned that Thaddeus had been right about the trees. Mrs. Gardner was the next to see it from the window as she watched the swollen boughs of a maple against a moonlit sky. The boughs surely moved, and there was no wind. It must be the sap. Strangeness had come into everything growing now. Yet it was none of Nahum's family at all who made the next discovery. Familiarity had dulled them, and what they could not see was glimpsed by a timid windmill salesman from Bolton who drove by one night in ignorance of the country legends. What he told in Arkham was given a short paragraph in the *Gazette;* and it was there that all the farmers, Nahum included, saw it first. The night had been dark and the buggy-lamps faint, but around a farm in the valley which everyone knew from the account must be Nahum's the darkness had been less thick. A dim though distinct luminosity seemed to inhere in all the vegetation, grass, leaves, and blossoms alike, while at one moment a detached piece of the phosphorescence appeared to stir furtively in the yard near the barn.

The grass had so far seemed untouched, and the cows were freely pastured in the lot near the house, but toward the end of May the milk began to be bad. Then Nahum had the cows driven to the uplands, after which this trouble ceased. Not long after this the change in grass and leaves became apparent to the eye. All the verdure was going grey, and was developing a highly singular quality of brittleness. Ammi was now the only person who ever visited the place, and his visits were becoming fewer and fewer. When school closed the Gardners were virtually cut off from the world, and sometimes let Ammi do their errands in town. They were failing curiously both physically and mentally, and no one was surprised when the news of Mrs. Gardner's madness stole around.

It happened in June, about the anniversary of the meteor's fall, and the poor woman screamed about things in the air which she could not describe. In her raving there was not a single specific noun, but only verbs and pronouns. Things moved and changed and fluttered, and ears tingled to impulses which were not wholly sounds. Something was taken away—she was being drained of something—something was fastening itself on her that ought not to be—someone must make it keep off—nothing was ever still in the night—the walls and windows shifted. Nahum did not send her to the county asylum, but let her wander about the house as long as she was harmless to herself and others. Even when her expression changed he did nothing. But when the boys grew afraid of her, and Thaddeus nearly fainted at the way she made faces at him, he decided to keep her locked in the attic. By July she had ceased to speak and crawled on all fours, and before that month was over Nahum got the mad notion that she was slightly luminous in the dark, as he now clearly saw was the case with the nearby vegetation.

It was a little before this that the horses had stampeded. Something had aroused them in the night, and their neighing and kicking in the stalls had been terrible. There seemed virtually nothing to do to calm them, and when Nahum opened the stable door they all bolted out like frightened woodland deer. It took a week to track all four, and when found they were seen to be quite useless and unmanageable. Something had snapped in their brains, and each one had to be shot for its own good. Nahum borrowed a horse from Ammi for his haying, but found it would not approach the barn. It shied, balked, and whinnied, and in the end he could do nothing but drive it into the yard while the men used their own strength to get the heavy wagon near enough the hayloft for convenient pitching. And all the while the vegetation was turning grey and brittle. Even the flowers whose hues had been so strange were greying now, and the fruit was coming out grey and dwarfed and tasteless. The asters and goldenrod bloomed grey and distorted, and the roses and zinneas and hollyhocks in the front yard were such blasphemous-looking things that Nahum's oldest boy Zenas cut them down. The strangely puffed insects died about that time, even the bees that had left their hives and taken to the woods.

By September all the vegetation was fast crumbling to a greyish powder, and Nahum feared that the trees would die before the poison was out of the soil. His wife now had spells of terrific screaming, and he and the boys were in a constant state of nervous tension. They shunned people now, and when school opened the boys did not go. But it was Ammi, on one of his rare visits, who first realised that the well water was no longer good. It had an evil taste that was not exactly fetid nor exactly salty, and Ammi advised his friend to dig another well on higher ground to use till the soil was good again. Nahum, however, ignored the warning, for he had by that time become calloused to strange and unpleasant things. He and the boys continued to use the tainted supply, drinking it as listlessly and mechanically as they ate their meagre and ill-cooked meals and did their thankless and monotonous chores through the aimless days. There was something of stolid resignation about them all, as if they walked half in another world between lines of nameless guards to a certain and familiar doom.

Thaddeus went mad in September after a visit to the well. He had gone with a pail and had come back empty-handed, shrieking and waving his arms, and sometimes lapsing into an inane titter or a whisper about "the moving colours down there." Two in one family was pretty bad, but Nahum was very brave about it. He let the boy run about for a week until he began stumbling and hurting himself, and then he shut him in an attic room across the hall from his mother's. The way they screamed at each other from behind their locked doors was very terrible, especially to little Merwin, who fancied they talked in some terrible language that was not of earth. Merwin was getting frightfully imaginative, and his restlessness was worse after the shutting away of the brother who had been his greatest playmate.

Almost at the same time the mortality among the livestock commenced. Poultry turned greyish and died very quickly, their meat being found dry and noisome upon cutting. Hogs grew inordinately fat, then suddenly began to undergo loathsome changes which no one could explain. Their meat was of course useless, and Nahum was at his wit's end. No rural veterinary would approach his place, and the city veterinary from Arkham was openly baffled. The swine began growing grey and brittle and falling to pieces before they died, and their eyes and muzzles developed singular alterations. It was very inexplicable, for they had never been fed from the tainted vegetation. Then something struck the cows. Certain areas or sometimes the whole body would be uncannily shrivelled or compressed, and atrocious collapses or disintegrations were common. In the last stages—and death was always the result—there would be a greying and turning brittle like that which beset the hogs. There could be no question of poison, for all the cases occurred in a locked and undisturbed barn. No bites of prowling things could have brought the virus, for what live beast of earth can pass through solid obstacles? It must be only natural disease—yet what disease could wreak such results was beyond any mind's guessing. When the harvest came there was not an animal surviving on the place, for the stock and poultry were dead and the dogs had run away. These dogs, three in number, had all vanished one night and were never heard of again. The five cats had left some time before, but their going was scarcely noticed since there now seemed to be no mice, and only Mrs. Gardner had made pets of the graceful felines.

On the nineteenth of October Nahum staggered into Ammi's house with hideous news. The death had come to poor Thaddeus in his attic room, and it had come in a way which could not be told. Nahum had dug a grave in the railed family plot behind the farm, and had put therein what he found. There could have been nothing from outside, for the small barred window and locked door were intact; but it was much as it had been in the barn. Ammi and his wife consoled the stricken man as best they could, but shuddered as they did so. Stark terror seemed to cling around the Gardners and all they touched, and the very presence of one in the house was a breath from regions unnamed and unnamable. Ammi accompanied Nahum home with the greatest reluctance, and did what he might to calm the hysterical sobbing of little Merwin. Zenas needed no calming. He had come of late to do nothing but stare into space and obey what his father told him; and Ammi thought that his fate was very merciful. Now and then Merwin's screams were answered faintly from the attic, and in response to an inquiring look Nahum said that his wife was getting very feeble. When night approached, Ammi managed to get away; for not even friendship could make him stay in that spot when the faint glow of the vegetation began and the trees may or may not have swayed without wind. It was really lucky for Ammi that he was not more imaginative. Even as things were, his mind was bent ever so slightly; but had he been able to connect and reflect upon all the portents around him he must inevitably have turned a total maniac. In the twilight he hastened home, the screams of the mad woman and the nervous child ringing horribly in his ears.

Three days later Nahum lurched into Ammi's kitchen in the early morning, and in the absence of his host stammered out a desperate tale once more, while Mrs. Pierce listened in a clutching fright. It was little Merwin this time. He was gone. He had gone out late at night with a lantern and pail for water, and had never come back. He'd been going to pieces for days, and hardly knew what he was about. Screamed at everything. There had been a frantic shriek from the yard then, but before the father could get to the door, the boy was gone. There was no glow from the lantern he had taken, and of the child himself no trace. At the time Nahum thought the lantern and pail were gone too; but when dawn came, and the man had plodded back from his all-night search of the woods and fields, he had found some very curious things near the well. There was a crushed and apparently somewhat melted mass of iron which had certainly been the lantern; while a bent bail and twisted iron hoops beside it, both half-fused, seemed to hint at the remnants of the pail. That was all. Nahum was past imagining, Mrs. Pierce was blank, and Ammi, when he had reached home and heard the tale, could give no guess. Merwin was gone, and there would be no use in telling the people around, who shunned all Gardners now. No use, either, in telling the city people at Arkham who laughed at everything. Thad had gone, and now Mernie was gone. Something was creeping and creeping and waiting to be seen and felt and heard. Nahum would go soon, and he wanted Ammi to look after his wife and Zenas if they survived him. It must all be a judgment of some sort; though he could not fancy what for, since he had always walked uprightly in the Lord's ways so far as he knew.

For over two weeks Ammi saw nothing of Nahum; and then, worried about what might have happened, he overcame his fears and paid the Gardner place a visit. There was no smoke from the great chimney, and for a moment the visitor was apprehensive of the worst. The aspect of the whole farm was shocking—greyish withered grass and leaves on the ground, vines falling in brittle wreckage from archaic walls and gables, and great bare trees clawing up at the grey November sky with a studied malevolence which Ammi could not but feel had come from some subtle change in the tilt of the branches. But Nahum was alive, after all. He was weak, and lying on a couch in the low-ceiled kitchen, but perfectly conscious and able to give simple orders to Zenas. The room was deadly cold; and as Ammi visibly shivered, the host shouted huskily to Zenas for more wood. Wood, indeed, was sorely needed; since the cavernous fireplace was unlit and empty, with a cloud of soot blowing about in the chill wind that came down the chimney. Presently Nahum asked him if the extra wood had made him any more comfortable, and then Ammi saw what had happened. The stoutest cord had broken at last, and the hapless farmer's mind was proof against more sorrow.

Questioning tactfully, Ammi could get no clear data at all about the missing Zenas. "In the well—he lives in the well—" was all that the clouded father would say. Then there flashed across the visitor's mind a sudden thought of the mad wife, and he changed his line of inquiry. "Nabby? Why, here she is!" was the surprised response of poor Nahum, and Ammi soon saw that he must search for himself. Leaving the harmless babbler on the couch, he took the keys from their nail beside the door and climbed the creaking stairs to the attic. It was very close and noisome up there, and no sound could be heard from any direction. Of the four doors in sight, only one was locked, and on this he tried various keys on the ring he had taken. The third key proved the right one, and after some fumbling Ammi threw open the low white door.

It was quite dark inside, for the window was small and half-obscured by the crude wooden bars; and Ammi could see nothing at all on the wide-planked floor. The stench was beyond enduring, and before proceeding further he had to retreat to another room and return with his lungs filled with breathable air. When he did enter he saw something dark in the corner, and upon seeing it more clearly he screamed outright. While he screamed he thought a momentary cloud eclipsed the window, and a second later he felt himself brushed as if by some hateful current of vapour. Strange colours danced before his eyes; and had not a present horror numbed him he would have thought of the globule in the meteor that the geologists' hammer had shattered, and of the morbid vegetation that had sprouted in the spring. As it was he thought only of the blasphemous monstrosity which confronted him, and which all too clearly had shared the nameless fate of young Thaddeus and the livestock. But the terrible thing about this horror was that it very slowly and perceptibly moved as it continued to crumble.

Ammi would give me no added particulars to this scene, but the shape in the corner does not reappear in his tale as a moving object. There are things which cannot be mentioned, and what is done in common humanity is sometimes cruelly judged by the law. I gathered that no moving thing was left in that attic room, and that to leave anything capable of motion there would have been a deed so monstrous as to damn any accountable being to eternal torment. Anyone but a stolid farmer would have fainted or gone mad, but Ammi walked conscious through that low doorway and locked the accursed secret behind him. There would be Nahum to deal with now; he must be fed and tended, and removed to some place where he could be cared for.

Commencing his descent of the dark stairs. Ammi heard a thud below him. He even thought a scream had been suddenly choked off, and recalled nervously the clammy vapour which had brushed by him in that frightful room above. What presence had his cry and entry started up? Halted by some vague fear, he heard still further sounds below. Indubitably there was a sort of heavy dragging, and a most detestably sticky noise as of some fiendish and unclean species of suction. With an associative sense goaded to feverish heights, he thought unaccountably of what he had seen upstairs. Good God! What eldritch dream-world was this into which he had blundered? He dared move neither backward nor forward, but stood there trembling at the black curve of the boxed-in staircase. Every trifle of the scene burned itself into his brain. The sounds, the sense of dread expectancy, the darkness, the steepness of the narrow steps—and merciful heaven! . . . the faint but unmistakable luminosity of all the woodwork in sight; steps, sides, exposed laths, and beams alike!

Then there burst forth a frantic whinny from Ammi's horse outside, followed at once by a clatter which told of a frenzied runaway. In another moment horse and buggy had gone beyond earshot, leaving the frightened man on the dark stairs to guess what had sent them. But that was not all. There had been another sound out there. A sort of liquid splash—water—it must have been the well. He had left Hero untied near it, and a buggy-wheel must have brushed the coping and knocked in a stone. And still the pale phosphorescence glowed in that detestably ancient woodwork. God! how old the house was! Most of it built before 1670, and the gambrel roof not later than 1730.

A feeble scratching on the floor downstairs now sounded distinctly, and Ammi's grip tightened on a heavy stick he had picked up in the attic for some purpose. Slowly nerving himself, he finished his descent and walked boldly toward the kitchen. But he did not complete the walk, because what he sought was no longer there. It had come to meet him, and it was still alive after a fashion. Whether it had crawled or whether it had been dragged by any external force, Ammi could not say; but the death had been at it. Everything had happened in the last half-hour, but collapse, greying, and disintegration were already far advanced. There was a horrible brittleness, and dry fragments were scaling off. Ammi could not touch it, but looked horrifiedly into the distorted parody that had been a face. "What was it, Nahum—what was it?" He whispered, and the cleft, bulging lips were just able to crackle out a final answer.

"Nothin' . . . nothin' . . . the colour . . . it burns . . . cold an' wet . . . but it burns . . . it lived in the well . . . I seen it . . . a kind o' smoke . . . jest like the flowers last spring . . . the well shone at night . . . Thad an' Mernie an' Zenas . . . everything alive . . . suckin' the life out of everthing . . . in that stone . . . it must a' come in that stone . . . pizened the whole place . . . dun't know what it wants . . . that round thing them men from the college dug outen the stone . . . they smashed it . . . it was that same colour . . . jest the same, like the flowers an' plants . . . must a' ben more of 'em . . . seeds . . . seeds . . . they growed . . . I seen it the fust time this week . . . must a' got strong on Zenas . . . he was a big boy, full o' life . . . it beats down your mind an' then gits ye . . . burns ye up . . . in the well water . . . you was right about that . . . evil water . . . Zenas never come back from the well . . . can't git away . . . draws ye . . . ye know summ'at's comin', but 'tain't no use . . . I seen it time an' agin senct Zenas was took . . . whar's Nabby, Ammi? . . . my head's no good . . . dun't know how long senct I fed her . . . it'll git her ef we ain't keerful . . . jest a colour . . . her face is gettin' to hev that colour sometimes towards night . . . an' it burns an' sucks . . . it come from some place whar things ain't as they is here . . . one o' them professors said so . . . he was right . . . look out, Ammi, it'll do suthin' more . . . sucks the life out . . ."

But that was all. That which spoke could speak no more because it had completely caved in. Ammi laid a red-checked tablecloth over what was left and reeled out the back door into the fields. He climbed the slope to the ten-acre pasture and stumbled home by the north road and the woods. He could not pass that well from which his horse had run away. He had looked at it through the window, and had seen that no stone was missing from the rim. Then the lurching buggy had not dislodged anything after all—the splash had been something else—something which went into the well after it had done with poor Nahum. . . .

When Ammi reached his house the horse and buggy had arrived before him and thrown his wife into fits of anxiety. Reassuring her without explanations, he set out at once for Arkham and notified the authorities that the Gardner family was no more. He indulged in no details, but merely told of the deaths of Nahum and Nabby, that of Thaddeus being already known, and mentioned that the cause seemed to be the same strange ailment which had killed the livestock. He also stated that Merwin and Zenas had disappeared. There was considerable questioning at the police station, and in the end Ammi was compelled to take three officers to the Gardner farm, together with the coroner, the medical examiner, and the veterinary who had treated the diseased animals. He went much against his will, for the afternoon was advancing and he feared the fall of night over that accursed place, but it was some comfort to have so many people with him.

The six men drove out in a democrat-wagon, following Ammi's buggy, and arrived at the pest-ridden farmhouse about four o'clock. Used as the officers were to gruesome experiences, not one remained unmoved at what was found in the attic and under the red-checked tablecloth on the floor below. The whole aspect of the farm with its grey desolation was terrible enough, but those two crumbling objects were beyond all bounds. No one could look long at them, and even the medical examiner admitted that there was very little to examine. Specimens could be analysed, of course, so he busied himself in obtaining them—and here it develops that a very puzzling aftermath occurred at the college laboratory where the two phials of dust were finally taken. Under the spectroscope both samples gave off an unknown spectrum, in which many of the baffling bands were precisely like those which the strange meteor had yielded in the previous year. The property of emitting this spectrum vanished in a month, the dust thereafter consisting mainly of alkaline phosphates and carbonates.

Ammi would not have told the men about the well if he had thought they meant to do anything then and there. It was getting toward sunset, and he was anxious to be away. But he could not help glancing nervously at the stony curb by the great sweep, and when a detective questioned him he admitted that Nahum had feared something down there—so much so that he had never even thought of searching it for Merwin or Zenas. After that nothing would do but that they empty and explore the well immediately, so Ammi had to wait trembling while pail after pail of rank water was hauled up and splashed on the soaking ground outside. The men sniffed in disgust at the fluid, and toward the last held their noses against the foetor they were uncovering. It was not so long a job as they had feared it would be, since the water was phenomenally low. There is no need to speak too exactly of what they found. Merwin and Zenas were both there, in part, though the vestiges were mainly skeletal. There were also a small deer and a large dog in about the same state, and a number of bones of small animals. The ooze and slime at the bottom seemed inexplicably porous and bubbling, and a man who descended on handholds with a long pole found that he could sink the wooden shaft to any depth in the mud of the floor without meeting any solid obstruction.

Twilight had now fallen, and lanterns were brought from the house. Then, when it was seen that nothing further could be gained from the well, everyone went indoors and conferred in the ancient sitting-room while the intermittent light of a spectral half-moon played wanly on the grey desolation outside. The men were frankly nonplussed by the entire case, and could find no convincing common element to link the strange vegetable conditions, the unknown disease of livestock and humans, and the unaccountable deaths of Merwin and Zenas in the tainted well. They had heard the common country talk, it is true; but could not believe that anything contrary to natural law had occurred. No doubt the meteor had poisoned the soil, but the illness of persons and animals who had eaten nothing grown in that soil was another matter. Was it the well water? Very possibly. It might be a good idea to analyze it. But what peculiar madness could have made both boys jump into the well? Their deeds were so similar—and the fragments showed that they had both suffered from the grey brittle death. Why was everything so grey and brittle?

It was the coroner, seated near a window overlooking the yard, who first noticed the glow about the well. Night had fully set in, and all the abhorrent grounds seemed faintly luminous with more than the fitful moonbeams; but this new glow was something definite and distinct, and appeared to shoot up from the black pit like a softened ray from a searchlight, giving dull reflections in the little ground pools where the water had been emptied. It had a very queer colour, and as all the men clustered round the window Ammi gave a violent start. For this strange beam of ghastly miasma was to him of no unfamiliar hue. He had seen that colour before, and feared to think what it might mean. He had seen it in the nasty brittle globule in that aërolite two summers ago, had seen it in the crazy vegetation of the springtime, and had thought he had seen it for an instant that very morning against the small barred window of that terrible attic room where nameless things had happened. It had flashed there a second, and a clammy and hateful current of vapour had brushed past him—and then poor Nahum had been taken by something of that colour. He had said so at the last—said it was like the globule and the plants. After that had come the runaway in the yard and the splash in the well—and now that well was belching forth to the night a pale insidious beam of the same daemoniac tint.

It does credit to the alertness of Ammi's mind that he puzzled even at that tense moment over a point which was essentially scientific. He could not but wonder at his gleaning of the same impression from a vapour glimpsed in the daytime, against a window opening on the morning sky, and from a nocturnal exhalation seen as a phosphorescent mist against the black and blasted landscape. It wasn't right—it was against Nature—and he thought of those terrible last words of his stricken friend, "It come from some place whar things ain't as they is here . . . one o' them professors said so. . . ."

All three horses outside, tied to a pair of shrivelled saplings by the road, were now neighing and pawing frantically. The wagon driver started for the door to do something, but Ammi laid a shaky hand on his shoulder. "Dun't go out thar," he whispered. "They's more to this nor what we know. Nahum said somethin' lived in the well that sucks your life out. He said it must be some'at growed from a round ball like one we all seen in the meteor stone that fell a year ago June. Sucks an' burns, he said, an' is jest a cloud of colour like that light out thar now, that ye can hardly see an' can't tell what it is. Nahum thought it feeds on everything livin' an' gits stronger all the time. He said he seen it this last week. It must be somethin' from away off in the sky like the men from the college last year says the meteor stone was. The way it's made an' the way it works ain't like no way o' God's world. It's some'at from beyond."

So the men paused indecisively as the light from the well grew stronger and the hitched horses pawed and whinnied in increasing frenzy. It was truly an awful moment; with terror in that ancient and accursed house itself, four monstrous sets of fragments—two from the house and two from the well—in the woodshed behind, and that shaft of unknown and unholy iridescence from the slimy depths in front. Ammi had restrained the driver on impulse, forgetting how uninjured he himself was after the clammy brushing of that coloured vapour in the attic room, but perhaps it is just as well that he acted as he did. No one will ever know what was abroad that night; and though the blasphemy from beyond had not so far hurt any human of unweakened mind, there is no telling what it might not have done at that last moment, and with its seemingly increased strength and the special signs of purpose it was soon to display beneath the half-clouded moonlit sky.

All at once one of the detectives at the window gave a short, sharp gasp. The others looked at him, and then quickly followed his own gaze upward to the point at which its idle straying had been suddenly arrested. There was no need for words. What had been disputed in country gossip was disputable no longer, and it is because of the thing which every man of that party agreed in whispering later on that the strange days are never talked about in Arkham. It is necessary to premise that there was no wind at that hour of the evening. One did arise not long afterward, but there was absolutely none then. Even the dry tips of the lingering hedge-mustard, grey and blighted, and the fringe on the roof of the standing democrat-wagon were unstirred. And yet amid that tense, godless calm the high bare boughs of all the trees in the yard were moving. They were twitching morbidly and spasmodically, clawing in convulsive and epileptic madness at the moonlit clouds; scratching impotently in the noxious air as if jerked by some alien and bodiless line of linkage with subterrene horrors writhing and struggling below the black roots.

Not a man breathed for several seconds. Then a cloud of darker depth passed over the moon, and the silhouette of clutching branches faded out momentarily. At this there was a general cry; muffled with awe, but husky and almost identical from every throat. For the terror had not faded with the silhouette, and in a fearsome instant of deeper darkness the watchers saw wriggling at that treetop height a thousand tiny points of faint and unhallowed radiance, tipping each bough like the fire of St. Elmo or the flames that came down on the apostles' heads at Pentecost. It was a monstrous constellation of unnatural light, like a glutted swarm of corpse-fed fireflies dancing hellish sarabands over an accursed marsh; and its colour was that same nameless intrusion which Ammi had come to recognise and dread. All the while the shaft of phosphorescence from the well was getting brighter and brighter, bringing to the minds of the huddled men a sense of doom and abnormality which far outraced any image their conscious minds could form. It was no longer *shining* out, it was *pouring* out; and as the shapeless stream of unplaceable colour left the well it seemed to flow directly into the sky.

The veterinary shivered, and walked to the front door to drop the heavy extra bar across it. Ammi shook no less, and had to tug and point for lack of a controllable voice when he wished to draw notice to the growing luminosity of the trees. The neighing and stamping of the horses had become utterly frightful, but not a soul of that group in the old house would have ventured forth for any earthly reward. With the moments the shining of the trees increased, while their restless branches seemed to strain more and more toward verticality. The wood of the well-sweep was shining now, and presently a policeman dumbly pointed to some wooden sheds and beehives near the stone wall on the west. They were commencing to shine, too, though the tethered vehicles of the visitors seemed so far unaffected. Then there was a wild commotion and clopping in the road, and as Ammi quenched the lamp for better seeing they realised that the span of frantic greys had broke their sapling and run off with the democrat-wagon.

The shock served to loosen several tongues, and embarrassed whispers were exchanged. "It spreads on everything organic that's been around here," muttered the medical examiner. No one replied, but the man who had been in the well gave a hint that his long pole must have stirred up something intangible. "It was awful," he added. "There was no bottom at all. Just ooze and bubbles and the feeling of something lurking under there." Ammi's horse still pawed and screamed deafeningly in the road outside, and nearly drowned its owner's faint quaver as he mumbled his formless reflections. "It come from that stone . . . it growed down thar . . . it got everything livin' . . . it fed itself on 'em, mind and body . . . Thad an' Mernie, Zenas an' Nabby . . . Nahum was the last . . . they all drunk the water . . . it got strong on 'em . . . it come from beyond, whar things ain't like they be here . . . now it's goin' home. . . ."

At this point, as the column of unknown colour flared suddenly stronger and began to weave itself into fantastic suggestions of shape which each spectator later described differently, there came from poor tethered Hero such a sound as no man before or since ever heard from a horse. Every person in that low-pitched sitting room stopped his ears, and Ammi turned away from the window in horror and nausea. Words could not convey it—when Ammi looked out again the hapless beast lay huddled inert on the moonlit ground between the splintered shafts of the buggy. That was the last of Hero till they buried him next day. But the present was no time to mourn, for almost at this instant a detective silently called attention to something terrible in the very room with them. In the absence of the lamplight it was clear that a faint phosphorescence had begun to pervade the entire apartment. It glowed on the broad-planked floor and the fragment of rag carpet, and shimmered over the sashes of the small-paned windows. It ran up and down the exposed corner-posts, coruscated about the shelf and mantel, and infected the very doors and furniture. Each minute saw it strengthen, and at last it was very plain that healthy living things must leave that house.

Ammi showed them the back door and the path up through the fields to the ten-acre pasture. They walked and stumbled as in a dream, and did not dare look back till they were far away on the high ground. They were glad of the path, for they could not have gone the front way, by that well. It was bad enough passing the glowing barn and sheds, and those shining orchard trees with their gnarled, fiendish contours; but thank heaven the branches did their worst twisting high up. The moon went under some very black clouds as they crossed the rustic bridge over Chapman's Brook, and it was blind groping from there to the open meadows.

When they looked back toward the valley and the distant Gardner place at the bottom they saw a fearsome sight. At the farm was shining with the hideous unknown blend of colour; trees, buildings, and even such grass and herbage as had not been wholly changed to lethal grey brittleness. The boughs were all straining skyward, tipped with tongues of foul flame, and lambent tricklings of the same monstrous fire were creeping about the ridgepoles of the house, barn and sheds. It was a scene from a vision of Fuseli, and over all the rest reigned that riot of luminous amorphousness, that alien and undimensioned rainbow of cryptic poison from the well—seething, feeling, lapping, reaching, scintillating, straining, and malignly bubbling in its cosmic and unrecognisable chromaticism.

Then without warning the hideous thing shot vertically up toward the sky like a rocket or meteor, leaving behind no trail and disappearing through a round and curiously regular hole in the clouds before any man could gasp or cry out. No watcher can ever forget that sight, and Ammi stared blankly at the stars of Cygnus, Deneb twinkling above the others, where the unknown colour had melted into the Milky Way. But his gaze was the next moment called swiftly to earth by the crackling in the valley. It was just that. Only a wooden ripping and crackling, not an explosion, as so many others of the party vowed. Yet the outcome was the same, for in one feverish, kaleidoscopic instant there burst up from that doomed and accursed farm a gleamingly eruptive cataclysm of unnatural sparks and substance; blurring the glance of the few who saw it, and sending forth to the zenith a bombarding cloudburst of such coloured and fantastic fragments as our universe must needs disown. Through quickly reclosing vapours they followed the great morbidity that had vanished, and in another second they had vanished too. Behind and below was only a darkness to which the men dared not return, and all about was a mounting wind which seemed to sweep down in black, frore gusts from interstellar space. It shrieked and howled, and lashed the fields and distorted woods in a mad cosmic frenzy, till soon the trembling party realised it would be no use waiting for the moon to show what was left down there at Nahum's.

Too awed even to hint theories, the seven shaking men trudged back toward Arkham by the north road. Ammi was worse than his fellows, and begged them to see him inside his own kitchen, instead of keeping straight on to town. He did not wish to cross the nighted, wind-whipped woods alone to his home on the main road. For he had had an added shock that the others were spared, and was crushed forever with a brooding fear he dared not even mention for many years to come. As the rest of the watchers on that tempestuous hill had stolidly set their faces toward the road, Ammi had looked back an instant at the shadowed valley of desolation so lately sheltering his ill-starred friend. And from that stricken, faraway spot he had seen something feebly rise, only to sink down again upon the place from which the great shapeless horror had shot into the sky. It was just a colour—but not any colour of our earth or heavens. And because Ammi recognised that colour, and knew that this last faint remnant must still lurk down there in the well, he has never been quite right since.

Ammi would never go near the place again. It is over half a century now since the horror happened, but he has never been there, and will be glad when the new reservoir blots it out. I shall be glad, too, for I do not like the way the sunlight changed colour around the mouth of that abandoned well I passed. I hope the water will always be very deep—but even so, I shall never drink it. I do not think I shall visit the Arkham country hereafter. Three of the men who had been with Ammi returned the next morning to see the ruins by daylight, but there were not any real ruins. Only the bricks of the chimney, the stones of the cellar, some mineral and metallic litter here and there, and the rim of that nefandous well. Save for Ammi's dead horse, which they towed away and buried, and the buggy which they shortly returned to him, everything that had ever been living had gone. Five eldritch acres of dusty grey desert remained, nor has anything ever grown there since. To this day it sprawls open to the sky like a great spot eaten by acid in the woods and fields, and the few who have ever dared glimpse it in spite of the rural tales have named it "the blasted heath."

The rural tales are queer. They might be even queerer if city men and college chemists could be interested enough to analyse the water from that disused well, or the grey dust that no wind seems ever to disperse. Botanists, too, ought to study the stunted flora on the borders of that spot, for they might shed light on the country notion that the blight is spreading—little by little, perhaps an inch a year. People say the colour of the neighboring herbage is not quite right in the spring, and that wild things leave queer prints in the light winter snow. Snow never seems quite so heavy on the blasted heath as it is elsewhere. Horses—the few that are left in this motor age—grow skittish in the silent valley; and hunters cannot depend on their dogs too near the splotch of greyish dust.

They say the mental influences are very bad, too. Numbers went queer in the years after Nahum's taking, and always they lacked the power to get away. Then the stronger-minded folk all left the region, and only the foreigners tried to live in the crumbling old homesteads. They could not stay, though; and one sometimes wonders what insight beyond ours their wild, weird stores of whispered magic have given them. Their dreams at night, they protest, are very horrible in that grotesque country; and surely the very look of the dark realm is enough to stir a morbid fancy. No traveller has ever escaped a sense of strangeness in those deep ravines, and artists shiver as they paint thick woods whose mystery is as much of the spirit as of the eye. I myself am curious about the sensation I derived from my one lone walk before Ammi told me his tale. When twilight came I had vaguely wished some clouds would gather, for an odd timidity about the deep skyey voids above had crept into my soul.

Do not ask me for my opinion. I do not know—that is all. There was no one but Ammi to question; for Arkham people will not talk about the strange days, and all three professors who saw the aërolite and its coloured globule are dead. There were other globules—depend upon that. One must have fed itself and escaped, and probably there was another which was too late. No doubt it is still down the well—I know there was something wrong with the sunlight I saw above that miasmal brink. The rustics say the blight creeps an inch a year, so perhaps there is a kind of growth or nourishment even now. But whatever demon hatchling is there, it must be tethered to something or else it would quickly spread. Is it fastened to the roots of those trees that claw the air? One of the current Arkham tales is about fat oaks that shine and move as they ought not to do at night.

What it is, only God knows. In terms of matter I suppose the thing Ammi described would be called a gas, but this gas obeyed laws that are not of our cosmos. This was no fruit of such worlds and suns as shine on the telescopes and photographic plates of our observatories. This was no breath from the skies whose motions and dimensions our astronomers measure or deem too vast to measure. It was just a colour out of space—a frightful messenger from unformed realms of infinity beyond all Nature as we know it; from realms whose mere existence stuns the brain and numbs us with the black extra-cosmic gulfs it throws open before our frenzied eyes.

I doubt very much if Ammi consciously lied to me, and I do not think his tale was all a freak of madness as the townsfolk had forewarned. Something terrible came to the hills and valleys on that meteor, and something terrible—though I know not in what proportion—still remains. I shall be glad to see the water come. Meanwhile I hope nothing will happen to Ammi. He saw so much of the thing—and its influence was so insidious. Why has he never been able to move away? How clearly he recalled those dying words of Nahum's—"can't git away . . . draws ye . . . ye know summ'at's comin', but 'tain't no use. . . ." Ammi is such a good old man—when the reservoir gang gets to work I must write the chief engineer to keep a sharp watch on him. I would hate to think of him as the grey, twisted, brittle monstrosity which persists more and more in troubling my sleep.